THE
REDEEMERS

THE
REDEEMERS

ACE ATKINS

corsair

CORSAIR

First published in the United States of America in 2015 by G. P. Putnam's Sons,
an imprint of Penguin Random House LLC

First published in Great Britain in 2015 by Corsair

1 3 5 7 9 10 8 6 4 2

Copyright © 2015 by Ace Atkins

The moral right of the author has been asserted.

The author gratefully acknowledges Chris Knight for use of a verse from
'In The Mean Time' from the album *Little Victories*.
'In The Mean Time'
Written by Chris Knight
Enough Rope Music (ASCAP)
Find out more about Chris at www.chrisknight.net.

A CIP catalogue record for this book
is available from the British Library.

ISBN: 978-1-4721-5162-9 (trade paperback)
ISBN: 978-1-4721-5163-6 (ebook)

Printed and bound in Great Britain by CPI Group (UK) Ltd., Croydon, CR0 4YY

Papers used by Corsair are from well-managed forests and
other responsible sources

MIX
Paper from
responsible sources
FSC
www.fsc.org   FSC® C104740

Corsair
An imprint of
Little, Brown Book Group
Carmelite House
50 Victoria Embankment
London EC4Y 0DZ

An Hachette UK Company
www.hachette.co.uk

www.littlebrown.co.uk

For Tom Freeland

Render unto Caesar no more than you got to
Keep the Lord in your heart, and keep your powder dry.
But do you good in mean time
While you're waiting on a good time, draw the line.

—Chris Knight "In the Mean Time"

If we take prisoners, we keep 'em separate till we have
had time to examine them, so they can't cook up a story
between 'em.

—Rogers' Rangers Standing Order No. 5

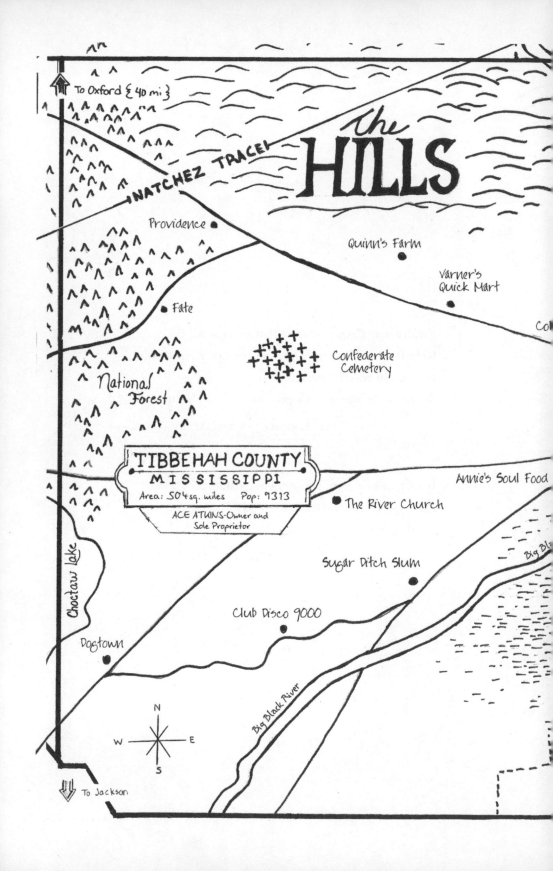

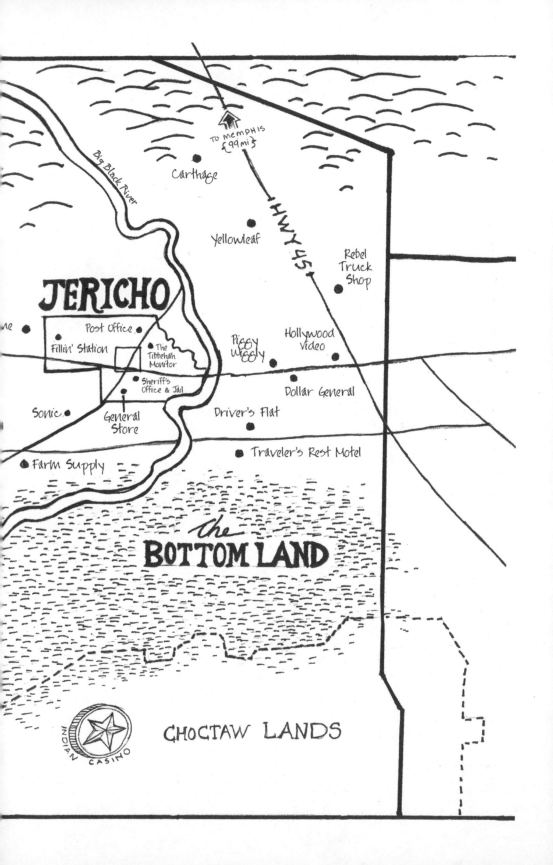

1.

Mickey Walls didn't bring up the subject until after he'd paid the Huddle House check and was walking out to his red Hummer parked on top of a ridge overlooking Highway 45. His buddy Kyle followed, working a toothpick in the side of his mouth, strolling like a man who didn't have nowhere to be, leaning against his truck, advertising HAZLEWOOD CONTRACTING. It was winter and colder than a witch's tit, and Mickey slipped his hands into his thick Carhartt jacket. He stood near the truck's tailgate and said, "I heard you had some problems with Larry Cobb."

"Shit," Kyle said, firing up a Marlboro. "To hell with that bastard."

"You were doing some dozer work for him and he jacked your ass?"

"He says I did a half-ass job," Kyle said. "That was a goddamn lie. When I come to talk to him, he sent out Debbi to talk. He's one sorry piece of shit."

"Why don't you sue him?"

"Cost more for a lawyer than I'd get."

"You could whip his ass."

"Larry's an old man," Kyle said. "He ain't worth it. You can't just go beating up some ole son of a bitch. That's like picking on a cripple.

What makes me madder than anything is that I thought I was his friend. Me and him used to hunt together. He even took me out to his place in Colorado and introduced me to his high-dollar friends. We'd shoot skeet and drink Coors Light in the Jacuzzi."

"I thought he was my friend, too," Mickey said.

"Till you and Tonya split up."

"I never done a damn thing to that man," he said. "And he knows his daughter is bat-shit crazy. She takes Xanax like they're Tic Tacs. Then he sued me for nearly a hundred grand, about bankrupted me just because our divorce didn't sit well with him and Debbi."

"Like I said," Kyle said. "That man's a genuine piece of shit."

The Huddle House hadn't been there long, opening up that summer with all the other places built after the tornado. People in Tibbehah County saying that twister may have been the best thing that happened since the Choctaws sold out. Even though seventeen people died, they now had a Subway, a KFC, and even a Walmart. Mickey leaned over the tailgate of the big truck, watching the traffic speeding by the exit on Highway 45. Kyle flicked away his spent Marlboro, firing up another. His skin was burnt-red, and he wore his graying hair cut long and stylish like some country music singer, along with a thin, wispy beard that was also turning gray. Kyle didn't know he was old. He still wore a leather puka shell necklace he'd bought down in Panama City Beach.

"Someone needs to put that man in his place," Mickey said.

Kyle turned from the traffic to look at his old buddy. His face didn't show nothing, light blue eyes looking right through him. "What are you thinking, man?"

"Shit, I don't know."

"Hell you don't," Kyle said. "You didn't call me for the fellowship and biscuits and gravy."

"I just think it's wrong, is all," Mickey said. "The way Larry Cobb has spent his whole life making money by wiping his ass with people in this town."

"You can either pray on it or shoot his ass."

Mickey shook his head. "What if there was another way?"

Kyle squinted through the smoke as he studied Mickey's face. Mickey knew he was interested, that he had him, even just a little. He'd been about half and half whether he was going to even mention the thing. But he knew he needed help, and Kyle Hazlewood was one of the few people he trusted in Tibbehah County, this busted-ass place ninety miles from Memphis and too damn close to Tupelo. He needed a friend right now, a man he could rely on to get the job done.

"He ever tell you about his special room?" Mickey said.

"You talking about that room off his closet?"

"Yes, sir."

"Where he keeps his found money."

"Is that what he called it?"

"I seen it," Kyle said, rubbing his nose. "Larry'd get drunk on Wild Turkey and he'd wander back there just to show you what he got. Man can't help himself. He got stacks and stacks of money. He told me it was because his daddy told him to never trust no banks."

"His daddy also told him don't pay no taxes, neither," Mickey said. "You know how much shit that man has done off the books with that logging operation?"

"How much?"

"Last time I seen it, it was more than a million."

"Holy shit," Kyle said. His cell phone ringing. He took it off his hip, saw the number, and turned it off. "Just what you thinking, man?"

Mickey turned back to the Huddle House, watching the waitress behind the glass refilling cups and talking with a couple old men in the back booth. A raggedy minivan pulled into the parking lot and a fat woman with a fat baby waddled on in to get their morning feed. Kyle hadn't moved. He was shivering a little, wearing that imitation-leather red-and-black motorcycle jacket he'd had for years. Mickey remembered when Kyle was the king of Tibbehah High, rolling around the town Square in his bad-ass El Camino. That same El Camino now sitting outside his work shed on blocks.

"I got a court-ordered judgment against me for a hundred grand," Mickey said. "I'm just saying it'd be funny to pay back Larry with his own goddamn money."

"You talking about robbing him?"

"No, sir," he said. "I'm talking about taking what's ours. I got a plan, but need you to be a part of it."

"I don't know, man," Kyle said. "That's a high-tech safe. He paid a couple thousand for it at the Costco in Memphis. It ain't opening with no crowbar."

Mickey pushed himself away from the big truck. "You don't need a crowbar if you got the combination."

"How the hell you know that?"

"I used to be his favorite son-in-law."

"You were his only son-in-law."

"I'm just talking," Mickey said. "I just wanted to see if you're interested first. Me and you been pals a long time. And when I heard Larry had cornholed you, too . . . Well, I just started thinking on the situation and how to make things right."

"What if the combo don't work?"

"I got a backup plan," Mickey said. "But one step at a time. I just need to know, are you in?"

The wind kicked up Kyle's long graying hair, the pinpoint of the Marlboro glowing in the morning cold. Trucks and cars sped up and down Highway 45, passing Tibbehah like it wasn't no more than a speck on a map. Mickey had wanted to buy him a new jacket for Christmas, but then he'd forgot. If this here deal worked out, Kyle could buy something made of real leather this time. Maybe he could help Kyle pull himself out of the shit. That was the least he could do.

"How 'bout I let you know?" Kyle said.

"Think on it."

"I will."

"We deserve better," Mickey said.

"I done some things I ain't proud of," Kyle said. "Drugs, drinking, and shit. But nothing like this. I ain't no criminal."

"Shit, you know stealing from a thief ain't stealing at all."

"What is it, then?"

Mickey rubbed his face and spit on the eroding ridge. "Justice."

Quinn Colson sat behind the wheel of his official sheriff's truck, a big F-250 diesel nicknamed the Big Green Machine, looking out at a tired old apartment complex in South Memphis. There were signs advertising move-in specials and monthly rentals, with an entire wing of the apartments gutted, no doors or windows, a big dumpster below toppling with trash. The complex was on Winchester, a half mile from the FedEx facility, and every few minutes a big jet would take off, rattling the truck, the apartments, and anything under its path. Lillie Virgil had come up with him, as she was the one who'd helped him track down what he needed, since she had once worked as a cop in Memphis. They talked a little while they waited. Quinn saying that all the planes reminded him of his last deployment, a tent city outside an airfield in Afghanistan.

"You were telling me something?" she said. "About some kids you met there?"

"I talk too much."

"You make goddamn Gary Cooper seem like a Chatty Cathy," she said. "Talk to me, Quinn. What else do we have to do but wait and watch?"

"You mind if I fire up a cigar?"

"Yes, sir, I do," Lillie said. "They smell like shit. Besides, you want those folks to see the smoke coming from the cracked windows?"

"Hell," Quinn said. "You really think they'd notice?"

Quinn glanced down at the ashtray and a half-smoked La Gloria Cubana Black. Seemed like a damn shame to leave it, but he'd rather leave it than listen to Lillie complain. Lillie was what you'd call a strong personality, nearly as tall as him, twice as mean, and perhaps the best shot in north Mississippi. Probably all of Mississippi. Before she'd became a cop, she'd been a star shooter for the Ole Miss Rifle Team. Her unruly brown hair was twisted up into a bun, and any hint of her femininity covered up with a bulky hunting jacket and ball cap.

They'd left their uniforms and badges back in Tibbehah County. He didn't want anyone to confuse why he was working in another state as a Mississippi sheriff.

"My last two deployments were at Camp Eggers," Quinn said. "I just got an email from a kid in my platoon. He was talking about things that happened there and those kids. I shouldn't have brought it up."

"God damn it, Quinn," Lillie said. "Just tell me the fucking story."

"The Afghan kids sold trinkets outside the gates. You know, necklaces, teapots, sometimes old weapons they'd found. They didn't go to school. They made money for their families, shuffling between two forward operating bases at Eggers and Camp ISAF."

"How old were they?" Lillie asked.

"There were two brothers," Quinn said. "Abraham and Abdullah. I think they were ten and twelve. And their friends Noah, who was about their age, and Miriam. Miriam was a cute little girl. Precocious. She couldn't have been more than seven or eight. Not much older than Jason."

"Was this part of winning hearts and minds?"

"U.S. Army Rangers don't do a lot of that," Quinn said. "Mainly, we just shoot bad guys and blow shit up. When we'd return from a mission, I'd buy stuff from those kids and send it home. I got to know them. That's all."

Quinn turned on the big truck's motor to get the heat going again. He caught a glance of his face in the rearview mirror, all hard planes and angles from his distant Choctaw roots, and his hair buzzed on the sides with a half inch on top. He was a wiry and lean man, still hard from ten years in the service. The expression on his face wasn't pleasant. Next to him, Lillie rested her shoulder against the passenger door and its fogged-up window. In profile, Lillie had a very pretty face, although to tell her she was pretty might be construed as an insult. Wearing makeup, letting down her hair, or wearing girly clothes wasn't a big part of her life. She never gave a damn about what people whispered about her.

"You send that shit home to your sister?" Lillie asked.

"Mainly, to my mom," Quinn said. "And Anna Lee, when I got drunk. The deployment was the longest I'd been on. I got to know those kids pretty well. I'd give them a few bucks on Thursdays before Jumu'ah. That's the Muslims' holy day of prayer."

"No shit, Quinn," Lillie said. "I read."

In the darkness, Quinn sat behind the wheel, watching that door on the second-floor unit. Watching people come and go, making mental notes of how many, how long, and what each one of them looked like in great detail. He knew Lillie was doing the same, waiting for the right moment. If it hadn't been for Lillie's contacts in Memphis, they'd have never found this place. Never found her. A true shithole in a neighborhood called Holiday City.

"What happened to the kids?" Lillie said. "There's got to be a damn reason you brought it up. You don't bring up shit unless it's got a god-damn point."

"When I went back to the base a second time," Quinn said, "the kids were still there. They remembered me. I brought them food from the mess hall, even though it was against regulations. My mother knew about them from letters. She took up a donation at the church and sent some clothes. On Christmas Eve, they presented me with an old threadbare scarf. They said it was from their families for my mother's Christmas present."

"I didn't think Muslims gave a flying fuck about Christmas."

"I didn't, either," Quinn said. "Maybe that's why it meant so much to me."

"And now?"

"Maybe more."

"What happened to them?" Lillie said.

Quinn and Lillie watched two Hispanic males walk up an outside stairwell to the second floor. They knocked on the apartment door and were let inside. Quinn was silent for a long time. He felt his breath tighten, muscles tense across his upper back and arms. Lillie had leaned forward, her eyes flicking across the scene in front of her. He'd asked her not to bring her service weapon but knew she had it on her anyway. Lillie didn't go to Walmart without her gun.

"I want to go with you."

"That could get you in a shitload of trouble," Quinn said. "A Mississippi deputy has no business in Memphis."

"And what about the sheriff?"

"Considering I got all of two days left in my position?" Quinn said. "To hell with it."

"So," Lillie said. "The kids. Abraham, Abdullah. Noah and Miriam. What happened to them?"

"Last time I saw them was on my final deployment," Quinn said. "That wasn't long before I came back to Tibbehah and that mess with my uncle. They were all pretty sad I was going home. But I promised

I'd go back. I worried about Abraham. He was particularly upset. He hugged me around my waist, not wanting to let me go. I promised I'd bring him back something really special."

"And you never came back," she said. "Because of all the shit we got into after your uncle died."

Quinn shook his head. "Two months after I left, a suicide bomber pulled up to the front gates. All the kids were killed except Abdullah."

Quinn could hear Lillie swallow. She didn't speak. When he turned to her, tough, mean-ass Lillie Virgil had been crying and wiped her face. He didn't say a word, concentrating on the two Hispanic men walking out with a black male. The black male was in his thirties, skinny, smoking a long cigarette and counting out cash with his fingers. Quinn took a long breath and reached under his seat for the familiar shape of an axe handle he'd brought from his shed.

"You stay here."

"Fuck that."

"Stay here," he said. "I need you to keep watch."

"OK," she said. "But don't kill anyone if you can help it."

"Appreciate the advice."

"I wish you'd let me go," Lillie said. "I'd wipe the floor with all those rotten sonsabitches."

"Caddy's my sister," Quinn said, reaching for the door and gripping the axe handle. "It's about time I brought her home."

2.

Johnny Stagg didn't give two shits for hunting. Why the hell would a fella get up at the crack of dawn and wait with his pecker in hand for some skittish animal to show itself? If Stagg wanted some red meat, all he had to do was go down to the Piggly Wiggly and find a T-bone, vacuum-packaged neat and clean and ready for the grill. This didn't make no sense at all. But there he was, up at four-thirty and on Rusty Wise's land at five-thirty, eating the sausage-and-biscuit he'd brought from his Rebel Truck Stop and talking about sitting in a deer stand for the next six hours like he didn't have nothing better to do. Rusty Wise was set to be Tibbehah's next sheriff next week, and Stagg, being the president of the Board of Supervisors, thought a little quality time was in order.

He borrowed a bolt-action Browning .270 off his right-hand man, Ringold, and drove on out a rutted dirt road in his Cadillac Eldorado. Wise, being the buttoned-up insurance man he was, had been waiting. And after a little hot coffee and biscuit, spraying doe piss on their boots and loading up their guns in a Bad Boy Buggy, they were off down a narrow fire road. Sun hadn't even begun to rise.

The stand sat up on eight-foot sections of four-by-fours. Inside were two old metal chairs, and Wise had brought a little propane unit for heat. They sat down in their big thick jackets and pants, stretched tight with thermal underwear, and waited for daylight to shine on the man's green field. Wise real proud of the green field, bragging about it all fall, all through election time, talking about winter wheat, rapeseed, and even some turnips. Stagg found out deer sure did like turnips. If he were a drinking man, Stagg would've blamed being drunk on agreeing to come on out to the hunt.

"You comfortable?" Wise said.

"Yes, sir."

"You don't need to call me sir."

"How about sheriff?" Stagg said.

Wise grinned bigger than shit.

Wise was a thick-bodied little cuss with bright red hair and fleshy red cheeks. He was built like a spark plug, and for two years had been a cop down in Columbus. Stagg knew what he'd done didn't amount to much more than writing parking tickets. And, sure, there'd been an incident with some nigger robbing a BP station, when ole Rusty had pissed himself. But Stagg had seen more in the fella. They'd talked about him running against Colson. He'd even come out to Johnny's annual Good Ole Boy that September. They'd shook on the deal over a plate of barbecue chicken. There had been an understanding.

"My freezer's full, Mr. Stagg," Wise said. "I shoot one and it's yours."

"Appreciate that."

"Ain't nothing like deer meat," Wise said. "I got a man who mixes in some pork fat and it makes some good sausage. Not to mention the backstrap. Better than any filet you'd get up in Memphis."

"You don't say."

"My boy got his first kill on Thanksgiving Day," Wise said. "Wadn't much. Just some little spike. My boy told me later he thought it was a doe. But when he smeared that blood across his face, he sure was proud. I don't think he's stopped grinning."

"How's your daddy doing?"

"He's good," Wise said. "Appreciate you asking. He's going back into insurance while I make the transition. He knew I was never cut out for it. Being a lawman was in my blood. I thought about being a cop every day since I left my job."

"You'll make a fine sheriff."

"Thanks, Mr. Stagg."

Stagg didn't bring much that morning: a sack of biscuits from his truck stop, a thermos of black coffee, Ringold's gun, and a legal-sized manila envelope bulging thick and tight.

The men didn't talk for a long while. And when they spoke, they talked in whispers. After about thirty minutes, Stagg did what he came to do, tossing the bulging envelope down on the slats of the stand's floors.

"What's that?" Wise said, rubbing his gun with an oil rag.

"Something you musta dropped out on the trail."

Wise leaned over, gun in lap, and grabbed the envelope. He opened the top and glanced inside. He looked back at Stagg. His dumb, grinning face grew real serious. "I didn't drop this."

"Christmas is expensive," Stagg said. "And you having kids and all. I bet there'll be some Visa bills come the first."

Wise closed the top of the envelope and resealed it. Stagg leaned back into the seat, seeing just the thinnest line of dawn cross over the tops of the greens. He smiled, already thinking on getting on back to the Rebel Truck Stop, making some calls up to Memphis. Things that needed to be done now that the jungle up there was good and shook-up.

Stagg's head snapped back when he heard the thick envelope land back on the slatted floor in front of him.

"Appreciate that, Mr. Stagg," Wise—fucking Rusty Wise—said. "But that ain't my style. This ain't like when my granddaddy was Supervisor. I was to run this whole deal straight and true. I made a promise to my wife when we were up in Gatlinburg a few weeks back. I told her I'd be the same man I'd been selling insurance. I don't need nothing to sweeten the pot."

"That ain't sweetening the pot, Rusty," Stagg said. "Just a little welcome gift."

"Like when you tried to give that big Dodge diesel to Quinn Colson?"

"Quinn didn't know how to show us any respect," Stagg said. "He was an outsider. Just as dumb as his stuntman daddy."

"I appreciate Quinn," Wise said. "I appreciate what he's done to help this county. I didn't run against him for any other reason than I think I can do a better job. I think I'm a better administrator than Colson. This town will never be the same after that F5 rocked our world. People died. Everything got its guts ripped out. But you and I know things can never go back to the old days. We got money coming in. People aren't staying in Jericho because they got nowhere else to go anymore."

"Pick up that money."

Wise shook his head, Stagg remembering when the boy had gotten some kind of award as a Little League pitcher and came up to the Rebel for an ice cream celebration. Hell, that seemed like Monday of last week. "This is from me to you," Stagg said. "This ain't from the taxpayers. This is to make things easier coming in from a nice-paying job. I just want me and you to be friends."

Wise studied Stagg's face and he nodded slowly but didn't pick up

ACE ATKINS

the money. Something caught his eye and he reached for the rifle in
his lap. He picked it up and brought it to his shoulder, training his eye
on an eight-point buck prissy-walking in the frost on those greens.
The buck was thick and big, but the antlers didn't seem to fit his size.
Stagg didn't see much worth in that one, hearing the hooves make
prints on the thick greens, a bright yellow morning pouring across a
little twisty creek and some rolling hills and on into the darkness of
the forest.

Stagg needed to take a piss. But now he had Wise all ready to shoot.
Stagg kept his rifle in his lap as he saw two more deer appear, two fat-
tened does following this fella out from the darkness. The buck stood
tall and alert while the does started to graze. Wise had his rifle set right
on that old boy. Stagg took a deep breath, waiting for that shot. Wise
closed one eye, everything cold and still, even a swallow seemed to echo
in the little wooden room.

Wise squeezed the trigger, the shot cracking hard, and that big buck
turned and twisted, speeding for hell or high water back over the creek,
running broken and scattershot over the greens until he fell, heavy and
busted, in a bed of turnip leaves. The does were gone.

Wise set down his gun. He turned to eye Stagg and then looked
down at the money.

"This why you came?" Wise said.

"I guess I ain't a hunting man."

"But you'll eat the meat?"

"Sure."

"Then help me drag this deer back to the Bad Boy Buggy and we
can head on to town," Wise said. "This buck will be my gift to you.
Might be a good way of starting off the year."

Stagg stood up, feeling some stiffness in his knees, and held his
rifle in his hand. The rifle feeling strange and foreign to him. He'd
much rather be sitting behind his desk and handling his affairs in a

closed room. Being out here in nature and the wide-openness of it made him feel strange. His stale, rotten breath came out like a cloud in front of him.

"I do wish you'd reconsider," Stagg said.

"I know," Wise said. "But this is how things got to be, sir."

Stagg followed him down the homemade ladder of the stand, knowing he'd just laid it all on the wrong fella.

S top the truck," Caddy screamed from the backseat.

The sun was coming up along Highway 78, over the state line, but not far out of Memphis. Quinn didn't answer, but Lillie Virgil turned around in the passenger seat and then turned back to Quinn. "You better," she said. "She looks real sick."

"Nothing I can do about it."

"I think she's gonna fucking puke."

"Let her puke," Quinn said. "I'm not stopping until we get back to Jericho."

"Jesus Christ, Quinn," Lillie said. "You really want to clean up that mess?"

"She'll try and run."

"Hell, no she won't."

Caddy started to make retching sounds from the backseat. "God damn it," Quinn said. A road sign said next exit was in a quarter mile, and Quinn looked up to the rearview mirror and told Caddy to hold on. "There's a filling station. We can get out and walk. Get you some fresh air. But don't even think about going anywhere."

Quinn eased the truck into the exit lane and turned right up into an Exxon station facing the highway. The pumps were empty, but the inside of the convenience store was lit up like a bright box. The truck wasn't even stopped before Caddy had opened the door and hopped out, running, Quinn thinking for a moment she would try to run away, but then she stopped in some high yellow weeds and bent at the waist.

"I told you," Lillie said. "That's not good."

"No, ma'am."

"What the fuck is she on?"

"I saw tinfoil and lighters laying around," he said. "Her fingers are black with soot. Looked like a goddamn opium den in there."

"You were in there a while. I was headed up to that shithole when I saw you come down those steps, carrying her in your arms."

"Yep."

"What happened?"

"A few folks needed an attitude adjustment."

"No shit," Lillie said. "There's blood all over your shirt."

"It's not mine," Quinn said. He reached for the door handle and stepped out into the brightening December morning. The chill cut up and over a hill filled with aluminum cans, fast-food wrappers, and beer bottles. Caddy had puked and now she was trying to quit the heaves. Quinn stepped up and put a hand on his sister's back.

"Oh my God," she said, kept saying. "Oh my God. Those boys. You. Oh my God."

"Everything is OK, Caddy."

"Are they dead?" she said. "Is everyone dead?"

"No, ma'am."

"Why?"

"Because they weren't worth it."

Caddy straightened up, wiping her eyes with her filthy hand, weak sun in her face. She didn't look much like the sister he'd known. Her blonde hair had grown out long and stringy and she looked to have lost a good deal of weight. Her face was skeletal and hollow, with black circles under her eyes. There were sores and scabs on her arms, and a few on her neck. It had been a long year and a half, after losing her house in the storm and watching her boyfriend be shot and killed.

"You have blood on you," she said. "All the blood."

"It'll wash out."

"Are you OK?"

"I'm fine."

"What was that?" she said. "What were you swinging? What was that?"

"An ole axe handle," he said. "Just something to get those men's attention."

"I didn't want you up there," she said. "I didn't want you to see me like this. *Oh God. Oh God.* I'm a waste. I'm just all the hell used up."

"Bullshit."

"I want to be dead," she said. "I want to be dead. Don't you fucking understand?"

"And how would that work out for Jason?"

"Oh God," she said. "Oh God. Jesus. Jesus. What am I?"

"You're alive," he said. "You just got lost. I'm here. I got you. You understand? I got you."

Quinn kept his hand on Caddy's back. He turned to look over his shoulder and saw Lillie Virgil, standing tall and confident, outside the truck, with hands in her jacket pockets, ball cap pulled down in her eyes. Quinn reached down and grabbed Caddy's hand, thinking of leading her through the Big Woods all those years ago, when real evil entered their lives, and kept on following her ever since. His hands were still shaking a little bit. Three men coming at him with some kind of ownership over his sister had brought on a rage he seldom liked to let loose.

"Come on."

Caddy wouldn't move. "I don't want him to see me like this."

"You don't have to see Jason until you're ready," he said. "We'll get you all cleaned up."

"You can't clean up all this shit. All the shit I've done. Don't you want to know?"

Caddy's whole body was shaking, and he reached around her shoulders and hugged her in close. Caddy had always been much smaller than Quinn. He kissed the top of her head, smelling the foul scent of body odor and cigarette smoke. The cherry perfume used to cover it all up doing a poor job.

"You've been gone almost a month," he said. "Jason doesn't give a shit what you look like. He doesn't care where you've been."

Caddy shook her head, but she let Quinn lead her away from the trash-strewn hill and back to Lillie Virgil and the safety of the Big Green Machine. The eighteen-wheelers blew past on their way to Memphis and down to Mobile. Quinn walked in step with his sister slowly, her whole body quivering under his arm as she started to cry. She'd left everything—her mother and father, her brother, her son, and even an outreach ministry that, for a time, had seemed to have been not only her salvation but salvation for a lot of others after the storm.

"Come on," Quinn said. "Let's go home."

"I don't know what all happened," she said. "I don't remember."

"Good."

"I'm sorry, Quinn," she said. "I fucked up. I fucked up bad. Just leave me here. No one has to know."

"Nope."

"You damn bastard," she said. "Why do you just keep coming back?"

"Our daddy comes back after thirty years and it's all on me?" Quinn said. "Dealing with him and Jean? To hell with that."

"I'll fuck up again," she said. "It'll happen again."

"Maybe." Quinn wrapped his arm over her shoulder and they started moving toward the big truck. Caddy looked up into his eyes as they walked and gave a blank smile. He held her close and tight. They moved together, Quinn feeling good, until his sister threw up on his cowboy boots. He stepped back as she dry-heaved.

"Jesus," she said. "Jesus."

"Slow steps, Caddy," he said. "Slow steps."

3.

Mickey Walls was just about done loading a truck with two thousand square feet of Brazilian cherry flooring when god-damn Debbi Cobb pushed her way through the showroom and back into the warehouse wanting to know just who in the fuck did he think he was. Mickey was smoking Marlboro Reds with his best installer, a fella named Lee Salter, who'd just gotten back from a six-month stretch in Parchman, and wasn't in any mood to square off with his ex-mother-in-law over one missed alimony check.

"My daughter has too much class to beg you for what's coming to her," Debbi said, chomping on some gum.

"Hello, Debbi," Mickey said. "Sure is good to see you. How about we step into my office?"

"I'd rather stay right here while you go write me a check."

"Come on," he said. "I made some coffee. Let's talk."

"About all you're good for," Debbi said. "Talk."

But she turned, noticing but not acknowledging Lee's old weathered ass giving her a good look-over. Mickey knew Debbi liked it. Why else would a woman pushing sixty wear a pair of painted-on black jeans with fancy-ass pockets, a black-and-silver-striped top reading BEBE, and silver heels showing off her purple-painted toenails? Her hair was high and puffy, with blonde streaks in all that dyed brown, and she had on a pair of big designer sunglasses that looked like a pair of welding goggles. As she followed him back into the showroom, Lee puckered his lips and narrowed his eyes. Mickey figured that six-month stretch must have been six months too long.

"I thought Lee was in prison," Debbi said, popping that gum.

"He just got out."

"And you hired him back?"

"Lee's the best man I have."

"Didn't he expose himself to a checkout girl at the Piggly Wiggly?"

"He was relieving himself in the parking lot."

"Not the way I heard it."

"No?" Mickey said. "Well. Yeah, I guess the judge wasn't buying it, either. Sit down. You still like that fancy hazelnut stuff in your coffee?"

Debbi took off her sunglasses, spit out her gum, and sat down. Mickey filled a Styrofoam cup, mixed in a little Coffee-mate, and handed it over to her. She took it but didn't thank him, holding the coffee in her hand, as Mickey took a seat behind a desk loaded down with more work orders than he could keep up with, stacked under a runner-up trophy from an over-forty softball league.

"It's been busy, Debbi," Mickey said. "You know?"

"Didn't you tell Tonya that you'd 'get her later,' since she was living right next door to her momma and daddy and she didn't need the money?"

"No, ma'am," Mickey said, slipping on a pair of half-glasses that hung from around his neck. He stretched out his legs under the desk, reading the delivery-and-installation list for the rest of the week. "I never said anything of the sort. We made an agreement during the separation. She'll get the check. I am just a little late, is all. Business has been slow."

"Bullshit," Debbi said. "You just got done sayin' you're busy. We got more building going on in this town that we can keep up with. It's like Jericho got a damn do-over after the storm. Larry's got the mill running day and night. Most of the timber is staying right here in Tibbehah."

"Good for ole Larry."

"Good for you," Debbi said. "How much of your business comes from heart pine planks from our mill?"

"A fair bit."

"More than that," she said. "Larry wants you to think about your future."

"Is that what it come to?" Mickey said. "A silly-ass threat?"

"I know you hate Larry," Debbi said. "And he don't like you much, either. You two always fought over who Tonya loved best. But let me tell you something right now. The real reason y'all hate each other is because y'all are just alike. You're like a couple dogs pissing on the same tree branch."

"Pissing on Tonya?"

"You know what I mean," Debbi said. "Me and you always got along because we are just different enough that we can communicate. I know Larry and I know you. That's why I came here this morning, all nice and pleasant, just wanting to know when you were going to get straight with my daughter."

"Correction," Mickey said, standing, stretching out his aching back from loading all that cherrywood. "You marched onto the loading dock and said to me who the fuck do I think I am and then threatened about where my flooring supply is gonna be coming from."

"I can't help but tell the truth," Debbi said, taking a little sip of the free coffee. "I shoot straight. You and Larry's the ones who shake hands, jackass around, and drink your goddamn Dickel, but, not five minutes after one of you is gone, y'all talking shit about one another."

"How's that coffee?"

"I had better coffee at the Quick Mart."

"Sorry about that."

"I appreciate the gesture," Debbi said, standing up to her full five-foot-two, including the nails and hair and five pounds of makeup and jewelry. "Just get straight with Tonya. OK? Last thing I want is for you and Larry to get into a goddamn wrestling match like Thanksgiving. All that did was scare the kids and the dogs. You broke my favorite wineglass and the legs off a handmade coffee table."

"That was unfortunate."

"It was the Dickel," Debbi said. "We'll leave it at that."

"Larry called me a pussy hound in front of my three-year-old niece."

"And so you jumped on him."

"He just sat there cocky as hell, sitting back in that La-Z-Boy and pointing at me with his crooked finger."

"What he said was that you have BIG DAWG written on the side of your tool trailer and that it should have read something else. He never said 'pussy hound.'"

"Well," Mickey said. "I heard it."

"You heard the Dickel sloshing around between your ears."

Mickey let out a long breath and shook his head. You couldn't reason with a Cobb. *Any of them.* Picking Tonya Cobb as Mrs. Walls number three was a hell of a bad bet. But Tonya was newly divorced herself and a hot little number, not looking a damn thing like her fat, red-faced daddy or painted-up momma. Tonya had gotten the hell out of Jericho and then come back a couple years before the storm to open a combination coffee shop and tanning parlor. She was stick thin, blonde, and had a pair, about as real as a set of Goodyears, that stuck out like torpedoes. She and he had partied a hell of a lot on his boat down in Gulf Shores, gone to a Jason Aldean concert at the Hangout, and eaten shrimp with their fingers out on Robinson Island. Damn, he'd been drunk as hell when they'd gotten engaged. Can't fault a man for that.

"Good-bye, Mickey," Debbi said as Mickey walked past her to the door. She leaned in, expecting a kiss on her cheek after dog-cussing him in front of his employees. Damn, if he couldn't help himself, bending down and kissing the woman's cheek, covered in a good inch of makeup. Debbi probably bought the stuff in tubs like it was spackling. "Do right by Tonya."

Do right by Tonya? Mickey wanted to tell her about the time her little angel tried to kill him for the third time. She'd poured paint thinner into his whiskey and served it up to him in a crystal glass as if he couldn't tell the difference. But he kept his mouth shut, glad to see Debbi on her way, watching her short old ass switching and swaying in those black jeans down the hall.

The Cobbs wanted alimony on top of the goddamn settlement Larry got for that horseshit business deal. These people wouldn't leave him alone until they'd picked him dry or they were ruined themselves.

And Mickey Walls wasn't one to sit around with his thumb jacked up his damn ass. He searched through his desk for the number he needed for some professional help.

C addy's a real mess," Luke Stevens said. "I'm glad you went up there and found her. I don't think she would've lasted another day."

"Wasn't me," Quinn said. "Lillie called in a few favors with her Memphis people. Tracked a number to a throwaway phone she'd been using. It put us in the neighborhood, and, after that, it didn't take us too long."

"She was nodding off in the waiting room," Luke said, standing in the hall in his hospital coat. "Low on fluids, nothing in her stomach. She nodded off again, she might not have woken up. Y'all need to get her into treatment. If she goes back to where she's been, she's not coming back."

Luke and Quinn used to be friends. They'd known each other since second grade. Luke's dad had been the town doctor, while Quinn's daddy had gone off to Hollywood to be a stuntman. They had played together, fished together, played high school football for the Wildcats. And they both had loved the same girl, growing up. Anna Lee Amsden had been Quinn's first and only love until he joined the service. But she'd gotten married to Luke, had a child, and all looked right until Quinn came back to Jericho and complicated matters a good bit.

"I gave her a shot that will help with the withdrawal," Luke said. "And I gave her a scrip for Valium to help her sleep and clonidine for the anxiety. She probably would be a lot more comfortable, and safer, in a detox clinic, if she's going to get better. But that's got to be her call. You can't force her with a gun."

"I don't think she's ever getting better," Quinn said. "I think she's fried her mind."

The men stood together in front of an old flickering television playing *Family Feud* in the Tibbehah General waiting room. Lots of old magazines lay on beaten tables between couches and chairs with ripped upholstery. Black-and-white pictures hung on the wall from when the hospital first opened in 1968, with young men and women who were now old or dead. Luke was a shaggy-haired, handsome guy, who liked to duck-hunt and ran marathons. He'd gone to Vanderbilt and Tulane while Quinn had been running and gunning in Trashcanistan. Quinn often wondered if Luke suspected anything about him and Anna Lee. Maybe he was too proud to confront them.

"It's not her fault," Luke said. "It's not just a weakness. She went back to needing this high because of some kind of stressor, maybe a reminder of when she was using before. Do you know what she was doing in Memphis?"

"Nope."

"Or who she might've seen?"

"I don't know anything about her life up there," Quinn said. "She's never talked about it. Some very bad things happened to her when we were kids. You know all about that. The situation with her boyfriend getting murdered certainly didn't help her mind-set. I asked her about Memphis. She wouldn't say."

"I guess we all keep some secrets."

Quinn nodded. *Here it comes.*

A black man in nurse's scrubs walked into the room and Luke held up his hand and told him he'd be right there. An ambulance pulled up outside the portico. Luke didn't move an inch. A couple EMTs hopped out of the ambulance and busted open the back doors. Quinn stood tall and waited.

"So she just up and disappeared?" Luke said.

"Right before Thanksgiving, there was a service out at The River to remember Jamey Dixon," Quinn said. "I don't think it set well with her. She got pretty upset. We talked the day after, and I thought everything was OK. She was really in love with that son of a bitch."

"That'll do it."

"And then she goes back to what she'd been before Jamey?"

"I'm not a psychologist, but that sounds about right."

"Caddy."

"She says she's not going to another goddamn detox center," Luke said. "I'd gather the family together and try and change her mind. Like I said, she's a mess. She came within a few hours of killing herself."

"Going from preacher to junkie is a hard fall."

"How are things out at The River?" Luke said. "I heard it's all shut up."

"Diane Tull's taken it over for a while," Quinn said. "She's taking care of the spring planting. They got a visiting preacher from Ackerman to come and help out. He's a crazy-ass hippie like the rest of them."

"So where will you take Caddy?" Luke said.

"Back to the farm," Quinn said. "She's always found peace there. My mom and I can take turns watching her until we get a plan and she agrees. I can take her wherever she needs to go when she's ready. I'm guessing she'll want to see Jason first. That's the one thing that will keep her strong."

"You think that's such a good idea?" Luke said. "For Jason?"

"Nope."

Luke nodded, thoughtful, looking as if he had something on his mind. Quinn stood there, waiting for Luke to go get Caddy or tell him more about how to handle his junkie sister. But instead he took off his expensive glasses and cleaned them with a Kleenex that he pulled from his coat pocket. The buzzer for the wrong answer sounded on the *Family Feud* and then the host talked about the other family having a chance to steal. They were wanting to *Name something that you have to catch.*

"Appreciate it, Luke," Quinn said. "I appreciate your help." He offered his hand.

Luke didn't accept it. He looked at it as if it were dog shit. The hospital doors were open, an old woman on a gurney was being wheeled in by the EMTs. A cold wind shot into the waiting room, ruffling the crappy old magazines and scattering the stale-antiseptic smell of the room. "You need to know, I'm looking for another job far away from this county."

Quinn nodded.

"I can't stay around this mess," he said. "You and Anna Lee, y'all do what you want."

Quinn placed his right hand in his jeans pocket and waited for Luke to either punch him or shoot him. He deserved both. The buzzer sounded again on the game show. The old woman on the gurney talking nonsense about having no one to feed her chickens anymore and now the coyotes were back. She disappeared down a long hall lined with yellow tile.

"I never thought of us as great friends," Luke said. "But I had always thought of you as an honorable man."

Quinn nodded.

"The instructions for the meds will be on the bottle," he said. "I gave Caddy my cell number. But I don't want you calling me or contacting me ever again. And if you ever try and get in the way of my relationship with my daughter, I'll come for you. I don't give a shit if you were an Army Ranger or MMA superstar. Do you understand me?"

Quinn looked Luke in the eye. Luke's face was hot with blood, his chin quivered.

All Quinn could do is nod and say, "I'm sorry."

"To hell you are," Luke said. "Don't kid yourself. My wife is the only reason you came back to Jericho. You wanted her and now you have her, Quinn Colson. Good luck with that."

4.

Johnny Stagg had brought on a right-hand man not long after the storm, an ex-military soldier of fortune named Ringold who'd come with a résumé so long that Stagg needed a flowchart. He was young-looking but bald, with a full black beard and sleeve tattoos of skulls, daggers, and maps of places on the other side of the earth. Stagg never talked to him about the places he'd been or the things he'd done, all he needed to know was that Ringold was good with a pistol and would protect Johnny's old ass when the bullets started to fly. After some trouble with a crew of shitbirds on scooters from over on Choctaw Lake—the goddamn Born Losers Motorcycle Club—the man had proven his worth. Now Ringold had taken on more, working direct with Stagg on running the Rebel Truck Stop and the ladies next door at the Booby Trap. The man not only knew how to fight but had a head for business. Stagg liked Ringold better than his worthless son, who was now over in Atlanta selling used cars and luxury watches and pretending he'd never heard of a place called Jericho, Mississippi.

Only problem he'd had with Ringold is that the man liked to drink.

"How'd it go last night?" Stagg said. "Any trouble?"

"Smooth night," Ringold said. "We had a couple kids up from State that kept on getting onstage with Laquita and dancing. One of them took her bikini top and was wearing it like a hat, putting the cups over his ears and tying the string up under his chin."

"Them Bulldogs don't have no respect for strippers."

"Ole Miss kids are just as bad," Ringold said. "They just tip better."

"Yeah," Stagg said. "But God bless them Rebels. Those boys will call a naked woman 'ma'am.'"

They were in the kitchen of the Rebel Truck Stop as the breakfast rush was slowing and the lunch rush was about to begin. Plates of eggs and grits slapped on the long stainless steel counter were moving on over to the world-famous chicken-fried steak with mashed potatoes and gravy. The Rebel was doing a pretty good share of barbecue business these days with chopped pork and rib plates. Truckers all up and down 45 knew and appreciated Johnny's place. Good to have the help of Ringold making sure toilets were flushed and the waitresses served a meal with a smile. He needed to give the boy some kind of title like assistant manager or something.

Stagg moved on over to the big brick pit and pulled a little of the charred meat from a side of pork. A big black guy everyone called Midnight Man watched Stagg, seeing what the boss thought of the smoking he'd started before the sun had started to rise. The meat had that nice pink ring on the outer flesh and fell right off the bone. He winked at Midnight Man and followed Ringold out of the kitchen and the sound of sizzling bacon and burgers and the clatter of dishes going through the wash.

Ringold held the swinging door for him, Stagg passing and patting Miss Baylee-Ann nice on the rump as she carried a pot full of hot coffee.

"How'd the hunt go?" Ringold asked.

"Rusty Wise ain't the man I thought he was."

"How so?"

Stagg leaned in and whispered, "I tried to be friendly and he went on and got uppity," Stagg said. "Started talking about integrity."

"Doesn't the man sell insurance?"

"Exactly what I'm talking about here."

They were in the dining area, about half full of truckers and travelers, hunkered down the counter and in a few booths facing the big metal roof overhanging the gas pumps. It was good to be seen, something Johnny had passed on to Ringold. A man starts being absent from his business and he might as well go ahead and pull his pants around his ankles and wait for Cornhole City. You had to let every cook, dishwasher, waitress, cashier, and janitor know that you were the man around here. And if they wanted to go and get greedy, you'd damn well know their names.

"Maybe he's just gotten nervous," Ringold said. "The man's never had this kind of responsibility. He'll relax when he gets into the routine. You caught him just after Christmas and before he's settled into the job."

"Really?" Stagg said. "I don't think he's gonna be no different than Colson. I think I've been wasting my fucking time."

Stagg moved on through the store that sold the cowboy boots and hats, western wear and such, and through the convenience store, with its junk food, cold beer, and souvenirs commemorating passing through Mississippi. Coffee mugs, toothpick holders, and those little silver spoons that you collect from every state. These had a magnolia leaf and a hummingbird on the handle, something an old woman would crap her drawers to get.

Stagg picked up a toothpick right before he hit the side door, moving out by the gas pumps and crossing the big wide-open space of the empty truckers' lot that would be filled tonight. He and Ringold walked side by side, their shadows blackening the edge of the cracked concrete while they made their way over to the corrugated tin building with the unlit neon reading BOOBY TRAP.

"You want me to talk to him?" Ringold said.

"No, sir," Stagg said. "Not yet. I'll let you know if it comes to that."

Ringold nodded, feet moving off the concrete and onto the crushed gravel lot and up to the locked side door of the Booby Trap. A printout was taped to the door saying ALL GIRL REVUE FROM 8 TILL 8 FRI TO SAT. CLOSED ON SUNDAYS TO GIVE THANKS!

Stagg unlocked the two dead bolts and stepped into a big room that wasn't any different, and built on the same plan, as a metal horse barn. He flicked on the overhead lamps, lighting up a place that was always noisy and dark, playing modern music that Stagg didn't understand and hated to hear. If he thought them boys would throw dollars to Pat Boone, he sure as hell would play it. The light showed no mercy on the ole Trap, industrial carpet showing stains and imitation-leather chairs with big rips sealed with silver duct tape.

Stagg spotted a half-full ashtray on a table and shook his head, not saying a word to Ringold. He dumped it out in a canister and then moved behind the big bar to fix himself a Dr Pepper with grenadine and a couple cherries.

Ringold did not ask for a drink. Nor did Stagg offer.

"What concerns me about Rusty Wise is how far he may go," Stagg said, and added some ice and shook the glass to make the drink colder. "Me and him got to be real friendly before the election. I made some casual, offhand remarks to him about the way the Rebel worked, the way business here affected this whole community. He's lived here most of his life and he didn't seem interested in changing things. Even god-damn Colson didn't mess with the economics of Tibbehah."

"You think he might shut you down?" Ringold said. He reached across the bar for a bottle of his go-to baby juice, Old No. 7, and poured him a tall order in a short glass.

"I think he's working with the Feds," Stagg said.

Ringold drank down a little of the whiskey. He looked up but didn't say a thing.

"Me and you both know the Feds are watching this place," Stagg said. "You yourself saw them slick-suited boys from Oxford using video that night. Now we got a new sheriff coming in, changing the way he talks to me and the understanding we have. I think he's the goddamn point person for those turds. Think about it. He shuts down me, the Rebel, all we done, and he becomes Buford Pusser for the ages."

"I think he's nervous, is all," Ringold said. "He doesn't know what to make of you."

Stagg took a sip and pulled in some ice, crunching it with his back teeth, the only real teeth in his whole head, already wearing down and getting old like the rest of him. He thought on things, shook the glass to chill the Dr Pepper and cherry juice more. "Them Feds got rid of my dear ole pal Bobby Campo. Got him shuffled off to the federal pen. And then the Mexes took out Houston's black ass. I saw his goddamn head in the bed of a truck. Now where you think they're looking? They want me and the sonsabitches Mexicans and I'm the easiest to pick off first. Or try and turn me."

"I think you're giving Rusty Wise more credit than he deserves," Ringold said, finishing off his whiskey like it was ice water. "I heard he once pissed himself when he had to draw his gun during a robbery."

"Yeah?" Stagg said. "I heard that story, too. Robber didn't even have a gun, was carrying a damn pocketknife. We tried to hush it up during the election."

Ringold sat down on a stool, removed his jacket, and sat his muscular tattooed arms across the bar. He wasn't facing Stagg but looking at himself in the mirror. He stroked that big wild-man beard and ran a hand over that bald head. God damn, that boy liked himself.

"Keep an eye on Rusty for me?" Stagg said. "Maybe do some of that shit you were trained to do? Follow him around? Maybe put some bugs in his house to hear his conversations?"

"Yeah, I could do that, Mr. Stagg."

"Good," Stagg said. "'Cause if he's turning on his own folks, me and him need to talk. We don't give a shit for federal people down here. Never have. That's not our way."

Y ou found her where?" Jason Colson asked.

"Memphis," Quinn said. "Last night. You don't want to know the rest."

"I'd like to know," the old man said, smaller and more wiry than Quinn, with slick gray hair and a short gray mustache and goatee, still handsome, but weathered in kind of a cowboy way. "She's my daughter."

Quinn didn't care for his father's tone, as the man had been estranged from the family, from Jericho, for more than twenty years. He'd been a semi-famous stuntman on the West Coast well before Quinn was born, working as a top man at Hal Needham's Stunts Unlimited, and had doubled for Burt Reynolds for a number of years. He was always in and out of his family's life, and then one day he was gone for good. As children, Caddy and Quinn couldn't know that there were other circumstances that last time, people who wanted him dead. Jason quietly came back to Mississippi years ago without them knowing, working horses in a town called Pocahontas.

Now every time Quinn turned down his dirt road to the old farmhouse, he spotted Jason Colson's single-wide, his old GMC truck, and a

cherry-red Pontiac Firebird up on blocks. The Firebird moved wherever Jason moved, as it had once been featured in *Hooper*, the same car
they'd driven through Armageddon and then pretended to jump over a
river in Alabama.

"Can I see her?" Jason said.

"Sure," Quinn said. "But I'd wait a few hours. She took some pills
and laid down. I think she's out. She's been through a lot."

"But you won't tell me what?"

"Shit," Quinn said. "I don't know the details. I told you that."

They stood face-to-face on the big wraparound porch of the old tin-
roof farmhouse, the day bright and sunny, not a cloud in the blue sky,
but brisk and cold. Quinn and Jason both wore heavy coats. Jason wore
a cowboy hat. He could pull it off, the black Stetson pulled down low
on his craggy face. Quinn's cattle dog, Hondo, rested nearby, with his
patchwork black-and-gray coat ruffling in the wind. Hondo breathed
slow and easy, his flank rising and falling.

"You ask Caddy," Quinn said, looking back to the back field and
the big burn pile of busted timber and branches that sat about halfway
between the old house and his dad's trailer. "Maybe she'll be straight
with you."

"Drugs?"

"Some."

"Men?"

"Why don't you ask her, Jason," Quinn said, checking his cell to see
if he had any missed calls. He was set to go on night duty at six. Two
more nights to go. His chief deputy, Lillie, running the day shift.
They'd switch off at six.

"I really wish you'd quit calling me that," Jason said in his hoarse,
whiskey-soaked voice.

"Hell," Quinn said. "It's your name, and your grandson's name. It's
a fine name. I don't mean any disrespect."

"You don't have to call me Dad, but at least call me Mr. Colson."

"All right, Mr. Colson," Quinn said. "Let your daughter sleep it off for a while. I'm going inside to make up a late breakfast. I haven't eaten since lunch yesterday. Come on, Hondo."

The dog jumped to his feet after hearing his name and the word *breakfast*. He shook the dust from his coat.

"OK, then," Jason said, cheek twitching a little. "Fine. I got some work to do."

"Like what?"

"Like finishing that half-done barn or fixing those outbuildings turned to shit."

"They turned to shit fifty years ago," he said. "They can wait."

"Your Uncle Hamp must've been the laziest man God ever created."

"I make no apologies for him," Quinn said. "Or me."

"You can't keep an animal in those barns," Jason said. "They got snakes in all 'em. One of them is about to fall over."

"What does it matter?" Quinn said. "I just got tools and some equipment in there."

"Horses."

"Horses?" Quinn said. "Shit. We don't need horses. I don't have time for horses."

"I got four back in Pocahontas," Jason said. "And I'm not as friendly with the woman keeping them as I used to be. She wants them gone. Or for me to start paying her."

"Jesus," Quinn said.

"They won't be any trouble," Jason said, his eyes the lightest blue, almost weird-looking up close. "I can turn them out with your cows."

"Shit."

"And I can teach little Jason to ride," Jason said. "How would that be? You know he'd love it."

"Let me think on it," Quinn said. "My mind needs a break this morning. Is that OK? Can I just get a damn break for five minutes?"

"Yes, sir," Jason said, pulling up the collar on his sherpa Levi's jacket. "Not a problem. I don't want to be any trouble." Quinn watched his father turn and move toward the steps of the porch. The cows wandered far out into the pasture, plenty of space for a few more.

"Hey," Quinn said.

"Yeah?"

"You want some breakfast? Mr. Colson."

Jason turned and looked over his shoulder. He smiled. "I don't want to be any trouble."

"You already said that," Quinn said. "Come on." He opened the kitchen door wide and waited for his father to pass.

"Where is she?"

"My room."

"Where will you sleep?"

"Upstairs," Quinn said. "In one of the bunks with Hondo, until she comes out of it. Or goes somewhere to get help."

The old man took off his black hat and set it crown down on the table. Quinn reached into an old 1940s refrigerator made by International Harvester, retooled by a guy up in Memphis. He started frying up four pieces of bacon in a black skillet, and laid out several eggs and some bread. As the meat started to sizzle, Quinn set his backside against the sink, crossed his arms over his chest, and turned to his father. "I need to ask you something."

"Anything."

"I don't even know how to start."

"Not about Caddy?"

"No."

"Your momma?"

"God, no," Quinn said. "She'd kill me if I talked personal matters with you."

"Your job?"

"Just listen," Quinn said. "Over the summer, I got involved with two different women."

"And you want to keep them both?" Jason said, serious as can be. "I had a deal like that going out in Los Angeles. They were roommates, a couple hippies. One of them had spent some time with Gram Parsons before he passed. And I had suspicions about her knowing Charles Manson. I slept with one eye open."

Quinn held up his hand. "I only kept one," Quinn said. "The other one isn't talking to me right now."

"You're talking about Ophelia Bundren," Jason said. "That nice girl from the funeral home. Hell, I knew y'all had split up. Everybody in town knows that. Don't blame you. Didn't she throw a fork at your head?"

"No, sir."

"I thought she did," Jason said, thinking on it. "When we cooked out steaks on your birthday?"

"It was a knife," Quinn said. "She's very good with knives. It stuck straight in the kitchen wall."

"Good God," Jason said. "What'd you do to piss her off?"

"The worst thing I could."

"What's that?"

"Told her the truth," Quinn said. "We weren't ever getting married. She wasn't the one."

"Did she know about this other gal?"

"Nope," he said. "That happened later. And before her, too, I guess. But it had been coming on for a long while."

"I know the woman you're talking about," Jason said, grinning.

"Y'all have been trying to sneak around. But neither of you are too good at it. Damn, she's a fine-looking woman."

Quinn nodded. He walked to the sink and filled up a coffeepot with water and spooned in some grounds in the percolator.

"But careful," Jason Colson said. "She looks like the kind of woman who'd tear a man's heart into shreds."

5.

I f he was real honest with himself, and didn't let Jesus or his kin get
in the way, Chase Clanton had to say the most important thing in his
whole damn rotten life was University of Alabama football. He'd
been a Tide fan since he was born, his momma making sure of it, never
really knowing how his daddy stood on lots of things: family, politics,
religion, or important matters like knowing whether he pulled for Auburn or Alabama. One of the first memories Chase ever had was watching the great Gene Stallings, that old rawboned Texan, roaming the
sidelines to beat the hell out of Michigan in the Outback Bowl. His
Uncle Peewee always said he was full of shit, as Chase was only two
years old. But Chase remembers it clear as yesterday, as that was the last
big team before those lean years, before they brought in the second
coming of Bear Bryant—Nick Saban—to again take their place as the
football machine they'd been back during the glory days.

Uncle Peewee was a Tide fan, too. He even had a red Ford Econoline van customized with special seats covered in houndstooth check
and a mural airbrushed on the side of a shirtless AJ McCarron, and
Nick Saban, and a smiling Jesus Christ, and, in the background, Coach
Bryant riding an elephant to victory, with the stats to back it up. *323*

Wins. Six National Titles. Uncle Peewee sure loved that van, although they were taking his other one tonight, the one just like it, only it was black and had the VIN number scratched off the door. The plates were stolen, and everything they needed was inside a black duffel bag—the drills, hammers, and assorted picks—just in case they had to bail. Since his daddy took off and his momma had gotten fat and hooked up to the oxygen, Uncle Peewee had looked out for Chase.

Not only had they tailgated together at Bryant-Denny sixteen times but he'd become Chase's own private junior college, teaching him things, ways of life, that his daddy couldn't or never knew.

"You stick in the van," Peewee said, hunched over the wheel. "You hear anything on that police scanner or someone coming down the road, you call me on that walkie-talkie. But don't say shit 'cause some-one might be listening in. You never know who might be tuned to our channel. You just do the way we talked about it. You remember?"

"Yes, sir," Chase said. "I think someone is comin' and I say 'Roll Tide.'"

"That's right, boy. That's right."

Uncle Peewee was a fat man, wasn't any getting around that, with fat arms and fat legs and a midsection big as a whiskey barrel. He wore big gold-framed glasses and had wild hair that he never combed, mak-ing him seem like a cartoon owl. Didn't help that he also ate a lot of pork plates from the Ole Kountry Kabin out on Highway 17. He liked to smoke extra-long Pall Malls, and on Friday nights he'd sometimes smoke a few joints with Chase, telling him stories about running with the Dixie Mafia, back when they meant something, and even more sto-ries about all the women he'd laid. If he were to take Uncle Peewee's word as gospel, then he figured Uncle Peewee must've screwed over a thousand women in his life. When Chase called him on it over the summer, Uncle Peewee just nodded his head, said that was probably true, and figured he still had time for a thousand more.

"You don't have to worry too much," Peewee said, hitting a hard pothole in the highway, jarring their asses up and down. "I been watching this house last two nights. Nobody's checking their mail, and they got them lights on a timer. No dogs. Only an alarm that hooks up to the telephone line. I can cut the line before I break in the back door."

"What if there's nothing worth stealing?" Chase said.

"I been doing this twice as long as you been alive," Peewee said, staring down that line in the middle of the highway from behind thick glasses. "I ain't never been in a house that didn't have something worth stealing."

"How much you want to get tonight?"

"I can go back to taking her easy for a while if I get a couple thousand," Peewee said. "That of course is minus your cut. Way I figure, that two thousand will give me just enough to fuel up my van and head down to New Orleans for an ole-fashioned pussy party."

"You sure like the ladies."

"No, sir," Uncle Peewee said. "I love the ladies. Gonna buy me an extra-large box of condoms at Sam's Club, a big ole bottle of butter spray, and a pair of handcuffs. I ain't coming back to Gordo till the money runs out."

"I wouldn't mind seeing the Sugar Bowl."

"If this house is like I think, I'll get us four tickets on the fifty-yard line."

"Four?"

"Two for you and me," Uncle Peewee said. "And two for them strippers we gonna meet."

"You and your strippers."

"I respect strippers," Uncle Peewee said, staring straight ahead, looking for the exit they'd be taking inside the Birmingham city limits. "They respect my money and I respect their titties. What I call a fair and truthful arrangement."

On his right hand, Peewee had three large gold rings. One of them with the initials PWS for "Peewee Sparks," Peewee being the youngest member of the infamous Sparks brothers, three of them in prison and one of them dead. Chase's momma was the baby, a lot younger than Peewee. She told Chase she didn't start dating till she was sixteen on account of everyone in Gordo was afraid of her family. When Chase's dad got her pregnant after some Bible retreat in Panama City Beach, Uncle Peewee gave him the option of getting married at seventeen or getting his pecker sawed off with a pocketknife. Chase took some comfort knowing his daddy wasn't as stupid as some folks said.

"You think you'll let me come with you the next time?" Chase said. "I don't like just sitting in the car. Makes my ass hurt."

"You can come with me when you can bust a safe. Took me nearly ten years before I got good enough."

"How'd you learn?"

"Same as you," Peewee said. "I tagged along with this ole fella from up in Corinth, Mississippi, who'd run with Towhead White. Before that, he'd learned the trade direct from the master, a real mean redheaded motherfucker named Head Revel, in Phenix City. This going back some years—a long time back."

"Momma doesn't know what you're doing."

"Oh, she knows."

"She says she doesn't," Chase said. "I think she just likes me going to your house so I ain't sitting around playing Call of Duty all day. She says I'm stealing the TV, keeping her from watching her stories. You know how much she loves *Days of Our Lives*."

"You see that sign up there?"

"What sign?"

"That sign coming up on the right," he said. "My glasses are dirty."

"Mountain Brook."

"That's it," Peewee said. "Always like to hit a house with two Mercedes in the garage."

"Why don't we steal the cars?"

"Been there, done that," Peewee said. "Ain't no decent chop shops in west Alabama no more. We cross over into Mississippi and then they get us on federal. Ain't worth the risk. I'm no car man. I'm a safe man."

Chase smiled as the black van turned onto a gentle curve and then wrapped back under the highway bridge. They passed through a little downtown full of jewelry stores, fancy-ass clothes stores, and restaurants, all looking like pictures he'd seen of Germany. Uncle Peewee reached for his pack of cigarettes and lighter. As he got one going, he tossed Chase a folded-up piece of yellow paper with directions and an address on it. "All right, tell me where I'm turning next."

"Yes, sir."

"Remember what I said about the walkie-talkie."

"Yes, sir."

"And don't forget what I said about the snatch down in NOLA, neither," Uncle Peewee said, cracking a window and driving low and slow. "Ain't nothing like it nowhere."

In the console by his cigarettes and Bic lighter, his cell phone buzzed and shook, vibrating the loose change and bottle caps around it. Peewee picked it up for a minute and then turned it off. Chase didn't see a name, just a location. JERICHO, MS. Wherever the hell that happened to be.

If you think I'm hanging around for this shit show," Lillie said, "you're wrong as hell."

"So you've told me," Quinn said, looking up as he loaded more boxes, making sure the office was cleared by tomorrow. He didn't have much—mainly, some books, some personal photographs, and a dozen or so weapons. "It's not a bad deal. Rusty wants to keep you on as assistant sheriff at more pay than you're getting now."

"Well, I'm not working for that moron," Lillie said. "He's got no business being in law enforcement. That son of a bitch just tried to sell me a life insurance policy this spring at the Fillin' Station. Did you see his ad on those fucking billboards on Highway 45? With his kids, wife, and goddamn dog?"

"Unfortunately, most of this county doesn't agree with you," Quinn said. "I appreciate your loyalty, but you need to think about your family. You've got a mortgage and a daughter. Saying 'Fuck it' isn't as easy as it used to be."

"Rusty said he'd hire you on, too?"

"He did," Quinn said. "But I think he was just being polite. I can find other work."

"In Jericho?" Lillie said. "I hear they're looking for greeters at the new Walmart. You can wear one of those PROUD VETERAN hats with American flag pins. Folks can salute you as they're leaving with their big-screen TVs and buckets of beef jerky."

"Overseas work," Quinn said. "An old friend from the Regiment does some consulting back in the AFG. I've been in touch."

"But you won't go back to the Army?"

"I haven't ruled it out," Quinn said, reaching for a stack of books on his desk. The *Nick Adams Stories*, the *Legends of King Arthur*, *Greek Myths*, and a field guide to tracking animals. "I'd have to go back through selection. But I could return to Fort Benning and instruct."

"I thought you hated the idea of being an instructor," Lillie said. "When I came to find you at Fort Benning, you said you'd rather—"

Quinn held up his hand. "Things have changed from what we discussed. I'm getting older. I got to go back to what I know best."

"Shooting people?"

"Something like that," Quinn said. "Rangers do other things, too. We do a shit ton of push-ups, sit-ups, and run all day long."

"Thank God, you didn't shoot those bastards this morning," Lillie said. "We'd still be filling out paperwork."

"Is that all that would bother you?"

Lillie nodded, moving closer to the desk. She was back in uniform, slick SHERIFF's OFFICE coat, dark green ball cap with a star logo, and shitkicker boots. "How's Caddy?"

"Resting."

"What'd Luke say?"

"He said if you hadn't found her, she'd be dead," Quinn said. "I appreciate you pulling in those favors."

"She's my friend, too," Lillie said. "A royally fucked-up friend is still a friend. Is she with your momma?"

"No, my dad's watching her," Quinn said. "Momma's coming over tonight."

"And little Jason?"

"Keeping him far away," Quinn said. "We're working on getting her into a good place in Tupelo. But she says she won't go. She alternates saying she's fine and saying she doesn't deserve to live. She's a goddamn mess, Lillie. I don't know what to do. I want to just force her into the detox, but I think she'll try and escape."

"I'd do what Luke says," Lillie said. "He's smart. Maybe the smartest guy I know. I'd trust him."

"That's what I hear."

"Y'all get into it?"

Quinn shrugged. He walked over to a far wall and pulled a framed flag that his friend Colonel George Reynolds had presented him. The flag had flown at Camp Spann in Afghanistan, where Quinn's platoon had operated for a few weeks. There had been a lot of patrols. A Ranger private from Tennessee had gotten his leg blown off and there was a hell of a fight to get him back to the camp before he bled to death. The flag had been flown to honor Quinn for his integrity and commitment.

"What's your dad saying about this whole mess?" Lillie asked.

"Not much," Quinn said. "We ate bacon and eggs, and he told me about a three-way he'd had with some hippie women up in the Hollywood Hills."

"Jason Colson," Lillie said. "A real charmer."

Quinn taped up the box. He set it beside four others by the door. The door was one of those old-fashioned ones with a frosted-glass pane at the top reading QUINN COLSON, SHERIFF. Before that, he'd had to scrape the name of his dead uncle off the same glass. Now it would go to Rusty Wise, and things just kind of marched on like that. You come back home, shoot it out with some skinheads in the woods, run off a bunch of Mexican gunners, chase down some escaped convicts, see the town through a tornado, solve a couple horrific old murders, run off a biker gang, and the voters send you packing anyway.

Three pink slips had been set on his desk by the new dispatcher, a black woman named Cleotha who'd been in Quinn's high school class. All the slips read "Anna Lee Stevens." Quinn looked up at Lillie to see if she'd noticed. "Don't quit until you've found a new job," Quinn said. "Promise me that."

"There's an opening with Memphis PD," Lillie said. "Sex crimes. But you know I fucking hate Memphis. I don't want to raise my daughter in that shithole. Just being up there last night brought on some bad memories. About the only thing good about Memphis is the Grizzlies and barbecue."

"You're not selling me out for staying on," Quinn said. "You were here before I came home and you'll be here long after I've gone."

"Don't talk like that."

"Things have grown complicated since I moved back to Jericho."

"That's an understatement."

"Personal things."

"No shit," she said, looking down at the pink callback slips. "You think I don't know?"

"Might be best if I leave town for a while," Quinn said.

"That's bullshit," Lillie said. "I'm sorry about your sister, and I'm sorry about this political shitstorm that kicked you out of office. But, other than that, it seems like things are going fine. You have a good family. You got a great dog, a decent truck. You're getting laid regular."

"Lillie . . ."

"Am I lying?"

Quinn didn't say anything.

"Nobody figured you came home for this fucking job."

6.

ickey hadn't picked up a dirty pair of drawers since Tonya Cobb left him. He just kept on buying packs of new Hanes boxer shorts at Walmart and leaving the spent ones on the floor. He hoped one day she'd come back to their big ranch house and get the message that she just didn't matter. He didn't pick up much else, either. There were the same old cans of Bud Light and Hunt Bros. pizza boxes racked up on the coffee table right by the television set. And the television set was new, too. He just went for it, getting that eighty-inch plasma to watch State games and episodes of *Swamp Pawn* and *Dallas Cowboys Cheerleaders: Making the Team*. A man hasn't lived until he's seen those tatas bouncing around on an eighty-inch. Mickey was finally living like he'd meant to live. Nobody telling him his business.

He was headed to work late, Lee Salter calling at eight, saying he couldn't get the goddamn luan to seal right, and Mickey saying it didn't have to be perfect, it just had to lay flat for the linoleum. Lee said the problem wasn't the luan but the damn sealant. Mickey knew Lee just wasn't getting what he'd been taught and told him to go get some biscuits and he'd meet him at the house.

"Mickey?" Lee had asked.

"Yeah?"

"What the hell is luan anyway?"

"It's Filipino for cheap-ass wood."

The thing about being the boss, the owner of Walls Flooring, was that he didn't have to get on his knees as much as he used to. His monkeys did that for him. But he had a reputation, Walls being the business where WE MAKE THINGS RIGHT. OR YOUR MONEY BACK. Mickey figured that was about the whole point of living. *Making things right.* Maybe that's why he just couldn't get out of his mind what goddamn Larry Cobb had done. Mickey would sit up in the middle of the night and see Cobb's craggy face and want to punch the fucking air. *God damn it.*

Mickey changed into his clothes, the nice ones, the ones that showed he was successful. The clean Carhartt pants, the Pete Millar plain shirt, and the wooly vest made by True Grit. He might wear cheap drawers, but, on the outside, people knew Mickey Walls was somebody. The eighty-inch was on, playing the CBS morning show out of Tupelo, as he buttoned up the shirt and zipped up the vest. He reached for his cowboy killers and lit up the first one of the day. He should have told Lee to get him a sausage biscuit, too. And he was just about to call him back when he heard a knock on the garage door.

Kyle Hazlewood was standing out at the garage by Mickey's red Hummer, wearing that same confused hangdog expression as yesterday, and the same old leather racing jacket, now worn as hell around the collar.

"I went by the office," Kyle said. "You weren't there."

"No shit," Mickey said. "'Cause I'm here."

"What's eating your ass?"

"Come on," Mickey said. "Come on in. I'm just pissed-off 'cause I hadn't eaten and forgot to tell Lee to get me a sausage biscuit. And I got a hangover to boot."

"I can run you up to the Sonic," Mickey said. "They got those burritos with eggs and tater tots in 'em. They ain't too bad. Hey, man, can I get a cigarette off you?"

"Yeah, sure," Mickey said, holding the door open. "Smokes on the table. You been thinking on things?"

Kyle nodded, dropped his head, and walked up into Mickey's kitchen. He didn't have any coffee on account of forgetting to buy some, the refrigerator was bare as hell, nothing in there but a few cartons of the yogurt that made you need to shit. It had been cold last night and Mickey had kept the water running so the pipes didn't freeze. They were still running. *Tap . . . Tap . . . Tap . . .*

"I hear what you're saying," Kyle said, lighting up.

"Good."

"About Larry."

"Yeah?"

"He's a real cocksucker."

"Sure thing, man."

"I mean, Larry Cobb is one prismatic son of a bitch."

"Yeah?" Mickey said. "What exactly does that mean?"

"You know, like a prism, a crystal," Kyle said. "You twist him around and he's a son of a bitch from every angle. What they call multifaceted."

"Just what I said," Mickey said. "Am I now making some sense?"

"I figure," Kyle said. "But I don't know if there's enough time. You're talking about tomorrow night? What if we get in there and you can't open the safe? You said it's been a few months. Larry's probably gone and changed the lock after you and Tonya broke up. You ain't exactly his special son-in-law no more."

"Yeah," Mickey said, "I know. I know. But the reason I wanted you to come along is that I can't be in no way associated with this. Someone busts into goddamn Larry Cobb's safe and the first thing Quinn Colson is gonna to do is knock on my front door."

"He ain't the sheriff."

51

"I think he's sheriff for another week or two," Mickey said. "I seen him cruising around last night in that big-ass green truck. I can't have him or that Lillie Virgil interfering with my business and my world and wanting to know when and where I was at while someone was giving it high and hard to that son of a bitch Larry Cobb."

Kyle rubbed his thin, graying beard and shook his head. "God damn," Kyle said. "If you're wanting me to go at this thing alone . . . I ain't crazy. You got to have two people to watch the road, see who's coming. Also just to carry all that money. No telling what's in that safe—"

"Already thought about that," Mickey said, holding up his hand. "I'm not leaving you alone. I'm just saying I can't be around it. You know goddamn well that Larry looks to me if someone has farted in the lumberyard. He blames me for the Bulldogs losing, for his dinner getting burnt, and that fucking global warming."

"He doesn't believe in that shit," Kyle said. "He told me that himself. He said it was just lies from liberal Yankees and part of the homosexual agenda."

"Yeah," Mickey said, firing up another cowboy killer. "That sounds about like the wisdom of Larry Cobb."

"So," Kyle said, "if you can't be around this and I'm needing some help, how the hell we gonna bust out a million bucks from that safe and not get our asses a ticket to Parchman? I'm too damn old and tired to get cornholed by some black degenerate."

"We need help with opening the safe and transferring the money he's got," Mickey said. "I mean, you ain't gonna just go drop it off at Jericho First National in a bunch of Piggly Wiggly sacks. We need to connect with folks who've done this before."

"I don't know any real criminals," Kyle said. "Not any good ones anyway. My daddy once knocked over a fillin' station in Meridian back in '73. He got three years on The Farm on account of getting thirty-two fifty and a Zagnut bar."

"I didn't, neither," Mickey said, pointing the lit end of the Marlboro at Kyle. "But I know someone who does. They put me in touch with a real professional."

"Someone on your crew?"

"No, sir," Mickey said. "My goddamn ex-wife."

"Misty?"

"Afraid so."

"She ain't mentally stable, Mickey," Kyle said. "What the hell, man? You told me that yourself."

"Maybe," Mickey said. "But she's loyal. She'd come and tend to me right this moment."

"Who the hell does she know?"

"I ever tell you she's a Sparks?"

"Like them crazy-ass Alabama boys?" Kyle said. "Those mother-fuckers are a bunch of killers. Come on, man, I ain't working with any goddamn Sparks. They'll plug one in the back of my ear before I hear 'em coming. I said I'd help you, not work with any of the goddamn Sparks."

"Her uncle ain't like that," Mickey said. "He's not one of the Killin' Sparks. His name is Peewee. He's strictly a safe man. He's got skills. He says he can work a safe like a monkey cracking open a peanut."

"I don't know," Kyle said. "Shit. I'm not so sure."

"Peewee says he knows a half-dozen boys like to be in on a job like this. He called it a real honeypot."

"You already called him?" Kyle said. "You called him after me and you talked? I thought this was only about making things right. About me and you getting back at Larry Cobb."

"It is."

"But a Sparks?" Kyle said. "Man, come on."

"Will you just meet him?" Mickey said. "Just meet him. He's all right. I drank some beer with him at a family reunion for Misty's people. We sat behind a Baptist church and rolled us a fat one, talking about Jimmy Buffett and shit."

"Misty know what's up?"

"God, no."

"Why'd she think you needed to talk to her uncle?"

"Work," Mickey said. "I said I needed a hand over the Alabama border laying some heart pine and to put me in touch with her people."

"Shit," Kyle said. "Robbing? It ain't our style, man."

"Come on, bud," Mickey said. "Don't get no better than this."

Y ou told him," Quinn said. "Didn't you?"

Anna Lee Amsden—still hard to think of her as Anna Lee Stevens, Luke's wife—didn't say anything. They stood in front of the half-moon gravel drive outside Quinn's old farmhouse, with its white siding, leaded-glass windows, and silver tin roof. She'd been waiting for him as soon as he'd come off night patrol. Quinn had on a heavy winter coat and a ball cap, at first asking her if she wanted to come inside. When she said she didn't, he just went ahead and asked about how Luke found out about them. "It's twenty degrees," Quinn said. "Let me make a fire and some coffee."

"I have to get home."

"That's the way it goes?" Quinn said. "You clean your conscience and leave it to all work out?"

"I haven't liked myself much lately."

"I wish you'd told me first," Quinn said. "I might have been ready to duck."

"Luke wouldn't hit you."

"He might have."

"And how much damage would that have done?" Anna Lee said. "Luke might've broken a finger on your head."

"Come on inside," Quinn said. "I've been on for the last fourteen hours. We can sit and talk. And then you can go. OK by you? It takes two hours to heat that old house."

"I think we better keep what needs to be said outside," Anna Lee said. "Besides, I don't want to disturb Caddy. Is she still sleeping?"

"Yeah," Quinn said. "Dad's watching her."

"This is a bad time," Anna Lee said. "We need to slow down, make some sense of things. I don't want anyone else hurt by us."

Quinn nodded and told her that was bullshit. Anna Lee put her fingers up to her mouth and shook her head, looking good as always in faded Levi's, cowboy boots, and an old trucker's jacket over a scoop-necked black sweater. The sweater down low enough to show off her perfect, delicate collarbone and the thin gold chain with the gold cross around her neck. Quinn reached out a hand and she shook her blonde head.

"I sleep fine," Quinn said.

"That's a hell of a thing to say."

"It's the way I feel."

"I feel awful," Anna Lee said. "It's wrong."

"Never felt wrong to me," Quinn said. "I came back here for you."

"You came back to bury your Uncle Hamp," she said. "And then got this old house, and all your family troubles, and, before anyone knew it, you'd blown away a half-dozen evil folks at Hell Creek."

"Yeah," Quinn said. "But I came back to see you. Lillie Virgil told me that today. She's known a long time."

"Of course she has," Anna Lee said, smiling just a bit. Quinn walked up on her, closing the space, putting his hand around her narrow waist and sliding a hand into her back pocket just like he'd done back in high school. She could change what she wanted and lie to herself, her family, and Jesus, but there had never been a damn thing that could come between them. Everything that Quinn had done since stepping back in Tibbehah County had been a big game. She was why he was here, and she had to feel it the same as he did.

"Come inside."

"God damn you."

He pulled her in close, inside his coat, and she stayed there for several moments, shivering, before speaking. "Is Caddy OK?" she said.

"No."

"Is she going to get help?"

"I don't know," Quinn said. "I'm trying to talk her into it. It's the best for her. And best for Jason. She's ripping that kid's guts out."

"I'm sorry," Anna Lee said, moving in closer under the jacket. "I'm real sorry."

"You know what?" Quinn said. "I'm glad it's out. Who the hell do I need to impress around here? I'm glad you told him."

"Luke's leaving town."

"When?"

"He's gone," she said. "He told me about what happened with Caddy and then with you. He's packed and gone to Memphis. He said he's not coming back and we'll work out visitation. It's no bluff."

"Good."

Anna Lee pulled away, away from Quinn, and stepped back to stare him down with those hard brown eyes. "Are you sure?"

"Yes, ma'am."

"Now what?"

"Reminds me of a fella back home who fell out of a ten-story building."

"We don't have ten-story buildings in Jericho."

"You know what he said?" Quinn said.

"What?"

"So far, so good."

"That doesn't give me a lot of comfort, Quinn," Anna Lee said. "Slow and easy. OK?"

"Yes, ma'am," Quinn said, pulling her even closer, kissing her. "I'll do my best."

7.

Johnny Stagg had been holding court in his red vinyl booth at the
Rebel for nearly two hours, glad-handing and arranging favors for
county employees and the like, by the time Larry Cobb showed
up, wanting two eggs sunny-side up and two pieces of well-done bacon
with no toast. Cobb told Stagg he'd been trying to watch the carbs and
that he and Debbi had been on this diet they learned about from watching Dr. Phil, wanting to know if Stagg ever watched the program.

"I don't watch a lot of TV, Larry," he said, taking a sip of coffee. "If
I do, it's the television news or a good ole-fashioned Western."

"Me and Debbi watch Dr. Phil and that other guy, the one who
knows Oprah, too. He's the real doctor, wears scrubs and all. He talks
about how exercise and good eating can add ten years to a man. Debbi
and me been working our whole lives—hard work—to earn what we
got. Last thing I need is another heart attack to keep me away from
fishing or the ski slopes. We're going back to that time-share in Aspen
in February. You should fly up to Colorado sometime, Johnny. I think
you'd just love it."

"I been there," Stagg said. "Lots of rich women in fur coats and men
dressed up like queers. No thank you, sir."

The waitress set down a ceramic mug for Cobb and walked off, checking on other tables, giving Stagg the privacy that everyone knew he needed at the corner booth. If Johnny had company, everyone knew to set down the food, or coffee, and walk away. Let Johnny tend to his business. The truck stop was filled this morning, eighteen-wheelers backed up nearly ten slots for the diesel pumps, credit card receipts unrolling, register bells jingling.

"So how you been, Larry?"

"Fine," Cobb said. "I ain't complainin'."

"You sounded worried on the telephone."

"Nah," Cobb said. "I ain't worried. Just trying to get things straight. Make sure everything's working out with the bridge. I hadn't heard a word in two months. I just figured that . . . Well, you know."

"That it was a done deal?"

"Yeah," Larry Cobb, that greedy son of a bitch, said. "Yeah, that's about it."

"It is."

Cobb was a man of medium height and impressive girth. He hadn't done manual labor since the eighties but shuffled his feet and bounded around as if he were a big man on account of his thickness. He had a big fat stomach and big fat arms that he'd cross over the bulk with a lot of self-satisfaction. He was bald, with white hair ringing his head, and kept his white beard just short enough not to look like a redneck Santa Claus. Two of his teeth were gold, and he'd taken to wearing a Mississippi State jacket just to show he didn't care a whit for Johnny's beloved Ole Miss. Mainly, he just lorded over his world—a single-wide trailer out back of north Mississippi's biggest lumberyard.

"Johnny, I appreciate the business and all, but a man's got to go and plan ahead. You know? I got to turn down business to take on a project like this. And I got other folks, equipment people up in Memphis, who are wanting to go ahead and get paid. I mean, you can't just talk about building a big highway bridge on a Monday and start work on a Tuesday. We need to start clearing them woods."

"I'm pretty sure I know how this all works, Larry," Stagg said. "Maybe the reason that you and Debbi can fly up to Colo-rado and queer around with all them California folks like Mississippi come to town."

"I didn't mean nothing, Johnny," Cobb said. "It's just that it's been—"

"Two months."

"Yeah—"

"Eight weeks."

"Well," Cobb said, a plate with two eggs and bacon sliding in front of him. The way the cook had arranged the plate made the breakfast look like a man's face. Two yolks for eyes, and a big wide bacon grin, burnt to a crisp just like Larry Cobb's big old fat ass liked it. "Yeah," Cobb said, slurping on his coffee, bent over the breakfast and shoveling it into his mouth. Making those *Mmm-mmm* sounds. Son of a bitch.

The place in front of Johnny Stagg was clean, a rolled-up paper napkin around the silverware, an unsoiled place mat showing a cartoon image of Mississippi and all the famous things that happened across the state. Elvis in Tupelo. Faulkner in Oxford. And Faith Hill over in Ridgeland. Stagg sure loved to hear that woman sing. He was a true fan of her talent and her beauty.

"You want me to butter your bread for you?" Stagg said.

Cobb sat up just a little straighter and eyed Johnny, getting the message, putting down the knife and fork and licking his lips. He nodded and nodded as he thought, wiping his mouth with a napkin. "Easy for you," Cobb said. "Ain't it? You don't have no physical investment in the project."

Stagg grinned, looking over Cobb's shoulder, and spotted Sam

Bishop, Jr., Tibbehah County Supervisor for District 1, walk through the door. Stagg waved at Bishop and Bishop waved back, coming in with his wife and two daughters, taking a booth toward the front door. Christmas lights and fake holly hung over the glass. The waitress walking right on up and bringing them some ice waters.

"Sorry, I had something in my ear," Stagg said. "You were saying how I'm not a part of some business around here?"

"Smile all you want, but it ain't your money," Cobb said. "It's a hell of an investment for me and Debbi. We had to make some hard decisions, family matters, to come up with that kind of cash. We even had to cut back on our tithes at First Baptist."

"Bullshit."

"Excuse me?"

"I said, you're full of shit, Larry Cobb," Stagg said. "You know what it costs to do business with the State of Mississippi and you became a rich man because of it. Go and give the hardworkin' redneck shuck to one of your truckers you ain't paying right."

Cobb gave him a hard look, which wasn't much since the man had pig eyes and no chin. Stagg took a drink of water, the ice melting but still clicking in the glass. He shrugged it off, and Cobb's hard look turned to a grin, trying to be a hard-on just for the hell of it. Now that he saw Stagg couldn't get a guarantee on that dirty money any faster, he would switch over to the old, portly, hardworkin' man and go right back to chawing on the breakfast. Sure enough, Cobb just shook his head and picked up a piece of burnt bacon. "Just makes me nervous," Cobb said. "You know how that goes?"

"Eat up, Larry," Stagg said. "You been eating up in this county trough a long time. This is the first time I ever heard any complaint about your seat at the table."

Cobb swallowed and nodded. "During that storm and cleanup, me and you shared and shared alike," he said. "Made rich men even richer. That durn storm was the best thing that ever happened to either of us."

Stagg turned a fork around a circle on the Formica table, looking up to Larry Cobb. "You want me to get you a microphone so you can broadcast our business to everyone in north Mississippi?"

"No," Cobb said, cutting into his eggs, busting the yolk. "But don't you ever make me out to be some kind of charity case. Me and you shared plenty over these years. We all got a little dirt on us."

"Go on. Go on. Spell it on out."

"Hell, I don't know," Cobb said, yellow running down his white-bearded chin, snorting in some air. "Just pass me some of them jelly packs. Will you, Stagg?"

Stagg eyed the bloated piece of shit on the left side of him and chose the right side of the big red booth to make his departure. He got out, made sure the Ole Miss sweater-vest was flat over his chinos, and stood above Cobb. Cobb didn't look up, hunkered over the wheel and sopping up everything on his plate. At the swinging door to the kitchen, Ringold leaned against the cash register, sipping on coffee. He met Stagg's eye and nodded.

Stagg nodded back, hit the front door, and walked around to his office.

W ell," Peewee Sparks said. "Fuck a duck."

"How much?" Chase asked, browsing through the Gold Mine pawnshop off Interstate 65, somewhere south of Birmingham. The Gold Mine hadn't opened up yet, the barred door locked behind them, lights off overhead but shining bright in the glass cases, with their jewelry, pistols, rare coins, DVD players, and shit made during the Civil War.

"We can walk out of here with three grand," Peewee said. "But I could burn though that in fifteen minutes at Temptations on Bourbon Street. That's just an introduction to those women doing serious business. Not to mention your cut is a damn third."

"How about this other deal you're talking about?" Chase said. "The one in Mississippi?"

"Don't know enough about it," Peewee said. "Could be something. Could be jack shit. People always trying to shit you in this world, kid."

"I say we do it."

"Oh, you do," Peewee said, his crazy owl hair sticking up wild, the lenses of his big gold glasses dirty. "I sure do appreciate the advice since you don't know nothing about it."

"I ain't telling you what to do," Chase said, spotting a real sweet little gun, a silver .32 with a pearl grip inlaid with a joker playing card. "I'm just saying let's move on. It ain't like we can drive back to Mountain Brook and tell those people we'd been lied to."

"We'll see," Peewee said. "I've been dreaming about raw oysters and titties for weeks."

"Can you ask that fella what he'll take for that pistol?"

"What pistol?"

"One right there," Chase said. "In the glass case. It's got a really fancy grip on it with the joker card. It looks like something out of a comic book."

"Thought you'd like one with the Bear on it."

"They make one like that?"

"Shit, I'm just funnin' you." The older man reached into his sagging blue jeans and brought out a blue bandanna. He sneezed into it, wiped his nose, and then used the same rag to clean his glasses. He hitched up his blue jeans, sagging down under his stomach. "I don't mess with guns. You want to buy the gun, you talk to the man. But I'm not gonna be the one to buy you the pistol that gets you killed."

"How you figure?"

"I ain't telling your momma that," Peewee said. "Everyone always talking about how the Sparks boys are bat-shit, they ain't never met your momma. She makes all her brothers seem like goddamn Ruritans."

"Sure," Chase said. "That's fine with me. Just give me what I got coming."

Peewee waddled back past the glass counters and through a shower curtain hanging over a back doorway. Chase heard the men talking low and kind of mumbled. For a second, he thought he might just be able to slip a hand under the glass counter and get the gun. But he spotted a lock, and when he glanced around the showroom at its four corners— all the stereos, TVs, DVDS, computers, leather jackets, and tools—he spotted no less than five fucking security cameras. Uncle Peewee was right. *Fuck a damn duck.*

Peewee wandered out, counting out hundred-dollar bills in his hand and sucking on a lollipop. He handed Chase a green sucker and then counted out a thousand into the boy's waiting hands. Peewee tucked the rest of the roll down deep into his underwear and then scratched the stubble on his chin. He was wearing a red-and-green plaid shirt over the T-shirt Chase had given him for Christmas. It was of the Grinch and that little old brown dog of his, the one that got screwed, always having to do the heavy lifting. The shirt read GRINCH BETTER HAVE MY PRESENTS.

"We headin' over to Mississippi?" Chase said.

"I said, I don't know."

"We might just see what they got to offer."

"I might fart the theme to *Green Acres* out my ass," Peewee said. "Or I might not. I just said it's something."

"Something is good when you ain't got nothing."

"Boy," Peewee said. "You ain't never held a woman's coot. And you ain't never felt that much cash in your hand. Be grateful."

"I am," Chase said. "I appreciate it. I just figured it wouldn't hurt having a gun. Especially if we're gonna cross the border."

"You ever been out of Alabama?"

"No, sir."

"Haw, haw," Peewee said. "Shit, do what you want. I'm gonna walk right over to that Cracker Barrel, take me a dump in a clean stall, and then get a Uncle Herschel's Favorite with country ham and an extra order of hash brown casserole."

"OK."

"You really want that little peashooter?" Peewee said. "How about you just wait on something bigger?"

"I just like how it looks, is all," Chase said. "It'll do right."

"Don't give a shit what name your daddy gave you," Peewee said, fluorescent lights flickering on over their heads. "You are a Sparks."

A foreign fella, who was Chinese or Mongolian or from Hawaii, walked on past them to the front door and turned on a couple neon signs and unlocked the door. Chase nodded at his Uncle Peewee and turned back to the man, fluorescents still trying to come to life. He nodded to his uncle and his uncle turned and walked away and out the door, strolling across the parking lot over to the Cracker Barrel. Chase moved up to the gun display and unwrapped his free sucker. "Excuse me, sir?" Chase said. "You speak any English?"

Quinn borrowed Caddy's truck, a beaten-to-shit '72 Ford that he'd bought while at Fort Benning, to drive north on the Natchez Trace without being spotted. He brought with him a couple good cigars, La Gloria Cubana Blacks, and a couple tall coffees from the Fillin' Station diner. The Trace took him up into the rolling hills of Tibbehah County, past the turnoff to his farm and the hamlets of Fate and Providence, and on into southern Lee County and a visitors' center with public bathrooms and a covered area with a view of the mounds where the Chickasaw had buried their dead and made temples to their warriors. As usual, it was empty. And, as expected, the lean, bald man with the beard was waiting for him.

"You know, they didn't even have shovels," the man said. "Did the whole damn thing with baskets, filled with dirt."

"True dedication," Quinn said, and passed along the cigar and the coffee. "And here we are. A millennium later and still looking at 'em."

Ringold cut the end of the cigar with a pocketknife and borrowed Quinn's Zippo to get it going. He leaned against a protective rail while Quinn had a seat on an old picnic table, both drinking coffee and watching frost melt off the trio of mounds. A few cars passed on the Trace. No one stopped. The cigars burned nice and warm in the cold. The smoke lifted and broke apart in the wind. Quinn rested his elbows on his knees. "How's it coming?"

"Son of a bitch is getting paranoid," Ringold said. "The other day he thought the sheriff-elect was working with the Feds. I had to laugh. And this morning it was the guy who owns the lumber mill, Larry Cobb. He accused Cobb of a shakedown. Said the man was threatening him."

"How's that?" Quinn asked.

"I asked Stagg the same thing and he said it was more in Cobb's attitude than his words. They got some kind of deal on that new bridge going across the Big Black. Stagg's got Cobb's company on rigged bid. The bid hasn't come through and Cobb wants to know about his seed money."

"You get all this solid?"

"Shit no," Ringold said. "We have his office tapped. But like I said, he's gotten squirrelly as hell. Nervous. Doesn't know how to use a computer. Won't use the landline. He'll only talk to folks face-to-face. I got a lot on the man. But I want everything."

"How much longer?"

"He's real careful what he says," Ringold said. "Talks in that Johnny Stagg code. Stuff that could be reinterpreted to a jury. We could shut down his dope business out at that ole airfield right now. But the pay-offs to state officials isn't as clear as we'd like. That's why I was sent here."

"Remind me again how you fellas are making a case against a man who's run wild for more than two decades?"

"Same way you eat an elephant," Ringold said, blowing some smoke into the cold wind. "One bite at a time."

"I never knew Larry to do much more than timber," Quinn said. "He's crooked as hell, but particular about his business. Since when is he into bridge building?"

"Didn't you hear?" Ringold said. "He started a cleanup-and-construction company after the tornado—him and Stagg. I told you about all that. All of it seems to be on the level. They did do the jobs they promised to do. Never had any competition on the jobs."

"Of course not," Quinn said, shrugged, the tip of the cigar glowing a bright orange. A hard, cold wind lifted up off the roadside as a couple more cars drove slow and steady on past. In the clearing, two large does snuck out from the edge of the woods, heads up, ears twitching, catching the scent of the smoke and scampering back into the darkness.

"What do you know about Cobb?"

"He's the uncle of a woman I know," Quinn said. "One of the richest men in town. Church deacon. Civic leader. Oh, and he hates the shit out of black people and thinks his success in business was a gift from God."

"Is he as bad as Stagg?"

"He's a cheater," Quinn said. "Some might say a liar. But I don't think he's got ole Johnny's ambition. And truth be known, he's not as smart."

Ringold nodded, smoking, watching the wide-open empty field. The deer were long gone after the smoke hit their nostrils and sent them hightailing it far away. Quinn had been trying to teach his nephew Jason about smells as they walked the woods. He'd told him to walk lightly without leaving a mark, not letting yourself be known to the animals, or even plants, around them. Walk soft. That way, you could be part of the whole woods, feel it and sense it. It didn't matter if you were hunting or passing through, you treated the woods, the natural world, with a sense of respect.

"Nothing changes after you step down," Ringold said. "You got that?"

"Shit," Quinn said. "Like a neutered hound."

"You can do things, talk to people, outside your work. Outside your duties."

"OK."

"Let me ask you something."

Quinn looked up and ashed his cigar at the edge of the picnic table. Ringold took a puff on his and then rubbed his thick, almost biblical-looking beard. "Does all this seem familiar to you?" he said. "Folks blindly listening to whoever is in charge without asking a thing? Drug running. Political corruption. Bullshit road projects and nation building."

"Tibbehah and Trashcanistan?"

"Yes, sir," Ringold said. "Nobody gives a shit as long as they can sit on their ass and watch football on Saturday and stuff themselves after church on Sunday."

"Southerners aren't real good on change," Quinn said. "Or calling out the folks in power. In case you need a reminder."

"I'm not Southern."

"No kidding," Quinn said. "Just where are you from anyway, Mr. Ringold?"

Ringold smiled, thumbed the side of his nose, and turned his back, walking away. "Appreciate the smoke, Quinn," Ringold said. "You're too good for these folks."

"Maybe," Quinn said. "But a man's never too good for his family."

8.

Hello, Momma," Quinn said as he walked into his farmhouse and removed his ranch coat and dark green ball cap, hanging them on a single hook. He lifted the Beretta 9 off his belt and locked it away in the side drawer of his office desk, while Jean Colson followed him, drying her hands on a dish towel, a worried look on her face. She had on a gold scarf draped around her neck and an oversized green sweater dotted with snowflakes and gold ornaments. She was a slightly heavy but beautiful woman with a lot of red hair and love for all things Elvis Presley. A long time ago she'd ridden around north Mississippi on the back of Jason Colson's Harley, wearing hot pants and boots.

"She wants to see him," Jean said. "All she's been talking about this morning is little Jason. I think it's a terrible idea. She looks like hell."

"She sure does."

"No six-year-old boy needs to see his momma like that," Jean said. "It might do her some good, but it will scare the boy."

"Roger that," Quinn said. "We all need to keep them far apart. I don't care what Caddy wants right now. She's not in her right mind."

"Oh, Lord," Jean said. "This whole thing's a mess. You want some coffee?"

"Yes, ma'am."

"I finally got her to sleep in your room," Jean said over her shoulder. "Hope that's OK. Luke told me to double those pills if they weren't working. It made her tired, but she wouldn't stop talking. Kept on rambling on about things that didn't make any sense. She was remembering some trip you and her took to Opryland as kids. You recall that?"

"I do."

"Where was I?"

"That was after you and Dad had separated," Quinn said. "Uncle Hamp drove us to Nashville to meet up with Dad. We got to see the Oak Ridge Boys open for Dolly Parton."

"Did you meet Dolly?"

"Dad got us backstage passes."

"Of course he knows her, too," Jean said. "He probably has played with her big titties."

"Mom."

"Well, would it surprise you?"

Quinn had no answer as he followed his mother back through the long shot of the house, morning light streaming through leaded-glass windows, to the kitchen. She had a fire going in an old black stove, the room smelling of burning red oak and fresh coffee. Quinn sat down at the kitchen table, covered in red-and-white-checked oilcloth, and his mother brought him the coffee. He kicked off his cowboy boots. It had been a long night on patrol. Two drunks. One domestic. And an arson at an abandoned convenience store. Fire department was handling that mess.

"Did Luke say anything else?" Quinn said.

"He said if she didn't get professional help, she'd go right back to where you found her."

"And Caddy thinks she's fine."

"She says she just slipped," Jean said. "Says she's back on track since

ACE ATKINS

praying on it. Said she'd started to think about what happened in the storm, with her house being torn up. And with—"

"Jamey Dixon."

"You bet," Jean said. "That'd throw anyone for a loop."

Quinn drank some coffee and looked out a side window at a half-dozen peach, apple, and pear trees neatly aligned down a sloping hill. His cattle dog Hondo trotted through the thick of them, covered in mud and shit from his daily messing with the cows. Despite all Quinn's attempts, man cannot change a dog's instincts. Hondo was a tough, strong Australian shepherd with two different-colored eyes, one of the smartest animals he'd ever known.

"I found this place in Tupelo," Quinn said. "Actually, Lillie found it. It's a nice facility not far from the mall. Lillie checked out the staff and called some folks at Tupelo PD for recs."

"Well, we can't force her," Jean said. "You know how Caddy can get. You force her into something and she's gonna take another path. Luke said it has to be her idea."

"Bullshit."

"Don't you dare talk to me like that, Quinn Colson," Jean said. "This hasn't been easy. She'd been so good. Done so well with coming back last time. I thought all this was over. And now I'm back raising Jason. I love that boy, but I'm not his mother."

"I guess it's time for the finger-pointing and tears," Quinn said.

"What's that mean?"

"Intervention."

Jean put her hand to her mouth, nodding and thinking. After a few moments, she said, "I guess we should bring in Diane Tull, too. Boom and Lillie. Ophelia, of course."

"Maybe not Ophelia."

"Why's that? She's Caddy's friend."

"Have you forgotten about the steak dinner?" Quinn said. "That knife thrown in my kitchen wall?"

"Can you blame her?" Jean said. "You just told her that you didn't have deep feelings for her. That you didn't ever see y'all getting married. Ophelia wasn't trying to hit you with that damn knife. She was just trying to make a point."

"Appreciate that, Momma."

"OK," she said, still thinking about the list. "Well, Jason can't be there, but he can write a letter."

"Which Jason?"

"The good one."

"You don't think her own father should be there?"

"Jason Colson hasn't earned a place at our table," Jean said. "He forfeited that right about twenty years ago to go chase tail around Hollywood and race dirt bikes in the desert."

"Or he could have stayed in Jericho and been hung from the tallest tree by a motorcycle-riding group of thugs," Quinn said. "And have all of us threatened and harassed. Things were more complicated then and you know it."

Jean Colson shrugged and looked out at the field, out at the orchard, where Hondo had disappeared. Soon Quinn heard scratching at the back kitchen door. And Jean got up, walked to the door, and let in the dog. Quinn told her she better not, on account of the dog being covered in cow shit and most likely heading right for the couch to take a rest.

"Then why do you let him in this house?" Jean said.

"After I hose him down," Quinn said. "That dog can't resist cow shit."

"Not a lot of difference between a dog and a man."

Quinn raised his coffee mug. "So when?"

"Sooner, the better?" Jean said.

"Tonight?"

She nodded with a weak half smile and turned back to the farm sink, nearly overflowing with soap bubbles, and continued with the dishes. From the window, Quinn could see way out in the pasture to the silhouette of his father, working on that old cherry-red Firebird. The older man's body bent over the engine, taking inventory of rusted parts that he didn't have the money to replace.

Lillie Virgil had already had a hell of a morning even before coming on the day shift. Her three-year-old Rose had woken up at a quarter to five, screaming and terrified with a nightmare, and then after Lillie had gotten her calm, the phone rang, waking the child again, crying and wanting Lillie. She finally said to hell with it, getting up, making breakfast for them both, and then, before they were headed out the door to day care, a plate of eggs and fruit got dumped across Lillie's uniform. Change of clothes, change of attitude, and race across town, and she was still late by fifteen minutes. Her hair was damp from the shower but pulled back into a neat bun; she was wearing a pair of Levi's and a fresh uniform shirt, the one with the star on the pocket and the embroidered title *Assistant Sheriff*, under a warm satiny jacket with TIB-BEHAH SHERIFF on the back.

The big door of the County Barn was open, and inside the metal-frame building she saw her vehicle up on a lift and Boom Kimbrough under it with an orange bucket. The barn smelled like gasoline, diesel, and engine grease, the place where all the county's vehicles were fueled up and maintained and where backhoes, bulldozers, and mountains of crushed rocks sat waiting for the roads that haven't been paved yet.

"Don't smoke," he said. "I'm draining out the gas."

"Fuel pump?"

"Yes, ma'am," Boom said in his deep but somewhat soft voice for a man who was six-foot-six and two hundred and sixty pounds. Boom had dark skin and a wide, flat face. He moved slowly, with a lot of purpose, and spoke in careful, deliberate ways, often communicating more with his eyes than his mouth. One of his arms had been severed at the elbow while delivering water for the National Guard in Iraq. He wore a prosthetic hand with fittings for various tools he needed as a mechanic.

"How long?"

"Right after lunch," Boom said. "Unless there's more."

"There's always more."

"Not always," Boom said. "Fuel pumps in these Jeeps are always going out. Surprised this didn't happen two years ago."

"Maybe I'll get a new vehicle?"

"Doubt it," Boom said. "New sheriff said he was cutting the budget. Figure my ass is gone."

"You work for the county supervisors."

"You know how I got this job," Boom said, fitting a flat-bladed tool into his hand, reaching up under the Jeep, and scraping away. He used another hand to twist and pry and he came down with a fuel-soaked pump in his hand, dripping gas.

"I'm gone, too," Lillie said.

"What did Rusty say?"

"Doesn't matter what Rusty says," Lillie said. "Quinn's out and so am I. Besides, I'd really rather not raise my daughter in Tibbehah County. Both of my parents are dead. Most of my kin who have sense have moved away. What the hell are you doing here?"

"Fixing shit."

"Besides fixing shit?"

Boom wandered over to a long tool bench and set the bad pump on a dirty rag. He craned a light overhead and began to write down something in a notebook. "My dad's alive, most my brothers and sisters still live here. I leave and things don't get done at my dad's farm. At the church."

"Screw 'em."

"Way it works."

"How the hell could this goddamn place do this to Quinn?" Lillie said, slipping her hands deep into her coat pockets. A chill coming in through the open bay door, despite heaters burning bright from the ceiling.

"You hear from Miss Jean?" Boom said.

"About the intervention?" Lillie said.

Boom nodded. He crossed his good arm over his chest and held the upper part of what was left of the bad one. Behind him, all of his tools had a place, gleaming silver and bright in the lamplight. On this year's *Playboy* calendar, Miss December wore a red bikini and frolicked pool-side.

"You going?" Boom asked.

"I don't think Caddy Colson gives a shit what I have to say."

"But Miss Jean—"

"OK," Lillie said. "Son of a bitch."

"All you got to do is be there," Boom said. "No one is asking you to hold hands and sing and shit."

"I guarantee there will be plenty of church folks around," Lillie said. "Quinn and Jean don't think they know about Caddy and where she's been. But, come on. They all know she's a mess, back on drugs. I heard she was wasted out at The River right before Thanksgiving. She was unraveling. Couldn't keep her shit straight."

"You blame her?" Boom said, slitting open a box and pulling out a new pump. He set it on the table, picked up a hanging light, and hooked it under the Jeep to shine the light bright and deep. "Besides," Boom said. "Miss Jean is cooking. I ain't missing that."

"Do all mechanics keep calendars of women posing as sex objects?"

Boom fitted a new tool under his hand and nodded. "Most I know."

Lillie nodded. "That one's got a pair of aftermarkets up top, not to mention no hips. A woman's got to have hips."

"Didn't notice." Boom looked to the calendar and studied it a bit as he tightened the prosthetic. "So I'll be seeing you tonight?"

"Hell, yes."

Mickey drove into Jericho and parked out on the town Square, the centerpiece being a big white gazebo and a big marble monument to all the local soldiers who'd died, from the Civil War to all that recent business overseas. The oak trees were bare but full of white lights from Christmas, the shops open for business, which still seemed strange to him, as most of downtown Jericho had been barren for his whole life. Even that shitty old movie theater where that crazy-ass preacher had been hung from a homemade cross was open for business again, showing new and old movies for two dollars a ticket. The side of the downtown that had been taken out by the twister now had a Greek restaurant and two women's shops. And there was still the Western Wear shop, Doris's Flowers, and a big coin laundry that was jam-packed this morning. Mickey got out and walked across the street to the little place his ex owned. For some reason, Tonya thought Jericho could really use a combination coffee shop and tanning parlor.

And there she was leaning over the counter, talking to Betty Jo Mize, who ran the local newspaper, glancing up once at him and then returning to her conversation. Despite it being late December, the girl was as brown as a nut. She'd be the same way buck-ass naked. Her skin looked like some kind of stained wood against that gray baseball shirt with red sleeves. Her blonde hair as bleached as her big toothy smile. Her hair was cut up and styled like that woman on television with all those kids, like a barber had taken an axe and chopped off a good hunk.

Miss Mize had a Styrofoam cup in her hand as she passed him. He smiled at the old woman and she spoke back, her being friendly with him since he'd laid down some high-traffic wall-to-wall at the *Tibbehah Monitor* office last year. As she went out the door, Mickey grinned and set his elbows across the counter.

Tonya put her hands on her hips. "What the hell?"

"I just want some coffee."

"Hell you do."

"Your momma come by yesterday to see me," Mickey said. "Do you know what she said?"

"Good riddance?"

"Nope," Mickey said. "She wanted to know 'Who the fuck did I think I was?' Where does an old woman learn to talk like that?"

"Before she married Daddy, she drove trucks. And after she married Daddy, she drove a backhoe. If she couldn't dog-cuss those boys out at the lumberyard, they'd walk right over her. You know that."

"She didn't need to come to my place of work."

"Did it hurt your feelings?" Tonya said, smiling just a bit. The first time she'd smiled since he'd walked in the door.

"No," he said. "Your momma couldn't do that. What hurt my feelings is that you told her I was late on alimony. That hurt me real bad."

"You are late," she said. "You owe me money."

Mickey tried to look sad, shaking his head. He glanced away and tried to give her a soft, kind of wistful smile, the way he'd done when they first started going out. He'd give her that sad look and say he couldn't believe she didn't want to go to bed with him. He'd been so lonely since his wife had left, but that she didn't give him no love at all anyway. He told Tonya that the woman had shattered his heart.

Tonya wasn't buying it anymore, walking out from behind the counter and over to a little table where someone had left a couple mugs and a half-eaten muffin. He found himself talking to her back.

"It's not that I don't owe you," he said, "I do. That's why I came here. I brought you a check. I just finished on a big job. Them people hadn't paid me a dime till this morning."

"Then why are your feelings hurt, Mickey?" Tonya said, tossing the muffin and setting the dirty mugs on the counter. "'Cause of what happened a couple weeks back?"

"No," he said. "I mean, yes. Hell, yes. I mean, I didn't think you'd turn on me like that. What happened was really beautiful."

"Come on," she said. "Must have been the song playing in your truck. I don't recall nothing beautiful about giving you a quick hand job outside the Southern Star."

"Meant something to me."

Tonya shook her head, smiling to herself, finding Mickey kind of funny. And that was fine. He didn't have any problems with that. As long as she wasn't pissed at him. She was pissed at him, everything was going to turn to shit. All he wanted was a little room to work.

He looked her over, in those tight jeans with those bejeweled ass pockets and that tight baseball shirt with the words COWBOY UP written across her titties. She stared back, knowing something was turning in his mind. "What?" she said. "What is it?"

He reached into his wallet and pulled out a cashier's check, getting it official, as she might not have accepted one from Walls Flooring.

"You sure are tan."

"No shit, Mickey."

"And you smell nice."

"I'm not going out to your truck," she said. "That wasn't me. That was the Jäger working."

"I don't want you in my truck," he said. "How'd you like to ride down to the beach with me for New Year's?"

She crossed her arms over her chest and just stared. She looked doubtful as hell, but she was listening. Just as he was about to lay it on out, some fat woman in sunglasses and a big heavy coat walked out from a back room. He bet her big ass was the color of a belt. She thanked Tonya and headed out the front door, waddling as she walked.

"Go on."

"I don't want to spend the New Year in Jericho," he said. "Florida Georgia Line is headlining at the Flora-Bama. You know how much I like that song 'Sun Daze.'"

"So?"

"So?" he said. "I hadn't forgot those times." He leaned into the counter, noticing that a cup of coffee cost three dollars and five tanning sessions cost thirty. He wondered if you could drink the coffee while you tanned, and, if you did, could you get some kind of discount.

"You are two months late on alimony, walk in here complaining about my momma being a real bitch, and now you think I'm going to jump in your truck and head down to the Gulf for some quick hot sex and country music?"

Mickey's mouth hung open for a second. And then he closed it. "That's about the long and tall of it."

Tonya rubbed her hand over her face, lightly enough not to smear all that makeup. She looked up at the ceiling as if dear God himself was going to answer if she should head down to the Flora-Bama. She stared at him long and hard for half a minute until two Chinese women from the restaurant across the street walked in, talking Chinese between themselves.

"What do you say?" Mickey said, giving her a big old smile.

"OK," Tonya said.

"We're going to have a hell of a time."

She pointed the folded-up check at his head. "We better."

9.

Mickey Walls had ball games to watch and beer to drink, now that damn-near everything was teed up. He picked up a case of Bud Light at the Piggly Wiggly—finally being able to buy beer in Jericho even if it was illegal to buy it cold—and drove on back to his ranch house and eighty-inch television. He was about to turn down his long driveway when he saw a black van parked outside, lights on in his house. When he got closer, he put down the windows and heard music. Someone was playing Hank Williams, Jr., like it was the goddamn Fourth of July and had even turned on the Christmas lights along his fence and the little glowing Nativity scene he'd gotten from his aunt in Arkansas to put the Christ in Christmas. Mickey was about to call the damn sheriff but then started thinking it must be that knucklehead Lee Salter, thinking he'd been serious about inviting him over for the bowl games. He probably just let himself in and was burning down a joint, his mind not quite right and not realizing what he was doing was breaking and entering.

If he called the sheriff, he'd never get down to thawing out some Tony's pizzas and icing down that beer. Goddamn Lee.

He parked and walked up the front steps. His front door stood open, letting out some wafting smoke that didn't smell like weed. More like someone burning bacon. He coughed and waved away the smoke. Through the haze, he saw a young dude, maybe seventeen or eighteen, sitting on his couch and calling out some dumb-ass quarterback for throwing the stupidest interception in history.

"Who the fuck are you?"

"Me?" the boy said.

"Hell, yes, 'you,'" Mickey said. "What are you doing in my house?"

He looked up to see a fat man stepping from his kitchen with a plate of bacon and eggs and a bottle of Jim Beam under his arm. He had glasses and wild hair and the picture of the fucking Grinch on his T-shirt like some kind of child would wear. He didn't say nothing, didn't apologize, only walked over to the big La-Z-Boy—Mickey's seat—and made himself comfortable. When he got settled, he said, "I got some extra bacon. It's a little burnt."

"I said, who the fuck are y'all?" Mickey shouted over Hank Jr., who was bellowing loud enough to wake the dead, the music turned up and the ball game turned down. "I'm calling the fucking sheriff."

"Don't do that," the man said. "Don't you recognize me? I'm Misty's Uncle Peewee."

"Son of a bitch."

"You bet," Peewee said. "It's been a year or two."

"And who the hell is the kid?"

"My nephew, but no relation to Misty," Peewee said, forking some bacon and eggs in his mouth. "Chase, say hello."

"Hello," Chase said, the kid looking Mickey over with his big cow eyes and opening his big dumb mouth. "Can I have some of that beer?"

Mickey didn't know what to say to that. He just looked to the kid and said, "It ain't cold yet."

"I don't care."

"You want a warm beer?" Mickey said.

"If I can have it," Chase said.

"Can I ask what y'all are doing in my house?"

Peewee Sparks lifted up one end of his backside and let out a fart. He didn't break stride as he forked some more bacon and eggs into his mouth. "You got a pizza in there. Didn't figure you'd want us touching it, as it's the only thing in there. Reason I made the bacon and eggs."

"Didn't expect you till tomorrow," Mickey said. "You said we were straight. Didn't want us to be seen together. We done worked out that whole deal on the telephone."

"We were driving along close by and Chase said damn, why don't we just drive on over to Jericho tonight," Peewee said. "Let's go ahead and get that shit done right now."

"We can't tonight," Mickey said. "You said you had to get your tools."

"I got my tools."

"And you said you were coming alone."

"What?" he said. "You mean Chase? He ain't nothing. Are you, boy? He just my goddamn protégé. He's watching me work so he can do what I do someday."

"Sit in other folks' chairs and fart?"

"Been in the car for a while," Peewee said. "Gas backed up a little. Say, pass me one of them beers."

"Son of a bitch," Mickey said, feeling a swell of worry and fear flood his body. He thought he just might throw up. This man was supposed to be a pro. The best. Not just some fat man in a Grinch shirt about to shit his britches. He didn't seem to be the man he recalled from the Sparks family reunion. "Someone might see you."

"That's why we go on tonight."

"We can't."

"Why not?"

"'Cause they're at home," Mickey said. "Didn't you listen? They leave tomorrow night for a big high-rollers' party in Tunica. We can't go tonight. The plan was never tonight."

Peewee nodded, put the plate down on the floor, and kicked back the lever on the La-Z-Boy, looking at the television and listening to Hank Jr. He rested his hands over his fat stomach and said, "OK, tomorrow it is. Now, how about some of that pizza and a beer. We got some thinking on things to do."

The kid Chase smiled big and wide, shaking his head like his uncle sure was one tough old character. *Shit. This wasn't good at all.*

The man drove a black Crown Vic, with tinted windows and a special tag noting he was law enforcement. He slowed a bit in front of the Booby Trap Lounge, Stagg walking around the back of the vehicle to crawl in the passenger's side. The man didn't even turn to look at him, knocking the car in gear, reaching down with his right hand to tune down the radio set for troop headquarters of the Mississippi Highway Patrol. It took a couple minutes, not until they were cruising at a hundred-plus miles per hour on Highway 45, before the Trooper turned to Stagg and said, "What's that motherfucker want now?"

"Some assurance this here deal is going through," Stagg said. "I told him this kind of business takes time and he told me so did the cornholin'. I really don't have much patience for Cobb's dumb ass. But I threw in with him after the storm because I had to. He was the only one with the equipment ready to go."

"He say anything about that?"

"Yeah," Stagg said. "He was acting like we owed him something. Christ, you mind crackin' a window or something? It must be ninety degrees in here."

The Trooper reached down again and lowered the heater, Stagg already sweating up a lot under his red sweater and hundred-dollar dress shirt. They soon hit the Lee County line, the Trooper not slowing a bit, actually speeding up, taking the Crown Vic to around one-fifteen. He was a lean, square-jawed man who'd kept a silver crew cut ever since Stagg met him down in Jackson with Senator Vardaman. The Trooper did things like that. Favors for a U.S. senator. He also guarded football coaches for Ole Miss and made sure they were protected and got to where they needed to go. Discretion, the Trooper said, was why he'd been the go-to man for the last couple decades.

"Everything's fine," the Trooper said. "You tell that dumb son of a bitch that they can't announce a fucking project until the start of the new quarter. Doesn't he know the way that government works?"

"He's a logger," Stagg said. "Runs the biggest mill in three counties. His head is as thick as an ole oak. He thinks this is gonna work like the storm money."

"Wasn't that federal?"

"Most."

"Then you need to educate him, Mr. Stagg," the Trooper said. "Them boys in Jackson don't write no IOUs."

Stagg nodded, the Crown Vic flying down the highway, running light on the rails, the motor growling, the interior still feeling like the inside of a goddamn sauna. Only a sick man would keep his car so hot, and the man was dressed in full Highway Patrol gear. He had on sunglasses, no expression, hair looking like a gray box on his head. "When's that new sheriff taking over?" the Trooper asked.

"Supposed to be on the fifteenth," Stagg said. "But us supervisors decided it best for all concerned that he go ahead and take over first day of the year. Quinn Colson's already cleaning out his desk."

The Trooper reached down in the pocket of his uniform and fingered out a little Skoal. He had a half-full Dixie cup in the cup holder that he reached down to spit into. "Hallelujah."

"Don't go and thank Jesus yet," Stagg said. "We don't know what we got."

"Can't be worse than that son of a bitch Colson," the Trooper said. "How the fuck you let a man like that be sheriff?"

"I may influence it, but I don't control the ballot box, sir."

"Since when?"

Just then, Stagg looked up in time to see a big purple billboard with the image of Jesus Christ looking skyward. The sign read IS HE IN YOU? The Trooper didn't seem to notice as he spit in the cup and set it back in the holder. The billboard had a listing for a website where the true world suckers could donate some money for some phony-ass ministry. Football coaches and preachers had the easiest shuck in the world. People were supposed to shut their mouths and listen and pass the plate for the ministry. Pass the plate, if you wanted your team to win the game. At least with football coaches you could fire their asses if you didn't get results. As one of Ole Miss's top fifty donors, Johnny T. Stagg sure made sure they changed out their coaches as regular as lightbulbs. He'd yet to get a National Championship ring on his hand.

"Where does it all end?" the Trooper said, sounding like he was talking to himself.

"Excuse me?"

"All this shit in Tibbehah," the Trooper said. "You better get your leash tighter, Stagg. You nearly got fucked two ways from Sunday by them bikers out of Tennessee and now you're letting some turd in Jericho tell you how to do business. When you'd get so soft?"

Stagg didn't speak until he was ready. He reached into his vest pocket for a peppermint, unwrapped it, and stuck it in his mouth. He sucked on it as he thought, then crunched it up with his back teeth. "How about you head back south," Stagg said. "Our talk is done."

"I didn't mean nothing, Stagg," the Trooper said. "Shit. Don't get your panties into a wad."

"Since when did the messenger think he's calling the shots?"

"I never do."

"Me and you got the same friends," Stagg said. "And I expect you to come through when called. But don't go to try and give me any advice, sir, or I'll make sure you go back to writing tickets to cocksuckers in rest stop bathrooms. You understand me?"

The problem with Mississippi State," Chase Clanton said, pointing his fingers at the center of Mickey Walls's chest, "was that y'all had to go and get yourselves a black quarterback. Studies have proven that you can't have no black man running the offense. You ain't never gonna see that type of shit with the Tide."

"It was a good year," Mickey said. "That boy got the job done."

"Maybe," Chase said, settling into Walls's nice house, the big kitchen, the big-ass TV, and a nice stockpile of dirty DVDs he found. Some looked to be homemade. "But I don't like it. It ain't good for recruiting. You get a boy like goddamn AJ McCarron taking snaps and every blue chip in the country will want to go to Tuscaloosa. You see that woman he got? I seen her half nekkid on the Internet. I'm not lying. You got a computer and I'll show 'em to you. Uncle Peewee found 'em for me. I'll tell you what, they'll warm you on a cold night like tonight. Hey! Hey, y'all got some more beer?"

"No," Mr. Walls said. "Y'all drank it all."

"No problem," Chase said. "How about a Mountain Dew or a Pepsi?"

"Help yourself," Mr. Walls said, trying to walk away from the kitchen while Chase still had things on his mind.

"Things can happen," Chase said. "Like last year, the fucking Auburn game. About the worst day in my entire life. I was sitting there, watching the game at a Buffalo Wild Wings in Dothan, and I see that ball sail in the air, knowing it wasn't gonna put them ahead but appreciating Saban for making the effort. Next thing I know, that black bastard took that ball, cheating like a son of a bitch and running it for a touchdown. Tide players didn't even know what was going on. You want to tell me how that's fair?"

"Because it's legal to run back a missed field goal."

"Yeah?" Chase said. "Well, maybe. But when the other team don't know it, I say that's goddamn cheating. I cried like a baby that night. Felt like someone in my family had died. I seen AJ walking off the field with that smokin'-hot piece of ass. He probably didn't even try and get himself some pussy after all that shit. She probably just held him and made him feel better. Those goddamn stupid Auburn people. Ain't nothing but a cow college."

"You go to college, Chase?" Mr. Walls said, leaning against the counter, nursing on his third Jack and Coke. He was a rich man, an accomplished man, and Chase could tell because of the V-neck sweater and Dockers. Only a rich man wears khaki-colored pants and clean shoes.

"You know, I thought about it," Chase said. "But I'm learning everything I need to, on account of my Uncle Peewee. He's teaching me shit that I can't learn in schools, if you know what I'm saying. Hey, you mind if I look in your refrigerator for that Pepsi?"

"Only got Coke," Mr. Walls said. "Are y'all headed back tonight?"

"I don't know," Chase said. "I guess we'll ask Peewee when he come out of the shitter. Damn, that pizza tasted good goin' down, but it sure did tear up my stomach. You think maybe it's gone bad or something? You can't keep food frozen forever. We had some deer meat that got rotten last summer and gave my whole damn family the squirts."

The toilet flushed and Uncle Peewee walked on out, hitching up his big pants and wandering into the kitchen. "Y'all got any more beer?"

"Already asked him," Chase said. "Mr. Walls said we drank it all."

"Then you got a store around here?" Peewee said. "I can make a run for us. We got work to do. Hard to think sober."

"You two can't stay here," Mr. Walls said, getting real serious real quick. "Your big-ass van is parked right outside my house. You want to keep it here all tonight and all day tomorrow? That's not too smart. That's not what we talked about. This ain't the plan at all."

"Shit," Peewee said. "We can park it around back. Don't see any reason for us to drive back to Gordo tonight if we're here right now. That way, we can make a dry run over to that fella's house and see what's shaking. Lay it all out. Plan. Be smart. All of us get educated on what needs to be done."

"What's shaking," Mr. Walls said, acting to Chase like some snotty Yankee, "is that they're not gone. We agreed for you to meet my friend and y'all would take care of it. I'm not gonna be a hundred miles from here. I'm the first one the law will look to. This is y'all's deal. And you get the cut and then get the fuck out of here."

Peewee lifted up the bottle of Jack Daniel's and poured some out into a red Solo cup. "OK," Peewee said. "OK. I know this ain't what's planned, but it's the deal we got now. I can pull my vehicle around back. Unless you got folks coming, ain't no one can see it. And then me and you need to drive past the place. Ain't no harm in that. But I need to know where me and my boy are headed tomorrow night. It may be a honey trap, like you said, but I ain't getting fucked over in Mississippi. I want to get fucked, I'll go over to Montgomery for that shit. I also need to know the make and model of the safe."

"I don't know."

"You don't?" Uncle Peewee said. "Christ Almighty. But can you find out?"

"All I know is that it said 'Bighorn' on it," Mr. Walls said, taking a deep breath like worried men do. "Had a drawing of a ram or something on it."

"Yeah," Peewee said. "I know it. Made by Rhino. How big?"

Mr. Walls put down his drink and leveled his hand at chest-high.

"Gun safe," Peewee said. "Holds about twenty-five rifles and shit. Digital lock with a nine-volt battery. Thirteen cubic feet, with a three-spoke handle on it. Looks like an old-time bank safe. Right?"

"Yeah," Mickey said. "Sounds right to me."

"Damn thing weighs about five hundred pounds," he said. "Door is about five inches thick, with external hinges."

"Can you bust it?"

"I thought you had the combo?"

"*If* the combo doesn't work," Mr. Walls said, swallowing some more Jack and Coke. "That's why I reached out, Mr. Sparks. I don't think you've been listening."

"Yes, sir," Peewee said, Chase noticing his glasses had gotten a little smudged, "I have. Ain't a safe made I can't bust."

"I told you," Chase said, grinning wide. "I fucking told you! My uncle knows safes better than anyone. Now, that's doing your goddamn thinking like a white man."

Mr. Walls's face turned sour, Chase wondering if he hadn't gotten some of that bad pizza with rotten pepperonis. He turned and walked from the room and then out a side door, leaving it open and the cold air rushing inside like a son of a bitch. He looked to his Uncle Peewee and Uncle Peewee, being the smartest man he'd ever met, just shrugged and finished Mr. Walls's drink.

10.

Quinn had walked outside his mother's home, the inside getting too heated, too much talk, too many accusations, and Caddy jumping from being ashamed to pissed-off. Boom was outside, too, after saying his part to Caddy, and now leaning against Quinn's truck, the one he'd rebuilt and refined as an answer to a brand-new monster Stagg had first offered Quinn as a bribe. Now all that seemed long ago. Quinn planned on driving it the final time tomorrow on New Year's Eve before turning in the vehicle at the County Barn and heading on into whatever was next.

"How's it coming?" Boom said.

"Terrible."

"Who's talking now?"

"Momma," Quinn said. "Again."

"That might take a while."

"Yes, sir."

Quinn reached into his old ranch coat and pulled out two cigars and offered one to Boom. Boom declined and Quinn trimmed the end of his and cracked open his old lighter. They sat outside, leaning against the Big Green Machine, not once lamenting the loss, worrying about where the old truck was going or where Quinn would go.

"I don't like what I said," Boom said. "I could have done better."

"What are you talking about?"

"I tried to talk to her as one addict to another," he said. "I tried to compare me being a drunk to her being addicted to whatever shit she's on."

"Heroin."

"Yeah," he said. "Didn't sound right. I think she thought I was preaching to her. I'm no fucking preacher."

"Neither of us are," Quinn said. "Thank God."

"But Caddy," Boom said. "She got that in her. She was headed that way. Leading all those people, doing all those things at The River. She was good at it. Her ass fell hard."

Quinn nodded. Ithaca Street, the road of middle-class houses off the Jericho Square, was still and cold. All the yards still decked out for Christmas, with lights on the houses, around the windows and doors, inflated reindeer and snowmen in front, light-up plastic Santa displays mixed in with ones of Baby Jesus. Sometimes it looked like Santa himself had been there at the holy birth. An old couple down the road had bright lights that winked on and off to the small sounds of electronic Christmas carols. The night was as cold as it had been so far, and Quinn's cigar smoke drifted up and away without scattering or falling apart, twisting up over the colored lights across the road.

"How'd you do it?" Quinn said. "How'd you beat things?"

"That's what I was trying to explain to Caddy," Boom said. "Tell her she got to quit hating herself. I told her all of this shit comes from wanting to kill yourself. Some people do it fast and some do it real slow. I was on slow."

"You hadn't relapsed."

"I got a purpose," Boom said. "I got tired of feeling sorry for myself, on account of what happened. I had to buy into what you were saying, and my family was saying, even that woman I talk to up at the VA. You know?"

"What's that?"

"Getting to that new normal," Boom said. "Ain't nothing going to jump back to what you want. You take what you given. That's what Caddy facing. She kept on moving after the storm, kept busy as hell, so busy it would have killed some folks. She raised money, handed out food and clothes to the folks in Tibbehah, and she was fine until things slowed down. When things got slow, she had to look at her situation. And there she was, missing something, like I missed my goddamn right arm."

"Dixon."

"Yes, sir," Boom said. "You know she was right about him. He took that bullet. He didn't have to go, be there when you gone to go to get Caddy and Jason. That son of a bitch stepped up, owned up to what needed to be done for your sister. She probably loved him even more for that."

"I shouldn't have let him go," Quinn said. "And I never even found out who shot him. That's the least I could have done for her. I think it was the not knowing what happened, who pulled the trigger, that's been pulling at her. I just never knew."

"But we all know who called it."

Quinn nodded, studying the end of the cigar, glowing red-hot. He ashed the tip, the electronic music playing soft down the street. Lights winking on and off. He could see the shapes and movements of family behind the curtains of the dining room, moving in and out. He waited for the sound of plates crashing, and maybe some yelling, but there was nothing, Jean probably still saying her piece, maybe reading that letter that Jason had written his mother earlier that day. Quinn had read it and the whole thing had ripped him up. He never wanted to read something like that ever again. How in the hell could his sister refuse to get better, why would someone want to stay in the swamp, not crawl out, not improve, not keep moving on. Caddy had been wounded bad time and again. She just never got the chance to heal without something breaking her apart soon after.

"I hate to see this truck go," Boom said, patting the hood as if it were a horse. "Lots of hours, lots of work."

"Rusty will get some good use out of it."

"I don't know," Boom said. "I don't think he wants it. Maybe you can make an offer to the supervisors. You can buy it from the county."

"Maybe."

"Take it to wherever you're going."

"Who said I'm going anywhere?"

"You ain't sitting around Tibbehah with your thumb jacked up your ass," Boom said. "And you ain't no farmer."

"I'm looking into some things."

"Mmm-hmm."

"Got to make a living."

"Me, too," Boom said. "I appreciate all you done to get me working again. I wish we could have done the same for Caddy. You can tell she feels like it's all over. The River. Whatever life she had planned with Dixon. She loves Jason, I know that. But she's all cracked-up, man."

The front door opened and Jean Colson stepped outside. She waved Quinn forward. She was crying hard. But she was smiling.

Quinn looked to Boom. And Boom nodded back.

Caddy had agreed to get help.

Lillie Virgil helped clean up after the intervention with Caddy. Miss Jean was still in the living room with Caddy, Quinn, and Diane Tull, a family friend who'd taken over Caddy's role at The River.

Jason Colson, the old one, had been there, too, but didn't say much. He only said he loved Caddy, as if that was all he'd been permitted. None of the family was doing much good until Miss Jean unfolded that letter little Jason had written in purple ink, only having to get two or three sentences into the thing, about how he missed his happy momma and was sad when she was gone, when Caddy started to cry. Caddy had broken down completely, Lillie knowing it was the place where someone like Caddy needed to be. To look at herself right in the goddamn mirror, nod, and admit she was truly and absolutely fucked-up and needed a hand.

She could go to Tupelo tomorrow. Quinn would take her.

"Who's on duty tonight?" Anna Lee Stevens asked, both of them working elbow to elbow in the kitchen, Lillie rinsing the shit off the plates and Anna Lee loading the dishwasher.

"Kenny," Lillie said. "Ike McCaslin. I'm headed back on in an hour. I got to check on Rose. Babysitter is watching her and Jason."

"I better be getting on, too," Anna Lee said. "My mom has been over at the house for three hours now."

"Where's Luke?" Lillie asked, but damn well knowing the answer. Playing dumb was sometimes the best way to find the truth.

Anna Lee opened her mouth and took a deep breath, holding a flowered plate in hand, and then closed it. "Working," she said.

Lillie nodded and then scraped off some more of the food they had put out, no one really touching the food, not feeling like it was some kind of party, except for Quinn and Caddy's Uncle Van. Life was a goddamn party for Uncle Van. First thing he did was walk over to the dining room table and make a big turkey sandwich with cheese on a little dinner roll. He looked stoned as hell, being the kind of individual who had a hard time facing the world with a clear head.

"This was good," Anna Lee said. "I'm proud of her."

"What else could she do?"

"Leave," Anna Lee said. "Not face the truth. She's done that before."

Lillie nodded, finding it a little hard to wash dishes with a gun on her hip, the Glock knocking into the sink when she turned to hand a glass over to Anna Lee.

"I don't know how this sounds," Anna Lee said, "but Caddy has always seemed to be playing a part. The way she was in high school. You knew her better than I did. But you know what she was like. The things she did to shock people. She got off on that."

"It was an act," Lillie said. "If she can outshock someone, act like she doesn't give a shit, then you can't hurt her. That's why she did what she did with boys. The reason she went up to Memphis and did the things she did there. She had to prove to everyone in this town how tough she was. But she's softhearted. I don't think she was acting these last couple years; who she became, who she was trying to be."

"You don't think all the religion, the good doing and all that, was all because of Jamey Dixon?"

Lillie rinsed a final plate. She heard Boom say something and heard laughter that she took to be a good sign, a family resolved to what they had and moving on. She shook her head. "I think that's the real Caddy," Lillie said. "Dixon was the one who found her."

"The murderer?"

"I don't know what he was," Lillie said. "I just know what he did for my friend."

Anna Lee didn't talk for a while, finishing up with the dishes while Lillie wiped the counters clean. Lillie watched her as she pulled her phone from her purse, texting someone, and then turning back to ask if she could do anything else.

"No," Lillie said. "It's fine."

"I didn't mean to talk bad about Caddy," Anna Lee said, standing there as perfect as she'd always been. Strawberry blonde, small-bodied, in a black sweater and jeans. Lillie bet her goddamn red purse cost five hundred dollars. She and Lillie had always wanted different things in life.

"I know."

"I just want her to know herself," Anna Lee said. "Her addiction is hurting everyone and she needs to admit it."

"Is that a fact?"

Anna Lee pulled that red bag over her shoulder and pulled her bangs from her eyes, staring at Lillie as if she was bringing Lillie into focus. "Excuse me?"

"I just think honesty is a fine thing," Lillie said. "I think it's good to be truthful with kids. I think it's also good to be truthful with your friends."

"Of course."

Lillie wiped her hands on a paper towel and tossed it in the garbage. "How about I walk out with you?"

Anna Lee said her good-byes, hugging Caddy tight. Caddy, wearing sweatpants and an oversized sweatshirt, said, "God bless you."

Lillie put a hand over her mouth, waiting for Anna Lee to move toward the door, Lillie not bothering to put a coat on over her heavy uniform top. Most of the folks who'd been there had left, leaving spaces in between Anna Lee's little Honda and Lillie's official Jeep Cherokee. Lillie walked with her to the car, stopping on the Colsons' lawn, the entire house lit up bright and shining by old-fashioned multicolored lights over the dormers and squared around the windows.

"Don't hurt him."

"What?"

"Quinn," Lillie said. "I hope you know what you're doing."

"I don't know—" Anna Lee started but then realizing that she better stop. "Well, I guess. I guess you can think whatever you want."

Lillie crossed her arms over her chest, over the silver star, and looked Anna Lee right in the eye. "You better be honest about your plans," she said. "You want to fuck him, fine. But you leave him like you did before and I'll come for you."

"What?"

"I will whip your bony ass, Anna Lee Amsden," Lillie said. "I don't know what keeps on drawing y'all together. But he's too goddamn good for you."

Mickey Walls pulled into the gravel lot beside Calvary Methodist Church and killed the engine of his red Hummer. His headlights shone across the old graveyard, spreading out under a half-dozen old trees. Most of the headstones were from a hundred years ago, skinny pieces of rock jutting out of the ground, crooked and broken. Some of the stones had worn down to shards of what they'd once been, sunbleached roses on the graves, a few little Confederate and American flags on sticks for the veterans. The cemetery was old, but people were still being buried there.

He sat there about ten minutes until a single headlight shone down the road and then turned into the little white church. The light went out, the door slammed, and Kyle Hazlewood was looking at Mickey from the other side of the passenger window. He knocked twice and Mickey reached over to let him on inside. "God damn, it's cold," Kyle said. "Why'd you want me to come way the hell out here?"

"You want us seen together?"

"Shit, people see us together all the time."

"Yeah," Mickey said. "But not the night before. I don't want folks to think we're sitting around plotting this thing with Larry Cobb."

"Then what are we doing?"

"We're plotting the damn thing," Mickey said. "Right? Are we still good?"

"I don't know, man."

"Shit," Mickey said. "I damn well knew it. I've been trying to call you all damn day and you wouldn't answer. I knew you were backing out."

"I ain't backing out," Kyle said, rubbing his thin beard, everything about him smelling of cigarette smoke. "Not yet. I just don't know why it can't be just you and me. Why you'd go and bring these Alabama boys into the mix?"

"'Cause I need 'em," Mickey said. "I need one of them anyway. The other is just some kid, kin to the Sparks. He just follows his uncle around and talks about Alabama football. He also drank all my damn beer."

Kyle didn't say anything. He had on a pair of brown Carhartt overalls splattered with mud up to his knees. He even had some mud stuck in his goatee that he was picking at while he stared out into the blackness of the graveyard, not saying a damn thing. *Thinking*. Mickey let him think, let him take all the time he needed. 'Cause he sure as hell needed Kyle running the show. If not, he knew he wasn't going to be able to trust someone like Peewee Sparks.

"Tell me again why you can't be there," Kyle said.

"'Cause Larry Cobb is going to point his finger right at me," Mickey said. "You know that's true. First thing he's gonna say when he gets home from Tunica and sees his safe's been busted is 'Mickey Walls just fucked me in the ass.'"

"Yeah," Kyle said. "I guess that's true."

"You damn well know it's true."

"But these other boys," Kyle said, getting some more mud from his beard, letting down the window and flicking the dirt out onto the gravel, cold air coming on in the cab. "I mean, shit. You know."

"Yeah."

"God damn," Kyle said, "I don't know them from Adam's house cat. You want me to work with a fucking Sparks and some kid. I don't want to get back-shot for a few thousand dollars."

"Ain't a few thousand," Mickey said. "It's a million."

"Could be a dang billion, but I can't spend it when I'm lying face-down in the damn dirt," Kyle said. "Why don't we just lay off on this thing for a couple months, go at it again when Larry and Debbi are out of town for a while? Just me and you head on in there and take care of business. That way, we won't have to work with no fucking criminals."

"I see what you're saying," Mickey said. "But which one of us is going to crack up a five-hundred-pound safe? You got them talents? You see what I mean?"

"Yeah," Kyle said. "I guess. But who the hell's this kid? What's he got to do with anything? That's just another person in the mix know-ing our business."

"Sparks says the kid is learning to be a safecracker," Mickey said. "He tails him around to get some on-the-job training. Like some kind of damn apprentice. Don't worry, the kid won't screw you. He's dumber than shit. Thinks Bear Bryant is a bigger deal than Jesus Christ."

"Hold up," Kyle said, reaching into his overalls and coming up with a pack of cigarettes, pulling out a cowboy killer and lighting up. "Those motherfuckers are here?"

"Weren't supposed to be," Mickey said. "But, yeah. They came on over to my house. They want to ride by Cobb's house tonight, check things out and lay out some plans. I'd like you to be there, too."

"Man, I just got off a ten-hour deal down in Ackerman running PVC for a half mile. I don't have time for that. Not now."

"Tomorrow," Mickey said. "It's got to be tomorrow. The boys are here. Debbi and Larry are gone. I'm out of town."

"I know," Kyle said, blowing smoke out into the cold. "You're gonna be doing tequila shots off Tonya's big brown titties while I'm jacking around with a couple crooks at midnight. Just don't seem fair."

"We split it even."

"You said that."

"I'm only paying those boys ten grand."

"Ten grand total or ten grand apiece?"

"Sparks wants twenty for the whole deal," Mickey said. "I'm not splitting hairs with him. That's why you got to be there. I don't want him counting up that money. He's got no idea how much is in that safe. He thinks it's just some payroll or something from the mill. I want you to be there, shoulder to shoulder, when he gets the safe open. You grab everything in that son of a bitch—rings, jewelry, guns. Don't matter. If you don't get it all, it's going to prove the folks who did this knew about the hidey-hole."

"Shit."

"Come on, man," Mickey said. "That money is dirty as hell. He's been cheating folks like me and you his whole damn life. Him and goddamn Johnny Stagg's as thick as thieves. There ain't no telling what all's in that safe. Dirty, dirty money."

Kyle nodded, not saying a word. He reclined the seat and lay back into the headrest, a cigarette held in his lips, staring up at the truck cab. The cold air blew into the cab from the cracked window, clearing out the smoke.

"It's time for Cobb to get what's coming to him."

Kyle nodded.

Mickey offered his hand, and Kyle, head still tilted back, cigarette held loose, reached out to shake it.

"This is gonna change everything, man," Mickey said. "Now, listen up. OK? This is how I see things are going to need to work tomorrow night."

11.

Quinn and his dad took little Jason to the barbershop early the next morning. Jean was dealing with Caddy, getting her packed for her time in Tupelo, and Quinn and big Jason thought the barber might get the boy's mind on something other than worry. It was strange to watch Jason up in that spinning chair, head tilted down, as a new barber trimmed the kid's curly Afro short and close to his head. Old Mr. Jim had been cutting Jason's hair his entire life, but now Mr. Jim had sold off his business of fifty years to a somewhat younger man from Yalobusha County while he lived out his final days on oxygen, watching daytime television. The younger man had hired two women to work with him, and although Quinn had no problem with female barbers, the entire shop had changed. Most of the deer heads and mounted fish had been taken down. No more girlie calendars, and only one football schedule mounted on the wall. The shop was swept clean. The ancient couches and folding chairs had been replaced with newer stuff.

Jason giggled as the clippers touched the nape of his neck.

Quinn sat next to his dad. Across the way was Mr. Varner, who'd just walked in the door, bringing coffee to the new barber, whose name was Don. The two women who waited at their own stations for walk-ins sat in their chairs, reading magazines. One woman scowled at Mr. Varner, who lit up a six-inch-long cigarette and blew out the smoke. He was an old U.S. Marine and hadn't changed his standard-issue haircut since his days on Parris Island and in the jungles of Vietnam.

"Boy's grown," Varner said, his voice gravelly from thousands of cigarettes.

"Yes, sir," Quinn said.

"Almost didn't recognize him," Varner said, looking up to Jason in the chair. "Looked like a high schooler to me."

Jason smiled. The elder Jason shuffled in his chair a bit, as he and Luther Varner had never been on the friendliest terms. Varner had always thought of Quinn's dad as some kind of commie hippie. Jason's stories of working stunts for Burt Reynolds and Hal Needham while seducing *Playboy* bunnies impressed plenty others but couldn't have mattered less to Varner. Just the word *California* was usually enough for Varner to excuse himself from the conversation.

"How you been, Quinn?" Varner said.

"Getting along."

"Big day."

"Same as any."

"To hell with this place," Jason said, looking up from a copy of *Car and Driver*. "Damn supervisors making three times the sheriff salary. Tell me there isn't something wrong with that picture."

"You looking for work, Mr. Colson?" Luther asked, squinting through the smoke. He leaned forward on his weathered forearms, decorated with faded skull and dagger tattoos. "I hear you're good with horses."

"I am."

"I know some folks who could use some help."

"Appreciate that, Mr. Varner," Jason said. Quinn hung back,

watching the two old men ping-ponging over who had the right to hold court at the barbershop. "But Quinn and I have some pretty good plans for next year."

"Oh yeah?" Varner said, blowing out some more smoke. "And what's that?"

"Farming."

"Farming, huh?" Varner said. "You and Quinn?"

"Yes, sir," Jason said. "Watermelons, mainly. I've been doing my homework and know a boy over in Pocahontas who made out pretty good. Of course Quinn has enough land to do a decent bit of corn and cotton. But a watermelon farm is where I see us making a solid living."

Luther Varner sat there on the couch, ramrod straight, and ashed his cigarette into an empty coffee cup. He kept speaking to Jason but looked to Quinn. "Well, I wish y'all the best with all that."

Varner had done six tours in Vietnam as a sniper. He once told Quinn that slowing down, quitting fighting, and getting back to what he'd been before was the hardest part. If Quinn had asked, Varner would've jumped up at that very moment to fetch the nearest gun to join whatever fight was out there. The old man smiled some more at Quinn while the older Jason, dressed in a black T-shirt with a cow skull on it and a fringed leather vest, ran down the highlights of what he'd learned about watermelon production. "What folks don't do down here but they do out west is rely on horse manure. I figure with me bringing in horses and getting going, that won't be a problem."

"I'm not sure about the horses yet," Quinn said. "We might start with a few. See how it goes."

"So you're saying the secret to this business is horseshit," Luther said.

Jason gave a wry smile, stroked his gray beard, and said, "Yeah, I guess that's about the heart of it. Horseshit is pretty much how I make my way, Mr. Varner."

Varner smiled and nodded. He winked at Quinn. Quinn didn't say anything, knowing the old man could read his mind and knew that he wasn't ready to put down the gun.

Up on the spinning chair, little Jason hadn't been paying attention to their talk, making small talk instead with Mr. Don. Mr. Don asked him about what he'd gotten for Christmas and whether or not he was going to be starting T-ball in the spring.

"At the VFW, you were talking about some overseas work," Varner said. "With your Ranger buddy in Tennessee."

"That's still on the table."

"Not if y'all got a full-time farm," Varner said. "My daughter has been running a farm for the last five years and hasn't taken a single day off."

Quinn nodded. The barber pulled the cape from Jason and shook loose the trimmed hairs onto the floor. Jason bounded out of the seat and waited for Don to offer him some candy and gum from his bucket. Mr. Jim had done the same when Quinn had been Jason's age. Don seemed to be a good man, and despite the upgraded decor, he was keeping the same spirit of the barbershop.

"Everything tracking at the home front?" Varner asked.

"Been a rough winter," Quinn said.

"Everything's going to be fine," Jason said, smiling and then taking his grandson's place in the barber's chair. His long gray hair hit down to his shoulders, his goatee long enough to be held in the old man's fist.

Quinn moved over to beside Mr. Varner, picking up Jason's magazine and glancing through it. Varner spoke to the ground, low enough that only Quinn could hear him. "I were you, I'd pack my bags come Monday and put Jericho in your rearview," Varner said. "But do me a favor."

"Yes, sir."

"You stumble on some good overseas work, let me know," Varner said. "I sure do itch for it."

Johnny Stagg met the Bohannon brothers, K-Bo and Short Box, at a hot-wings restaurant they owned off Elvis Presley Boulevard, about a mile from Graceland and next door to a twenty-four-hour car wash. The Bohannons were Craig Houston's cousins and right-hand men, running the show after Houston's head ended up in the truck bed of some Mexican cartel folks. "It was a shame what happened to Craig," Stagg said. "He was a fine man."

"Ain't nobody deserve that shit," K-Bo said. "Couldn't even bury him right. Didn't ever find the body. Just the gotdamn head."

"Disgraceful."

The brothers were twins. *Identical.* The only way Stagg could tell them apart was that K-Bo had a razor-thin beard and one earring. Short Box didn't have a beard and had diamonds in each ear. Other than that, they had the same chiseled face, thick neck, and general stocky football player build. They even wore the same V-neck black T-shirts just to confuse folks.

"That's what we got," Short Box said. "Not gonna stop till we all dead. We in a battle."

"It's y'all's world, too," Stagg said. "These people are animals. Don't have green cards, don't give two shits for America. This is your home turf. I ain't never making a deal with those fucking bean-eaters."

"Craig worked with them," K-Bo said. "You see where that shit got him?"

Stagg nodded, knowing that it wasn't his work with the cartel that separated his head from the rest of him. It was working with Stagg and his Mississippi connections instead that took out Craig Houston's ass.

Now he had the Bohannons, two of the meanest motherfuckers in South Memphis, when they weren't making hot wings or waxing cars. Stagg figured they'd do just fine.

"You want some wings, Mr. Stagg?" Short Box said. "Best in Memphis two years in a row. We got our picture in the *Flyer* and everything."

"No, thank you, sir," Stagg said. "I got an ulcer. Me and spicy food don't mix. Have to drink a glass of milk every night before bedtime."

"Got some honey-glazed and garlic that will sit right with you," Short Box said. "I can make up a fresh batch. Hey." He pointed to the skinny girl watching TV behind the counter and snapped his fingers. The girl rushed up to the table, pen and pad in hand.

"This is our sister, LaTasha," he said. "Say hello, LaTasha."

She rolled her eyes at her brother.

"Appreciate it, miss," Stagg said, grinning, making good with these two shitbirds. "But I got to get going in a minute. I just wanted to come on up and say hello."

Short Box jerked his head at his sister and she wandered back behind the counter to watch a big-screen television roll some highlights from last night's Grizzlies game. K-Bo was listening to, but half watching, the television, too. He slapped the table hard enough that Stagg flinched a bit.

"Damn," K-Bo said. "Check that shit out."

Stagg didn't move or turn his head to the game, just kept on grinning, waiting for these two boys to get the full appreciation of why he'd make the trip. He hadn't come up to Memphis since the trouble with those bikers. And he wanted to make sure the Bohannons weren't tempted to throw in with all the Mexes buzzing about town. They threw in with the cartel, Tibbehah County and all Stagg had built wouldn't mean jack shit.

"Have any of those Mex boys sought y'all out?" Stagg said.

K-Bo shook his head. "Had some shit happen a couple months back," he said, eyes on the television. "They lit up a pool hall we got on Lamar. By the Pirtle's Chicken. Folks saw a big-ass truck rolling the fuck out of there. Had a picture of Jesus and Mary on the tailgate. Ain't nobody but a Mexican spray-paint Jesus and his momma on they truck."

"Damn right," Short Box said.

"What'd y'all do?" Stagg said.

"Paid a visit to the gotdamn cha-cha club where they all hang out," Short Box said. "What do they call that shit? That music they listen to sound like a polka. We shot the shit out of their world. Ain't been no trouble since. What about down in Miss-ssippi?"

"Lots of them a couple counties over," Stagg said. "My understanding is, they got things running smooth on I-55. Everything coming in straight from New Orleans. People in Louisiana don't have a bit of class."

"Where you get your shit, Mr. Stagg?" K-Bo said, looking at him now.

"Wouldn't y'all like to know?" Stagg said, grinning. "Then you wouldn't need this ole country boy."

"You ain't like most peckerwoods, Stagg," Short Box said. "Craig said he always trusted you. That means something. You OK, for a white man."

"Sure do appreciate that, Short Box."

"But we ain't gonna lie to you," K-Bo said. "Mexes been cutting into our world real deep. They get shit fast and cheap. You know what I'm saying? I ain't naming names, but there are some folks in this town who only care about money. They don't give a shit about Craig Houston and what he used to do for people. They forgot all the money he gave out to families, to churches, helping people when they down."

"God rest his soul."

"But we straight with you, Mr. Stagg," Short Box said. "You're cool."

Stagg grinned. Outside the hand-painted plate-glass window, he watched Ringold lean against his cherry-red Eldorado. He had his arms crossed over his chest, glancing back to the hot-wings joint every few moments, one hand in his pocket and the other stroking his Moses beard. Stagg realized that the only thing coming between him getting his ass chimichanga-ed was that hardheaded military boy and these twin black hoods. It was getting to the point he couldn't even rely on the good old boys down in Jackson. Stagg offered his hand to the Bo-hannons. They shook it, K-Bo smiling, still watching the game, paying attention to the highlights from last night, not meeting his eyes. "Hell, yeah," he said. "You see that shit? God damn."

"Really something," Stagg said, not turning to watch.

"Maybe we can get down to Tibbehah soon," Short Box said. "Meet some of those fine women you keep out at the truck stop. Champagne and titties, just like last time."

"Y'all are welcome anytime," he said.

Stagg excused himself. As he walked out the door and out to the parking lot facing EP, he wondered if working with goddamn idiots wasn't going to be what killed him.

T hat's it," Mickey Walls said, pointing. "Right at the top of the hill." Kyle had been riding them around in his truck that morning, showing the Alabama boys back roads and talking about timing, where and when to meet, and how the whole deal was supposed to work. Mickey was in a time crunch—he had to pick up Tonya in thirty minutes or the whole thing was off. That girl was just waiting for him to fuck up.

"Don't look like much," the boy Chase Clanton said, riding shotgun, staring up at the single-story brick ranch looking over the lumber mill. "I thought these folks were rich. I was expecting some big-ass mansion like on *Dallas* or some shit."

"You see all those logs?" Mickey said, sitting in the backseat with Peewee Sparks's fat ass.

"Yes, sir," Chase said.

"Well, that whole yard belongs to Larry Cobb," he said. "Every stick."

"Damn," Chase said. "That's a lot of timber."

"No shit, kid," Mickey said, smelling Sparks's bad breath every time he exhaled or coughed as they rode around Jericho. He just kept on imagining holding that first cold beer at the Flora-Bama tonight, a kick-ass concert, and getting laid on the beach. *Baby you a song, / You make me wanna roll my windows down and cruise.* Hell, yeah.

"Biggest lumber mill in three counties," Mickey said. "Cobb may be a supreme asshole, but does just fine for himself. So just listen to your uncle back here and shut the hell up."

"Hey, man," Chase said, turning to the backseat. "I don't need your shit."

Peewee ignored him, leaning forward between the front seats and poking his finger toward the Cobb house and the long gravel road. "Only one road up there?"

"Yep," Mickey said.

"Any gates?"

"They got a gate by the road," Mickey said, catching Kyle's eye in his rearview mirror. "And it will be locked. But it doesn't matter. The reason I want y'all to go tonight is that I know for a fact the man who checks on the lumber ain't going to be doing shit. He's a lazy-ass drunk and will be passed out by midnight. Kyle's handling that. Y'all can park in the yard and walk up to the house."

"Carl don't show, most nights," Kyle said. "He'll be passed out at home. I'm headed over later to give him a bottle of Rebel Yell to make sure."

"So your boy is goin' drinking and then keep watch for Johnny Law while me and Chase take care of the hard work?" Sparks said, snorting. "What's your name again?"

"Kyle," he said, arm hanging out the window, pulling it back in to take a hit off his cigarette. "Damn, he just said it."

"Kyle what?" Sparks said.

Kyle glanced up to his rearview again, not answering.

"That's all you need to know," Mickey said. "No need to pass out fucking business cards 'round here. I told you, Kyle's one of my best friends. Me and him have known each other since we were ten years old. He's representing me on this deal tonight. Whatever he says goes. Ain't no difference between him and a foreman. Kyle's in charge. Understand?"

"I don't know if I like the sound of that," Peewee said. "A foreman should be the man on the site who's got the most experience. That's the way it should work. How many safes you busted, man?"

Kyle didn't answer, rolling the steering wheel under his right hand, tires crunching hard on gravel, as he U-turned and headed back into Jericho. The mountains of logs and timber corralled by a long chainlink fence ran along the road until they hit the highway and Kyle sped off.

"This isn't a question of experience," Mickey said. "Y'all ain't installing cabinetry. You boys wouldn't know about this hidey-hole if it wasn't for me. And if it wasn't for me being on such bad terms with Larry Cobb, I'd be right there beside you. But Kyle being here is the next best thing. Once you bust that safe open, Kyle will hand off the money we agreed on."

"You said twenty grand," Peewee said.

"That's right."

"What about for Chase?" Peewee said.

"You can deal with him on your own," Mickey said. "Whatever you think is fair."

"What I think is fair is another five thousand dollars," Peewee said.

"Shit," Mickey said. "Come on, now."

Kyle dragged on the cigarette and then tossed the butt out the window. Mickey knew he was getting ornery, rethinking this whole thing. "Son of a bitch," Kyle said, and rolled down Cotton Road past the Hollywood Video and the Sonic. "What if it's empty?"

"It's not going to be empty, man," Mickey said. "That's Larry Cobb's hidey-hole. You know that. The place he keeps his dirty money and all his damn secrets."

"If it's empty, it ain't our problem," Peewee said. "You hired me to break it open. I break it open and you get squat, I get paid the same."

"Agreed," Mickey said. "I'll leave some money with Kyle, if that happens. But you'll only get that extra five if it's loaded. I never asked for you to bring this kid with you."

"I ain't no kid," Chase said. "I'm eighteen years old. I screwed more women and kicked more ass than you ever have. But don't worry. If you say this ole bastard driving is the coach, then I agree he's the coach. I know how to use the goddamn playbook."

"Whatever happens, no one calls me," Mickey said. "Once you let me out of this truck, none of us can speak to each other for a while."

"Fine by me," Chase said. "I'm tired of talking to y'all already."

Kyle slowed down his truck a little as they shot past a Tibbehah County sheriff's cruiser speeding in the opposite direction past the softball fields. Jericho was soon behind them, and he turned the truck onto the county road heading out to Mickey's house, passing more farms and trailers, old cars, and cows. Peewee Sparks sat silent beside him, scenery whizzing by while he picked his nose and wiped his finger on his trousers. He coughed a little and straightened in his seat.

"Y'all got anything else in this town besides churches and funeral homes?" Sparks said.

"Sure," Mickey said. "Why?"

"Well, I don't plan on getting caught in neither."

12.

re all those things true about Colson's dad?" Rusty Wise asked.
"What things?" Lillie said.

"About how he used to be real famous," Rusty said. "That he was the go-to stuntman for action pictures back in the seventies and eighties. Did he really jump a rocket car over a river in that movie with Burt Reynolds and Jan-Michael Vincent?"

"Hooper."

"Yeah, *Hooper*," Rusty said. "Was that really him?"

"They didn't actually jump that car," Lillie said. "It was special effects with a miniature. You can see it's fake if you slow down the movie frame by frame. He's a lot better in this trucker movie called *White Line Fever*. That man wasn't scared of nothing. Listen, it's good to see you this morning, Rusty. But can I help you with something?"

Rusty Wise sat on the old flowered couch that had belonged to her dead mother, like every other stick of furniture she owned, and sipped on some coffee from a flowered cup. While they talked, Lillie's three-year-old daughter Rose played with her new Doc McStuffins, the doll attending to the medical care of a couple stuffed animals and one toy monster truck. The little girl wore pajamas, and Lillie wore sweatpants and a navy Ole Miss T-shirt. She hadn't expected Rusty that morning, but there he was, bright and early, knocking on her front door and wanting to talk. She hoped this wasn't the way he operated.

"I just wanted to connect before tomorrow," he said. "Make sure you were all set."

"Of course."

"Well." Rusty, a little butterball of a man with fiery red hair, took a sip of coffee and paused. He was already wearing a TIBBEHAH COUNTY SHERIFF golf shirt and had a gun on his hip. "I guess I just had heard a few things from the grapevine about you maybe moving on from the sheriff's office. Something about a job up in Memphis?"

"People sure do love to run their mouths."

"Is it true?"

Rusty smiled as he held the small flowered cup with both hands as if warming himself. Rose fixed a wobbling wheel on the monster truck and pushed it alongside the two stuffed animals. Another satisfied patient for Doc McStuffins. The child had been born in Mexico to unknown parents and had come to Lillie two years ago after a bust of some local shitbirds trying to sell kids on the Internet. Lillie had dark thoughts about those people and tried to not to think on it too long. But she did pray every night that someday they'd be caught and tried for their actions.

"Maybe," Lillie said. "Better schools. More opportunity."

"I can't fault you for that," Rusty said. "I didn't come over here to put some pressure on you, trying to make you stay. I just wanted to let you know that you'd be a big help if you'd just commit to seeing through the year."

"Can't do that, Rusty," Lillie said. "I don't know if I'll ever leave Jericho. But I committed to Quinn to stay on as long as he was around. Now that's over and I'm trying to examine some things. I hadn't been back here too long when my mother died. I'm still living in her house surrounded by her things. I haven't even had time to clean out all the closets."

"I understand," Rusty said. "But I'm offering the same kind of deal you had with Quinn. I got no issue at all with the way you live your life. That's a personal matter."

"Come again?" Lillie said, lifting Rose off the floor and rolling the truck down the hallway so she would chase after it. Lillie wanted the child out of earshot in case she had to unload some profanity on Rusty Wise. She knew it was coming sooner or later. Rose carried the doll by its loose arm while she moved down the hallway. Lillie turned up the volume on the television, playing the morning show out of Tupelo.

"I just don't want you thinking I'm one of those people who have problems with it," Rusty said, laughing. "That's your own deal as long as you don't go marching in parades, waving flags, or something."

"I have no idea what you're talking about."

Rusty gave a little snort. "Oh come on, now. I'm no Bible-beater. I'm just looking for the right folks to do the job. You're the best one around here."

Lillie shook her head, looking Rusty right in the eye. She smiled and laughed a little, wrapping her arms over her chest. "Are you saying you don't mind if I'm a Methodist?" she said. "Because it might really cause some trouble in the sheriff's office if someone saw me drinking cold beer on Sunday. I also believe women can be in positions of power. Is that OK by you?"

"Fine by me," Rusty said, dumb smile on his face, cheeks glowing as red as embers. He swallowed, trying to look relaxed but not doing a good job at it. "I didn't mean anything. I was just coming over to say that it was all right. Whatever you do. I mean, on your own private time. Long as it isn't something that's all out in the public eye, I don't see where they'd be any problems. You obviously didn't have any issues with the adoption board. Everything worked out good for little Rose. Didn't it?"

Lillie stood up and reached down to tighten the string in the waistband of her sweatpants. She pushed up the T-shirt sleeves on each arm and walked toward Rusty. He slurped his coffee while she took a wide stance and asked, "You done with that coffee?"

"Yes, ma'am."

"Good," Lillie said. "Because I got shit to do."

"I didn't—"

Lillie held up the flat of her right hand in an effort to tell Rusty to shut the hell up. She turned to see Rose, oblivious to the conversation, standing two feet from the television, the weatherman predicting a gorgeous kickoff to the New Year, but with a cold front on the horizon.

As Rusty stood up, shaking his head, saying, "Aw, hell," she spotted their reflection in an old beveled mirror behind him. Lillie stood there, broad-shouldered and tall, hair in a ponytail and not a speck of makeup on, and the little round man, maybe a head shorter than her, was already wearing his gun, his shirt two sizes too small.

"How about we keep this between you and me?" Rusty said.

Lillie walked ahead of him and held the front door open wide. "Sounds good, Sheriff," she said. "See you tomorrow."

Quinn drove Caddy to Tupelo.

They hadn't spoken for about twenty miles, her head propped against his passenger window, the radio playing "Behind Closed Doors," Charlie Rich singing the old favorite with a smooth and easy confidence. Quinn had always loved to hear that man sing.

"You should have let me see my son," Caddy finally said. "That was wrong."

"It would've been wrong for him to see the shape you're in."

"You and Momma are just talking shit."

"Nope," Quinn said. "You'll be glad later. He knows you're well. And safe. That's all he needs to know right now."

"Whatever."

"You were going to pray on it last night," Quinn said. "Is that all you came up with?"

"Don't throw Jesus in my face," she said. "You, of all people."

"I'm not giving you a lecture," Quinn said. "How about you do me the same courtesy?"

Caddy snorted and shook her head, bringing her legs up into the big seat and pulling her knees close to her chest. "The thing is, everyone in that room last night has their own problems," she said. "When's the last time you've seen Momma without a glass of wine in her hand? Or Uncle Van when he wasn't stoned? We all like things that aren't good for us."

"Human nature," Quinn said. "Difference is, those things aren't going to kill us. At least not yet. Luke says you should have died."

"Luke is a tender heart," Caddy said. "I don't care what he thinks, and women don't find that attractive."

They passed signs for the Brice's Cross Roads Battlefield, where a thousand-plus Union soldiers had died or were taken prisoner by Nathan Bedford Forrest's much smaller forces. When Quinn was a kid, he used to imagine being part of the boys who'd stalled the cavalry on that muddy road, making the Yankee infantry double-time it to catch up, bone-tired and on half rations. The graves of the soldiers who died that day were buried out back of the new church, one they had built long after the battle. Now the site was just an acre surrounded by gas stations and fast food and nail salons.

As they passed, Caddy gave a sloppy salute in reference to what Quinn had done as a kid.

"This won't be long."

"Someone will bring a guitar," Caddy said. "Someone always has a guitar at these fucking places."

"I thought you cared for that stuff," Quinn said. "The singing, old-time hymns."

"My brain is fried," she said. "How can you believe a word that comes out of my mouth?"

Quinn drove on, turning off the main road, following the signs to the clinic where he'd check in Caddy for detox. The radio played Ferlin Husky, "I Wouldn't Treat a Dog Like You're Treating Me."

"Why do you listen to that?" Caddy said. "All that old music. You know, they've made music in the last fifty years that might be a little better."

"Name one."

"I know why you like that old stuff," Caddy said. "Because it reminds you of Uncle Hamp's house and all those old records he kept in wooden crates. You used to put them on when we were kids, the adults sending us back to the junk room to play while they carried on, drinking, talking bad about each other, whispering things about the world that we shouldn't know."

Quinn kept on driving, seeing the flat, low brick complex coming into sight down the road. He slowed. Caddy closed her eyes and swallowed. She looked better than she had the other night, but not much. The sores all over her arms and face had scabbed over, making her look as if she'd been in a street fight. She had on old faded jeans and an oversized man's flannel shirt that Quinn was pretty sure belonged to Jamey Dixon.

He parked the truck and killed the engine, the DJ announcing the next song was Johnny Paycheck singing "Green, Green Grass of Home," the man saying this was his favorite version of the old standard.

"Momma would fight the man on that," Caddy said. "Elvis. Elvis. Elvis. No wonder we are all so fucked-up."

Quinn shut his mouth.

"Oh, I'm sorry," she said. "You're the good one. Oh, favorite son."

"Jesus Christ," Quinn said. "Can I at least carry your bag while you tell me to go to hell?"

Caddy swallowed and nodded. She slipped on a pair of very large and dark sunglasses. The glasses hid half of her face. Quinn got out of the truck and reached into the back for the bag, reminding him of the little pink suitcase she'd brought with her following her brother into the Big Woods.

"You might want to talk to these people about what happened when we were kids."

"I don't know what I need to talk about."

"It doesn't matter if things come out," Quinn said. "You don't need to protect me for what happened."

"Did you do what I asked?"

Quinn reached into his jacket and brought out two packs of cigarettes and a new lighter. For the first time in a while, his sister smiled, leaning forward and kissing him on his cheek.

"You do love me," she said.

"No shit, Caddy," he said, picking up her two bags and walking toward the front door of the detox center.

D o we really need to wear masks?" Chase said. "I feel pretty god-damn stupid."

"You're going to feel even dumber when the cops get you on a surveillance camera," his Uncle Peewee said. "Or when some witness picks you out. Would you rather wear a ski mask or something?"

"You got one?"

"Nah," he said. "Ain't no skiing in Mississippi. Just this shit Mr. Walls got for us."

Mr. Walls had told Chase he'd picked up the masks earlier that year at the Dollar Store for a Halloween party that he never went to. Maybe if he'd chosen something else, something scary, it wouldn't have made him feel so dumb. But the goddamn Teenage Mutant Ninja Turtles, his Uncle Peewee wearing the Donatello mask. Shit, it was too damn much. He was even wearing the fucking purple bandanna that came with it and flipping around a pair of plastic nunchucks, saying he knew some moves from this guy over in Columbus who'd been a real-life Green Beret.

Walls was gone. Already halfway down to the beach.

Soon it would be dark. And wouldn't be too long before that Kyle fella would come on over and they'd all pile into his uncle's van. Peewee had said they could use some walkie-talkies in the truck, but Kyle had said the law might be listening in. So they'd agreed just to use their phones, in case something was going on. Other than that, everyone was supposed to stay quiet until the door opened on that safe.

Peewee had pushed the mask off his face and set it on top of his head. He'd helped himself to a cold Coors and was sitting in Mr. Walls's easy chair, watching a damn porno movie. Chase had watched some of it, but he wasn't buying none of it. Just 'cause the girl kept on saying, "Oh my God. Oh my God." Shit, that didn't mean a thing. At one point, the girl looked up at the cameraman like she was asking when is this damn donkey gonna quit riding my asshole.

"I want to find me a woman like that," Peewee said, a little high but not drunk, looking silly as hell with a kid's mask on his head. "Down at Temptations."

"Hell, that woman is a fat-ass."

"How old are you, Chase?"

"Eighteen," he said.

"You don't know nothing about real women yet," he said. "I bet you like all them stickly skinny girls with those big blow-up boobies. Wait till you get older and you're gonna appreciate some shaking goin' on."

"I'm hungry."

"Mr. Walls got some cereal," he said. "Eat some of that shit."

"I don't want any more fucking Frosted Flakes," he said. "Give me the keys. I saw a Sonic back in town. I want a cheeseburger. I'll bring you back one."

"Think," Peewee said. "Think on it, son. How many folks you want seeing our getaway vehicle. Good Lord in Heaven. You sure got the brains of your daddy."

"You never told me you knew my daddy."

"Me and him run together before he got sent on to Kilby," Peewee said. "You might think about going on and seeing him sometime."

"Hell, no."

"That may be for the best," Peewee said. "The man has gone and turned queer. Dresses up like a woman and slow-dances with the biggest niggers in the joint."

Chase opened his mouth. And then he closed it.

"Ha, ha, ha," Peewee said. "Shit, man. I'm just messing with you. Your daddy ain't no fucking queer. Not that I know about. He's just a real asshole."

"Momma won't tell me what he did."

"He busted a man's head open at some beer joint," Peewee said. "It was a fair fight, but the fella died."

Chase nodded, picking up his own mask off the kitchen table, it being Raphael. He slipped the elastic band over the back of his head and slid the mask down over his face, now seeing the world through eyeholes. Uncle Peewee was right. He could see just fine.

He reached around and touched the small of his back, where he kept his new gun. The little .32 felt snug and tight, hanging right there in his waistband and under his drawers. Everyone who'd been telling him no guns tonight—Peewee, Mickey Walls, and that dumb fucking hick Kyle—could all smooch his redneck ass. He wasn't showing up at this party empty-handed.

He was too damn smart for that.

13.

Quinn was into his last hour, his last patrol as sheriff, when he spotted the black woman in the white nightgown wandering along Jericho Road. The closer he got, the more he realized it had to be Miss Magnolia, an elderly woman with dementia who often locked herself inside her own house, or wandered off into the woods, and many times carried a little .22 no one would take away from her. Quinn approached the woman with caution, as he eased the Big Green Machine onto the side of the road and walked out behind her. She didn't slow a bit, picking up her feet in the tall brown grass, walking with purpose to god-knows-where.

Quinn called her name.

She didn't stop.

Quinn called her name again and the woman stopped cold. Her right hand appeared to be empty, but he couldn't see the left. He recalled she often carried the pistol in her left when he'd made welfare checks on her late at night.

He walked up to her, coming from behind her shoulder, the thin, gauzy material of the nightgown, made for a woman much younger, billowing up and around them in the brisk wind. Her blued cataract eyes gave him a blank stare. She was barefoot and holding the little pistol. The sun was going down over the low rolling hills, the light a faded orange.

Quinn quickly snatched the .22 from her hand so fast, the loss barely registered.

"Mr. Beckett?" she said, calling Quinn the name of his dead uncle.

"Yes, ma'am." No need to fight it.

"He done it again."

"Yes, ma'am."

"That son of a bitch gone out drinking," she said, almost spitting the words. "Whoring."

"Yes, ma'am."

"I'm going to shoot him this time," she said. "I swear on it."

"Who?" Quinn said.

"Who do you think?" she said. "James. Once he gets to drinking, he's gonna get laid. Has to get laid."

"Mr. James has been gone for some time," Quinn said, looking down at the little old woman, hand on her shoulder.

"I know," she said. "That's why I'm gonna shoot his ass."

"He's dead, ma'am."

"Lord," she said. "What happened?"

"He died about forty years ago," Quinn said. "I heard he had a heart attack. Long time ago."

She stared at him, weathered face, clouded eyes, not knowing what to say. Her dry mouth then formed the words to ask, "What kind of nonsense are you talking, boy? I used to change your diapers."

"That was my uncle."

"You don't get out of my way, Hamp Beckett, I'm going to the nearest tree and switching your ass red."

The night was coming on fast, dark clouds moving in from the Delta, folks talking about rain and sleet through New Year's Day. He took off his old coat, the one that had belonged to his uncle, maybe making the confusion complete, and set it across her brittle shoulder bones. The faded tobacco brown ranch coat reached the old woman's knees.

"I'm going to kill him."

"Your grandson called," Quinn said. "He's worried about you. He came to bring you supper."

"I don't have no grandkids."

"Come on back with me," Quinn said. "It's cold."

"Won't stop me," she said. "Won't stop me shooting his pecker clean off."

"I understand."

The old woman turned her head, a different light coming into her eyes, watching Quinn's face, a moment of something like embarrassment that quickly went away. "I am cold."

"It's going to sleet tonight."

"Man shouldn't be whoring," she said.

"No, ma'am," Quinn said, leading her back to the truck. The wind coming on hard at their back, Quinn in shirtsleeves rolled to his forearms, as he took the radio off his belt and called in to dispatch.

He had to lift the old woman, as light as a bird, off the ground and set her in the passenger seat. When he started the truck, she turned to him and smiled. "I know you," she said. "What do they call you?"

"Quinn."

"I know your uncle," she said. "Fine man. Fine man."

When Mickey Walls and Tonya got down to Gulf Shores, they skipped the condo and went right to Lulu's. They'd been listening to Jimmy Buffett and Kenny Chesney the whole way down, and all Mickey could think about was one of them Cheeseburgers in Paradise and a cold deluxe margarita. The windows and doors had been covered with heavy plastic, and they had a few big industrial heaters glowing red up under the ceiling, the restaurant made to look like some kind of Key West beach house. A band onstage was singing "A Pirate Looks at Forty" just as they got their drinks, and by the time they'd ordered some crab claws with dippin' sauce, he had Tonya on the dance floor to "Fins," Mickey making his hands into a shark fin and dipping back and forth around Tonya. She had her eyes closed, holding on to that margarita for dear life and not spilling a drop.

Mickey ran out of breath a couple songs later, knowing he was going to be getting on that P90x exercise plan next year, and they went back to their little table facing barges on the Intercoastal.

"You're getting old," Tonya said, smiling, straw in her mouth. "I bet you'll be snoring before midnight."

"Bull," Mickey said. "Shit."

"We'll see," she said, playing around with the straw on her lips. "Let me ask you something."

"Shoot," he said, reaching for one of the crab claws, already grown a little cold while they were on the dance floor.

"Why'd you ask me down here anyway?"

"Do I need a reason?"

"All my friends say I'm crazy," Tonya said. "The ones I told anyway. They can't believe I'd be spending New Year's Eve with the ex-husband that I supposedly hate."

"You hate me?"

"I hated you and I wouldn't have come."

Might have been the margarita soaking into his brain, but, god damn, Tonya looked good tonight. She didn't seem to have a trace of Larry Cobb in her, only seeming like a younger and thinner version of her mother. Her big chest just swelled in that dress, under a red motorcycle jacket with sparkly jewels on the shoulder. Those big old linemen calves were nowhere to be seen in some tall blue-and-pink cowboy boots. Lots of makeup and hair spray. She smelled good.

"What are you looking at?"

"You just look good, is all," he said. "I need a reason?"

"I just want us to get one thing straight," she said. "Me coming down here doesn't mean that we can have sex. I came down with an old friend, just like you offered. So no matter how drunk we get, we're both keeping our pants on."

"Hell," Mickey said. "I know. Shit."

He checked out his watch—getting to be about six o'clock. The Alabama boys would just be getting ready to go over and lighten Larry Cobb's load. He smiled and finished off the margarita. The band had taken a break, speakers overhead playing some good old classic Garth Brooks. "Friends in Low Places." He had to laugh, as he thumped out the song on the table and sang along.

She reached for his fingers, the place where he'd had that wedding ring still showing off as white as a whale's belly. "You understand," she said. "Right?"

"No sex."

"No, sir."

"Just dancing and laughing."

"Old friends."

He nodded. Sure would have made things easier if she hadn't come along all tan and smelling so damn good. Mickey turned in time to see three women walking in, singing along with Garth, drunk as goats, and heading up to the bar. The girls couldn't have been long out of high school, tight bodies and short skirts. He bet girls like that could go all night long. As soon as he could touch that money, able to enjoy it, he and Kyle might head down to the Keys to do some bonefishing.

The young women ordered a line of shots, knocking them back like those high times wouldn't ever end.

"I sure am glad we didn't stay in Jericho," she said. "I probably would've just watched the ball drop with my momma and daddy like always."

"They wanted you to go to Tunica?"

Tonya wasn't listening, snapping her fingers for the waitress, another round, maybe go ahead and order those burgers. "They changed their mind," she said. "Daddy wanted to go on and get back tonight. Momma said he'd already lost five hundred dollars playing blackjack."

Mickey swallowed and stood up. "I'll be right back."

When Quinn got back to the sheriff's office, there was a cake and sparkling grape juice.

And almost every deputy on the payroll: Kenny, Ike McCaslin, Cullison, and Watts. A few friends had joined them to say good-bye: Boom, Diane Tull, Luther Varner, and the only two county supervisors he respected, Sam Bishop and Bobby Pickens. Betty Jo Mize from the *Tibbehah Monitor* took pictures and said she was working on a story about Quinn's last night on the job. She said she planned to run Quinn's picture big and tall as a real *Screw you* to all the ungrateful bastards who'd turned their back during the election. "You flip them all the bird and I swear I'll run it on the front page."

"You want to say a few words?" asked Kenny.

Quinn smiled and faced the little gathering in the sheriff's office. "Appreciate it."

"That's Quinn Colson," Betty Jo Mize said. "A real quote machine."

"Y'all didn't have to come out," Quinn said. "Just locking up some guns and writing reports."

"To hell with that mess," Mize said. "I wouldn't file one more of those things."

"I actually have two," Quinn said.

"Hurry up, then," Mize said. "You got a whole lot more folks waiting on you at the Southern Star. I refuse to toast you with grape juice. This little send-off is purely for the teetotalers."

Quinn shook a lot of hands and drank a little grape juice. A lot of people made apologies for the county, saying Quinn was too good for them. Some just wanted to know what he was going to do next. Quinn would just shrug and say "Hunt" because he really wasn't sure beyond next week. There was a chance of some contract security work in Afghanistan with his old friend Colonel Reynolds. He could make enough money in a couple months to live the rest of the year. But tonight he'd only thought of making a fire in his old rock fireplace, sitting in with some good bourbon and getting into a new book his mother had bought him on Stonewall Jackson. He'd always admired the man's tactics, even though the Colson family had come from Jones County—the Free State of Jones, since it voted against secession—and had joined up with a Union regiment.

"I'm going to miss seeing Hondo," Kenny said. "I don't think Rusty even has a dog. Don't know if I can work for a man who doesn't own a dog."

"His wife has a shih tzu."

"That ain't no dog," Kenny said. "That's a dust mop."

"Maybe he'll get a police dog," Quinn said. "He could put you in charge of the K-9 unit."

"Hondo is the smartest dog I ever known."

"Yes, sir."

"Me and him been friends since before you got home from the war," Kenny said. "He's got a lot of sense. Not just with cattle, but people. I swear, he bares his teeth every time he smells Johnny Stagg."

Quinn nodded, Kenny looking like he had something more to say. The party was breaking up, deputies headed back on duty and the rest home to their families before the rain and sleet started. He put his hand on Kenny's back and told the man he appreciated all he'd done.

"I was just thinking about when my folks died and all the mess around the tornado," Kenny said. "When you and Boom came out to the house and we found Momma."

Quinn reached out and shook the man's hand. Kenny, a portly fella in his wrinkled tan uniform, looked like he just might cry and Quinn really didn't want to see it. They were saved by the new dispatcher, Cleotha, who walked into the room and asked Quinn if he could get some deputies out to the lumberyard. "Mr. Cobb just called and can't get in touch with his night watchman," she said. "Wanted some extra patrols out that way. You know, I don't like that man. He talk to me like I work for him."

"I'll check it out on the way out of town."

"Shit, no," Kenny said, winking at Quinn. "Get on to your party."

Quinn shrugged and nodded.

"Yes, sir," Kenny said. "Have a few for me. I hope you get good and stinking drunk, Quinn. Call me if you need a ride home."

Quinn thanked everyone, wrote the last two reports, and locked up the Big Green Machine in the parking lot. His last act as sheriff of Tibbehah County was to unpin the star on his chest, lay it on the desk, and turn out the light on his way out.

14.

H ey, you," Peewee said. "What the hell's your name again?"

The guy named Kyle Hazlewood shot Uncle Peewee a look from the back of the van and said, "My goddamn name is Kyle. I told you that fifteen times. Don't you forget it again."

"OK, Kyle," Peewee said, sitting behind the wheel of his van, staring up the twisty gravel road to the house they were about to rob. "You sit here in the yard. Me and my nephew are gonna truck on up to the house. You better call if you see anything. I don't want Johnny Law anywhere near my ass."

"Wait, wait, wait," Kyle said. "Hold on one fucking minute. That wasn't the deal. That wasn't what we'd discussed with Mickey. The deal was you and me was going to the house. The flunky kid can sit down here in the van with his dick in his hand. That don't take no special talent."

Chase Clanton had had about enough of this bastard's low talk. *Dick in his hand? What kind of talk was that?* He looked at the skinny dude, with that thin-ass beard, and said, "You hold on one dang minute. I ain't no one's flunky. I'm a fucking apprentice. If I'm going to be doing my apprentice shit, I got to watch my dang uncle break into this house.

I got to see him bust this safe. Ain't no apprenticing if I'm sitting in a van. Any bastard can do that."

The fella Kyle raised up, tall as he could in the back of the van, and for a good moment Chase was pretty sure the old monkey was going to start swinging. But instead, moved on up to the front seat of the van, parked in the far corner of the big lumber mills. They'd snipped open the chain lock on the front gate and hung a new lock in its place. "Son of a bitch," he said. "Son of a bitch." He started to kick the shit out of the dashboard with his work boots, kicking so damn hard that the glove box opened up.

"What the hell?" Peewee said. "Shit, man. You're fucking up my vehicle."

"Y'all are going to fuck this up," he said. "I'm gone. I'm out of here. I'll walk home. I done my part. I got the guard drunk as a goat."

"Wait," Peewee said. "Wait. Hold on one damn minute. If you're gonna be all pissed-off and shit about things, you can just go up there with us. I don't expect it's going to take long at all. We head on up together."

"Someone's supposed to watch the van."

"If someone takes note, we're screwed anyway," Peewee said. "Right? I mean, we're gonna have to haul ass on foot. If we got Johnny Law rooting around, I think a better place would be up on that hill. We got problems, we take that back road that ole Mickey was telling us about."

"Leave the kid here."

"Boy's right," Peewee said. "He's supposed to watch what I do. We work together. He's a fucking assistant. He knows my tools, my methods. Like a doctor and a nurse. It's all precision work. You wouldn't get it."

"Shit," Kyle said, the man not buying it. Chase started wondering why the hell this old dude Kyle was here anyway, other than babysitting him and Uncle Peewee. He offered not a damn thing to this job. He had no skills, no talents, other than bitching about who was going to watch a fucked-up old van in the lumberyard.

"We all go," Peewee said, lighting up a smoke, fanning out the match. "All right? You all right with that?"

Chase didn't figure on anyone noticing the van anyway, the whole lumberyard like a damn maze of logs piled up five stories high, and long metal buildings, open at both ends, where they kept the milled timber. They'd parked the van outside the building, but Chase didn't see any reason why they couldn't hide the vehicle inside. Uncle Peewee was right. You needed a man to watch the road, and he and the older fella could take turns outside the house. Watching the road would be a hell of a lot better up on that hill, looking down on the highway.

They backed up the van into the metal building and all piled out, night coming on cold and hard. Uncle Peewee opened up the back of the van and waited for Chase to grab the big bag full of screwdrivers, pliers, and crowbars. It was heavy, maybe twenty-five pounds, and it fell solid on his back as he lifted it up on his shoulder. Peewee crushed out his cigarette. Kyle lit up one himself, not being able to hold off until they got up the damn hill. The man smelled like a fucking ashtray.

"Hold up," Peewee said, plucking the cigarette out of the man's mouth and snatching Chase up by the front of his coat. He pulled them both into the shadow of the long building just as a car showed up at the mouth of the opposite opening and flashed a spotlight, crazy and wild, all over the timber.

The car—Chase now seeing it was a dang patrol car—kept on moving, not driving into the building but circling on out, moving toward a back gate somewhere.

"I thought you changed up the lock?" Kyle said. "What the hell?"

"This yard got four gates," he said. "I can't change 'em all. They didn't see us."

"How do you know?" Kyle said.

"You see his flashers?"

"No," Kyle said.

"Then he didn't see us," Peewee said. "Come on. Let's go. We can see it all up top."

"I was just thinking the same thing," Chase said.

"Smart going," Peewee said. "Now carry my shit on up that road."

The extra girls, hired on just for the annual New Year's Brews and Titties bash at the Booby Trap, had been trucked in from the Indian casino in the county south of Tibbehah. A ruthless old red-headed bitch by the name of Fannie Hathcock ran the whores down there and had been agreeable with Johnny Stagg on making a deal. Stagg could have a dozen girls who knew how to work the pole and a man's rod for five hundred each. Stagg was pretty sure that Hathcock would be sending along her second-stringers as always but was pleasantly surprised to see a crop of not-bad-looking Mexicans and white girls unload off an old yellow bus he'd sent down, TIBBEHAH COUNTY SCHOOLS written along its side.

Ringold had driven the rig. He got down after the flow of girls walked across the blacktop, through the sleet starting to fall, and into the warmth and red light of the club. He had on a leather coat with the collar up, a green Carhartt knit cap on his bald head.

"You sure you got the right ones?"

"I bargained for the right talent," Ringold said. "First ones she sent out wouldn't do. Strung-out. Old and tattooed."

"These girls speak English?"

"A few."

"The thing I respect about the Mexicans is they know how to work," Stagg said. "White girls do OK, but they got an attitude."

"Maybe these girls have an attitude but you can't tell what they're saying."

"Maybe," Stagg said. "I guess I'm wondering what kind of deals Fannie Hathcock is making with those boys in Memphis. I feel like we're being sandwiched here. She didn't come across that talent by making a trip down to a Tijuana donkey show. She's getting 'em trucked in."

"I didn't ask her," Ringold said, both men standing in the parking lot, the neon glow of the sign of the mud-flap girl casting red, yellow, and blue over the slick pavement.

"She say anything about me?"

"Only talked money," Ringold said.

"That's Fannie."

"You two have a history?" Ringold said.

"Oh, yes, sir," Stagg said. "You could say that."

The men walked in out of the sleet and through the front door of the club, pulsing with dance music. The club already filling up with college boys from Starkville, lonely truckers, and horny fellas from Memphis. They had clubs in Memphis, but the Booby Trap was known to offer more mileage from their girls than places in Shelby County. You made a deal with a girl at Stagg's place and arrangements could be made for the hot pillow joint across the road that Stagg also owned. The air in the club smelled of smoke, sweat, coconut body oil, and money.

"You hear about that party they're throwin' for Colson?"

"Must've lost my invite," Stagg said. "You think we should send some girls over in appreciation?"

"Maybe some Jack Daniel's and barbecue, too."

"Why the hell not," Stagg said. "Get ole Midnight Man to drive over a bottle of booze and some barbecue. I got no more truck with that fella. I hope he does OK, now he's unemployed."

"I hear he's leaving town."

Stagg reached into his coat pocket for a fresh toothpick and set it between his teeth. "Damn shame."

The Booby Trap had three main stages and then a special VIP Suite out past the toilets where you could hire a girl to sit in your lap and rub you for good luck. A dance cost twenty-five dollars per song, but you could get two for forty, which Stagg thought was more than fair. One of the new girls, a slender young Mex, had already taken to the main stage and was spinning down the gold pole upside down as if she'd been born to it. Maybe she had. Maybe she'd just popped out her momma's cooch and took hold of it in some crib down in Nuevo Laredo.

Stagg took a seat at the end of the bar as Ringold wandered to the house phone to call up Midnight Man about the pork plate and whiskey. The bartender brought Stagg over a Dr Pepper with extra ice and extra cherries. He sipped the drink as the girls danced and moved. A fat trucker, big and round-faced as a gorilla, had wandered up to the edge of the stage, fanning a big wad of cash. His goddamn head looked as big as a medicine ball as he grinned and tucked money into the Mexican girl's G-string, some song playing overhead about chilling on a dirt road, him laid-back, swerving like he's George Jones. Shit, that dumbass singing wouldn't know the Possum from a possum's pecker. Stagg got up and walked to the DJ stand and told the man to start playing "Tennessee Whiskey."

"What?" the DJ said.

"George-goddamn-Jones," Stagg said. "Play it now or you can go back to cleaning out truckers' toilets."

The boy found the song real fast and maybe it did slow down the mood of the party. Some of the younger folks griping, Stagg hearing them groan, but in all—full credit to the Mexican gals and even, he was glad to see, one white girl—they just rolled with it. Moving those slender hips and big ole titties to that sweet old anthem.

Stagg toasted them with his sweet Dr Pepper, taking a cherry from the ice and sucking it for a long while before it came loose from the stem.

The inside of the Southern Star was warm and crowded for Quinn's farewell, packed with familiar faces of family and old friends. A beer appeared in his hand the moment he walked in the door. Someone took his ball cap and old jacket and he was led toward the stage, where Diane Tull sang the song he'd been named for, "The Mighty Quinn." But she didn't sing it fast and upbeat like Dylan's version, but slow and melodic, like a version he'd heard from Kristofferson that he liked a great deal. Folks patted him on the back, they brought him shots of Jack Daniel's and one tequila, and he accepted them all, not to be polite, but because he was a Ranger and he'd never known a Ranger to refuse a free drink. Diane launched into Waylon's "Slow Rollin' Low," and then Quinn found himself cornered by his Uncle Van, who started telling him a long, elaborate story about how much his Uncle Jerry wanted to make it, too, but he'd been saddled with trucking some transformers over to Valdosta and wouldn't be back to Jericho until the second. Quinn's father was there and soon joined them, saving him from a story Uncle Van was about to tell about how mean their daddy had been. Although Quinn had never known his grandfather—the man died when he was two—he had to agree that no kid wanted to cross the old man when he was high on shine. The Colson family had been notorious moonshine runners back in the day.

Jason took his son by the elbow and moved him over to the bar, where he ordered two beers, acting as if he was buying, although Quinn knew all draft and wine was free that night. Someone had collected some cash for the send-off and Quinn was pretty sure it had been Lillie, maybe Diane Tull, or even Jean Colson, although his mother couldn't make it tonight on account of watching little Jason. Quinn's dad talked a lot about the farm as if it would be a salvation for both of them. And Quinn had a pretty good buzz going when Jason told him that he'd be bringing over the horses next week. There was talk of an early planting of collards and then tilling up another acre or two just for corn. Jason had plans for that corn, using most of it for feed for the horses and the chickens. Chickens? Yes, chickens. Guineas, too, Jason said. You know, they eat ticks. Best damn eggs you'll ever eat, if you can find the bastards. Quinn nodding, sipping on a tall Yalobusha draft, feeling good, maybe not so bad about the new arrangement. He knew it was the beer or Diane Tull singing an a cappella "Hope You're Feelin' Me (Like I'm Feelin' You)," and then being joined by J.T., who ran a local garage and body repair shop, and Uncle Van himself on bass.

Quinn glanced across the room in time to see Ophelia Bundren. She had her curly brown hair up in a loose ponytail, long bangs dropping across her eyes. She held a beer and was laughing with a man Quinn didn't recognize. Over the man's shoulder, Ophelia met his eye and gave him a weak smile. Quinn smiled back, recalling some really good times, thoughts of them moving in together, making a real go of it. He hadn't seen her since that bad wreck in November when those Ole Miss kids got killed.

Boom was there, too. But his friend hadn't talked to him yet. He was on the other side of the bar talking up a pretty young woman who worked at the courthouse. Quinn nodded to Boom and Boom nodded back.

"Don't waste a good thing," his father said. And Quinn looked at him, not knowing what the hell he was talking about. All he could think about was chickens, horses, and pig shit. God, had he said something about pigs, too? But his father repeated it at the edge of the bar and nudged his shoulder, Quinn looking in the same direction and seeing Anna Lee standing there, watching Diane Tull and her boys play. The neon light in the bar made her strawberry blonde hair seem more of a deep red, head cocked back, moving a little with the music, in a tall-collared white coat and jeans. She still had on those big diamond earrings she'd gotten from Luke. Quinn heard his dad talking more about something between him and his mother, Quinn wanting to hear what he was saying but was being pulled to the center of the bar. More hands on his back. "You done good." "Sure gonna miss you." "See you at church." Quinn kept moving, spotting Ophelia across the bar again, her walking toward him. He smiled at her, turning full in her direction, wondering if things didn't have to be so tough between them, and then found himself nose to nose with Anna Lee.

"Brought you something," she said. "Set it on the bar."

"Strychnine?"

"Ninety proof, seventeen-year-old."

Ophelia saw them together and ducked in another direction, taking Jason Colson by the arm and laughing at something he said. She met Quinn's eyes once more and then walked away and toward the front door.

"Didn't expect you to be here."

"How could I not?" Anna Lee said.

There was a lot of sound, a lot of movement, but Quinn didn't hear any of it. Those big earrings sure could sparkle. Boom stood in the corner, blasted face shielded in shadow. He watched Quinn, shook his head ever so slightly, and turned away.

"People will talk," Quinn said.

Anna Lee looked at him good and hard, chin lifted, eyes on him. "I don't give a good goddamn," she said. "How about you?"

. . .

F uck, man," Chase said, not feeling real good about what he was
seeing in that closet. "Shit. Shit. Shit."

"That cussin' ain't helpin', son," Peewee said, half-glasses on, studying the red digits on the big safe's keypad. "Can someone go fetch me a
glass of water?"

"What the hell you need water for?" Kyle said, rubbing his graying
beard as if it were magic or something. "How's water gonna help you
open up that safe? You gonna try and flood that money out?"

"I need me a water for my damn dry throat," Peewee said. "I got to
be steady and cool about things. How about you just excuse yourself for
a while? This goddamn closet is getting too cramped. How many fucking flannel shirts and overalls can a man own? I can't even think on
things with all this shit around me."

"Think on what?" Kyle said. "Christ Almighty! We tried the combo
Mickey gave us and it ain't worth a shit. And now his expert safecracker,
his backup plan, doesn't know what the hell to do."

"Did I say that?" Peewee said, getting up, slow and pained, off one
knee, where he'd been studying the lock. "Did I say that? I said go get
me a goddamn glass of water and let me get my mind right. You ain't
no more help than a dog licking his balls while you on a hunt."

Kyle dog-cussed Peewee a bit and left the closet, Chase not knowing
what the hell they were talking about the closet being small. The closet
was twice as big as the damn room where he'd grown up in back in
Gordo. Shit, it was still nicer than where he lived now. A big top section, with hunting shirts and flannels and dress shirts, and a bottom
section, with Carhartt pants and fancy boots made out of snake hide
and crocodile. Uncle Peewee went back to his knee again, just like football players did to pray after the big game, studying that dial on that

gun safe. Chase couldn't wait for that old boy Kyle to watch his uncle crack that son of a bitch and try to talk with a big helping of dog shit in his mouth. That sure would be something.

"You know you don't have to wear that thing inside," Peewee said. "Damn, son."

"What?"

"The fucking turtle mask," Peewee said. "I swear to you, I'm not so sure that we're kin sometimes. I think you got too much of your daddy in you."

"I don't know why you're saying all that mess about my daddy," Chase said. "You said yourself you didn't know him that well. He might've been a good man."

"Lots of good men over in Kilby," Peewee said. "And crooks dumber than shit, too."

Kyle walked back into the closet, holding a plastic cup from Sonic. Peewee was sweating, hand a little shaky as he reached for it and told Kyle thank you, he didn't mean to cuss him none. "I just get a little edgy when I'm trying to think without some weed. Hey, boy? You go down and get me a little smoke down in the van? It's over the visor."

Kyle stood in the doorway, mouth looking like it was about to hit the damn floor. "Wait one minute. Are you saying we all need to stick around in a house we just busted into while your boy goes down and fetches you a joint? Are you shitting me, man?"

"You want me to think? Or not?"

"What I want is for you to admit that you don't know jack shit about safes and that you tricked Mickey into thinking that you're Butch Cassidy. You thought you were just going to kick open that back door, use his code, and walk out with some cash? How's that deal sounding to you now?"

"Why don't you just calm down," Peewee said, tapping in some numbers. "Hell. I can't even hear myself think. Both of y'all get out of here. I need to be alone with this baby. How we doing for time, Chase?"

"Been in here twenty minutes," Chase said.

"Well," Peewee said. "We counted on an hour. Them folks gonna be gone till tomorrow. If you hadn't figured it out, this is Plan B we're working on. Give me a second. Y'all just clear out and let the master do his thing."

"Don't you have a pair of them things a doctor uses to hear people's hearts?" Chase said.

"You talking about a stethoscope?"

"I guess."

"It don't help if you don't have no tumblers," Peewee said. "Just get me a hammer and a chisel."

"Oh my God," Kyle said from the other room. "A fucking hammer? Are you shitting me?"

Peewee looked to be in pain on that one knee, glancing up from where he was working, nodding his head toward the other room. "Keep that bastard away from me, son," he whispered. "This is professional work here. You understand? He's messing with my mind."

"Yes, sir," Chase said.

Chase walked back out into the big room and sat down on the floor, where he could keep Kyle from coming in and out. They'd kept the lights off and he had to use his flashlight to read old copies of *Field & Stream* and *Guns & Ammo*. He found a section in the back of *G&A* about women with big titties shooting firearms to raise money for veterans. All the girls wore bikinis and got to shooting damn machine guns and bazookas and shit. He sure wished he could see them on video and get all the vibrating action of them pulling the trigger, recoil, and such.

"Hey, man," he said to Kyle. Kyle sulking, leaning against a wall, smoking a damn cigarette in the dark. "You got to see this shit."

"We been here almost an hour."

There was the tap-tap-tapping sound of the hammer and chisel in the rich man's closet. A few times Chase heard Uncle Peewee say "Shit" and once say "Hot damn." But the "Hot damn" was soon followed by an "Oh, shit" and he knew he wasn't getting any closer to opening that son of a bitch. About fifteen minutes later, Chase had moved on to reading an article, "Best Days of the Rut," when Peewee walked out, mopping his face with a handkerchief, thick eyeglasses fogged all to hell. "God damn," he said. "I ain't seen nothing like it. That son of a bitch is thicker than I thought. Locked up tight."

"It's a safe," said Kyle from the shadows, smoke all in the room now. "It's what they do."

"I never met a safe acted this way," Peewee said. "I need some more muscle. This one is a like a woman who just don't want to put out."

"How much muscle?" Kyle said.

"Shit, man," Peewee said. "I'm about tapped out. But I don't think a man can do it."

"Can you blow it?"

"You mean, like, explosives?" Peewee said, using his sweaty handkerchief to clean his glasses. "I ain't got none."

"Great."

"How about a jackhammer or some shit?" Chase said. "Them things could bust that door wide open."

"You know where to get one?" Kyle said.

Chase shook his head. He closed the magazine, a picture of a big fat doe staring up with big doe eyes, and got up off the floor. He looked at the time, knowing that Mr. Kyle was right. They'd just farted away a dang hour and hadn't so much as budged that door. He sniffed and moved the turtle mask back over his face. He figured they maybe should be heading on to Gordo right now. He was too young to end up like his daddy.

"Fuck it," Kyle said. "I got something will open it up."

"What is it?"

"Ever heard of the Jaws of Life?" Kyle said, stepping up close to where he stood with Peewee. He blew smoke in both of their dang faces.

"Like firefighters use on wrecked cars?" Peewee said, pig-snorting a bit. "Shit. How the hell we gonna find one of them?"

"Because you're looking at the chief of his volunteer fire department," Kyle said, plugging another smoke into his mouth, lighting up. "You two Alabama shitbirds stay here and keep watch. I'll be right back."

15.

ook at it," Mickey Walls said. "Ain't it beautiful?"

"It's fucking cold, is what it is," Tonya said. "Come on, let's go back to the bar. You owe me a shot of Jäger."

"I owe you two shots of Jäger," he said. "You beat me on that video game fair and square. Damn, you got a mean punch."

They stood together at the edge of the beach out back of the Flora-Bama Lounge, watching the waves hit the shore, frothy and cold, loud country music playing from the bandstand. Tonya had on her pink faux fur coat and Mickey wore his old Carhartt work coat over his Hawaiian shirt, refusing to admit they were in the dead of winter. He looked out at the Gulf of Mexico, moonlight turning the tips of waves all pretty and silver, and hugged his ex-wife tight to him. "How come you don't call me Big Daddy no more?"

"You want me to call you Big Daddy?"

"Well," he said. "I don't know. I guess. Sure."

"OK, Big Daddy, let's get our asses off the frozen beach and back to those space heaters and some warm booze," she said.

"How about we make it double or nothing?"

"Double what?"

"Double the drinks I owe you."

"I don't give a damn about those drinks," she said. "I can buy my own, Mickey Walls. I didn't come down here because I need free shit from you."

"What fun is in that?"

She grabbed the front of his work coat, the pink fake fur tickling his nose as he brought his lips down to her neck, tasting a bit of that salt after they'd done tequila body shots. Tonya snuggling right on up to him, breath smelling like booze, eyes hazy, not saying a word as he got a good hand on her ass and said, "Let's go swimming."

"You've lost your damn mind," she said, looking this way and that, down the miles of beach from Alabama on one side and Florida on the other. Not a soul. The Flora-Bama was a big old two-story boardwalk of pressure-treated pine wrapped in plastic. Hundreds of people were packed inside the four bars and two stages. Florida Georgia Line supposed to come onstage at eleven and would be counting down the New Year.

"It'd be our own little club," he said. "Let's get buck-ass nekkid and run on into the water, wash away all the bad shit that happened last year. It'll be like a damn baptism."

"A Flora-Bama baptism?"

"They do have a church service here on Sunday."

"You're crazy as hell," Tonya said, but looking up at him, grinning a little. Some devilment about her. "Do I have to take my bra and panties off, too?"

"Everything or it don't count," Mickey said, taking off his work coat, a forgotten little wrench jingling in his pocket, cold wind like a damn knife ruffling his silk shirt as he worked on the buttons and kicked off his boots. He stripped down to his boxers, the cold so hard and mean that it just numbed him all over. His last thought before taking down the boxers was about his pecker. He knew that thing would be crawled

147

up inside him like a scared turtle. But, fuck it. Fuck it all. It wasn't easy to make things right.

He took off his boxers. Tonya shook her head like she was talking to one *bad* boy and took off the pink coat and then the dress. It was too cold for some kind of debate and, a second later, they were nekkid as could be, hand in hand, shivering and laughing and waist-deep in the Gulf of Mexico on the last day of the year.

"God damn you," she said.

Mickey grabbed her and pulled her cold skin in tight, pressing her big tan boobies against him, thinking this was damn well going to be the year. Everything was going to work out. All the bad shit would just float on away down to Cancún. She was screaming and yelling and laughing, and he dipped them both under the water, more screams, and then they broke free, running like hell back onto the beach and pulling on their clothes. Teeth chattering, her lips turning blue but smiling, "Four drinks," she said, "Big Daddy."

"And then?" Mickey said, glad to be pulling his pants over a unit that had all but disappeared. Sand clinging to his bare feet.

She slipped into the pink coat. Wet hair and big teeth. Dark brown skin. But something off about her, makeup running down her eyes.

Something just didn't seem right.

"Come on," she said. "Come on."

He knew the smile just slid from his face.

Damn, he saw it. Those mean, lying eyes of her daddy. God damn Larry Cobb's ugly ass. He wobbled a little bit and made his way up toward the boardwalk. Tonya hadn't noticed he wasn't laughing anymore and raced ahead of him, shoes in hand, toward the bar and the free drinks she'd won from her Big Daddy.

Mickey picked up his boots and followed. Maybe another drink would help.

. . .

It's getting to be midnight," Chase said. "We better get the fuck out of here."

"Boy's got it," Peewee said. "He's got it."

"Shit," Chase said. "He can't get a grip. Them things are meant to cut into fucking cars, not safes. Those pinchers can't grab hold of a big ole safe like that. We need some kind of damn saw, something that can cut through that thick metal."

The generator Kyle had brought with him from the fire station was heavy as shit, noisy as hell, and Chase had to yell a bit as he was conversing with Uncle Peewee. Uncle Peewee had all but quit, sitting at the big fancy dining table of the folks they were robbing. He'd helped himself to their scotch and some Christmas cookies. He had green sprinkles stuck all around his mouth as if he'd just gone down on the Grinch himself.

"Well, we're gonna need some kind of miracle," Chase said. "Y'all need to start thinking about running the ole two-minute drill. You remember last year's LSU game when the Tide was down by a touchdown? Ole AJ switched things up in less than a gosh-dang minute. He damn marched their ass down the field in five plays. Five damn plays. How you like that?"

"This ain't football, son," Peewee said, licking his fingers. "It's robbing."

"I'm just saying we need a big play," he said. "All we're doing is farting around and fumbling. We need some momentum. Leadership. We got to see some daylight in that there safe. Ain't nobody taking charge."

"You want a drink or something?"

"I don't drink."

"Hell you don't."

"I drink beer," Chase said. "But that ain't like drinking alcohol or nothing. Beer never killed a man. Hey, hey. You hear that? Hold up."

Chase left Peewee in the dim-lit dining room with that fancy-ass table and chairs, pictures of some big-headed man with a gray beard with all his kids and shit, and walked on into the bedroom and that deluxe closet. He heard a popping noise, a squealing that sounded like a dying squirrel, and figured that maybe old Kyle sure as shit was getting close. You could feel all the pressure, nearly popping in the air, as that boy was down on both knees sticking those metal pinchers in the door. But the pinchers were still closed, needling into the frame, trying to run the machine in reverse, hoping to separate the pinchers and open those doors to glory.

"Hell-fucking-yes," Chase said.

"Won't budge."

"I heard it," Chase said. "Come on, now."

"What you heard is this damn machine going full tilt," he said. "If I could just get a little more grip, just edge a little more into that door. Hey, hey. You got a crowbar?"

"Peewee got one."

"Get it." Kyle's face was red as hell. But even though he was breathing hard, a lit cigarette hung from his mouth in true dedication. It bobbed up and down in his lips while he cussed. "God damn. Son of a bitch."

Chase got the crowbar from the bag and walked it back into the closet. There was a floor-to-ceiling mirror back there and from a long ways it appeared that four folks were working on that safe. He handed the bar to Kyle, Kyle snatching it away, and Chase stood a little taller and sucked in his little gut. He had on a hooded canvas coat over a ROLL TIDE hoodie. The smoke and sweat in that little room sure was getting to him. Kyle worked and worked with that crowbar, but didn't seem to get nothing, and tossed it on the floor.

Chase checked his watch. Ten minutes to midnight. Damn.

Kyle used his legs and feet to push those pinchers as far as they'd go into the safe's frame and pushed the lever. His face reddened more, sweating, cigarette bobbing and then falling from his mouth, as he gave one final all-out groan, the generator and pump on a real high whine, until he fell to his ass and caught the cigarette just as it burned a hole into his jacket. "Fuck. Fuck. Fuck."

"You tried," Chase said. "Hell of an effort. I mean it. Hell of an effort."

"Get your uncle in here," he said. "This ain't working."

"You want to try some more with that crowbar?"

"I said, go get that fat bastard and tell him to get in here now," he said. "Shit. Shit. Wait. What the hell's that?"

Gunfire was popping off all around them. *Crack-Crack-Crack.* Pistols, and then an automatic weapon on full blast. Kyle scrambled to his feet and ran to the generator to turn off the device. "It stopped. Wait."

More shots. Chase ran from the closet to get Peewee. This whole thing was headed south fast. Good thing Kyle had driven the van on up the dirt road. If they could just get on out to the vehicle, maybe they'd still have a chance. Sounded like a damn army out there.

Peewee was standing near a lamp and studying the bottle in his hand. He didn't look as if he had a concern in the world.

"Come on," Chase said. "Didn't you hear that shit? Come on. They're shooting at us."

Peewee looked up at him from under those wild, crazy eyebrows and shook his head. "Damn, son," he said. "It's New Year's Eve. People got an American right to fire off their weapons."

Chase turned back and saw Kyle wheel the big cutters and generator out of the bedroom. The man had heard what Peewee said and shook his head, knowing he'd been just as almighty stupid. "Think," Chase said. "This is when the game breaks down. We make mental mistakes

151

that'll cost us a game. We need that safe. We got to get it with us and then find a way to bust in."

Kyle nodded. He gathered up the orange electric cord in his hand.

Peewee moved on toward a back door that opened into the garage just as a light shone into the dark room, all of them hitting the carpet to dodge it. The flashlight circled over the far wall, and they heard footsteps on the walk outside and the halting sounds of the sleet. Whoever was walking around had on a radio, the radio making squawking sounds, as doorknobs rattled and someone knocked on the front door.

And they just kept on knocking.

Chase looked to his Uncle Peewee. Peewee grinned and put a long finger to his lips. This whole night just seemed funny as hell to the old man. That automatic weapon went off again. Six shots from the pistol.

The knocking stopped.

Happy New Year.

W hat kind of problems?" Mickey said into the phone.

"Big fucking problems," Kyle said.

"I don't like the way that sounds," Mickey said. "Not at all. Talk to me."

Tonya was on her knees in front of him, unbuckling his belt, and working on his zipper, when the cell had rung. They'd just gotten back to the condo, deciding the Flora-Bama was too much country for them, buying a bottle of Barefoot Bubbly and a pint of Beam at the liquor store across Beach Road. The condo was real nice, high-class, with a lot of paintings of seagulls, seashells, and smiling kids on the beach. Mickey was laid back into the sofa, watching a replay of the ball dropping in Times Square, and pressed mute on the remote. Tonya wouldn't stop fiddling with his pants. He knocked her hand away and she got up off her knees and stormed back to the kitchen, pouring herself some more champagne into her red Solo cup.

"These boys," Kyle said, talking low, Mickey knowing someone was listening. "These Alabama boys are full of shit. The old one. Peewee Sparks? Shit, man. He doesn't know any more about busting a safe than you or me. I had to go down to the fire station and get the fucking Jaws of Life and we still couldn't bust into it."

"Where are y'all now?"

"At Larry and Debbi's."

"Get out of there," Mickey said. "Get the fuck gone. Now. Didn't you get my message?"

"What message?"

"Shit." Mickey looked back to Tonya and held up a finger and made his way out the sliding doors to the balcony. The condo looked right out at the beach and the Gulf, as a cold-ass wind wrapped around the tall building. "Damn, Larry and Debbi are headed back tonight, man. Shit. Y'all are still there?"

"I didn't get no message."

"Larry was pissed because he lost too much at blackjack," Mickey said. "I had Tonya check up on them and she said they left Tunica about an hour ago. I figured y'all would be long gone by now. God damn. What have y'all been doing?"

"Trying to bust that easy-ass safe you been talking about," Kyle said. "The one you said you had the combo and, if the combo didn't work, you had the best safe man in north Alabama to bust it open. Dixie Mafia. A real-life Sparks."

"He can't do it?"

"Hell, no, he can't do it," Kyle said. "That's what I'm saying. Shit, man. We've been here for three fucking hours. I'm just calling to tell you we're gone."

"Hold up, hold up, hold up," Mickey said, pacing back and forth on the little balcony, hitching up his pants, zipping them up and buckling the belt. "How about a crowbar?"

"You think we ain't tried that? Come on, man."

"How about the sledgehammer," he said. "Just knock the holy fuck out of it. You can do that. You hit anything hard enough and it'll bust open."

"Not this," Kyle said. "I'm only calling to let you know we tried. But we're gone, man. I ain't going to Parchman for this. Fuck that shit. And don't you be calling me back for a long time. Understand? I ain't answering."

The sliding door opened and Tonya peeked outside, the curtains bustling about in the wind. "Everything OK?"

"Oh, yeah," Mickey said. "Just great. Just some work shit. Go on in. I'll be right there."

"It's New Year's, Big Daddy."

"I know," Mickey said. "I'll be there in a second."

Tonya looked sad, but shrugged and slid the door closed, staying on the other side of the glass. She smiled at Mickey, dropping that pink furry coat to the floor, and then working the straps of her dress off her shoulders. The dress dropped down to her ankles. She was wearing something pink and transparent, with only a gold ankle bracelet.

"Wait," Mickey said, whispering. "Wait. Can you move the safe? Just take it with you?"

"Had you forgotten I got an asthmatic fat man with me and some half-retard kid?" Kyle said. "I'm not Superman."

"What about a winch?"

Tonya turned off the television and turned on the stereo. She was switching the stations around, squatting there at the console in her Victoria's Secret bra and panties, until she found something to her liking. That song that Miranda did with Carrie Underwood, "Something

Bad," the video where Miranda and Carrie dress up in different cos-
tumes to rob a bank. For a second, Mickey wondered if Tonya didn't
know just what the hell was going on. But then she started dancing in
her underwear, with her red Solo cup filled with Barefoot Bubbly, and
he knew his mind was just screwing with him.

"I said, 'Hell, no,'" Kyle answered. "I'm gone. We tried, but now
you're saying Larry and Debbi are damn halfway back to Tibbehah.
Did I tell you some sheriff's deputies have been prowling around the
lumberyard, too? They just checked the front and back doors. You
know they saw the van. When Larry and Debbi get back and they see
the mess we've made, they're going to start asking a lot of questions."

"Van can disappear," Mickey said. "Sparks told me that ain't nothin'.
Just get that safe and I'll be back in Jericho by morning."

"Shit."

"Get the safe."

"How?" Kyle said. "How the hell am I going to pull a half-ton from
the back of a closet?"

"Figure it out," Mickey said. "We're neck-deep in this son of a bitch
now. I'm trusting you. I'm relying on you, brother. Everything we been
through. You're my best friend. I need you to come through and get
that fucking safe. That's why I put you in charge."

"You put me in charge so I'd do the work while you get to play with
Tonya Cobb's spray-tan ass and big brown tits."

"Bullshit, man," Mickey said. "Bullshit."

Tonya had pressed her butt cheeks against the glass and looked at
him upside down between her legs. She was crooking a finger with a
long red nail at him.

"God damn, Mickey," Kyle said. "You've gone and fucked me hard."

Mickey heard yelling and arguing and Kyle then saying he had to
go. They had something that just might work.

"How much time until Larry's home?" Kyle said.

"You got an hour," Mickey said. "Don't use the phone again. I'm comin'."

Mickey pushed open the door, snatched up his jacket from the bar-stool and his ring of keys off the kitchen counter. He headed to the door as Tonya ran behind him, yelling, thinking he was playing some kind of game. "Where you going?" she said. "We don't need them things. I'm still on the pill."

He wasn't listening, running past the elevator, and headed down the staircase. Just as he got to his truck and crawled behind the wheel, he spotted Tonya, still in her pink bra and panties, screaming at him from the fifth-floor railing. He was pretty sure she called him a mother-fucker but didn't care a bit. As he cranked the engine and backed out of the slot, he saw her open up his suitcase and start dumping all the clothes he'd packed over the railing: Hawaiian shirts, blue jeans, good underwear, and those good intentions, flying into the winter wind.

It was one o'clock. He'd be back in Jericho by daybreak.

16.

Anna Lee was asleep, naked except for a pair of white socks, in Quinn's bed. He'd awoken when Hondo nosed open the bedroom door, letting in the hall light, and then sat there on his haunches, studying Quinn. Quinn, getting the idea, standing to find his Levi's and a clean white tee from a pile of twisted clothes. From the window, he watched Hondo make his rounds in the cold rain, taking careful aim on each tree as if it wouldn't all be washed away come morning.

Quinn took an aspirin, drank water from the tap, and let the dog back in the door.

He shut Hondo out of the room and sat on the edge of the bed, covering up Anna Lee's bare shoulder. She stirred a bit, both of them falling asleep after a lot of clothes-tearing and moving from living room to kitchen to bedroom. His neck felt raw and bruised where Anna Lee had kissed him and then bit some. She'd gripped his wrists. She'd clawed at his back. The last few months had been tough, keeping apart. Tonight, all the cruel and hard stuff just broke free.

"Hi," she said, turning over on her back, staring at him.

He handed her the glass of water as she pushed up on her elbows, the sheet and the quilt covering a single breast, and drank a few sips. Anna Lee asked for more and Quinn returned to the kitchen and then back to the bedroom. An outdoor light shone on the side porch, letting in a soft white glow through the gauzy curtains. In the fireplace, the logs had burned down to a nice, even orange, the metal box radiating heat.

She set the glass on a side table and reached back with both hands to pull her hair back behind her ears. The sheet fallen away now, showing off her good shoulders and long arms, modesty not a factor. Anna Lee never being a shy girl who covered up. She'd always been proud of her strong body.

"Come back to bed," she said.

"Can you stay?" Quinn said. She'd never been able to stay. When they'd been teenagers, there'd been curfews. And, now, her daughter and a whole lot more responsibility.

"Mom knows I'm out all night."

"She knows where you are?"

Anna Lee nodded. Quinn moved in closer and rubbed her bare back and shoulders. She had sun freckles down her arms and across her chest. "How'd she feel about it?"

"Didn't say a word," Anna Lee said. "I swear to God."

"She never liked me much."

"Are we talking high school now?" she said. "When you stole the city fire truck or that time you flipped your truck mudding? You might've been the worst boy in the whole damn school."

"I wasn't the worst," Quinn said. "The worst boy in Tibbehah was Junior Lindsey. That dumb son of a bitch broke into the First Baptist Church and stole two television sets, a VCR, and a microwave. He held a damn party at his trailer so we could all watch *Under Siege 2*. He was smoking dope, doing karate, and telling us how he could whip Steven Seagal's ass anytime, anyplace."

"I'm not talking truly bad," she said. "I'm talking shit that makes a mother worry herself."

"You mean the kind of boy who'll talk you into getting buck-ass naked?" Quinn said. "Maybe gets you to go skinny-dipping with him in a creek one summer, play around a bit in the water, and then try things out, see how they worked."

"Yep," Anna Lee said. "That kind of boy. God help us. I really don't know how I didn't get pregnant."

"We were careful."

"That first time?" she said. "At the creek? That was careful?"

"I did my best," Quinn said. "Some wildlife might have been injured."

"Shit." Anna Lee laughed and then held her head. "I haven't had that much to drink in a long while. It's gonna suck tomorrow. Sweet Jesus."

Hondo scratched at the bedroom door, whining. Quinn got up and let him in, the dog finding the old wool rug where he slept by the fire, circling around four times and lying down. Quinn stood up, added a couple more logs. The dog lifted his head, sparks flying in the fireplace, and then set it back down.

"You feel bad?" Quinn said. Anna Lee pulling up the sheet and the cover back over her, turning on her side.

"No," she said. "Should I?"

"You will," Quinn said. "Soon as light hits, you'll be full of a hang-over and regret."

"No, sir."

"I can sleep on the couch," Quinn said, standing over her. "I won't make this tough. OK?"

Anna Lee watched his face and then smiled. "It's not the same," she said. "Not now."

"Time will tell."

"I'm not stupid," she said. "I know what your friends think of me. Lillie. Boom. Your momma and daddy. Shit. Everybody."

"Not Jason Colson," Quinn said. "He said you're a hot little pistol. Said I'd be a fool not to nail you down."

"Everyone thinks I'm going to fuck you up."

"If jumping out of airplanes and shooting people didn't fuck me up," Quinn said, "I think I can handle coming home. Coming back to this. To you."

"What?"

"The best tail in north Mississippi."

Anna Lee picked up a pillow and launched it at Quinn. He caught it and sat back down on the bed. "You bastard," she said.

"I know this is complicated as hell. Your divorce isn't final yet. They think you'll go back to Luke. Do right for your daughter."

"They aren't us," Anna Lee said. "This isn't their life. I think Caddy knows. Caddy understands what we have. She's told me so."

"Caddy's got enough shit to worry about."

Anna Lee nodded, not saying anything more, no one wanting to discuss Caddy's latest turn.

"We should go at things slow," Quinn said. "Everything is changing. Until it's all final."

"Luke knows," she said. "He told you himself. He understands I love you. He's mad and he's hurt, but he knows it's something that's never changed. I don't think he figured on you ever coming home."

Quinn nodded, fingering away the blonde hair from her brown eyes. He leaned down and kissed her, lingering there on her lips and breaking away slowly. "We'll get things right, the way they're supposed to be," he said. "OK?"

"This is right," she said. "You know it. I know it."

"We might be the only ones."

"This doesn't concern anybody else."

Quinn smiled, listening as the rain turned to sleet, pinging hard as hell on the tin roof. Anna Lee reached out and grabbed his hand, Quinn thinking he should leave the room and sleep on that couch. Let her make up her own mind in the morning light. As he stood, she pulled back the covers from her naked body, nothing on but that pair of tall white socks. "Show me how it's supposed to be, Quinn Colson," she said. "You make it right."

"Yes, ma'am," Quinn said. "I'll do my best."

Anna Lee smiled, pulling at him and tumbling with him into the old iron bed. Quinn unbuttoned his pants and pulled off his T-shirt. The sleet fell faster and harder above them, Quinn wondering if it just might tear off part of the old roof.

L illie had stopped by Miss Magnolia's house not long past midnight. She'd seen the front porch light and lights on in the old unpainted house—the old woman didn't seem to know when it was day or night. She'd promised Quinn to check on the woman, bringing her a sack of chicken biscuits from the Dixie Gas station. Miss Magnolia, pleased with the bounty, sat in her big recliner, a massive amount of pills and ointments on a TV tray beside her, eating while the TV played an episode of that old show *227*.

"Good biscuits," Miss Magnolia said. "You make these?"

"No, ma'am," Lillie said, holding her police radio in her lap. The whole house smelled of the propane that was burning off in a space heater on the wall. The woman smiling and laughing at the antics on the show. "That Jackée," she said. "Ain't she something?"

"Yes, ma'am," Lillie said. "You doing OK?"

"I am," she said. "'Course I am. Who told you I wasn't?"

"Sheriff told me you'd been wandering some," she said. "I don't want you going outside without your grandson. OK? It's sleeting out there tonight. Pretty rough and cold."

"Sleet?"

"Yes, ma'am."

"Fine man."

"Who's that?"

"The sheriff."

Lillie nodded, hearing dispatch sending Kenny to check out a traffic accident on 281. A car had slid off the road and into a ditch, no injuries, but the driver needed a tow. Lillie needed to get back on the road, on patrol, but knew she'd have to listen to Miss Magnolia ramble a bit about Hamp Beckett, as she couldn't tell the uncle from the nephew, not knowing if it was 1977 or 2014.

"He's taken a shine to you," she said. "I can see it."

"Sheriff Beckett is an old man, Miss Magnolia."

"Sheriff Beckett?" she said. "Who said something about Sheriff Beckett? That man died years ago. I'm talking about Quinn. Jason Colson's boy."

The radio popped on again, dispatcher telling Kenny to meet the vehicle's driver at the Shell station, where he'd walked. Kenny came back on the radio, giving a "Ten-four," annoyed he was having to reverse direction and head back into town. Miss Magnolia's blued cataract eyes had turned on her. She smiled, chin up, appraising Lillie. "You telling me you don't have no interest in that man?"

"In who?"

"In Quinn," she said. "Who the hell we talking about?"

"He's the sheriff," she said. "Or was the sheriff. I work for him. He's my boss."

"Mmm-hmm."

Lillie smiled at the old woman, the woman chewing away on her second biscuit, turning her head back to the TV, where Jackée was sick, lying on the sofa and holding a teddy bear. She told another woman that she had "aches, pains, and day-old nail polish." That seemed to make Miss Magnolia chuckle a bit. The old woman reached over to the TV tray for a bottle of some pills and unscrewed the top while she coughed a few times.

"If I was a young woman, I'd do him."

"I don't have any interest," Lillie said, feeling her face flush.

"I see how you look at him," she said. "I may be old, and sometimes I get confused. But that's just as plain as day."

"It's sleeting outside," Lillie said, standing. "Freezing weather. Can you lock yourself in, ma'am? I can check up in the morning."

"It is morning," she said. "Damn sunrise. I sure appreciate these biscuits. You know how to make 'em."

Lillie started to correct her but she decided against it, leaving the old woman turning back to the television and laughing along with something going on with that other old woman, the old woman from the sitcom, hanging outside her window and yelling at some kids. That seemed to really tickle Miss Magnolia.

Lillie got back into her Cherokee, checked off the wellness stop, and started the engine. Sleet tapped on the windshield as dispatch called for Tibbehah 2, Tibbehah 2 being her. She called back to dispatch, letting Cleotha know she was off the check and back on patrol. "Tibbehah 2, we've had two neighbor complaints of noise at Number 7 County Road 334."

"Didn't Kenny just check out the lumberyard?"

"Two more calls since then," Cleotha said. "We got a call that someone is driving a backhoe up the hill."

"Jesus Christ." Lillie shook her head, awaiting a certain type of drunkenness and stupidity that comes with working the New Year's Eve shift. She called Kenny on the radio and told him to meet her at the Cobbs' house. "Wait on me."

She hit the flashers and mashed the accelerator.

This is fucking awesome, man," Chase said. "Fucking awesome."

He was back down in the lumberyard, watching Kyle start up the backhoe and head on up toward the Cobbs', not worrying a damn bit about going to the main road but instead just crashing up and over a chain-link fence and hitting the gravel drive up to the house. Chase had his cell phone up to his ear, telling Uncle Peewee to get his ass ready.

"He got it started?"

"Hell, yeah, he got it started," Chase said. "He crashed through the fucking fence and is headed your way. He said to turn the van around and open them doors because he's gonna drop that safe inside like a fresh egg."

"Hot damn," Peewee said. "That boy's got big ole nuts."

"You think you can bust it?" Chase said. "If you got some more time and space? I know it was hard to work in that fucking closet."

"Hard to see," Peewee said. "Hard to manipulate that keypad. I get that safe back to my shop and I'll bust her open wider than a drunken cheerleader."

"And then we get down to New Orleans."

"Yes, sir," Peewee said. "Temptations, here we come!"

"And the Sugar Bowl?"

"Cold beer and warm whores, kid," Peewee said. "Now, come on and run up the hill before the law gets here. It sounds like a fucking John Wayne movie outside. You got to wake up half the county?"

"Yes, sir," Chase said, slipping the cell back in the front pocket of his

'Bama hoodie and following the trail of busted fence and ruts in the road, the backhoe rolling on ahead of him, turning the final curve of the hill up to the house. As Chase ran, the sleet fell like tiny little needles on his face, but he was so damn pumped-up, so fucking happy, that it didn't matter. He and Peewee had pulled it off. Sugar Bowl, here we come.

The cell phone and the gun were jingling in his pocket. He took out the gun, feeling tough and in charge, as he ran up the hill to that ranch house. He stood at the top of the drive, catching his breath, watching the soft light around the bushes and little trees. The house was one story, with a long, nice roof, brick walls, and red shutters. Lots of Christmas decorations around the door and windows, a plastic snowman lit up by the front door. Everything calm and peaceful in that sleet until damn crazy man Kyle headed right for the damn wall where the fat man's closet was. He didn't even hesitate, running that little backhoe right into the wall, knocking down bricks and part of the ceiling, using the scoop to push away all the mess in his way, all that clutter of timber and clothes, eating through half the room, rolling over a bed and chairs, flat-screen TV sparking off the fucking wall, until he got to something, let down the scoop again, and backed up and over all the shit, holding the safe in the bucket, coming backwards and then forwards over the lawn and dropping it nice and neat, with some kind of precision, in the back of the black van. Kyle backed up the backhoe, killed the engine, and helped Peewee shut the back doors.

"Come on, kid," Kyle yelled. "Let's get the fuck out of here."

Chase could hear the sirens—some law was sure as hell headed their way now. He dropped around to the side of the van, opening up the door and about to jump inside. Peewee cranked the motor and drove forward, not even waiting until Chase had both feet in the van and the door closed.

They didn't get a quarter way down that hill when those flashing lights met them. Through the windshield of the van, he saw a patrol car and blue lights. A door opened and a shadow got out, walking toward them.

"Fuckin' A," Peewee said.

There wasn't a way around the vehicle, only through it. But Peewee didn't have it in him. His lazy-ass uncle knocked the van into park and killed the engine. Chase was mad as hell now, opening up that side door and telling Kyle and Peewee to wait right there, he'd straighten out this whole mess.

"Hold up," Peewee said, turning back inside the van. "Shit. Hold up, boy. Don't you do it. Don't you fucking do it."

But it was too late. Chase had out his sweet little gun and headed right toward that shadow, walking with the weapon hanging low and out of sight behind his back.

17.

Lillie saw the blue flashers as she rounded the dirt road, Kenny's Crown Vic parked crooked in the dead center, driver's door wide open. Sleet falling heavy, windshield wipers working, her headlight spotlighting the cruiser. She called Kenny on the radio. No response. She called again. "Tibbehah 14?" she said. "What's your 20?"

Nothing. She called in to Cleotha and reached for her twelve-gauge, sheathed by the passenger seat and the gearbox. Lillie had on a heavy sherpa coat and a TIBBEHAH SHERIFF ball cap, the sleet pinging off the bill as she moved into the headlights with the gun, calling out for Kenny.

As she rounded his patrol car, she saw the big piece of road up on ahead, lit up by Kenny's headlights and flashers, and noted some rutted tire tracks not five feet away. It looked like a big truck might've been stuck and had to dig in deep to roll free. She called Kenny again.

The twisting road was quiet. She could only hear the windshield wipers on her Cherokee and the sleet. Cleotha was radioing on her handheld. No call back from Kenny on his cell. Lillie grabbed her mic and asked for all available deputies to head this way. Her stomach felt hollow and cold. She steadied her breath as she moved forward.

Out of the headlights and up the hill a ways, she called Cleotha on her cell and told her what she'd found. Lillie didn't want to broadcast to every busybody with a scanner that one of her deputies was missing. Art Watts and Ike McCaslin radioed they were headed her way.

"You want me to call Quinn?" Cleotha asked. Lillie didn't answer, putting down the phone, hearing something in a gulley, a rustling of leaves, movement. She turned on the speed light Quinn had made sure all the deputies attached to their shotguns. He said he didn't want any deputy fooling around with a flashlight on dark back roads. She marched forward, wind kicking loose some dead leaves from some skeletal trees. Up around the bend, she could see the Cobbs' ranch house, and down below were the lights of the lumberyard. The windshield wipers kept working as she walked forward, hearing her boots on the gravel road and more rustling down in the ravine.

She got to the edge of the road and pointed the barrel of the shotgun in the ditch, expecting to see a raccoon or an injured deer but instead saw Kenny on his belly, trying to crawl his way out but slipping and falling with each grasp. Lillie jumped into the ditch, using the weapon for its light, and helped Kenny slide down in the mud, checking his injuries. The right leg of his blue jeans a dark maroon, his face the goddamnedest shade of white, mouth working but dry and not forming words.

Lillie called in to dispatch for an ambulance. She got down to her knee, shotgun still clutched in her right hand, and using her left to hold Kenny's face, spoke to him. "Are they still here?" she said. "Where'd they go?"

"A kid," Kenny said. "Got shot by a fucking kid."

"Who?"

Kenny shook his head. Lillie heard the sirens of the other deputies, the lonely back road lit up in blue lights, car doors slamming, and she called out to them. "Down here," she said. "Kenny's shot."

Ike got a blanket from his cruiser and laid it on the road. He helped

Lillie pull Kenny from the mud while she pressed a towel to his leg. The towel turned a bright red while Art Watts was walking up the hill with his AR-15. She pulled off her belt and cinched it tight around Kenny's leg as a tourniquet.

Lillie asked about the vehicle the shooter drove. But Kenny just kept on repeating that the boy was an Alabama fan, wearing an Alabama shirt. "Fucking 'Bama turd," he said.

"Son of a bitch," Lillie said.

A minute later, Art called on the radio from the top of the hill. He said they had a break-in at the Cobbs', half the house looked to have been smashed in with a backhoe. She listened, let Ike respond to Art's call, while she kept on cinching Kenny's thigh, telling him he'd be just fine, everything would work out, although she wasn't so damn sure. She kept on waiting to hear those sirens, knowing he'd lost a lot of blood down in that ditch.

Ike responded, his black face sweating in the cold, and looked down to where Lillie helped his friend. "Cleotha wants to know if she should call Quinn?"

"OK." Lillie swallowed and nodded. "Can you get me another towel or something to use? This one's soaked all the way through."

Art walked back down the hill, AR-15 in hand and shaking his head. "It's a fucking mess up there, Lil."

Quinn lifted himself from bed, eased into his clothes, heavy jacket, and boots, and walked out into the cold to gather more firewood. Usually he would have stocked up for the night, not having to wake up Hondo or any company, but his company had bent his routine. He lifted up an armful of split and aged red oak, set out by the old smokehouse, and walked back to the house, Hondo following his footsteps. Hondo never giving a damn if it was day or night, always ready to hop in the truck or run a fool's errand. Even if it was seventeen degrees, dark, and whipping sleet around the house.

Even in the bad weather, the house looked just about perfect, perched atop a hill, smoke pouring from one of the three chimneys, porch lights lit. His great-great-grandfather on his mother's side built it in 1895 to grow crops and raise seven children. Tonight, the old house glowed for Quinn, knowing Anna Lee was in his bed. He started to think on how things might've worked, as it had probably been intended, if ten years of war and missed chances back home hadn't gotten in the way. She'd never been meant for Luke Stevens and Luke knew that. But there was a daughter for her and a surrogate son for him in Jason. And now with Caddy gone and the plans changing, he might have a full house this year. Maybe new children of his own to raise side by side a stepdaughter and a nephew.

Quinn liked that idea just fine. The old white farmhouse seemed to burst with warmth and light. He could make things work. He wouldn't even mind planting some crops with his father, seeing how that just might work out. Children, a farm to mend, maybe a wife. Isn't this what a man did after war? Slow the hell down. This goddamn county could take care of itself.

He had made his way up to the porch, setting down the extra wood by the front door, when the cell rang in his pocket.

Now, what the boy did was just fucking stupid," Uncle Peewee said. "Ain't no getting around that. But I'm not going to have some man I don't even know talking shit to my nephew. That boy is my kin and this here's my vehicle."

Chase listened to the defense from the back, where he rode with the safe on its side, skidding front to back as they took turns on country roads. He was proud of his uncle, speaking his mind to that hothead.

Kyle had called him about everything but a white man since Chase had saved all their asses.

"The kid shot a deputy," Kyle said. "I really don't care to get a lethal injection in the New Year. How about you, Mr. Sparks? You nail a fucking lawman and they'll track your ass for the rest of your life."

"Ain't nobody is going to nail no one for nothin'," Peewee said. "Nobody knows who did it. Boy was smart enough to wear a mask. If the man ain't dead, what's he going to say? He was shot by a goddamn turtle?"

"I was wearing that mask," Chase said. "Raphael."

"Shut the hell up, kid," Kyle said, not even having the decency to turn and look him in the face. "You just hopped out and took it on yourself to pull the trigger. I don't recall that when we were running down the plan."

"I don't recall the part about no lawman come sliding up on us like it was *The Dukes of Hazzard* and pulling his weapon on me."

"Did he pull it?"

"Well," Chase said. "He had a pistol in hand. I seen it. I'm sure. He told me to drop it or he was going to shoot. I sure as hell wasn't going to drop the gun. I just bought the damn thing."

"And so you killed him?"

"I don't know if he was dead," Chase said. "When Peewee kicked him in that ditch, he was cussing up a storm. Crying like a dang baby."

"I wore a mask, too," Peewee said.

"Donatello."

"Yes, sir," Peewee said. "That fucking turtle. We're all just turtles now. I know'd this cripple boy down in Millport who runs a chop shop when he ain't mud-racing. He'll have this van broke down to pieces before day's over."

"That's where y'all are headed?" Kyle said. "You're not taking this safe without me. What the hell you thinking?"

"Then come on, man," Peewee said. "I sure as shit don't want to be sitting 'round with my thumb up my ass and waiting for Johnny Law to find us. That cripple I know can bust open that safe before he takes apart this vehicle. Unless you want me to drop you off on the side of the road? If you want to go on and pay us out, that's just fine by me."

"Shut up, man," Kyle said. "Just shut the fuck up. I got a damn shop at my house and I got the tools to do it. I got a blowtorch and some rods. If we can bend that metal, I can get those cutters in deep. Besides, I got to get them back to the firehouse before someone sees they're gone. I can't be riding over to see some fucking cripple drag racer. That's all we need, one more dumb bastard in on this thing."

"You calling my uncle dumb, you gray-headed piece of shit?"

"Sparks," Kyle said, voice low and easy. "You don't call off that pup and I swear to you I'll toss him out the window."

Chase shifted a bit, trying to stand back, hand on the safe, right hand in the pouch of his hoodie. "I'd like to see you try, old man."

"Y'all calm down now," Peewee said, taking a turn down a dirt road, wheels bumping up and down. Windshield wipers scraping off the ice. "This ain't helping none. You say you got a toolshed."

"That's what I said."

"Ain't no need getting testy," Peewee said. "I'm just trying to think. Let me ask you this. Would the law have any reason to come and question you?"

"No," Kyle said. "Well, I don't know. It ain't no secret that me and Larry parted ways. But, no, I don't think they'd be looking at me first off. Mickey Walls was right. Law is going to look right at him. Nobody saw me. Kenny knows me. But I didn't get out of the van."

"Who's Kenny?" Chase said.

"The damn deputy you shot."

"And saved everyone's ass."

"I swear to it," Kyle said, not finishing his threat but instead lighting up. Blowing smoke and bullshit all inside the van. "Toss him right out the window."

"And you say you got a shop?" Peewee said.

"With a little heat and pressure, I can get that thing cracked open," Kyle said.

"I think I said the same thing to my second wife," Peewee said. "Haw, haw."

Nobody laughed. Chase didn't even crack a smile, even though he sometimes found his old uncle kind of funny. This was serious shit, serious business, and until they got that damn safe open, they all needed to keep focused and give a damn hundred and ten percent. "Fourth quarter, boys," Chase said. "Fourth quarter. Let's see who wants it more."

"Christ Almighty." Kyle let down the window, tossed out the cigarette, and started a new one.

18.

See these tracks," Lillie said, shining her Maglite into the dirt road ruts. "We're looking at a big truck carrying a real heavy load."

"What'd they take from the Cobbs?" Quinn said, walking with her outside the crime scene tape up the hill. Hondo followed them, keeping close and looking up at Quinn for directions. The dog liked crime scenes, sniffing about, liking all the sound and activity.

"I'm not sure," Lillie said. "Did I fail to mention someone drove a fucking backhoe through Larry and Debbi's bedroom?"

"Larry on someone's shit list?"

"How many folks in Tibbehah you know that like that man?"

"Maybe a couple."

"That aren't related?" Lillie asked.

"That narrows it a bit."

"Talked to the hospital," Lillie said. "They got Kenny in surgery. He's lost a shit ton of blood. But it's looking good. I got a belt up on his thigh early. Although he's not thinking straight. He told the EMTs he'd been ambushed by some fucking Ninja Turtles."

They walked side by side up the hill and onto the Cobbs' driveway.

Some MBI techs from Batesville had just shown up and were taking photos and video, picking through the mess. Ike McCaslin stood on a walkway up to the front door, making sure no one got into the house until the techs were done. More yellow tape had been strewn on the side of the one-story ranch house where there used to be a window and a room. Through the big hole, Quinn could see an upturned mattress and a dresser on its side, lots of clothes tossed across the carpet. Flashlight beams crisscrossed the darkness, some colored Christmas lights hanging crooked over the hole. Ike nodded to Lillie and Quinn.

He was a tall, very thin, almost gaunt-looking black man who'd put in nearly thirty years with the sheriff's office. He'd been a loyal friend to Quinn's uncle and a good deputy for Quinn. He was the kind of deputy who had the ability to ask a felon how his momma was doing as he laid on the handcuffs.

"Just got off the phone with Mr. Cobb," Ike said.

"Where is he?" Lillie asked.

"Tunica," Ike said. "Him and Debbi were coming back anyway. Cussing about getting ripped off. I didn't get two words out of my mouth and he asked about his closet. Wanting me to check his closet. I told the man it was kind of hard to tell where his closet at."

"What's he looking for?" Lillie said.

"Mr. Cobb said that he had a big-ass gun safe," Ike said. "I walked through there with that lady with MBI and there ain't no safe. Not anymore."

"He say what was inside?" Quinn asked.

"Nope."

"You ask?" Lillie asked.

"Figure it was guns."

"Lots of trouble just for some guns," Quinn said. "Where'd that backhoe come from?"

"Lumberyard," Ike said, pointing down the hill. "You can follow the trail it cut up through the trees. They stole it down here and rode it on up to the house. Larry Cobb's gonna shit a brick when he sees his house. His wife's lacy drawers flying in the wind like flags."

"What about the rest of the house?" Lillie said, turning toward the garage and a back door. "Anything else gone?"

"Nope," Ike said. "They left a couple good TVs. I saw some jewelry and things on the floor of the bedroom. Looks like they only came for that safe."

"Larry have any idea who?" Quinn said.

"Yes, sir," Ike said. "He said right off it was Mickey Walls. He said for us not to waste any time but go ahead and arrest his son-in-law. Or ex-son-in-law. Either way, Cobb said Mickey was out to get him."

"Lil?" Quinn asked.

She nodded. The sleet had stopped and there was only the cold wind now. Someone up on the hill, one of the Cobbs' neighbors, had a fire going and Quinn could smell the woodsmoke. He thought about Anna Lee back in his house in his warm bed, fire going in the stove. As they turned to the back of the house, Quinn spotted his old truck, the Big Green Machine, bucking and racing up the hill. Light bar flashing blue across the bare trees and over the muddy ground.

Rusty Wise jumped out of the truck, wearing a neatly pressed tan uniform and ball cap, and trotted on up to where Quinn stood with Lillie and Hondo. Hondo sniffed at the man as he got close. Rusty wasn't smiling. The star on his shirt gleamed bright in the porch light.

"How long ago this happen?" Rusty said.

"About an hour," Lillie said.

"You didn't think to call me?"

"Cleotha said she'd notify you."

Rusty looked to Quinn, up and down, boots to cap. He pushed his jaw toward the house and asked if they'd cleared the place.

"No one's in it," Lillie said. "Cobbs are missing a gun safe. And their bedroom."

"Gosh darn it," Rusty said, face turning a bright red. "How come no one called me? Today of all days."

"What's today?" Quinn asked, not being too helpful himself.

"According to the calendar, it's January first," Rusty said. "And I'm on the taxpayers' clock."

"You bet."

"I know you felt you had to come on out because of Kenny and all," Rusty said, rubbing the back of his neck. "But we're all good. We can take it from here. Right, Lillie?"

Lillie folded her arms over her chest. It was hard to see her eyes with the ball cap far down on her nose. She didn't say a word.

"Well," Rusty said, reaching down, petting Hondo on the head. "What a damn mess. Has anyone called ole Larry yet? Great Gosh Almighty."

Rusty walked over to Ike McCaslin, Ike pointing down toward some broken tree branches and the path of the backhoe that was now parked in the Cobbs' front lawn.

"Did he just say, 'Great Gosh Almighty'?" Lillie said.

"Yes, ma'am."

"Is he the sheriff or a fucking youth pastor?"

"He's a good man, Lil."

"Maybe."

"He doesn't want me here."

"I'm too old for hand-holding," Lillie said.

"You had to hold mine for a bit."

"Man looks like a fucking sausage squeezed into that uniform."

"Good luck," Quinn said. "I'm headed to the hospital."

"Quinn?"

He looked back.

"Can you at least find out about those Ninja Turtles?" she said. "I want to make sure Rusty is prepared for any gosh-darn thing that comes his way."

When you throw on the house lights, isn't everyone supposed to get the hell out of here?" Ringold asked.

"Yes, sir," Johnny Stagg said, looking at the mess the party had left. Not liking it a bit. "But you're not looking upon a crew of like-minded folks. You're looking at fornicators, deviants, and road trash blown up our way. It's just who we serve here. I've often thought of myself more a zookeeper than a bar owner. You just have to rattle the fucking cages and give a few direct pokes to get them moving on."

"I had to break up three fights tonight," Ringold said.

"Any of 'em give you trouble?"

Ringold just smiled behind that big black beard and took a sip of Coors. His bald head reflecting the fluorescent light.

"You go ahead and toss them stragglers out in the parking lot," Stagg said. "I got to get straight with my dancers. I'm always straight with them. But, Lord, how they love to play hidey-hole with that tip money."

"You gonna search them?"

"Any woman wants money bad enough to keep it in her orifice surely deserves keeping a dollar or two," Stagg said.

"Can I ask you something, Mr. Stagg?" Ringold said, not having to call him mister, but Stagg appreciated the gesture. Or maybe Ringold had just gotten high on all that free cold draft and was feeling like he was back in the service. Stagg his captain.

"Shoot."

"How do you stand it?" he said. "If you don't care for these people, is the money worth it?"

"First off, money is everything," Stagg said. "Don't make it any harder than that. You think any of those jackasses up in Oxford would let me eat and drink with them in the Grove if I didn't have money? I see their looks and their sly smiles. But they want to see me. Have to deal with me because I'm that Mr. Stagg, Mr. So-'n'-So, from Tibbehah County. They don't care what I do or what I own. Only that I'm rich."

"And this?"

Ringold leaned back against the bar, a bit reminiscent of maybe Jack Palance at some time or another, elbows behind him to hold his weight. He tipped the glass back, grinning, watching all the drunken fools try to make one last go of paradise. One more minute of booze and pussy. Johnny Stagg had seen it a hundred times, the reason he hadn't had a drop in more than thirty years. He reached into his back pocket, grabbed his Ace comb, and worked a bit on the ducktail and pompadour. He sucked his teeth and shook his head. The five frat boys trying to get the two strippers out to their car. The lonely farmer with cow shit on his boots who'd brought a dozen roses to some crack whore from Byhalia. And there was one of Tibbehah's own county supervisors trying to get a last-minute pecker pull from a black girl who wasn't two months into her eighteenth year. The man was a deacon at his church and the most outspoken opponent of Jericho legalizing cold beer a few years back.

"It's like a little aquarium, son," Stagg said. "I kind of enjoy sitting back most nights and just seeing what floats on in. You got it all. Human tragedy. Desperation. Fistfights. Blood, guts. Crying. Fucking. Man will do about anything in the world for whiskey and pussy. I always figured this place is like a trap. We bait it and they come on in."

"But you don't have to," Ringold said. "You turn a good profit at the Rebel. And with other business."

"Maybe I like it?"

"Do you?"

"Do you like what you do?" Stagg said, grinning. Ringold holding his eye, returning to the beer. Stagg thinking that this boy didn't care to be around him any more than those khaki-pants-wearing bastards in the Grove. Money, money, money. Sure can make the son of a manure salesman smell like Chanel No. 5.

Ringold wasn't listening. He'd turned his back to Stagg and walked on over to meet big old Midnight Man, who'd just ran off two horny truckers still trying to get inside the bar. Midnight Man was talking wild with his hands and pointing to Stagg. And Stagg wandered up and listened, thinking it was about some scuffle in the parking lot. But instead heard, "Someone robbed Mr. Cobb's place and shot a deputy."

Ringold turned to Stagg, listening and waiting for what he'd want him to do. Stagg swallowed hard and let out a breath.

"They kill Cobb?" Stagg said.

"Mr. Cobb wasn't there," Midnight Man said, standing as big as a two-ton ox, in a barbecue-splatted white T-shirt and an XXXL parka. "They got his safe, though. Ripped the goddamn thing clean out of the wall of his house."

"Shit," Ringold said.

"Yes, sir," Stagg said, nodding to Midnight Man, letting the man know he'd done good to tell them right off.

"What now?"

"Go find Cobb's stupid ass and find out what they got."

"You all right, Mr. Stagg?"

"I'm fine."

"Thought you didn't care much for Larry Cobb."

"We've done a lot of business with each other," Stagg said. "I'd prefer none of the dirt to rub off on me."

Stagg reached into his coat pocket for a napkin he'd kept from supper. He dabbed sweat off his forehead, feeling light, as if he was trapped in some kind of fucking heat box. You could smell all the trucker sweat, coconut perfume, and cigarettes. The smell of spent men and desperation. He couldn't breathe right until he'd stepped out in the cold and caught a hard wind coming off Highway 45. He cracked a peppermint candy into his mouth to relieve himself.

Within a minute, Ringold had walked outside to join him.

"I need you to find Larry Cobb and tell 'im we need to talk," Stagg said. "Don't let that sack of shit offer no excuses."

"Yes, sir."

Stagg walked back into the Trap and into his back office. He had another call to make. If ever it was time to break glass and get the Trooper on his side, it was now.

How about a cold one, kid?" Uncle Peewee asked. Chase smiled, took a can of Bud Light, and returned to the stack of concrete blocks where he'd been sitting. He'd been sitting there for damn-near two hours while Kyle what's-his-name worked on that old safe. Just a bunch of shredding and clanking, the old boy tearing at it, swearing at it with hammers, crowbars, and that big contraption he took from the firehouse. But he figured it must have paid off. Uncle Peewee wandered on out of the metal work shed with a smile on his face, his shirt unbuttoned wide and showing off his sweaty white belly. Man was sweating like a hog.

"We done it."

"You did it?"

"Yes, sir," Uncle Peewee said, raising his can of Bud to the boy. "We sure did. And, man. Holy shit."

"Lots?"

"More than they thought."

"How much?"

"That boy's still counting," he said. "But it's not just the cash. That ole bastard had antique guns, coins. One of them fucking Rolex watches. This one made out of real gold with diamonds."

"What about that?" Chase said. "That wasn't in the figuring. We get a cut of that shit?"

Peewee shrugged, swallowed some beer, and wiped his mouth with the back of his hand. He reached down to find his shirttail to clean off his dirty glasses. Looked like his uncle had been working hard. Chase had tried to help until that old Kyle, cigarette bobbing in his mouth, told him to go on and git. "Go outside and play with yourself," he'd said. Now, who the hell talks like that to a grown man? Play with yourself. Shit, man.

"We made a deal," Peewee said. "I ain't going back on it. He's cutting us in on ten grand apiece."

"How much you think is in there?"

"Might be a million," he said. "Might be more."

"After all we done?" Chase said. "What the hell?"

"I gave my word," Peewee said, lifting his chin, looking at him with big eyes in still-dirty glasses. "Means something to me."

"You're drunk."

"Hell you say."

"They get a million?" Chase said. "And we get shit."

"Kid," Peewee said. "Do you have any idea how much pussy a man can purchase with ten grand?"

"Hmm," Chase said, sliding down off those concrete blocks, hands deep in his pockets. "That's the difference between you and me. I don't pay for pussy."

"Wait till you get old and fat," Peewee said. "You'll toss out every penny you got."

Chase just shook his head and brushed past his uncle and into the work shed, where Kyle was unloading the safe and stacking all the shit he'd found on a workbench. The cash raised up about two feet and spread out about two feet square, more coming out of the metal box. Along the long wooden bench were several guns. Some of them looked like they went all the way back to the Civil War. A gold pocket watch. The fancy wristwatch with diamonds. A bunch of old coins, stacked neat and clean, in blue books. Some dang porno tapes. Not DVDs but damn old VHS, advertising women with big hair and big hairy pussies. A fat diamond ring and a red velvet box filled with diamond earrings as big as walnuts.

"Whew."

"Step back," Kyle said. He was sweating, too. His skinny-ass old-man body looking bony, a thin strip of gray hair down his chest.

"I ain't touching nothing."

"I'm taking inventory."

"Sure was a haul."

"And you'll get what you're gittin'."

"I understand."

Kyle got up off his knees, bare chest, dirty jeans, and work boots, and walked over to the bench for a fresh beer. He popped the top and looked to have drunk half of it straight down. He watched Chase, standing there, not doing a goddamn thing, with his hands in his 'Bama hoodie and trying not to make any trouble. But then Chase realized Kyle was wondering about the gun he'd used on the policeman. And maybe it was in the hoodie right now, waiting to take out old Kyle's gray ass and scoop up the rest for a trip back to Gordo. But, hell, it only made him laugh.

"What is it?" Kyle said.

"You think I'm going to shoot you."

"No."

"Sure you do," Chase said. "You're scared as a bitch."

Kyle reached on the counter for a pack of cigarettes, shuffled out one, and walked on over to where Chase stood. The old man slapped the dog shit out of Chase, sending his head reeling back, and reached into his hoodie pocket for the .32 he'd bought with his own goddamn money. Kyle stuck it in the small of his back, tucked into his belt, and returned to work.

"Wait outside," he said. "Tell your uncle that money is coming."

"Go fuck yourself."

Kyle didn't answer, just went back to unloading the cash and making his selfish little piles like a fat man at a buffet. Chase came on out back as Peewee was relieving himself on the blocks where he planned to sit. "You get the money?" he said, looking over his shoulders. "I'm getting ready to get gone, kid."

19.

W e appreciate you coming in, Mickey," Lillie Virgil said. "Come on in and take a seat."

"Can you tell me what the hell's going on?" Mickey said. "I hadn't been home an hour when two deputies come pounding on my door and telling me to put my pants on."

"Glad you have on pants," Lillie said, Mickey Walls moving on past her inside the sheriff's main office. "Makes things a little more professional."

"I told them I'd cooperate with whatever they need, but neither of them told me nothing the whole ride into town," he said. "You know I just got back from Gulf Shores? I went down there to party a bit with Tonya Cobb. You know Tonya."

"Of course I know Tonya," Lillie said, pulling a chair up to the desk that had been Quinn's. "She used to teach Sunday school at the First Baptist before she got into all that trouble with the youth pastor."

Mickey didn't answer, taking a seat as Rusty Wise walked into the room, holding a bottle of Coca-Cola. The room was empty except for the desk, a couple chairs. Nothing at all on the white walls but hooks.

"How was your trip?" Rusty said.

Lillie shot him a look, as both of them had agreed that she'd be the one who'd take over the questioning. It had been a long time since he'd been a cop and he had no experience as a detective. But he should at least know to let the suspect tell the story, not lead him or validate him in any way. Any son of a bitch who watched *Law & Order* could tell you that. Rusty gave a shy smile and moved back behind the desk but didn't sit down, just leaned over the back of a ladder-back chair, eyes watching Lillie.

"Larry Cobb's place got busted into last night."

"Sorry to hear it."

"Thought you might have heard something," she said. "You being close to the family and all. Maybe something that might help."

"Wish I could," Mickey said. "Larry and Debbi have been good to me. I was just down on the Gulf with Tonya. You know. Trying to work things out."

"Yeah, you told us that," Lillie said. "Several times."

Mickey just nodded, mouth hanging a little open, looking like a man who might have just hightailed it back from Gulf Shores over-night. He had on a wrinkled Hawaiian shirt under an old Carhartt jacket and gray sweatpants with boots. His breath smelled of liquor and he needed a shave. Cleotha was in her office right now making calls to the owners of the condo where he said he'd stayed.

"You drove all the way back at midnight?" Lillie said.

"Yeah," he said. "I got shit to do. Had a good time, but a few things needed my attention back home."

"Like what?" Rusty Wise said, leaning onto the back of the chair. "Long way to go in the middle of the night."

Mickey looked small and huddled-up in the chair in front of Quinn's old desk. His eyes shifted to where Lillie stood by the closed door and then back to Rusty. He closed his mouth and swallowed, rubbing the whiskers on his face. "Are y'all trying to say something here?" he said.

"I got no reason to rob nobody. You know that. Y'all both know me. I hadn't ever been in trouble with the law. Maybe two speeding tickets in ten years."

Rusty lifted a hand in a stop gesture and said, "Slow down. Slow down. Just asking, Mickey. We had a deputy shot last night."

"Shit," Mickey said. "Who?"

"Kenny."

"God damn," he said. "Son of a bitch."

"He's in rough shape," Lillie said, watching Mickey's hangdog face, trying to read something from any reaction. But he didn't change expression, dumb mouth hanging open again, small brown eyes looking ahead. "He's in his second surgery."

"Hell of a first day on the job," Rusty said, pushing his little fat self up off the chair and walking around the unfamiliar desk. "One of my deputies getting shot in a home invasion. You may not think you know something, but anything might help."

"Why the hell y'all want to talk to me?"

Rusty took a breath and looked to Lillie, turning it over to her. Lillie sat down on the edge of the desk, arms crossed, and said, "Larry Cobb said y'all haven't been the best of friends lately."

"Well," he said. "Shit. Doesn't mean I want to rob him. Or shoot a deputy."

"Nobody is accusing you of shooting Kenny," Rusty said. "Understand? We just thought you might heard something about what happened. From someone. Maybe folks who work for you who are out to get Larry?"

Mickey fingered something in his eye and laughed a bit. "Out to get Cobb?" he said. "How about you open up the Jericho and Tibbehah County phone book? I think he probably cheated or pissed off about everyone in it. I can't believe y'all came to me. Thinking I got something to do with this. You know me. Mickey Walls. I'm the carpet guy.

I fix houses. Mr. Big Shot. Shit, Lillie, I laid the honeycomb tile in your bathroom last year."

"And it's looking fine," she said. "Top-notch groutwork."

"This shit pisses me off," Mickey said. "It really does."

"So you hadn't heard anything?" Rusty said, standing up over by the window, looking out toward the chain-link of the county jail. The morning drunks and prisoners milling about in the dead brown-grass yard, smoking cigarettes, taking fried pies from their people through the holes in the fence. Lillie wished she had a cigarette right about now. She hadn't stopped since getting the call on Kenny.

"OK," Lillie said. "If it were you, who'd you try and talk to about what happened at Cobb's place?"

"I don't know," he said. "How the hell should I know?"

Lillie nodded at the cold Coke in his hand. "You want me to pop that top?"

Mickey leaned forward and set the bottle on the desk with a hard plunk. She could tell he was getting nervous with her and Rusty standing over him, asking all these questions, while he clearly looked tired as hell. Probably should give the man a break, let him go sleep a while, and then check back with him. From behind Mickey, Rusty Wise shrugged his shoulders. Useless. Completely useless. Quinn would've gotten something from him. He'd come a long way in four years, getting folks to trust him without aiming a gun.

Mickey looked ready to bolt. He hadn't been arrested. They had no reason to talk to him other than being the first name Larry Cobb mentioned. But she had one more thing. A good one, and she'd leave him with a little something to consider. For all she knew, he was innocent and had just driven home because Tonya Cobb wouldn't give it up last night. Even after probably downing a couple pitchers.

"You still run with Kyle Hazlewood?" she said, just leaving the information hanging there. It wasn't much, but they had two folks who'd seen Mickey and Kyle together lately. She also had learned that Kyle had threatened to kick Larry Cobb right in the pussy after he thought he'd been cheated. According to Cobb, Hazlewood had done a shit job on his property and Cobb wouldn't pay him.

"Some," Mickey said. "I hadn't seen him in a few months. Been too busy."

Lillie watched him hard and nodded, not saying anything for a good twenty seconds. "And you don't have any idea who'd want to get back at Cobb for something?"

"Why's it got to be getting back at him?" Mickey said, getting good and mad. "Shit, it was probably just a bunch of blacks from Tupelo looking for a place to rob and Cobb's place is good as any."

"You know what he kept in that safe?" Rusty said, smoothing down his brand-new sheriff's uniform and hitching up his belt.

"No," Mickey said.

"He never told you?" Rusty said.

"Nope," Mickey said. "Are we done here?"

C'mon, man," Kyle said. "You're the one who told me not to call. For any damn reason."

"I sure would've like to know y'all just shot a damn deputy."

"Wasn't me," Kyle said. "That ain't my deal. I was in the fucking van."

Mickey was driving his red Hummer around the Jericho Square, just kind of circling until he decided on where he'd head next. He wanted to go home, but what if some more law was waiting for him again? He knew they didn't have jack shit on him. They'd probably tracked Tonya down right after he left and asked where he was last night. Shit. Tonya. Last time he saw her brown tan ass, she was tossing his fucking luggage off a high-rise. But there were credit cards used, folks who'd seen them at the Flora-Bama. And his damn clothes were still there. Maybe it'd be best if he just hightailed it back down there, laid low till all this was over.

"Mickey?" Kyle said. "You fucking listening to me, man? I said that fat bastard Peewee Sparks nearly got us caught and his retard son done shot Kenny."

"It's his nephew."

"Hell, man," Kyle said. "I don't give a good goddamn. I want you to get on over here and help me with all this shit you wanted. I got my money. Rest is yours."

"What'd you get?"

"Nine hundred and sixty-six thousand."

"Dollars?"

"Shit, yes, dollars," Kyle said. "Ain't no Chuck E. Cheese tokens, man. And I got some of Larry's guns and watches. Jewelry and shit."

"Bury it," Mickey said. "Bury the money and go and toss all the other shit in the Big Black River. I don't give a damn. But that stuff. The personal stuff is what's gonna fuck us in the ass real hard."

"Where are you?"

"Just left the sheriff's office after a little heart-to-heart with Lillie Virgil and Rusty Wise."

"Who the hell is he?" Kyle said.

"The new sheriff out to make a name for himself."

"Where you want me to bury it?"

"How about where it can't be found."

Mickey aimed the Hummer onto Cotton Road and left the Square and headed back toward 45, seriously considering just going right on back to the beach. Tonya would be pissed. She was always pissed. But he'd call her on the way, say he'd gotten real scared because he was having deep feelings for her. And that scared him. Or some of that Dr. Phil shit. She'd pout a little. But then he'd give her what she'd been wanting later today and all would be forgiven.

"I got straight with Sparks."

"Good," Mickey said. "I hope to never see those people ever again. Reminds me of why I left my other wife."

"Mickey?"

"Yeah."

"I don't like this," Kyle said. "I didn't sign on for no shooting."

"Me, neither."

"Should have been just me and you," he said. "Why'd you involve these people? They ain't right in the head. Bunch of Alabama retards."

"I'll call you later."

"They gonna get us," Kyle said. "You do know that?"

Mickey ended the call and kept on driving east toward the highway. Not really sure what to do next. All he could do right now was drive.

Quinn's mother was cooking black-eyed peas for the New Year. That's just something you did, something every Southern woman did on the first of the year. She'd always cook them with some salty country ham and toss a dime in the pot, the person finding the dime being the one with the most luck for the year. He watched his mother over the stove, stirring, talking about going to visit Caddy in a couple weeks. "Would you like to come along?" she said. "I think she'd appreciate it."

"I'll come if Caddy wants it," he said. "I think she only cares if I bring her a carton of cigarettes."

"That's not true."

Quinn shrugged and got up to refill his coffee mug. He hadn't gone back to the farm since leaving the hospital to check on Kenny. He didn't feel like going home, sitting down with Hondo to watch a movie, or listening to his father try to make sense of the night before or talk about the year to come. He just wanted to go to his old home, the place where he grew up, and sit down for a cup of coffee and realize everything was out of his hands.

"Did you see Larry Cobb?"

"No," Quinn said. "But Anna Lee went over there to check on him and Debbi. Sometimes I can't believe she's related to those people."

"That's her dad's brother?"

"Debbi is her mother's sister," he said.

"That's right," she said, unbundling some collard greens and washing them in the sink.

"You even like black-eyed peas and collards?" Quinn said.

"Never really thought about it," Jean said, drying them in a paper towel, and started to cut off the leaves and toss them into a big pot of water. "It's just what you do. It's what we've always done."

"Anna Lee wants me to help."

"How would you help?"

"She says Larry is convinced it was Mickey Walls that ripped him off," Quinn said. "He didn't even hesitate when he heard his house had been broken into."

"Did more than that," Jean said. "Didn't they drive a tractor through his living room?"

"It was a backhoe," Quinn said. "They broke through the bedroom wall to get a safe. Pulled it out and left in a black van."

"And that's when they shot poor Kenny?"

"Yes, ma'am," Quinn said.

"What did Anna Lee say?" Jean asked. "Doesn't she know you're not the sheriff anymore?"

"She does," Quinn said. "But she believes I could help them out more than Rusty Wise. She doesn't care for Rusty and neither does Larry. She said Larry called Rusty a two-bit insurance man who doesn't have any goddamn sense."

"I guess Larry voted on you."

"I believe so."

"I wish she wouldn't try and get you involved," Jean said, turning up the burner on the stove. "I wish she'd just let you relax and finally enjoy your time being home."

"That'd be nice."

"I'll make some country-fried steak tonight," Jean said. "Will you tell Boom?"

"Of course," Quinn said. "He was disappointed we didn't get to eat at Caddy's intervention. He thought there would at least be some cakes or pie."

"Too worried to cook."

Quinn drank some coffee. He smiled at his mother. The kitchen wasn't the one he'd known as a kid. Everything had been ripped away during the tornado, replaced with bright pine cabinets and shiny stainless steel appliances. But the kitchen was still very much Jean, with her Elvis knickknacks, biblical sayings taped to the refrigerator, and pictures of Quinn, Caddy, and Little Jason hanging on the walls. Jean stirred the collards into the simmering water. She added some salt.

The house seemed empty with young Jason gone. Jean had sent him over to a friend's house this morning, wanting him to have some fun and not be around all this sadness.

"Caddy's going to be OK," he said. "Don't worry. She heals up quick."

Jean kept on stirring, not looking back, wiping her eyes.

"What's the matter?"

"I think she's too far gone," Jean said. "She's come back time and again. But I don't think she cares anymore. She told me herself. She's tired. She's ready to go on."

"Where?" Quinn said.

Jean didn't answer. They sat in the kitchen for a long while, not saying a word.

20.

S orry to hear about your troubles," Johnny Stagg told Larry Cobb, the man sitting still and quiet in a brown La-Z-Boy recliner. His bedroom was missing a wall and shit was strewn all over the place, sodden shirts, jeans and drawers, and paperback books, all frozen to the carpet. Cobb didn't seem to notice, just nodding and holding a bottle of Wild Turkey in his arms as if it were a newborn. The wind tossed around his thinning white hair.

"Appreciate that, Johnny," Cobb said, rubbing his goatee. His red cheeks blazing from the cold and the booze. "It's out of our hands now. Me and Debbi can't believe someone would do this. We're good people. Solid fucking citizens."

"Oh, yes, sir," Stagg said. "It's a head-scratcher."

Stagg figured Cobb was in shock, not moving a bit when he and Ringold parked outside the busted wall and walked on into the bedroom. Ringold milled about, using a stick to pick up stuff in his path: Larry's big white underpants, a broken picture of Tonya Cobb in a softball outfit, pink pajama bottoms. Reaching down for a book called *Become a Better You* by that bucktoothed preacher, Joel Osteen. He handed it to Stagg with a grin.

"Police said we could start cleaning up now," Cobb said. "It's not a crime scene no more. But Debbi is real upset. She went over to see her sister and niece, probably gonna stay there tonight. I got to secure this fucking wall with some Visqueen. Supposed to get some rain and sleet again tonight. Look at this shit. Look at this mess. Someone ran a fucking backhoe into the place where I sleep. How'd they know they weren't going to kill me?"

"Grace of God," Stagg said, tossing the book back on the ground.

"Well, they sure as hell knew what they were coming for," Cobb said, uncorking the Turkey and taking another swig. He pointed the bottle at Stagg. "Picked up my damn safe with the backhoe and skedaddled on out down the road. But I told that woman Lillie Virgil I'm pretty sure I know who did it."

"Who?"

"You know Mickey Walls?"

"Of course," Stagg said.

"He's the one," Cobb said, wiping some whiskey off his white chin. "He's out to get me. Told me so. Man's got hate in his heart. It wasn't enough that he ruined my daughter, but now he's going to go on and try and ruin me and Debbi. But he's out of luck. You know why?"

Ringold leaned against a closed door that opened into the house. Stagg caught his eye and said, "'Cause you and Debbi prayed on it."

"That's right," Cobb said. "Forgive as the Lord has forgiven you and me."

"You sure that's where you want to toss all your chips?" Stagg said.

"Yes, sir," Cobb said. "What am I gonna do, grab a gun and run out and shoot the boy dead? Me being the one to end up in jail? I got to find some peace in this, Johnny. If I don't, I think I'm going to lose my mind. I already had two heart attacks."

"How much?" Stagg said.

"What's that?" Cobb said, lost in thought, walking along with Jesus on the seashore in flowing robes, filled with his new, high-minded purpose.

"What'd they steal?"

"More than nine hundred grand, my guns, some jewels, and my daddy's pocket watch."

Stagg nodded, feeling odd standing in the middle of someone's bedroom but still out in the elements. There was an overturned bed, and a dresser right side up, carpet on the floor and the sky overhead. Stagg placed a hand in his trouser pocket. Cobb was right. It looked like it might start sleeting again.

"I'll get it back," Cobb said. "Every damn cent. It's God's will. Me and Debbi decided. A wicked man 'spends his days in prosperity but suddenly goes down to Sheol.' You know what *Sheol* is, Mr. Stagg?"

"I guess it's not a town near Pontotoc."

"It's the Hebrew word for the underworld," Cobb said. "It's fucking hell. Mickey Walls will live for all eternity in flames. The man screwed my daughter, tried to run my business into the ground, and now he's straight-up stolen from me. He took a vow in a church that we were family. He said things to me when we were drunk about me being better than his own daddy. Which ain't saying much. And now he does this? He destroys the place where me and Debbi sleep? Make love and watch television? If that ain't a fast track to hell, I don't know what is."

"Oh, yes, sir," Stagg said, standing near Cobb's La-Z-Boy. Ringold was listening but checking out the integrity of the walls, pushing at what was left of the roof with a stick. He had on his military pants and boots, and a padded blue jacket with a leather patch on the shoulder. Stagg couldn't see the gun rig he wore but knew it was close at hand.

"I commend you on your faith in both the Bible and that Wild Turkey," Stagg said. "But I don't give a goddamn how you think everything's meant to happen, Larry. What I care about is shit you've squirreled away in your damn safe, names and numbers that might incriminate me and some fine folks in Jackson."

Cobb looked up. He stared at Stagg with those little narrow pig eyes. "What?"

"I know you and Jesus got this all figured out," Stagg said. "But maybe you need some help."

"I don't follow," Cobb said, putting down the Wild Turkey and hitting the lever on the La-Z-Boy to bring his head up and his boots back to the ground.

"You need some fucking help holding Mickey Walls's nuts to the flame," Stagg said. "Because I know you. I know how you do business, and things you've let slip in our conversation. I know you keep records, documents of transactions. Foolish shit that I've warned you about. While you are one smart fucking squirrel, you ain't clever. And if your records and your account books talk about things that should never be mentioned, me and you and lots of other folks might be headed into some federal courthouse."

Cobb snorted. "You think a fucking thief cares about some stupid ledgers?" he said. "Mickey wanted my money. You know I won my court case against him. We settled out for a hundred grand. He come back to get the money from my safe. Whatever else is in there, he'll burn."

Stagg looked to Ringold, who'd sidled up by his shoulder. Cobb stood, using a lot of help with the armrests to get to his feet. "You willing to trust Jesus on that one?"

Cobb moved his hand over his white whiskers, stumbled on over to the edge of the room where the floor dropped off, and stood there, staring off into the trees and the lookout over his lumber mill, smoke billowing from one of his outbuildings. A lot of bright heat on a cold morning.

"Who's he talking about?" Ringold said. "Who is Walls?"

"Shit," Stagg said. "Let's go. I'll tell you everything you'll need to know."

W hat you got there?" Uncle Peewee said, hunkered over a laptop on the kitchen table since they got back to Gordo. He'd been switching from looking at titties to a swingers' dating site, where he went by the handle JUSBANGINU. Man had been using a damn picture of George Clooney for his profile pic.

"Nothin'." Chase was watching ESPN, drinking a Coors Light, and thumbing through some of those fancy books he'd found in the safe, along with the gold watch and earrings he'd took. He didn't have to ask nobody about it. He'd just done it. They'd worked the same as Kyle and deserved the same kind of reward.

They were in Peewee's trailer. He had four of them on a quarter acre in Gordo. Chase and his momma lived in one and Peewee rented the other two. The good thing about family was that every time the power company came to turn off the juice, Peewee would run a cord out back of his bathroom. That's what family was all about. Chase stopped reading and looked at the big gold watch on his wrist, shaking it. Wouldn't keep time worth a shit.

Chase looked up, hearing Peewee's hard breathing behind him. "That ain't yours."

"Ain't yours, neither."

"Where you'd get that?"

"It don't matter," Chase said, trying to ignore him. That peckerhead radio host from Birmingham was on TV, talking about how the Tide was going to put a whooping on Ohio State at the Sugar Bowl. That was a bad sign. Every time that peckerhead started to run his mouth about knowing things, it went the other way. *God damn it.*

"That was in the safe," Peewee said. "I seen it."

"Shit."

"What else you get?"

"Nothing."

Peewee slapped the Coors Light out of his hand and came around the couch to look down at him. Peewee trying to look tough in a pair of pajama bottoms and his Duck Dynasty T-shirt. He gave Chase a mean look while scratching his balls, blocking the TV set, the peckerhead on it running down a list of why Saban had a superior mind to Urban Meyer. Chase loved the Tide, but the TV man was giving Saban a good old-fashioned reach-around.

"Give it me."

"No, sir," Chase said. "It's mine."

"You better give me every fucking thing you took out of that safe except the money," Peewee said. "You hear me?"

He raised the back of his hand up just like his momma used to do, back when she gave a shit. Chase's Coors Light had bled out on the floor, leaving a big stain.

Chase looked up at him, knowing this was the time when lines had to be drawn. Peewee'd got to figure Chase was his own man. He'd done the job same as him. Peewee was no high-dollar safecracker. He was just a cheap thief.

"Hand it over."

"I said hell no."

For a second, he thought Peewee was damn pissing on him but then could smell the odor from the lighter fluid. The son of a bitch had squirted that shit all over him and was now standing above him flicking on his Zippo and looking down at Chase, wild-eyed.

"Yes, sir," Chase said, and snatched the fancy watch off his wrist.

"What else?"

"I got some big earrings," he said. "I stuck them in the back part of my commode."

"Go get them."

Chase stood up, smelling all that lighter fluid soaking into his clothes and skin. Peewee snatched the book out of his hands, flipping through the pages and seeing all the amounts, dates, names. A hell of a lot of them under the heading *Vardaman*.

"And this?" Peewee said. "You take this out to the trash barrel and burn it. You hear me? Why the hell you'd take it?"

Chase shrugged, seeing some of the lighter fluid soaking into the yellowed pages. "'Cause it was there."

"I can turn that money," Peewee said. "And I'll run the risk to do it. But I ain't getting burned for no watch or earrings. Don't ever take no souvenirs from a job. You understand? Unless you got a fence you can trust. This ain't no goddamn time to be testing relationships."

"Why?"

"You recall shooting a lawman?"

Chase dropped his head, nodded. Peewee handed him back the book but kept the watch. Chase noting Peewee slipping the gold and diamonds on his own fat wrist.

"Burn those books," he said. "Bring me back everything else."

At the Carthage Volunteer Fire Department, Lillie Virgil found Eddie Fudge making chili.

"I'm calling it five-alarm chili," Eddie said, opening the top of the Crock-Pot in the back kitchen. The department was nothing more than a metal shed, situated right next to an Assembly of God church.

"I figured you would," Lillie said.

"It's some bold stuff," Eddie said. "Some folks can't handle it. Especially women."

"You know women, Eddie," Lillie said. "We faint when there's heat."

Eddie was tall and thick, bald and bearded, and had taken to wearing ball caps too small for his head. He had on a white one today that told folks *With a Body Like Mine, Who Needs Hair?* He and Lillie had been in the same class at Tibbehah High. And when he wasn't out playing assistant fire chief, he fixed heating-and-cooling units. Sometimes he drove a school bus. "I used my own habaneros, a whole bottle of Louisiana hot sauce, and an entire cup of chili powder."

"And that's how you came by the name," Lillie said. "Clever."

"Want a taste?" he said, slipping the wooden spoon out of the pot and offering her some.

"Actually, I'm looking for Kyle Hazlewood," she said. "He wasn't at his house. Figured he might have stopped by here to play cards or wax the fire engine. Or whatever you boys do on your off days."

"Had a brush fire last week," Eddie said. "I know y'all think we just sit around and play with our hoses. But we got to be on call. You know how much I'd like a cold beer right now with this chili? But you never know when that cell phone's gonna ring."

"Don't I know it," Lillie said. "But Kyle. Have you seen him?"

"I haven't seen Kyle since that brush fire," he said. "Why? Something a-matter?"

"No," Lillie said. "Just had a quick question for him."

Eddie sipped from the spoon. "Wow. Ho-ly shit."

"Hot?"

"As two nekkid women in a pepper patch."

Lillie grinned. "That your own?"

"Nah," he said. "Fella over in Eupora told me that one. You can use it, if you like."

"Appreciate it," she said, turning back to the door. "Stay out of trouble, Eddie."

"Yes, ma'am."

Lillie shook her head and headed out of the kitchen and into the main shed, where they kept their four-wheel-drive fire engine, the red paint and chrome gleaming in the fluorescent lights. Lillie's boots thumped on concrete as she headed to the door. As she walked, a big tangled contraption set in the corner caught her eye. She'd been at accident scenes enough times to recognize the Jaws of Life and the compressor that worked it.

She got down to one knee and saw it was splattered in fresh mud and had several deep scratches in the paint. She called back to Eddie. "When did y'all get these?" she said.

Eddie came out, small bowl in hand, and walked over to see what Lillie was talking about. "Summer," he said.

"Y'all been training?"

"Not yet," he said. "I don't know what they're doing out. Someone's been fucking around with them."

"Why would anyone fuck around with the Jaws of Life?"

"Shit, someone probably used them as a bottle opener," he said. "They should have put it back where they found it. What if we had an emergency situation?"

Lillie nodded. "You ever had to use them?"

"Did some training couple years ago in Hernando," he said. "Hadn't used these. But they're pretty much the same thing."

"And they'll open anything?"

"Yes, ma'am," Eddie said. "Those pinchers can tear apart anything metal. Why?"

"I'm going out to my vehicle to get a camera to take some photos. OK? I'll be right back."

"What's going on?"

"Just thinking, is all."

"Do what you like," he said. "You sure you don't want some chili to go?"

"Only if you tell me how hot it really is," Lillie said.

"Two rats fucking in a wool sock can't generate this much heat."

"Wow," she said. "Make it to go. Some things are starting to come together for me."

21.

Jason Colson brought Quinn a cheeseburger and fries, chocolate shake on the side, from Sonic.

Quinn was sitting in a hard chair next to Kenny's bed at the hospital. He'd been out of surgery for an hour but was still asleep. Both Kenny's folks had been killed in the tornado. He had a sister in Columbus, but she hadn't made it to town yet.

"Thanks," Quinn said, his legs stretched straight out before him, boots crossed at the ankle.

"What's the word?"

"He's going to be fine," Quinn said. "But if Lillie hadn't found him, he would have died in that ditch."

"Jesus," Jason said, standing by Kenny's bed, Kenny off in dreamland. "Any idea who shot him?"

"He hasn't been conscious," Quinn said. "But Lillie's working on something. She'll find who did this."

"Is it true these bastards ran a fucking bulldozer through Larry Cobb's house?"

"It was a backhoe," Quinn said. "But, yes, sir."

"Hate to say it," Jason said. "I knew Larry back in high school and he wasn't worth a shit back then. You know that mill was his daddy's, and his daddy's before him."

Quinn reached into the sack and grabbed the cheeseburger and started to eat. Old habits of sleeping and eating when you can. Jason took a seat in the other free chair. Behind him was a framed Bible verse and a chart on how to measure your pain, 1 through 10. Blue was no pain. Bright red meant you hurt like a bitch.

"First, Caddy," Jason said. "Now Kenny. How you holding up?"

"Fine," Quinn said. "Nothing's wrong with me. Appreciate the lunch."

"Your momma called me," Jason said. "First reaction was that something had happened to you. I don't like getting calls like that from your momma. We haven't exactly been on good terms since I came back. I don't think she really wanted me back in Jericho."

"You don't say."

"I know, I know," Jason said. He was wearing his STUNTMAN UN-LIMITED jacket, red satin, along with a belt buckle the size of a dinner plate. It read *Skoal Bandit Racing*. "Hard to imagine. But I do think that woman will come around."

The last part surprised Quinn and he glanced up at his father. Jason shrugged. "Thought about riding over to Tupelo tomorrow. Check on Caddy."

"You can't," Quinn said. "Not until she's got that shit out of her system in detox. They also like to separate her from the family so she can focus and get with the program."

Jason nodded, sitting wide-legged on the chair, both father and son staring at Kenny, all shot-up and in la-la land. He had a lot of scrapes on his forehead and a busted lip from being in that ravine. A nurse came in and checked his vitals, saying hello and then turning to leave. Jason Colson appraised her backside on the way out. He raised his eyebrows.

"I guess you get used to this kind of thing," Jason said. "Folks getting injured. Shot-up."

"Some," Quinn said. "But usually we just tried to get them to the LZ and the hell out of the shooting."

"You lost a lot of buddies?"

"Yes, sir."

"Been over there, what, eight, ten times?"

"Thirteen deployments," Quinn said. "Ten years."

"Long time," Jason said, stroking that goatee, thinking on things. "I've lost some buds, too. Mainly drugs. Alcohol. One of my best friends—this was even before you were born—jumped off a nine-story building, doubling for George Kennedy. The sorry thing was, he'd already filmed the gag but went back to reshoot because someone had broken his world record. You know, for height. That's the ego we had back then. He landed the son of a bitch perfect, but the fucking air bag split and killed him. I can't even recall the name of the picture. I know Lee Majors was in it. We went on to work together for a long time on *Fall Guy*."

"Caddy and I met him," Quinn said, eating some fries. "Out on one of our L.A. trips."

"He was big shit back then," Jason said. "Women wouldn't leave his ass alone. I think they believed he had a bionic pecker."

"That would do it."

Jason smiled, nodding over to Kenny. "I'm glad he's gonna pull through," Jason said. "Always liked Kenny. I could tell how much respect he had for you. I think he'd walk straight through hell if you told him to."

"Yes, sir."

"You think Jean might let me pick up Jason later today?" Jason said. "I wanted to show him a reel of some of the gags I did in *Gator* and *Cannonball Run*. I think he'd get a kick out of it."

"Knowing his granddad is crazy?"

"You ever turn down a dare, son?" Jason said.

"No, sir."

Jason winked at him. "We just don't have it in us."

S orry, buddy," Mickey Walls said. "We're closed."

"That's OK," the man said, stepping into the warehouse behind the Walls Flooring showroom. "I don't need any flooring."

"Then what can I help you with?" Mickey said. "Like I said, we're closed."

"You Mickey Walls?"

The man was medium height and medium size, pretty much an unremarkable human being except for a big sprouting black beard on his otherwise hairless head. He wanted to say maybe he'd seen the fella somewhere, someplace. He looked familiar as hell.

"Yeah," Mickey said. "If you're gonna try and serve me with papers, why don't you take the day off. I'm not in the mood."

"I'm not the law," the man said.

"Oh yeah?" he said. "Then who are you?"

"I work for Mr. Stagg," the man said. "How about we take a little ride?"

"I'm good right here," Mickey said, standing tall in his shop. The ceiling raised up fifty feet in both directions, stacked with finished and unfinished hardwoods, rolls of laminate, and fine, high-traffic carpeting. Mickey didn't know what else to say, as he looked at the fella, who seemed as serious as could be, and so he lit a cigarette and fanned out the match. He tucked the cigarettes back in his shirt pocket and waited.

"This isn't a request."

"I don't have no truck with Johnny Stagg."

"Didn't say you did," the man said.

"If he wants to talk business, let's do it another day," Mickey said, smoke shooting out the side of his mouth. "We're fucking closed."

The man smiled like an old friend of the family and opened his coat to show a shiny blued pistol of impressive size. Just as fast, the man closed his coat. Oh, hell. Here we go, Mickey thought.

"What's your name?" Mickey said. "You never told me."

"That's right."

"But you speak for Stagg?"

"I do."

"OK," Mickey said, shaking his head. This day had been so damn fucked-up, what was one more thing. He wondered how he'd gotten on the wrong side or the right side of damn Johnny Stagg. "Why not?"

The man drove a jacked-up blue Ford Raptor, a truck made for off-roading and mud-riding. As they walked out into the cold, the man put on his ball cap and set his sunglasses on top of the brim. The big engine revved with a growl and they were off into the cold and gray. Mickey didn't have time for this kind of shit, worrying and trying to think just what he had done to piss off Johnny Stagg. He'd done some work for Stagg last year, but he'd done a solid job, as he did on all things. Like his business card told folks, *If You Don't Like It, We'll Make It Right.*

Whatever he did, he'd make right and then get on with his day. He had checked email and showered at the warehouse. He had a fresh change of clothes and a razor. He called Tonya eight times and left eight messages. She'd yet to call back.

"You had a busy night," the man said.

"Just got back from the beach," Mickey said. "I got a damn hangover that won't quit."

"Good for you," the man said. "But not as bad as your pals."

"What pals?"

"The ones who drove a backhoe into Larry Cobb's house and took his safe," the man said, driving slow and easy around Jericho and turning on toward two signs pointing to Choctaw Lake.

"I heard about it," Mickey said. "Don't have nothing to do with me."

"I'm not the law," the man said. "And I'm not here for a debate. Some other things were taken besides money."

"I said, I don't know nothing about—"

"Shut your mouth and listen," the man said, taking the Raptor up to fifty, sixty, as the little houses started to spread out. They passed a cemetery and then a few farms and Mr. Randolph's smithing shop. "There were two books."

"I said—"

"Shut up," the man said, just as easy as a man saying a prayer over supper. "We don't care about the money. We don't care what you've done or your trouble with Cobb. Just get us those books and we're good."

"How?"

The man stopped the big old truck on a dime, tires squealing and burning on the road. The big engine idling on the blacktop under the gray skies, bare trees, and endless rolling hills with muddy cows. "Get out."

"Here?"

"Get out," the man said. "Before I take offense."

"Who the hell are you?" Mickey said. "I don't give a good goddamn."

But then he caught the man's eyes and there was such a depth of fucking meanness that about the only thing to compare it with was a cottonmouth rared up. Mickey didn't like it. But he shut his mouth and grabbed the door handle. He stepped down from the truck.

He waited for some instructions or an idea of what to do next. But the man just reached over and pulled the door closed, U-turned on the big country road, and hit the accelerator back to town. A plume of black smoke left behind like a nasty insult to all Mickey had been through today. *Son of a bitch.*

He looked at the sky and shook his head. He started walking back to town, to his business and his cell phone. About a mile down the road it started to rain again. And, man, was it cold.

I don't know if some scratched-up tool is enough to roust Judge Lackey for a warrant," Rusty Wise said.

"Eddie Fudge said they'd never used them," Lillie said. "Not even for training. The things were dirty and moved from where they'd been kept. He was sure of it."

"You want to make that play on the word of Eddie Fudge?"

"Cases have been made on far less than the likes of Eddie Fudge," Lillie said.

They sat together in her Jeep Cherokee, where they'd met up by the Big Black River. The river looked cold and muddy, slowly moving under the big Erector set–looking bridge, while they talked in the heated car. Rusty kept on checking his cell phone while they spoke and Lillie was about a second away from snatching the thing out of his hands and tossing it into the water.

"I want to bring him in," Lillie said. "I can talk to him while you work on the warrant."

"I want to be there," Rusty said, scratching his cheek. "And then I'll decide about that warrant."

"Kyle Hazlewood has a tool shop behind his house," Lillie said. "If I'd stolen that safe, that's where he might have taken it. I'll try and get a look-see when I call on him."

"And if he doesn't go peacefully?"

"Then we'll know even more."

"OK," Rusty said, still looking down at his cell phone.

"Can I ask you something, Sheriff?" Lillie said.

"Shoot."

"What on earth is so fucking important to be texting about right now?" Lillie said. "You forgotten Kenny almost bled out in a ditch last night? Not to mention a major fucking burglary with almost a million bucks floating out there."

"Heck, Lillie," Rusty said. "Just telling my wife I can't make lunch. My mother-in-law was driving up from Meridian. She'd baked a chocolate pie for us."

"Well, thank the Lord you're on top of things," Lillie said. "You wouldn't want to have a chocolate pie emergency."

Rusty looked embarrassed. And more than a little pissed-off. Probably no one at the insurance office ever talked to him like that. But Lillie truly didn't give a shit. "I'll call Art and have him come out with me," Lillie said. "Unless you want to pick up Kyle with me."

"'Course I do," Rusty said. "Let's go."

"Mickey Walls was lying out his ass this morning," Lillie said. "Did you see how he was sweating?"

"Story checks out," Rusty said. "He couldn't fake being down there on the coast. We got his credit card receipts, and surveillance shows him coming and going at that condo. They sent stills."

"Couldn't have been any neater than if he planned it," Lillie said. Jesus, Rusty was the most trusting bastard she'd ever met. "He might've been giving Tonya Cobb the high hard one, but he's part of this shit. Screwing that woman doesn't make him clean."

"Lillie," Rusty said. "Do you always have to talk that way?"

"Does it make you nervous?"

"It just doesn't have to be like that," Rusty said. "You can get across the same point without using that kind of language. I'd prefer not to hear words I wouldn't want used in front of my pastor."

"Hmm," Lillie said. "What kind of nice words would you like me to use for shitbags running loose in our county, sir?"

"Durn it," Rusty said. "I don't know. That's not the point."

"This is a tough business, Sheriff," Lillie said. "We don't talk like it's a fucking church picnic. Shooting and robbing is dirty and nasty. I come at these boys hard as they come at me. *Comprende?*"

Rusty Wise put away his phone and shuffled in his seat. He didn't open his mouth.

"Why would Mickey Walls lie about talking with Kyle?" Lillie said. "Unless he had something to hide."

"Maybe he's nervous."

"I want those cell phone records, too," Lillie said. "Those dumb bastards probably been burning up some airtime. Fucking scheming. But we need more before we can get a warrant."

"Lillie?"

"If you don't like the way I talk, you don't like the way I am," she said. "Are you in or not?"

"OK," Rusty said. "Let's go. But one thing first."

"What's that?" Lillie said, cranking the engine and making a U away from the dirt patch by the river.

"Can I just please text my wife first?"

"She'll save you some pie," Lillie said, taking the Cherokee to up around seventy without the lights or flashers. "Don't you worry your pretty little head."

22.

Surprised to hear from you," Quinn said. "Don't you ever take a day off?"

"Been a little busy in Tibbehah," Ringold said. "How's the deputy?"

"Better," Quinn said. "When you called, I was at the hospital and he was awake but pretty out of it. Thought I was his momma for a little bit. And then he kept on talking about some dog they used to have and how he could really hunt."

The men had parked their trucks off the Natchez Trace and had met at the steps heading up to the top of the mounds. Ringold had been there when Quinn had arrived, smoking a cigar and reading a plaque about the first archaeological dig on the site back in 1992. He seemed very into a section about intrusive burials and the history of the Chickasaw Village.

"You got some Indian in you," Ringold said. "Don't you?"

"Choctaw," Quinn said. "On my mother's side."

"I can see it," Ringold said. "High cheekbones. You got a hard face."

"Appreciate that," Quinn said. "Goes with the head."

They got to the top of the mound and surveyed the wide-open acreage. From the top, you could definitely see the spots where the village had stood, a wide common area, which Quinn had read was a market, situated in the center. Ringold puffed on his cigar, "So what are you hearing about this mess from last night?"

"Shit, I figured Stagg's involved," Quinn said. "Right?"

"He about shit a brick when he heard Cobb had been robbed," Ringold said. "Had me track down Cobb on his way back from Tunica and set up a meeting. Stagg wanted to know what else was in the safe besides the money. Never really seemed to care about the amount of cash, only some bookkeeping he knew Cobb had stashed."

"Is that true?"

"Looks like it," Ringold said, blowing some smoke.

Quinn stuffed his hands in the pockets of his uncle's coat. His ball cap set low on his head, no longer TIBBEHAH SHERIFF but one he'd picked up in Columbus, Georgia, for Auburn University. Quinn had always been an Auburn fan while at Benning.

"This is what you've been talking about."

"If this is going to work," Ringold said. "If we're going to take down Stagg's ass for more than dealing drugs and guns, we're going to have to know his money connections. I've been working for him for two years now and he plays that shit close. I really don't know what he talks about with that old trooper, but it's something with that crook Senator Vardaman. Lots and lots of money, after the twister. That's when the real money started funneling in. Reason I got assigned in this godforsaken shithole."

"You're talking about my home," Quinn said.

"It needs to be fumigated."

"I tried," Quinn said. "There's nothing that Southerners hate more than self-examination."

"We can nail Stagg's ass," Ringold said. "So damn close."

"If you haven't heard, I'm no longer sheriff."

Ringold's cigar was about out. He studied the dead end and then used the heel of his shoe to scrape off the ash, setting what was left inside his coat pocket. He stood wide-legged, with his arms crossed over his chest. A little bit of his gun-hand wrist poked out and you could see the beginnings of all that scrawling tattoowork.

"You know a man named Mickey Walls?" Ringold said.

"I heard Cobb fingered him for the job," Quinn said. "I'm not so sure. Those boys have been in a pissing contest for the last year. Walls was married to Cobb's daughter and there was some bad blood after the divorce. I never made Mickey for a thief."

"You better think again," Ringold said. "It's him."

"How do you know?"

"Dumb bastard told me as much," Ringold said. "We had what you'd call a come-to-Jesus session. I told him he'd better come up with all of Cobb's bookkeeping or his ass was on the line."

"He deny it?"

"He tried," Ringold said. "But it's him. If he didn't do it himself, he knows who did it. I just want to find those books. We get some names and we can really go to work on some money transfers and Stagg's accounts."

"And then you can ride off into the sunset?" Quinn said.

"Never figured to stay around here forever, Sergeant."

"There's more to the place than the ugliness," Quinn said. "Maybe someday I can take you out hunting and fishing and you can know more than just that goddamn truck stop. Get out on Choctaw Lake and out into the National Forest."

"I'd like that."

"Folks like Stagg and Cobb haven't ripped all the guts out of the place," Quinn said. "There's still a lot left."

. . .

Mickey told Kyle he wanted to meet up at the First Baptist Church basement, down in the rec room, where they held Bible study and used to show Christian movies on Wednesday nights with microwave popcorn and Diet Rite. Mickey recalled seeing a movie a long time ago called *Years of the Beast* where folks are trying to scavenge like wild animals while the Antichrist is running the show of hypocrites. That thing scared the ever-living shit out of him. Mainly because his momma told him this was what the world would be like when he was her age. She said the world would become lawless and wild and that he'd have to fend for himself.

Right now, the rec room just looked kind of junky. The walls were made of old paneled wood, and the carpet was a threadbare green industrial that looked to have been laid about fifty years ago. It was so spotted and soiled, it looked like some kind of topographical map. If he'd known things had gotten crummy, he would have put down some new stuff for free. Hell, he would have been glad to do it. If he got through this thing, that was exactly what he was going to do. He'd lay wall-to-wall for free.

He pulled out a tape measure from his pocket and started looking at dimensions and was nearly done about thirty minutes later when Kyle showed up. The man didn't look happy, sweating and out of breath. He didn't say hello and shake Mickey's hand, only looked at him and said, "God damn, they know it. God damn, they know."

"Who?" Mickey said.

"The law," Kyle said. "I went down to the fire station for lunch and Eddie Fudge told me damn Lillie Virgil had just left. He was minding his own damn business, making chili, and she started asking all kinds of questions about why the Jaws of Life were out and who'd been using them."

"The jaws of what?"

"The goddamn Jaws of Life," Kyle said. "I had to borrow them from the firehouse to open the safe. I didn't have time to put them back or get them cleaned up. Lillie Virgil saw them. She took note. Eddie Fudge told me so."

"Fuck Eddie Fudge," Mickey said. "He doesn't know shit. And so what if you did use them things? If they can't find the safe and can't find the money, it just won't matter. What did you do with the safe?"

"Dumped it out in Choctaw Lake," Kyle said, waiting a second to burn another damn cigarette. "And hell, no. Nobody saw me. I know a road on the other side of the county that nobody uses. Ain't nobody gonna find that safe."

"Do you always have to smoke?" Mickey said. "I mean, son of a bitch. Kids play down here and shit."

Kyle looked at him through a cigarette haze as if he were talking in another language. "I don't like this," he said. "I don't like none of it. I hadn't gone home. I don't want to go home. If Lillie was sniffing around the firehouse, then she knows me and you are connected. And if she knows that, she's gonna want to pull me in and start asking questions. God damn that stupid shit for shooting Kenny. If he hadn't shot Kenny, I don't even think people would be looking that hard. I think folks might just be thinking that Larry Cobb got what he had coming. But, god damn, you don't shoot a cop. I see that damn kid again and I just might kill him."

"Kenny's gonna live," Mickey said. "We got bigger shit to worry about."

"Bigger than Parchman?" Kyle said, blowing smoke out his nose. "I doubt it, man. I seriously doubt it. My asshole is already clenching up."

"Johnny Stagg."

"What?"

"Stagg and Cobb do business," Mickey said, waving the haze of smoke out of the way. Light streaming in from the little windows, high in the basement but ground-level outside. "There was something in that safe. Some kind of fucking records that got his panties all in a twist. Something that could cause trouble for him and Cobb. You need to get it and bring it to me. I'll wait right here."

"No."

"No?" Mickey said. "What the hell you mean, no? I just got to ride around with that crazy bald-headed motherfucker that works for Stagg. You know the one with the big beard and all them tattoos? That son of a bitch is a card-carrying psychopath, I shit you not. He said he was gonna roast my nuts if I didn't give them back what they want."

"The boy took it," Kyle said. "Your boy Chase that shot the cop. He stole a Rolex and some earrings and took those books. They're real books. Two of them. Like old-fashioned leather ledgers they got at the courthouse. I didn't see much interest in them. I was going to burn them. I don't know why the hell the boy took them other than just to be a real and true retard."

"Shit."

"You bet."

"Now I got to drive over to Gordo and roust their ass while I got Johnny Law breathing down my neck."

"They pull you in again?"

"Just once," Mickey said. "I'm not going back without a lawyer. They don't have shit on me. They know my damn story checks out."

Kyle didn't say anything. He smoked down that Marlboro and started a new one. The basement was dark, musty-smelling, and cold. Mickey tried to recall a few scenes from that old movie he'd watched. He thought maybe one of the characters was a college professor and another a hippie or a Jew. The Antichrist was kind of like the president, but more like a king. He had a nice pin-striped suit and wore a carnation in his lapel. If he'd been black, Mickey would've figured maybe the End Times were right here and now. What was the world coming to?

"If the sheriff pulls you in, shut your mouth."

"If I don't say a word, or lawyer up, they're gonna know I was a part of this."

"What's the matter with you?" Mickey said. "They got jack shit. Nobody saw nothing."

"I'm not getting stuck with shooting a lawman."

"What are you going to do?" Mickey said, laughing. "Lay out the whole damn show?"

"I'm no thief," Kyle said. "I'm not a criminal. I never did this kind of thing in my life."

"Like I said, it ain't a crime. It's about making Larry Cobb taste some of his own shit. This is about getting right."

"I don't know," Kyle said. "I don't want to be into all this mess. I been upstairs for a while. I've been thinking it over. Praying on things. Maybe we should both go in and talk to Lillie Virgil. Explain what happened. You don't owe those Alabama boys a thing. They aren't nobody. They're nothing. Give the money back. Explain we were just trying to get back at Cobb."

Mickey knew his mouth was open. But he was unable to form the words to speak.

W e could've been killed," Debbi Cobb said. "Run over in the middle of the night, if we hadn't gone over to Tunica to play blackjack."

"Praise the Lord for Larry," Gail Amsden said, an empty glass of scotch and soda in hand. "Baby doll, would you go freshen up my drink? Been a long night for Momma."

Anna Lee snatched the glass and passed Quinn with a scowl, heading back to the kitchen. Quinn sat on the sofa, facing the two sisters, listening to Debbi Cobb tell about the wrecked home she'd found that morning. She had said more than once that she believed someone wanted Larry dead.

"Mickey?" Quinn said.

"Hell, no," Debbi said. "That's Larry talking. He blames Mickey every time his truck won't start or if his hemorrhoids act up. Those boys just flat out hate each other."

"Then who?" Quinn said.

"I thought you weren't the sheriff anymore," Gail said, reaching for the freshened drink.

"No, ma'am," Quinn said. "But Anna Lee asked me over."

"I bet she did."

Anna Lee shot a glance at her mother but exited the room without a word, heading down the long hall to her daughter's room. She didn't exactly slam the door as much as shut it with some emphasis. The old Victorian was big and cavernous, built by a railroad man during Reconstruction. Quinn could hear her talking to her daughter, Shelby, in the back room.

Gail Amsden crossed her legs, looking hard at Quinn and grinning. She looked a great deal like Anna Lee, with blonde hair and sleepy eyes. But the years had added some weight, and a nasty divorce had fine-tuned the attitude.

"I appreciate you coming," Debbi Cobb said. "You helped us when those goddamn meth heads were stealing copper. And when that dumb bastard Tim Weeks threatened to whip Larry's ass after he got fired. I don't know Rusty Wise from Adam's house cat. We used to have a policy on our home with his daddy. But that was a long time ago."

"He's a good man."

"Maybe," Debbi said. "But I know you. I know your momma and daddy. And this is serious business. Serious as hell. Someone wants my husband dead and they don't care if I'm with him. They probably want me dead, too. It reminds me of this movie I saw once with Judith Light. Or maybe it was Meredith Baxter-Birney. The woman on *Family Ties?* But she was an ordinary, good Christian housewife who found out her husband lived a double life. I can't remember everything that happened, but she cut in half some damn Yankee mobster with a twelve-gauge. I love Larry. God help me, I'd do the same thing."

"Larry's living a double life?"

"I don't know," she said. "I'm not sure what to call it. Are you sure you're not the law anymore?"

"No, ma'am," Quinn said, catching a satisfied glance from Gail, who took another swig of scotch. The ice rocking around in the highball glass.

"He's unemployed," Gail said.

"I wouldn't be telling you this if someone hadn't tried to kill us," Debbi said. "You got to promise me, Quinn, that what I say stays right here between you, Gail, and the Good Lord."

"Yes, ma'am," Quinn said, leaning forward in the seat, "I do."

"Folks don't know Larry's got interests more than just cutting and milling timber. I don't think that's a secret. He's big-time. You know he was named one of Mississippi's top hundred businessmen back in 2001?" Debbi said.

"How could I forget?" Gail said. "Y'all have it framed in your kitchen."

"Hush," Debbi said. "What I'm trying to say is that Larry has some powerful friends."

"Nothing wrong with that," Quinn said.

"I'm just not sure what they all do," Debbi said. "I'm pretty sure it's not all legal. You understand?"

"No, ma'am," Quinn said.

"Maybe I need to shut my mouth," Debbi said. "I should just shut my g.d. mouth. I don't want to get him in trouble. I love my husband and don't want my big boy killed. And I'd rather not die in the process."

"Understood," Quinn said. "But if you want me to help, you need to tell me all you know."

"Leave it to the police," Gail said.

"I only met these folks a few times at parties down in Jackson and down in Biloxi," she said, ignoring Gail. "Larry and them would say they were going fishing. And then he'd come back with a bag full of money. I'd ask him about the bass he was gonna catch and he wouldn't answer. He'd head right back to the safe and start packing in the money."

"I heard the thieves got nearly a million."

"That's right."

"Larry said it was for the grandchildren's college fund," Gail said.

"Larry's lying," Debbi said. "We got two grandsons and both of them are too stupid for high school. One of them already flunked out and is working at the mill, driving a forklift. The other just sits in his bedroom all day, playing video game football and looking at titties."

"Good Lord," Gail said. "How can you talk about your grandchildren that way?"

"Because it's the truth," Debbi said. "All this lying and hiding has gotten us into the shit we got now. Men busting through the walls of our house, stealing a gun safe loaded down with all that filthy money. That money is dirty. I don't want nothing of it. I hope to hell they never find it, if it's going to hurt my family."

"If it were me, I'd want that money back," Gail said, taking a sip of scotch to punctuate her point. "Would y'all like anything? I'm so rude, didn't even offer y'all coffee or a Coke. I can get you a beer, Quinn. I know how much you like beer."

Quinn didn't answer her. The woman getting up from her seat with a self-satisfied grin and walking back to the kitchen for more scotch to swill.

"Do you have names?" Quinn said.

"No."

"Do you have any idea on how Larry made that money?"

"I've asked a few times and he always laughs it off. Most of the time, he says he won it on blackjack. But that's a lie, too. Larry can't gamble worth a shit. He always loses. I don't think he can even count to twenty-one."

"Mrs. Cobb," Quinn said. "You got to give me something. This is not a Lifetime movie."

"Not until I'm dead," she said. "Someone slits my throat and it'll be *Midnight in Mississippi* or *Sheltered Secrets* or something like that."

Quinn smiled. "Who would play your part?"

"Maybe Delta Burke," Debbi said. "Before she gained all that weight. Just promise me that it will be a real Southern woman. I really can't stand some actress making us all sound like g.d. Scarlett O'Hara."

"Nobody's gonna kill you, Mrs. Cobb."

"And I don't want Larry going to jail."

"Not my job."

"Maybe I can get you some names," she said. "Talk to Larry some more before someone goes and shoots his dumb ass."

"Anyone I might know?"

"I don't want trouble."

"Johnny Stagg?" Quinn said.

Just as her sister came back with a fresh drink in one hand and a very long cigarette in the other, Debbi Cobb nodded.

"Just what did I miss?" Gail said.

23.

Mickey figured he could just get his cut of the money and leave town. He'd heard Costa Rica was nice, with the tropical drinks, monkeys, and such. A gringo could get lost down there in the jungle. Or he could stick it out, see what the law would do, while he talked more sense to Kyle. Kyle was having a case of the nerves, but he'd never give up Mickey. Kyle was the kind of man who'd run the line of Jäger shots, get buck-ass naked with some waitress in his truck, and then wake up the next morning praying to Jesus. That boy had quit drinking and quit raising hell so many times that when Kyle would start to witness to him, Mickey would just start laughing.

If he got back those papers or whatever shit the Alabama boys stole from Cobb, Kyle would mellow out and start thinking straight. Mickey needed Johnny Stagg off his ass to become a reasonable human being again.

Mickey was driving now, steering the truck with one hand and holding an open can of Bud Light with the other. It was gray and dark on the back roads of Tibbehah, winding high up in the hills beyond Fate and Providence and into the National Forest. He'd now called

Tonya for the thirtieth time with no answer and was on to message number fifteen for Peewee Sparks.

If Sparks didn't call him back by nightfall, Mickey figured he'd have to hightail it over to Gordo and do some reasoning in person. If him and his retard nephew tried to get tough, Mickey was prepared to go full-out redneck on their asses.

Mickey reached into the cardboard box for another beer, the gravel road crunching under his truck's tires. His radio was tuned to American Family Radio, the host talking about how the current president had plans to start looting folks' personal retirement. Sometimes Mickey figured his granddaddy had it right, take what you saved and hide it in coffee cans out in your yard.

The old logging road dovetailed into Highway 9, tires finding some solid purchase on the asphalt and zooming on down to Jericho. If he got what he needed, he could meet up with Kyle and then keep on heading south on 45 down to Mobile and then Gulf Shores. Tonya was still at the hotel, he'd bet every cent on it. If he could just see her in person, buy her a couple shots, then all would be forgiven.

He'd just lay low until this whole mess blew over. Maybe even find a way to hide some of that money down on the coast. He reached for his cell and thumbed down the number for Tonya. The phone rang and rang. He dialed up Peewee Sparks, knowing the number now by heart.

"Huh?" the man said.

"Shit, I've been trying to call you," Mickey said, running off the road and then righting the truck. "God damn, where you been?"

"Asleep," he said. "Who the hell is this?"

"You know who this is."

"No, I don't," Peewee said. "I ain't no fucking mind reader."

"Y'all took some shit that didn't belong to y'all."

Click.

Son of a bitch.

Mickey hit redial and after ten rings Peewee picked up but didn't say nothing. "Shit, it's Mickey, man. It ain't the law. I'm just trying to get some shit y'all weren't supposed to take."

Peewee didn't say anything, but Mickey could hear the fat man breathing into the phone.

"I don't want the jewelry or the fucking watch," Mickey said. "Just the papers. Y'all picked up some papers that are going to cause some other folks problems."

Silence.

"Son of a bitch, are you listening, you peckerwood motherfucker?"

A few seconds of silence. And then, "What kind of problems?"

"Bad problems," Mickey said. "For me and Kyle, too. Nobody was supposed to see that shit."

"Hmm."

"I can run over to Gordo or y'all can meet me in Birmingham or Tuscaloosa," he said. "Don't matter to me. But we got to have it back. Understand?"

"Sure," Peewee said, launching into a little coughing fit. "But let me ask you something. These folks who don't like trouble. Do they got a lot of money?"

"I don't have time for this shit."

"Me, neither," Peewee said, hanging up the phone.

Mickey ran off the road again, right by a big rolling pasture filled with a ton of cattle, throwing up grass and rock as he skidded to a stop. He hammered the ever-living shit out of his steering wheel and said, "Motherfucker. Shit. Shit. Shit."

None of these bastards had a bit of honor between them. They were going to hang his ass before he'd get a chance to spend a nickel of Larry's money.

. . .

Y ou don't believe someone's out to get Cobb," Boom Kimbrough
said.

"Nope," Quinn said.

"What did his wife say?"

"Debbi said he was tied in with some bad dudes from Jackson and
the coast," Quinn said, ashing his cigar in the tray of Boom's old pickup.
"She believes the Dixie Mafia came to kill Larry for what he knows."

"And what does Larry know?"

"Running a lumber mill and stealing from the county till."

"And who'd be pissed about that?"

"She believes Stagg's tied in with it," Quinn said. "But they chow
down at the same trough."

Boom had parked down the road from Mickey Walls's ranch house.
He'd found an old abandoned house with kudzu grown up and over
the roof and a half-dozen vehicles parked nearby, the kudzu creeping
over them, too. In winter, the kudzu withered and died and you could
almost make out the house under all that mess. Someone had jacked up
one of the old cars, left it on blocks, and stolen the wheels.

"You're doing this for Anna Lee," Boom said. "Make sure no one
hurts the Cobbs."

Quinn didn't say anything. He puffed on the cigar and reached for a
cup of coffee that'd he'd gotten when they met up at Dixie Gas. Boom
had on his tan county coveralls, BOOM K. embroidered on the pocket.
His right sleeve pinned to his shoulder.

"Then why?"

"Something I need was in that safe," Quinn said. "I think Mickey
Walls has it. And I want it back."

"OK."

"You're not going to ask what it is?"

"Don't care," Boom said. "But I'll help you fuck with Mickey."

"You don't like him."

"Shit," Boom said. "Hell, nah. He's a fat, cocky little racist. You?"

"I have no feelings about Mickey Walls," Quinn said, rolling the window down more. "But I'm not leaving Jericho until I make things right."

"For you?" Boom said. "Or is this about Stagg?"

"This shit's gone on too damn long."

Boom nodded. A few years ago, he'd walked with Quinn into a nest of white supremacists who'd camped up by Hell Creek. He'd never asked any questions then, either. Boom had just taken up a big .44 and waded right into the thick of the fighting. They'd been Stagg's people, but Stagg had walked right on out of the cannon fire without a mark.

"Whose house was this?" Quinn said.

"Benny Malone's."

"The bootlegger?"

"Yeah," Boom said.

"What happened to him?"

"He fucking died, man," Boom said. "Time didn't stop when you left."

"I keep on hearing that."

"But you gonna make up for it," Boom said. "Make things right."

"Before I leave."

"But you'll come back?"

"That's the plan," Quinn said. "Got to make some money. Wherever that might take me. Anna Lee's mother accused me today of being unemployed."

The roof of Benny Malone's house had fallen in, the windows busted out and the front door completely gone, leaving a black hole in the vegetation that resembled an open mouth. Quinn ashed his cigar again, studying its band. A small white car zipped past on the road, followed by a blue Chevy truck. Neither one of them Mickey Walls. Walls's big red Hummer wasn't too hard to spot.

"She never liked you," Boom said.

"She didn't think much of what I offered her daughter."

"Her momma just don't get it."

"Nope."

"You gonna make that right, too?"

"Anna Lee?"

"Yeah," Boom said. "Her and her kid."

"I'm gonna try."

L illie," Kyle Hazlewood said. "I swear to God, I got no idea what you're talking about."

"You didn't move those Jaws of Life last night?" Lillie said. "Maybe just to help someone out on something? We just need a little help, Kyle."

"I talked to Eddie Fudge," Kyle said. "I know you're trying to pull me into that thing that happened to Larry Cobb. Shit, Lillie, how long you and me knowed each other?"

"As long as I can recall," Lillie said. "You used to run with my brother, raise hell down in Columbus."

"Have I ever been arrested except for a couple DUIs and some drug shit when I was a kid?"

"No, sir," Lillie said, looking over her shoulder to Rusty Wise and then back to Kyle. "Not that I know about." They all sat together in the barren sheriff's office, as they'd sat earlier with Mickey Walls. Lillie had found Kyle sitting on his front porch, wrapped in a big horse blanket and smoking a cigarette. He looked cold, but was agreeable about coming in and talking. He almost seemed resigned to it, like he had been waiting on Lillie as she drove up in her county vehicle.

"You know me," he said. "Shit. Didn't those folks shoot Kenny? I worked fifteen years with Ken Senior. I was a pallbearer at his service. I cried as much as Kenny. What that family went through in that shit-storm. God help them. His mother was picked up like a rag doll and tossed a half mile away. Didn't she get impaled by a goddamn two-by-four?"

"Just because you let somebody borrow a tool doesn't mean you used it," Rusty Wise said. Lillie had instructed Wise to be the calm, patient one. Not exactly the good cop, but the understanding one. The guy who tried to talk sense and be rational. Lillie would do her best to work Kyle over. It wasn't hard for her. Busting their balls just came naturally.

"I didn't touch them things," Kyle said. "I did not borrow them. I had no cause to be at the firehouse. We didn't have a single call since Christmas."

"What happened on Christmas?" Lillie asked.

"Demetrius Clark set fire to his old lady's Kia," he said. "Don't you remember?"

"Oh, yeah," Lillie said. "Wasn't Demetrius's finest hour. She was his ride to work."

"Why'd he do it?"

"She was fucking ole Shane Gardner," Lillie said.

"Bull?"

"Yep."

"That's one big ugly son of a bitch," Kyle said. "Demetrius better watch his ass."

"Folks can do stupid shit when they get mad," Rusty said, thumping the top of his Copenhagen can. "If they'd just take a minute to think things over, their life might have gone a different way."

"Rusty," Kyle said. "Y'all ain't listening to me. I didn't bust into Larry Cobb's house. Y'all can check my house and look for all that god-damn cash. I look like I'm swimming in it?"

Lillie had been looking at the linoleum as he spoke, but her head jerked up at that last part. "Who said anything about cash, Kyle?"

"Y'all did."

"No, sir," Rusty said. "We never said word one of why we brought you in. We were just asking about property that belonged to the Tibbehah County Volunteer Fire."

"Come on, now," Kyle said. "Shit. Everyone in town knows Larry got about a million bucks taken from him. You think that's secret? What else would a man keep in his safe?"

"Guns, jewelry," Lillie said. "Nekkid pictures of his wife."

"I don't have none of that," Kyle said. "Hadn't seen none of that. Besides me working for the fire department, donating my time and sweat to help folks out, why do you think I'm a part of this mess? You want to give me one reason?"

Lillie lifted her eyes to Rusty. Rusty picked up a Styrofoam cup and spit in it, giving himself a dramatic little pause, looking Kyle over. Kyle did look rough as hell this morning. His thin beard was as gray as an old dog, but his longish hair—too long for a man his age—still had some brown in it. The whiskers not matching what was on top. The same way the puka shells on his neck, and the slick, worn motorcycle jacket, just didn't seem right with his bony, worn-out frame.

"You and Larry Cobb have a falling-out last month?" Rusty said. "Something about some dozerwork out on his land?"

"Yes, sir," Kyle said. "That's correct."

"And Larry wouldn't pay you?" Lillie said.

"He never was gonna pay me," Kyle said. "That's Cobb's way. He found something to criticize and make a point of so he wouldn't have to write a check. He's the cheapest son of a bitch I ever met in my life."

"Did it piss you off?" Lillie said.

"Hell, yes, it pissed me off."

"And you threatened to get back at him?" Rusty said.

Kyle's face flushed a high red. He nodded, flexing his jaw muscles. "That's right," Kyle said. "I told him that I was gonna whip his ass. This all being on the telephone. But I hadn't seen him since. I told him to keep out of my goddamn way. But you know what? If I'd seen him, I would have whipped his ass. I'd of done it, straight-up and man-to-man. I ain't into none of this sneaking around, breaking and entering. I got a problem with you and we work out that shit together."

Lillie swallowed. Rusty spit again, that seeming to be his best interrogation talent. Lillie got up and came around the desk, looking down at Kyle Hazlewood. The man looked dirty, worn-out. Black dirt under his fingernails and smelling like a damn ashtray. He didn't look like a man who got a good rest last night. Kyle looked bone-tired.

"Anyone see you last night?"

"My dogs."

"Besides your dogs."

"No, ma'am," he said. "I'm a working man. You think I'm out drinking whiskey and shooting guns on New Year's?"

"You got a girlfriend?"

"I did," Kyle said. "But there ain't no reason to bring her into this mess. She's already pissed-off at me as it is. I think she's dating the goddamn meat manager at the Piggly Wiggly. Said I never took her nowhere."

"Mickey Walls knows how to treat a lady," Lillie said. "He took Tonya Cobb down to the Flora-Bama last night. Drove all the way home this morning just to tend to some business. That is something."

"That's ole Mick."

"He tell you about it?" Lillie said.

"Mickey?"

Lillie nodded. Kyle shook his head and looked at the floor.

"Y'all haven't talked in a while, huh?"

Kyle shook his head, pulling out his pack of cigarettes from his red racing jacket, signaling it was time for him to be getting on. "Nah," Kyle said. "Me and him been really busy. Didn't know he and Tonya were back together. Good for them."

Lillie looked to Rusty and Rusty grinned a little before spitting in the cup again. He wiped his chin.

"You're right, Kyle, we have known each other a long while," Lillie said. "So I guess I should take you at your word you weren't at the fire-house last night. And that you and Mickey weren't hanging out at the Huddle House or the Sonic last week, either."

Kyle didn't say a word. Lillie shrugged and looked to Rusty Wise.

"Some of this just isn't adding up for me," Rusty said. "Can we come at it again? Start off real slow."

24.

He's going to break," Mickey Walls said to Peewee Sparks. Both of them having a serious man-to-man conversation in the back of Peewee's ROLL TIDE conversion van, parked at a McDonald's on U.S. Highway 82, right outside Columbus, Mississippi. "Doesn't even want to lawyer up first."

"They don't know nothing."

"Kyle thinks the sheriff knows that me and him been planning something," Mickey said. "They know he took that contraption from the firehouse yesterday to break into the safe. He's been sitting in the sheriff's office for the last two hours."

"So what if you and him been talking," Peewee said. "How the hell they gonna know what was said unless the dumb son of a bitch told them?"

"I don't know what he said."

"Even if they know y'all talked, what's it matter?" Peewee said. "Aren't y'all buddies and shit? I mean, god damn. That ain't nothing. What I want to know is, where is the fucking money?"

"Put up and buried deep."

"Good," Peewee said. "Good."

"What I need to know is, where are those books?" Mickey said. "If I don't have enough troubles with Kyle and my goddamn crazy-ass ex-wife, I got some bad dudes wanting to skin my ass alive. I don't have time for that shit."

"No kidding," Peewee said, talking to Mickey from the captain's chair, swiveling to and fro as they spoke. The man up in the high seat, in charge, and kind of bemused by the situation Mickey found himself in. Thank the Lord he didn't involve his dumb-ass nephew into this. But he sure as hell brought him along. He told the kid to go on in the McDonald's and get himself a double cheeseburger and fries and that they'd be done in a minute. "What's wrong with your ex?"

"I kind of left her down at the beach without any money and without a vehicle," Mickey said. "She was drunk and thought we were about to get into some romantic sex and all. And then I left after y'all couldn't get the safe out of the house. She finally answered my call after I'd called her about fifteen thousand times. She told me I might as well go fuck myself because that was the only action I'd be getting for a long while."

"She good-looking?" Peewee said, grinning. Licking his lips. He wore an old navy hoodie sweatshirt, a T-shirt with Bear Bryant's face popping out from the center, the hatted head prominent on Peewee's big expanding belly.

"Where are the fucking books, man?" Mickey said. "I don't need any shit. I was straight with y'all and want y'all to be straight with me."

"Is she good-looking?"

"What the fuck does that have to do with anything?"

"Just trying to get a visual," Peewee said. "Get her in my mind while you tell the story. What's wrong with that?"

Mickey swallowed, trying to slow down the blood pounding in his head right now. He was getting a fucking migraine right behind his left eye. He ground the heel of his hand into the socket and said, "She's blonde."

"Big tits?"

"Yep."

"Double D's?"

"C cup," Mickey said. "How many women you know with double D's?"

"What else?"

"She's tan."

"Tan all over?"

"Yes," Mickey said. "Even her ass crack is tan. Brown as a nut. Now, where the hell are those fucking books so we can separate? I ain't gonna lie to you. Things are not looking good. I want both of y'all to lay low and get off the grid. *Comprende?* Me and you ain't never talked."

"Me and the boy's headed down to New Orleans for the Sugar Bowl," Peewee said, zipping up the hoodie, covering a good bit of the Bear's face but leaving the famous hat exposed. "So don't you worry a bit about us. We long gone, bud."

The interior of the van was the same houndstooth pattern as the Bear's hat, the exterior painted a Crimson Tide red, with the faces of Alabama football greats airbrushed on the side. These boys were card-carrying morons. But they were Mickey's morons and he hoped to hell they had more sand than Kyle Hazlewood. Kyle had turned into a true, authentic disappointment.

"All right," Peewee said. "We're here. Let's talk about what this shit is worth to you."

"What's it worth?" Mickey said, raising his voice a good bit. "Your boy stole it from us."

"How's that?" Peewee said. "Who took what? What belongs to which one of us? Ain't none of this real clear in my head, Mr. Walls."

"How much?"

"Well," Peewee said. "I guess it boils down to that fact. You know, I was doing some thinking."

"Of course you were," Mickey said.

Just then, the sliding door to the van ripped open, giving Mickey's heart a start. But it was only Chase Clanton hopping up into the van with a big bottle wrapped in brown paper. "To hell with a cheeseburger," he said. "There's a liquor store next door. Didn't check my ID or nothin'. Come on, boys. Time to celebrate. I got us some Rebel Yell."

Y'all hungry?" Luther Varner said, working behind the register at his convenience store. "I made extra sausage biscuits for today. Peaches fried some chicken. I can get her to make some up fresh, too. Where you been? Hunting?"

"Just riding," Quinn said. "Killing time before supper tonight."

Quinn and Boom had just walked in from the cold, in their heavy jackets and boots, after waiting until dark for Mickey Walls to show at his house and then driving over to the carpet-and-flooring shop when he didn't. After he'd gotten the call from Varner, they'd left the shop and headed up north on 9. The glass case at the Quick Mart was filled with tamales, chicken, greens, green beans, hush puppies, and fries. Tonight, his mom was making those collards, black-eyed peas, and cornbread. He couldn't disappoint her.

Tall and lean, old, gray crew-cutted Luther Varner leaned over the counter, packs and packs of cigarettes, custom knives, and ammunition stacked behind him. The tattooed skull jarhead popped from his veiny forearm, a long cigarette between his fingers. "Y'all been looking for Kyle Hazlewood and Mickey Walls?"

Quinn nodded. Boom sidled up to him, his hand filled with some beef jerky and carrying a Mountain Dew in the crook of his arm. He set it down for Varner to ring up. Varner, still leaning over the counter, nodded his head to the back door, toward the kitchen where Miss Peaches cooked. If you lived in the north part of the county, Varner's was the last stop for supplies. A modern general store with an ICEE machine and two fancy coffeemakers that could make up the worst shit in north Mississippi.

"Can I ask what y'all are doing?" Varner said.

"Thinking of refinishing the heart pine at the house," Quinn said, smiling.

"Bullshit," Varner said. "Those two shitbirds are mixed up with this Cobb business."

"Haven't you heard," Quinn said. "I'm no longer sheriff."

"Yeah, I heard something like that," Varner said. "But I'll bet a hunnard dollars you still got a gun on your hip."

Quinn smiled.

"That shit don't go away," he said. "Never does."

"I'm asking around for a friend."

"Sure," Varner said, plugging the long cigarette in his mouth. "That's good. Because Peaches won't talk to no one else. Sure as shit not to some fat turd insurance adjuster."

The old black woman was still frying chicken in back of the store. She lifted up some brown chicken parts from the fryer and dumped them into an aluminum tray lined with paper towels. A big stainless steel bowl of coleslaw sat on a nearby table, a wooden spoon stuck in the center where she'd been stirring. Peaches was a big woman, with thick arms and chest, a plump face and gold glasses. As usual when she worked in the Quick Stop kitchen, she wore a red apron and a plastic cap over her hair.

After she put down the chicken, she walked over to Quinn and gave him a hug. "How your momma and them?"

"Good," Quinn said. "Everyone's fine. How about Bobby?"

"Just got him a job at FedEx," she said. "Gonna be driving a truck over in Batesville. But he'll get home twice a week. Got Mondays off. You want something to eat?"

"My mom's making supper."

"You saying your momma a better cook than me?" she said. "Don't you mess with me, Quinn Colson. I remember when you, Boom, and Bobby was in kindergarten. Playing grab ass out by the lake. Shootin' BB guns and raising hell."

"You really want me to be full at Miss Jean's house?"

Peaches smiled and picked up the tin of chicken, shaking it around on the paper towels to drain off the grease. "Luther tells me you been looking for Kyle Hazlewood?"

"Yes, ma'am."

"What's that boy into?"

"Not sure yet."

"Is this gonna get me into any trouble?" she said. "'Cause I don't need no headaches right now. If it comes down to it, I'll swear on it. But I watch my grandbabies after school. And if someone was to—"

"Miss Peaches, I'm not sheriff anymore," he said. "Just trying to make sense of something."

She nodded and grabbed a paper plate. She added a fried breast and some coleslaw, a handful of hot French fries. Boom had followed him into the back and Peaches didn't say a word to him as she made the same plate, only with more piled high, and handed it to him. "Y'all growing boys," she said. "Don't you dare tell Jean."

Boom took the plate to a little table by the fryers and started to eat.

"You talking about last night?" she said.

"Yes, ma'am."

"I seen Kyle outside the fire station in the middle of the night," she said. "He was loading up something into his truck. I didn't stop, but I waved at him. He just stared at me as I passed. Like he was mad as hell about something."

"You sure it was him?" Quinn said.

Peaches just stared long and hard at him. "I don't know what that boy was doing, but I knew it didn't look right."

"About what time was this, ma'am?"

C hase Clanton tilted back the bottle of Rebel Yell and took him a good, long swallow. Wiping his mouth with his shirtsleeve, he passed it back to Mickey Walls. The man drank most of the whiskey, relaxing in the back of the party van like they was old buds. Uncle Peewee swiveled to and fro in his captain's chair, trying to make plans, hatch ideas, on how this new deal was going to work out. "I ain't trying to rob you, Mr. Walls," Peewee said. "I'm just trying to fill my belly, make things right."

"Shit," Mickey said. "Just like every other son of a bitch in the world. 'Make things right.' You know what? I don't even give a good goddamn for the money. You know why I wanted to hit Cobb's house?"

"'Cause he got a million dollars?" Chase said. "And watches, guns, and shit?"

"Shhh," Peewee said. "Let him talk."

"The man rebuked my goddamn honor," Mickey said. "Here. Pass me back that bottle, kid. Shit. That's some rough stuff."

"You don't like it," Chase said, "then don't drink it."

Chase had been the one to buy the bottle and offer to share it. The man acting like it was his. Chase still didn't understand why he and Uncle Peewee had to drive all the way down to Columbus for them to meet. If the man wanted them books that goddamn bad, maybe he

should've driven his ass over to Gordo. He wasn't real wild about Peewee taking the wheel after downing a half bottle.

"I'll give you another ten thousand," Mickey said. "How's that
sound?"

"Fifty sounds better," Peewee said, not skipping a beat.

Mickey tilted back the whiskey and passed it on to Uncle Peewee.
Peewee chugging that bottle, Adam's apple bobbing up and down, like
he was drinking a pitcher of sweet tea. *Whew.*

"OK," Mickey said. "What the hell. Like I said, it ain't about the
money. I'm just trying to fix that son of a bitch for what he's done."

"What'd he do?" Peewee said, Chase not giving a good goddamn.
He found a good spot to lay down in the van between the center seats
and stared up at the roof. Uncle Peewee had pasted a bunch of *Playboy*
centerfolds up there and then covered 'em up with an inch of shellac.
The shellac had started to yellow and age, but you still could get a nice
look at all those women with big hair and titties. One hell of a view.

"Y'all ever heard of reclaimed wood?"

No one said anything.

"Well, I got the idea a few years ago to start tearing down ole barns
in the county that no one used anymore and selling the planks to rich
folks up in Memphis," Mickey said. "Me and my buddy Lee would strip
the wood and then Larry would run it through at the mill. We got to
be partners in the deal and were doing pretty good until me and Tonya
started getting into it."

"Who the hell's Tonya?" Chase asked.

"My ex-wife."

"The one he was screwing last night," Peewee said. "He said she got
big ole brown titties. I'd love to cover her ass in some butter spray.
Haw, haw."

Chase kept on looking up at all those California women he'd never meet, getting a little tickled about things being said, and started to laugh. "Big ole brown titties," he said. "What, is she Mexican?"

"Hell, no, she ain't Mexican," Mickey said. "I'm just saying me and Cobb had ourselves a partnership until he didn't like me no more."

"Why'd he sue you?" Peewee said.

"He accused me of cheating him and then got some goddamn CPA to root around in my asshole until he could make it so," Mickey said. "He was a liar. The damn accountant was a liar. It was a fucking witch hunt. Cobb didn't have no right to half the profits. He was only milling the timber. I was reclaiming the goddamn wood. I was transporting up to Memphis. I ran all the sales out of Walls Flooring. Half the installs I did myself."

Peewee handed Mickey the bottle, knowing the man sure could use some whiskey. Uncle Peewee was wise like that. A damn born leader, not unlike Gene Stallings. Mickey took a big old swallow and then passed it on to Chase. Chase raised it up and drank, Rebel Yell screaming down his throat and into his belly. "Whew," he said.

"You really think your boy is gonna crack?" Peewee said.

Mickey didn't say anything, staring straight ahead into the dark parking lot of the Mickey D's. Chase handed the old man the bottle to take another hit. Old Mickey Walls sure did look like shit warmed over, bad things that had happened, or might still happen, turning over in his mind.

"We can't have the law after our ass," Peewee said. "You can have them damn books. But I think we need to reconfigure our fucking situation."

"What do you mean?"

"I mean, right now ain't nobody ever heard of Peewee Sparks in Jericho, Mississippi, and I plan to keep it that way."

"I ain't saying shit," Mickey said.

"I trust you and know you are a man of honor." Peewee swiveled around a bit in the captain's chair, scratching his chin. "But I would prefer to keep our secret among the folks in this here van."

"Shit." Mickey snorted, glass-eyed. "And just how the hell do you aim on doing that?"

25.

They drove as they always did, Stagg in the passenger seat and the Trooper behind the wheel, running his cruiser upward toward ninety, then a hundred, as they headed south this time on Highway 45. The Trooper hadn't said a goddamn word since the Rebel, listening to Stagg lay out what had been going on with Larry Cobb and who probably took those books with all those facts and figures. The Trooper shuffled in his seat, reached up for his dip cup, spit, and said, "People wondered how long it would take for you to fuck yourself, Mr. Stagg."

"Excuse me, sir?"

"Things hadn't been right since the storm," the Trooper said. "You gotten sloppy."

"Did you hear a fucking word I said?" Stagg said. "It was Larry Cobb that got us into the shitter. It's his safe and his doings. I didn't know he'd been keeping books on our deals."

"But you suspected it," the Trooper said, mashing the accelerator, moving up and around two pickup trucks, dark night flashing by the windows. "Reason you called me first off. If you hadn't known, how come you hit the fire alarm?"

"I asked you to pass things on," Stagg said. "I don't want any more trouble. I want to make things right."

"You brought Cobb into this."

"Yes, sir."

"You vouched for him," the Trooper said. "I was at that party at the man's hunt lodge with the booze and cooze. You said Larry Cobb was a solid man and a fella we could all trust. You put your damn name on his. God damn it. Now you just might've fucked us all high and hard in the ass. Don't you get it? Son of a bitch."

"I never asked you to do nothing," Stagg said. "Besides, I don't ever recall you ever bein' a part of our dealings."

The Trooper nodded, spit in the cup, and took the cruiser on up to past a hundred. He reached down and fiddled with the heater, getting the air going hot and fast. Stagg feeling a little sick in his guts, reaching for the control to let down the window but finding it was stuck. The bastard noticed but didn't say nothing, just kept on dodging around all those cars, taking them down, out of the bottom, and into the next county, big signs for the Choctaw bingo parlors and luxury hotels and casinos. The world of Chief Billy and Fannie Hathcock.

"Can you let down the fucking window?" Stagg said.

The Trooper hit the control, window sliding down, and Stagg could breathe again, fingering at the second-to-top button on his dress shirt. Man tries to do the right thing, notify the right folks, and then he gets treated like he's the one who caused the mess. Ringold had given that Mickey Walls a long leash to fix it, but now Stagg wasn't so sure. If he turned over the whole thing to this buzz-cut leather brain, Tibbehah County could become a goddamn bloody mess.

"Man drank a bottle of Vardaman's finest hooch and then passed out on the toilet," the Trooper said. "He'd left one of your girls tied to the bedpost. She nearly had to nibble off her foot like a trapped coon."

"I never said the man had class," Stagg said. "I said he could get things done. Get everyone paid. He could get the equipment, put together a nice deal for all of us."

"God damn us."

"Just pass on the message."

"God damn you."

"I'm not dealing with you anymore," Stagg said. "Something's broken in your goddamn head. You do know that? Don't you ever speak to me like that."

The Trooper spit one more time into the Styrofoam cup and then turned the wheel hard and fast to the right, hitting the brakes, spinning out, leaving smoking tire across Highway 45. A goddamn semi barreling down the road, horn blaring, nearly broadsiding the cruiser. Stagg gritted his teeth and was about to tear the Trooper a new asshole when the man pulled a sidearm and stuck it right into Stagg's mouth.

"I don't need no one's brain splattered into my vehicle, Johnny," the Trooper said, more cars zipping around the cruiser. Blue lights flashing in the fast lane where he'd idled the vehicle sideways. "But you better come through with this shit. Don't you dare track mud into our fucking house. You ain't nothing but country come to town."

Stagg wanted to speak, but the barrel of the pistol was shoved deep into his throat. He could taste the blood from a cracked tooth.

"You understand the situation, Johnny Stagg?" the Trooper said. "We brought you in from the wild and you just shit all over the floor."

The thickness and metallic taste of the pistol brought tears to Stagg's eyes. He couldn't breathe and knocked the man's hand and the gun away.

Another eighteen-wheeler blew past, the Trooper's breath coming out rough and asthmatic like a smoker, before he knocked the vehicle in gear, crossed over the grassy median, and sped on back to Jericho.

. . .

How was supper?" Lillie asked.

"Country-fried steak with peas and greens," Quinn said. "One of the few things little Jason won't turn up his nose at. He sure hates her meat loaf."

"Can I admit something?"

"Shoot."

"I'm not fond of it, either," she said. "But her country-fried steak is top-notch. Especially when she uses the cubed deer meat."

"She did," Quinn said. "Processed it myself."

"Of course you did," Lillie said. "Probably made the hide into a coat. The antlers a gun rack."

They stood outside, shoulder to shoulder, against Lillie's green Jeep. Her passenger window was down and Quinn could hear the familiar radio patter from dispatch. Even on a full stomach, with enough money in the bank to last the rest of the year if he was careful, he still missed it. He liked the patrol, running the back roads of his county, checking on folks, keeping the world in order. Just a day off and he already felt sloppy as hell.

"She made you a plate," Quinn said.

"Why'd you think I came over?"

"You didn't get my message?"

Lillie shook her head. The front door opened and Jean waved to Lillie and Lillie waved back. She yelled that she had a plate for her and some coffee in a to-go cup. As she closed the front door, Lillie said everyone should have a momma like Jean Colson. Lillie reached into her Cherokee and snatched a pack of cigarettes. She tucked her hands deep in her green jacket while she smoked.

"I got you a witness who saw Kyle Hazlewood loading up the Jaws of Life."

"At the fire station?" Lillie said.

"Yes, ma'am."

"Thought you were going to take it easy."

"Anna Lee wanted me to check on things," Quinn said. "Her being related to the Cobbs."

"You're no different than the rest, Quinn," Lillie said, smiling. "Always working for pussy."

"I don't want to get in y'all's way."

"There's no 'y'all' to it," Lillie said. "As soon as I get a better job, I'm getting the fuck gone from Tibbehah County."

"What are you going to do?"

"Join up with the Wild West Medicine Show," Lillie said, blowing smoke from the side of her mouth. "Shoot cigarettes out of women's mouths. How the hell should I know? Be a cop? About the only thing I know. Who's the wit?"

"Miss Peaches."

"No shit," Lillie said. "You ever have her chicken? God damn, that's some good stuff."

"I told her you'd keep it confidential, if you could," Quinn said. "She's worried Kyle might try and mess her and her family. Her grand-kids."

"Kyle wouldn't kick a mean dog," Lillie said. "That's always been a problem. He won't speak up for himself. He lets people run flat over him. I remember one time his damn brother stole his brand-new truck and Kyle wouldn't even file a complaint. I know Mickey Walls was the one who talked him into this mess. Kyle is just goddamn stupid enough to fall for his bullshit—like half the women in Jericho."

"You think Hazlewood shot Kenny?"

"I don't know who shot Kenny," Lillie said. "But putting Kyle with the equipment sure does help. I think I can push Rusty to get a warrant."

"How's he doing?"

"You really want me to answer that?"

"Can't be as green as me when I started," Quinn said.

"You learned fast," she said. "You had it in you. Rusty is just another fucking politician. You can't make things change without upsetting folks. Rusty doesn't want anyone mad at him. He wants to glad-hand, bullshit about, and be everybody's buddy. I bet he gets a damn hard-on when he puts on his golf shirt with that embroidered star. He just wants to hold court down at the Fillin' Station and suck on his apple pie."

"Let me know how it goes," Quinn said. "Miss Peaches says she'll speak to you private."

Lillie nodded, flicked her spent cigarette into the road, and pushed herself off the side of the Cherokee. "Did Anna Lee tell you about our talk the other night?"

"No," Quinn said. "What did y'all talk about?"

"Nothing," Lillie said, smiling and patting Quinn's face. "Now go and get me my supper."

Ringold picked up Stagg down in Sugar Ditch, where the Trooper had let him out. At the Rebel, Johnny left him and made his way on into the Booby Trap, low time, a couple girls on the poles with a few hangdog truckers watching. He walked down the corridor to his office, unlocking the door and heading straight to the back room, where he brushed his teeth twice and gargled with Listerine. When he smiled in the mirror over the sink, he could see where the bastard chipped a tooth.

He hadn't felt so much humiliation and degradation since he'd been a boy and two older kids had beaten him bloody and then pissed all over his face. Another time, his daddy made him eat a dog turd for not finishing his supper, telling him he didn't have no respect for his family.

Stagg ran a finger inside his mouth and found that the veneer was about to slide off his old rotten tooth. *That goddamn son of a bitch.*

He picked up the phone and dialed the 601 area code for Jackson. He'd get this shit straight right here and now. After he left a message there, and on two other numbers, he called Ringold on his cell. Two minutes later, the boy walking in the door. Stagg feeling some kind of comfort in the man's protection and loyalty. The man stood ramrod straight at his desk, wearing a military green watch cap and black ski jacket.

"He threatened to kill me."

Ringold nodded.

"Man's a fucking sociopath."

"Probably."

"Girls he's been with," Stagg said. "Lord, my girls won't lie with him. Cigarette burns and sore cooters."

"What'd he say?"

"Let's clean up Cobb's mess and then I'll fix it."

"They just want you to feel small," Ringold said. "Like you don't matter. Just a piece of the machine."

"Who?"

"Mr. Stagg, I met plenty of them," Ringold said. "They use you. They use your county, your hospitality, wipe their asses with all you give them. I don't know why you do it."

"Well, I ain't doing it no more."

"They'd be nothing without you."

"Damn right."

"That nut job comes into this county again," Ringold said, "you just say the word."

Stagg fingered the busted tooth as he thought, the TVs showing feeds from the Rebel and the Trap lighting up the far wall, folks shoveling in his ham and eggs, buying up his diesel, tossing out dollar bills to see his girls' titties. Stagg swallowed, his mouth still tasting dirty and sickly. The room was dark and shadowed.

"Don't you kill the fucker yet," Stagg said. "How about you just shake that Walls boy for me first? I don't give a damn what you got to do, but help him get his mind right."

Ringold nodded. "Yes, sir."

"Mr. Ringold?"

"Yes, sir?"

"I appreciate you," Stagg said. "You understand that?"

Ringold nodded and left. Stagg sat in the dark office for a long while, watching the surveillance cameras and tasting that metallic dog shit in his mouth.

26.

Quinn drank black coffee and bourbon and smoked cigars late that night with his father and Boom Kimbrough. There was a big fire ring behind the farmhouse, built of old stones and burning bright with busted tree branches, big fat logs, and discarded bits of barn wood. Jason was telling Boom about the time he'd jumped a car off a dock and onto a barge in the Mississippi River for *White Lightning*, thinking that he'd broken his back, unable to move his legs for a couple hours after they pulled him out.

"Was it worth it?" Boom asked.

"Nearly killing myself for a paycheck?"

Boom nodded.

"I don't think I've ever felt more alive than when I was truly worried about dying."

"Not me," Boom said. "When I thought about dying, I thought, 'Oh, fucking shit, here we go. I'm about to fucking die.'"

"You remember the accident?" Jason said, tapping the ash off his cigar.

"Wasn't no accident," Boom said. "Motherfuckers laid out a whole road of IEDs for us. Only one worked. All of 'em went off and we wouldn't be having this conversation."

"Was it worth it?" Jason said.

"For the pay or to serve my country?"

Jason shrugged. "I guess to be a part of the war. America and all that?"

Boom drew hard on the cigar, the orange plug glowing bright in the corner of his mouth. "How about you ask me that in about twenty years, Mr. Colson? I kind of still miss my arm some."

Quinn reached into the fire ring and pulled out a blue, white-speckled pot filled with coffee. He poured a little into his mug of bourbon. Jason had bought him a nice bottle of Eagle Rare for Christmas that he'd just opened. He added some coffee to Boom's cup, bypassing Jason because he didn't care for coffee this late. A mean wind shot through the forest and down into the open back field.

"You see Lillie today?" Quinn asked Boom.

He shook his head. "Why?"

"She said she and Anna Lee had a talk, kind of leaving it there," Quinn said. "Like I was supposed to understand what she meant."

"Shit, I know what she meant," Boom said.

Jason Colson grinned wide. Quinn looked at his father, shaking his head. "It's not like that."

"Hell, anyone can see that woman is crazy about you," Jason said.

"Boom?" Quinn said. "You want to explain it?"

Boom shook his head, tapped his ash on a fire ring stone and looked across the blaze to Quinn. "Ain't easy to explain," Boom said. "I see it, too."

"Shit."

"I know Lillie keeps a big part of her world private," Boom said. "I can't recall her being out with a man. But I can't recall her being out with a woman, neither. I know she has friends in Memphis. I know she's got her own personal world that she doesn't want to share with anyone in Jericho. But let's just say she's like that."

"So she told off Anna Lee?" Quinn said. "Because Anna Lee didn't mention it."

"Nope," Boom said. "Knowing Lillie, I bet she said she'd whip her ass if she messed with your head again. Like I said, Lillie is looking out for you."

"She's my friend."

"Never fuck your friends," Jason said, toasting the men with his coffee mug. "Me and Susan Anton had a hell of a thing going. That's when she had this show with my buddy Mel Tillis. A country variety show. Got canceled after four weeks and Susan and I ended up at a bar on Hollywood Boulevard, drunk as hell and into each other's arms for comfort. Never was the same."

"It's not like that," Quinn said.

"And it shouldn't be," Boom said. "But no matter what Lillie is or ain't, she still cares about you. She wants you to be happy."

"What do you think?" Quinn said.

"About you and Anna Lee or about Lillie?" Boom said.

Quinn drank some of the bourbon and coffee, picking up the end of a shovel and moving the hot coals into the center of the ring, then moving some branches in closer. The smoke and heat from the fire, the smell of the cigars, relaxed Quinn. He preferred not having a roof overhead. Later on, he'd probably get a sleeping bag and he and Hondo could stay out until first light.

"Don't know about Lillie," Boom said. "Don't care."

"And Anna Lee?"

Boom looked at Jason and then back into the fire. He tapped the cigar again, the ash not growing much since the last time. He then just looked at Quinn with heavy eyes and said, "Ain't my business."

Jason stood up and kicked some stray embers, stomping them out.

He tossed his cigar into the center of the fire and touched the brim of his cowboy hat. "Morning's coming soon enough."

"Every day's a gift," Boom said.

"Damn right," Jason said, walking down a path he'd worn to his trailer, disappearing into the darkness beyond the fire. Quinn and Boom watched him go, the thought of Jason Colson being back home still odd to both of them.

"Who the fuck is Susan Anton?" Boom said.

The names on the stockings above Rusty Wise's fireplace read *Taylor*, *Tyler*, and *Skylar*. But Lillie already knew the kids' names from the ads Rusty had posted during the election. He ran on the ticket of being a strong family man. I LOVE MY WIFE AND KIDS bumper sticker kind of shit. Truth be known, Lillie wouldn't blame him if he didn't give two shits for his wife. She was pretty horrible. Chunky and mean, without a polite bone in her body. When Lillie had shown up at the front door, she'd just kind of rolled her eyes and gone back to the kitchen, where she was baking a pie and sipping on chardonnay. Maybe she should have been back in the living room taking down the goddamn stockings or the dead tree that looked sad and tired in the corner. Brown needles spread across the floor.

"Little late, isn't it?" Rusty said, drinking some coffee and watching his television show, something about World War II, in sweatpants and red socks. "I was about to turn in."

"I got something," Lillie said, exciting and ready to move. "More on Kyle. More on Mickey Walls."

"Can it wait till morning?"

"No," she said. "No, sir, it can't. We need to rustle up a search warrant on this shit. I just saw Kenny, and the nurse told me he won't be walking on that leg for another six months. Right now, I don't have much patience."

"Y'all OK?" said Rusty's horrendous wife in the kitchen, running a knife with icing around some cake, the glass of wine in hand.

"Fine," Rusty said. On the television, the battle for Remagen waged on with the capture of the Ludendorff Bridge. A lot of shelling, with all the action in black-and-white. A lot of talk about Adolf Hitler and something big about to happen called Operation Plunder.

"I got someone who saw Kyle Hazlewood loading up the Jaws of Life into his truck, same time as the Cobb robbery," Lillie said.

"Who?"

"Will it get me a warrant?"

"I don't know," Rusty said, scratching himself. "I mean, shoot. It's late. The judge is probably asleep. I don't want to start ticking folks off the first day on the job."

"Can't be having that."

"C'mon, Lillie," Rusty said. "You know what I mean. What else we got? That's just part of a theory you have of what he's been doing. Just 'cause he was messing around with fire station property doesn't mean he was involved in a felony."

"Yeah," Lillie said. "He was probably using those things to scratch his nut sack."

"Ah, heck. Come on, now. It's late. You got what? A couple folks who seen Mickey and Kyle talking. So you caught him in a lie right there."

"Why would he lie?" Lillie said. "Why would he say he and Mickey hadn't talked much when they'd been sharing a shake and fries over at the Sonic? And then cuddling up over at the Huddle House. It just doesn't make sense. We get a warrant to search his place, we might be able to make some sense of it."

Rusty sat down hard in his big recliner as some German commander set some charges on the bridge and then tried to blow it up. He mashed the button but nothing happened, as his troops were firing machine guns on the Allies. Rusty scratched himself some more, thinking, and then shook his head. "Why are you so set on Mickey? We know he was down at Gulf Shores. Everything checks out."

"For a total of six hours," Lillie said. "Just enough time for the break-in to happen, for the shit to hit the fan, and for Kenny to get shot."

"I'd appreciate you not using profanity in my home."

"God damn it," Lillie said. "Come on. Let's go, Rusty. You let those boys kick back a while and they'll have time to practice their stories. I nearly had Kyle today. He was so fucking close. He nearly told me. He didn't like what had happened to Kenny. He wants someone's ass for it."

"Lillie," Rusty said. "I got children in the next room playing Scrabble. This is a family day. I'm fine with getting up at any hour for police work, but I can't have you coming over here at all hours unless we got something solid and ready to move. Like I said."

"You don't want to push Judge Lackey," Lillie said. "You want him getting a good night's sleep. God forbid these fucking morons who shot Kenny might be inconvenienced. I have a witness who saw Kyle Hazlewood loading up the Jaws of Life just as the robbery was happening. Right before Kenny got shot. We know from Larry Cobb that Kyle and Mickey have intimate knowledge of his house and his safe. And probable cause to fuck up his world."

"So what do you want, Lillie?" Rusty said. "What is it?"

"I want a search warrant based on probable cause," Lillie said. "I want to search Kyle's house and his workshop for evidence that he was busting in that safe last night. I don't want to give him another minute to make peace with what he did to Kenny or hide his handiwork. Do you understand how time is of the goddamn essence?"

Just then, one of his children—Taylor, Tyler, or Skylar—walked into the room in her pajamas, wanting to known when Daddy would come back and finish playing Scrabble. Fucking Scrabble. Maybe Rusty could make a play for the word I-N-C-O-M-P-E-T-E-N-T.

"I'll be right there, sweet thing," he said, patting her on the fanny. "Man talk."

Rusty grinned. Lillie didn't acknowledge his stupidity. "Come on, Rusty," Lillie said. "Let's do this. Make something happen right off. Make a name for yourself."

Rusty nodded, considering it. On television, the bridge was captured intact and Hitler was pissed as hell about it. For the next ten days, Adolf ordered the Luftwaffe to shell the shit out of it. Lillie waited for Rusty, seeing if he'd put on some pants and get on with things. Instead, he rubbed his jaw to simulate thinking that just wasn't happening. "I don't know," he said. "I don't know."

"Fuck me," Lillie said. "Can we at least try and get a warrant for their phone records, try and establish their communications that night?"

"How about we talk tomorrow, Lil," Rusty said. "Right now, I'd like to just wait and see. I think it's going to be interesting as all get-out to see what those ole boys do next."

"So you want to dig it up now?" Kyle said. "Christ. It's ten o'clock, man. You said not to touch this shit for a good long while. Pretend like we ain't never had that money and that maybe someday, maybe in a few years, we could take it out."

"Well," Mickey said. "Things've changed. Johnny Law's right on your ass. We need to move it or lose it. Or you want to wait until they come over with a fucking search warrant."

Mickey and Kyle stood face-to-face out back of Kyle's house, on his busted-ass porch, Mickey parking in a vacant lot down the road and doubling back. Kyle had been waiting but not really prepared, in a tired old blue bathrobe, smoking Marlboros, and drinking a Bud Light. Underneath the robe, he seemed to be naked except for a pair of boxer shorts and cowboy boots.

"They wouldn't have found that money," Kyle said. "I know what I'm doing."

"How about you just humor me?"

"You take what's yours, but I'm leaving mine right where it's at."

"That's not thinking," Mickey said. "That's not thinking at all."

"Well, maybe I hadn't figured out what I'm gonna do."

"What the hell you mean?"

"Maybe I should just give it back to Cobb," Kyle said. "I ain't no thief."

"Son of a bitch."

"Do what you need to do."

"You give that money back and they'll know it was me who put you on to it."

"How you figure?" Kyle said.

"What are you gonna do? Just knock on Larry Cobb's door and say I sure am sorry I busted through your fucking house and stole your million dollars?" Mickey said. "You don't think they'll have a few more questions?"

"I'd never say your name," Kyle said. "You know that. But what happened later. The mess of the thing. With Kenny and all. Shit."

Unbelievable. *Fucking unbelievable.* Mickey should've never gotten Kyle involved in this, knowing how weak he could get, gone to pieces as soon as the law started asking some questions. Kyle was a good man. But, god damn, he'd never learned to lie. Everybody who has any sense knows how to lie. You get through life lying, telling people what they want to hear and keeping your ass out of trouble.

"You're fucking up," Mickey said. "You know that?"

Kyle swallowed. His reddened cheeks sunk against the bone when he inhaled from the cigarette. He pulled the robe closer around him in the cold, taking a little plastic flashlight from his pocket and walking down the porch steps. "Come on. Grab that shovel."

Mickey picked up a shovel set against a chair and followed Kyle deep into his backyard, passing an old swing set that had belonged to the man's kids before they moved to Gulfport, and down around the big tin work shed he'd built himself. Mickey carried the shovel in one hand, following Kyle to the edge of the woods and a long patch of rocky ground strewn with river pebbles. Kyle got down on his knees and clawed at the dirt and stones, uncovering a round plastic top about the same size as a pickle bucket.

"You put the money in a septic tank?" Mickey asked.

"Know anyone want to root around in there?"

"Shit," Mickey said.

"Yes, sir," he said, flicking the cigarette far away so it wouldn't connect with the methane. Mickey handed him the shovel and he scooped the edge of the lip and popped the top, bringing forth an ungodly stench that made his eyes water. He stood back, took a breath, and handed Mickey back the shovel on one bad, cold night.

"Oh, God," Mickey said. "Hell, that stinks."

"I doubled 'em up in some Ziplocs inside of trash bags," Kyle said. "I tied 'em all tight with some fishing line and ran the line to where the PVC runs to the inlet. You can't even see it. The line is two hundred test. For sportfishing. Same line me and you bought down at the Gulf this summer."

"Good times," Mickey said, gripping the handle of the shovel tighter, as his friend got down on his knees again and reached his arm up to his elbow into the shit tank, feeling around for the fishing line. The smell was something terrific. Thank God for the cold air blowing it on down the road.

"I ain't cut out for this," Kyle said. "I'll get the money to Larry in a way he won't know it was me. You can do whatever you want. Buy a fucking yacht and some hoochie momma to rub you to bed. I won't stand in your way."

Mickey watched his humped back, the digging arm. "Appreciate you, man," he said.

The wind had kicked up good and cold from the north, scattering Kyle's blue robe off his skinny old legs and cowboy boots. The man wasn't paying attention, reaching deeper into that black hole, feeling around for that lost line. Mickey stood above him holding the shovel, spade up to the stars, watching his friend and listening to the gurgling deep inside.

"How was the beach?" Kyle said.

"Me and Tonya took a dip in the Gulf," he said. "Ice-cold."

"I wouldn't care," Kyle said. "Wouldn't mind putting a boat in and trolling around for some of them big bull redfish. You know, before the season's over."

"I'd like that."

"Yeah?" Kyle asked, looking back over his shoulder. He smiled up at Mickey, looking relieved, as he kept on feeling around in the dark and back down in the hole.

"Sure thing."

"Damn, this line is cutting the whale out of me," Kyle said. "You mind giving me a hand? Pass me that shovel."

Mickey set his feet good, lifted the shovel far overhead, and came down hard and fast against Kyle's skull. The sound wasn't unlike an egg breaking. Mickey felt sick, not sure if it was from the sound or the smell, but steadied himself, walking away from the hole and reaching for his phone and dialing up Peewee Sparks. "Y'all still in for a disposal job?"

27.

Rusty Wise had only been sheriff for fifteen days now, but Lillie was a bit irked that he'd spent more of his time buying gear for the office and himself than he had tracking down the shitbird thieves who'd shot Kenny. Today, coming on mid-January, Rusty was finally doing something, getting off his ass and driving over to fucking Gordo, Alabama. He'd made sure to wear his new four-in-one tactical jacket, paying two hundred and fifty for it because of all its many secret pockets and the internal sherpa liner. "You can even zip up both sides, depending on what side you'd draw your weapon," he'd told Lillie on the drive. Already carrying that Glock 19 on his hip, star on that fucking jacket, like he'd been wearing them half his life.

They were in an empty room together that morning, not unlike every cinder-block shithole interview room in the country. Fluorescent lights. Busted linoleum floor. The local police had pulled in a man named Bryson Joseph Sparks, aka Peewee, for them last night. After Kyle Hazlewood went missing a couple weeks ago, Lillie pulled his phone records, showing him and this Peewee fella burning up some airtime on New Year's Eve.

"Either they are in love or in cahoots," Lillie said.

"I never saw Hazlewood running," Rusty said. "Shoot. You were right, Lil. We should have brought him in right off. We had probable cause."

Lillie closed her mouth and took a sip of weak-ass coffee the locals had given her. They sat there and waited a good long while until B. J. "Peewee" Sparks was walked into the room and sat down in a metal ladderback chair. Lillie introduced herself and Sheriff Wise, hating calling him that but knowing it would mean something to a guy like Sparks.

He was a hefty-looking turd, sloppy and wild-haired, wearing cokebottle glasses and a sweatshirt for Tabasco reading *Laissez les bons temps rouler.* "Heard you just got back from New Orleans, Mr. Sparks," Lillie said. "You have a good time?"

"Ain't nothing else to do down in that place," Sparks said. "Them people sure know how to live."

"I guess you know why we're here and why we wanted to talk to you?" Lillie said.

"No, ma'am," Sparks said. "No, I don't. But you sure are a tall drink a water. How tall are you?"

"Five-ten," Lillie said. "How tall are you?"

"Tall enough to climb a solid gal," Sparks said. "Haw, haw."

Rusty Wise's face went white, expecting Lillie to jump out of her chair and throttle the fat man's neck. But men like Peewee Sparks never bothered her. They almost always made dumb-ass sexist comments like that because of a lifetime of rejection from women, including their own mothers, and some form of impotency. Violence would only be wasted on a broke-dick fella like Mr. Sparks.

"We'd like to know about your relationship with Kyle Hazlewood and Mickey Walls," she said.

"Who?"

Lillie opened up a manila folder and pushed forward Kyle Hazlewood's phone records with all the calls they'd exchanged that night highlighted in yellow. The relationship to Kyle was known, but she didn't know anything about this shitbird and Mickey. But nine times out of ten, they'll let it slip somehow, step forward and let you know.

Peewee took off his thick glasses, cleaned them with his hot sauce sweatshirt, and put them on, glancing through the records. He nodded and looked back up at Lillie. "Kyle Hazlewood," he said. "I thought you said Lee Hazlewood. Like the singer. I couldn't figure out how you'd think I'd known him."

"And Kyle?"

"Ah, he's just an ole drinking buddy," Peewee said. "I done some work with him. He was interested in me working a Sheetrock job down in Eupora."

"No kidding," Lillie said. "Must have been a hell of an important job. Y'all exchanged twenty-two different calls on December thirty-first and the early morning of January first. What are y'all, the Sheet-rockers to the Stars?"

"Just some ole fella down in Eupora."

"What's his name?"

"Hell, I don't know. Why don't you ask Hazlewood?"

"Can't find Hazlewood," Lillie said.

"I'm sure he'll turn up."

Rusty Wise smiled, arms resting over his belly and his new coat, and said, "Have you heard from him?"

Sparks ran a hand over the back of his neck, shaking his head. "Can't say I have, Sheriff," he said. "Did y'all check his house?"

Lillie took a long breath. She bit the inside of her cheek and reached for the phone records, stacking them back in the folder. "So when you and Kyle were talking the other night—"

"Wasn't the other night, darling," Sparks said. "It was two weeks ago."

Lillie's cheek jumped a bit. But she kept on smiling and leaned forward, pointing to the name on her uniform. "My name is Lillie Virgil," she said. "I'm the assistant sheriff and chief investigator in Tibbehah County, Mississippi. Have you ever been to Tibbehah County, Mr. Sparks?"

Sparks chuckled a bit. "No, sir," he said. "I mean, ma'am."

"We've also been looking for a young man named Chase Clanton," Rusty said. "Police here tell us he's your nephew."

"That's right."

"Do you know why he and Mr. Hazlewood might've been talking?" Rusty said, rushing ahead a bit. He needed to let damn Sparks answer where he'd been the other night.

"Figure it must've been about the same job."

"And where can we find your nephew?" Lillie said.

"Shit," Sparks said. "I don't know."

"And do you know where you were on December thirty-first and the morning of January first?"

Sparks snickered, leaned back in the chair, and stretched, giving a big old fake yawn. "Yes, ma'am," he said. "Y'all know I could get a lawyer. But I don't have nothing to hide. I'll tell you whatever it is you want to know."

"OK," Lillie said.

Lillie waited. Thank the Lord, Rusty Wise did not speak while they waited for the fat son of a bitch to fill the silence. Shitbirds couldn't help but talk in a vacuum. Sparks licked the side of his mouth like he'd left some jelly there, shuffled in his seat, and looked straight at Lillie Virgil. "Darlin', I was out hunting up some pussy."

"Is that a fact?" Lillie said. "Where'd you go for that pussy, Mr. Sparks?"

"Down to the Waffle House," he said. "Picked up a gal."

"Just like that?"

"Just like that," Sparks said.

"Women can't resist you?"

"No, ma'am," he said. "We started a-talking and one thing just kind of led to another. One minute she's pouring the syrup and the next she's shaking my pecker."

"And where'd you go for all this fun?"

"Shit, I got a party van," he said. "We were fucking all night long. Woman couldn't get enough of me. She tied me up and whipped my ass with a belt. Woman was wild."

Lillie closed her eyes and dropped her head into her fingers, massaging her forehead. Another bad headache coming on strong. "And what was this lucky lady's name?"

"Never got no name," Sparks said. "But she was a rich woman from Birmingham. Drove a big old Cadillac. I knew from the way she putting that syrup on her pancakes that she was ready for some riding. I had some sex jelly in my van and a pair of handcuffs. Hot damn. We was on."

Lillie just stared at the fat old man the same way you watch animals on a nature show. She wondered how the Good Lord could have fashioned such an all-purpose, nearly perfect human idiot. She waited a little more to hear about that rich woman from Birmingham, but Sparks didn't finish the story. She just stared at him, knowing this was going absolutely nowhere.

"So y'all just knocked boots and went on your way."

"Women want it same as men," Peewee said. "It's in the science."

"Rusty, you think you'd be good enough to get me a fresh cup of coffee?" Lillie said. "I think we're gonna be here for a little while."

I brought coffee and cigarettes," Quinn said.

"What more does a girl need?" Caddy said.

"Y'all got a Starbucks just down the road. You think we'll ever get a Starbucks in Jericho?"

"That might spoil the authentic atmosphere of the town," Caddy said. "Next thing you know, we just might be civilized."

"Two sugars and a lot of cream."

"Marlboro Lights?"

"Hardpacks," Quinn said, handing her a carton. "Better than flowers."

"Momma would be mad," Caddy said. "But after all the shit I've put in my body, that's like a good helping of vitamins for my system."

They walked into a courtyard together, today being the first day Quinn had visited the facility. It was a bright and cold morning with some sun and a lot of wind. The courtyard was vacant, with a couple picnic tables and a few tilled-up flower gardens spotted with concrete figurines of Saint Francis, Jesus, a baby deer, and two rabbits. The beds were littered with cigarette butts. There was a lot of trash in the dead grass, where people had been eating and pacing the ground.

"Aren't you going to ask me how I'm doing?"

"Nope."

"How I've been? What do the doctors say? Have I kicked the shit and saved my soul?"

"How about we just sit down?" Quinn said, sitting at the picnic table and lifting the lid off his coffee. He smiled across the way at Caddy, his sister looking better but still very pale and washed-out, the color of her hair like dishwater, and some scabbed-over sores still spotting her neck and face. Didn't take her two seconds to tear into the pack and light a cigarette.

"Momma and Jason came by yesterday," she said. "First time I've seen my son in more than two months. How about you get one of those coffee mugs for me? 'Mother of the Year.'"

"He was glad to see you," Quinn said. "He loves you. He doesn't care where you've been."

"Maybe not now," Caddy said. "But soon he'll have thoughts about me. Hear things about how his mother is a fucking crack whore."

Quinn reached out and grabbed her hand, squeezing. The wind shot across the table and shook the bare trees and bushes, blowing some loose trash along the sidewalks. He drank some coffee and let Caddy smoke, as the first thing she'd said was to complain about having to bum cigarettes off a meth head who only cared for American Spirits.

"Daddy wanted to come with me today," Quinn said. "But, shit. I don't know."

"You have more of a problem with him than I do."

"He left us," Quinn said. "And bad things happened. We spent a lot of time a couple years back pulling out that stuff and examining it with that doctor in Memphis. I figured that shit is still a part of what's going on and, if we're going to face it, it's going to be me and you. No one else knows what happened."

"Who's alive."

"That's right."

"Can you do me a favor?"

"Sure," Quinn said.

"Can we not talk about it," Caddy said. "My mind feels like a tangled web. I don't want to walk that path into the Big Woods again. There's so much I don't really remember. You helped me remember and it helped facing it. But that door is closed again and I'd just as soon keep it closed until I can breathe a little. Is that all right?"

Quinn nodded, reaching across the table and squeezing her hand again. Caddy smiled at him, her mouth small and chapped. She let out a long breath and shook her head. "You're wearing the same coat."

Quinn watched her.

"I don't recall much," she said. "But I remember that coat. Uncle

Hamp carried me out. I can still smell that ole tobacco suede. He was a big man, wasn't he?"

"I know you don't want to till it up," Quinn said. "But I have a lot of friends who are like you. You realize you walked into a war zone when you were a kid. It eats at you and you'll do anything to quiet your mind. I just don't want you to think it makes you weak. God damn, Caddy, do you know how many friends I have from the Regiment who are sick right now? Sometimes you get out intact, but sometimes you bring back the disease with you. It takes a lot of time. And a lot of help."

"I thought I was beyond it," Caddy said. "But I lost something."

"Dixon?"

Caddy looked him dead in the eye, blowing out smoke. "A fucking purpose."

W
ell," Rusty Wise said, sitting in the passenger seat of Lillie's Jeep. "That was a gosh-dang waste of time."

"Rusty?"

"Yes, ma'am?"

"You do realize it's going to be tough as hell to be sheriff and remain such a nice, clean-mouth fella."

"I do."

"That the job might turn you, make you a little nastier, a little meaner, and that one morning you might just wake up yelling, 'God damn, son of a bitch'?"

"Could happen."

"There is hope," Lillie said, taking Highway 45 north, back up to the Jericho exit, passing Rebel Truck Stop billboards every half mile. BEST CHICKEN-FRIED STEAK IN MISSISSIPPI. NATIVE AMERICAN GIFTS. LINGERIE AND MORE.

"Did you get anything out of that?" Rusty said. "That man couldn't stop lying. Every word that came out of his mouth."

"Oh, you didn't buy that he was a massive poon hound and that women just couldn't wait to jump into his rolling party van?"

"Just like that," Rusty said. "Man says he walked into a Waffle House and walks out with some rich gal who just want to get it on with him."

"The man isn't exactly George Clooney."

"He's not even George Gobel," Rusty said, staring at the road ahead, fiddling with the zippers on his new jacket. "And, Good Lord. The smell of him. I don't think he's seen a bar of soap in ages. Dirty fingernails and hands. I couldn't stand another minute in that room with him."

"He liked you," Lillie said. "Told you to call him the next time he was in Gordo, that y'all could grab some beers."

"The next time I see that man, I want to be leading him into the courthouse."

"He did the job," Lillie said.

"Of course he did."

"But he wouldn't say shit if his mouth was full of it."

"And neither will Mickey Walls and neither will Kyle Hazlewood, wherever he's gone to. Why didn't we arrest Kyle, like you said? If we had him, we could have applied some good pressure, got a search warrant before he cleaned up his house and shop."

"Live and learn, skipper," Lillie said. "No telling where those turds took that safe to bust it open. No prints on the backhoe or in the Cobb house. They probably cleaned the shit out of Kyle's shop before we finally got to it."

"How many calls between them?"

"Two dozen calls between Sparks, Kyle, and Mickey, and that kid Chase Clanton."

"The chief in Gordo said that the boy had some kind of learning disability," Rusty said. "Said his daddy was some kind of hood, serving a twenty-year stretch for manslaughter."

"Good people," Lillie said. "Just good ole country people."

"Can I ask you something?"

"Shoot," Lillie said.

"Did this job change you? Being around so many liars and thieves? Killers and such?"

Lillie shook her head, letting down her side window and getting some fresh air into the Jeep. "Not really. I've always recognized the human circus and all the wonderful creeps you meet on the way to Oz."

"Even as a kid?"

"Yes, sir."

A sign read twenty-eight miles to Jericho, just before another Rebel Truck Stop billboard with a big-titted woman pressing a finger to her lips. PSST, SEE YOU AT THE BOOBY TRAP. The next billboard reading WHAT ARE YOUR EYES FIXED UPON? LET US FIX OUR EYES UPON JESUS!

"Jesus, titties, and guns," Lillie said. "How I love north Mississippi."

"Are other places that different?"

"You need to get out more, Rusty," Lillie said. "See the world."

Five miles to the Jericho exit, her cell phone rang. She picked it up and talked to Ike McCaslin for a good two minutes, then set the phone down on the console and stole a quick glance at Rusty Wise. She found a good place to slow down, a worn path in the median, to run down in a gulley and then turn back onto the southbound highway, heading down to Highway 82.

"What is it?"

"We ran those numbers for Hazlewood, Sparks, and Clanton," she said. "Not only were they talking but all of them were pinging off the same cell tower."

Rusty didn't say anything, holding on to the passenger door, as Lillie bucked up onto the road and mashed the accelerator. "There's only one tower near Cobb's place and all three were bouncing off it."

"Shit," Rusty said.

Lillie smiled. "Yes, sir," she said. "Let's go snatch up that fat bastard's ass and bring him back to Jericho."

"And call back Ike," Rusty said. "Tell him to get an arrest warrant for Hazlewood and Mickey Walls. Walls is a part of all this now."

28.

You know I've been here for damn-near eighteen hours?" Chase Clanton said. "I did everything a man can do at a fucking Flying J truck stop. I ate dinner and breakfast at Denny's, played twenty dollars' worth of quarters in that arcade, Pac-Man and Deer Hunter, done some laundry and took a hot shower."

"Good for you," Uncle Peewee said. The two, sitting side by side back at the Denny's, facing Daniel Payne Road, not but a few hundred feet from Interstate 65 outside Birmingham.

"Middle of all that, I was asked to leave the Denny's for complaining about the food, nearly got run over by a Kenworth, and got propositioned twice by two ole truckers who thought I had a mouth like a little girl. What kind of hellhole is this place?"

"It's a truck stop," Uncle Peewee said, chawing down on a Denny's hamburger. "Watch your wallet and your cornhole. These folks live on the hard side of the highway."

"Where we headed now?"

"Don't know," Peewee said. "But the police in Gordo have a warrant out for you and for me. When they pulled me in, I thought they were going to toss me in a cell. Instead, some big dyke deputy and dumb-ass sheriff played Twenty Questions about my whereabouts on New Year's Eve."

"You tell him?"

"Hell, no," Peewee said, reaching for a French fry. "Shit, man. You think your grandmomma raised her some retard? I told them a story that they can't prove or disprove. But it got them thinking about them being wrong. That maybe I wadn't in fucking Jericho, Mississippi, but in the back of my party van getting my knob shined."

"What?"

"Fucking," Peewee said. "I told them I met a woman and we were fucking."

Chase sucked on his chocolate milk shake, swiping the cherry and biting it off the stem. He imagined Uncle Peewee riding some young *Playboy* model in the back of the van, the whole thing shaking up and down, about to bust the shocks. In his mind, he could see his uncle's hairy back and bald spot, fat ass pumping that woman. The girl would be startled and gasping for air, moaning with pleasure. And Chase started to laugh, nearly choking on that cherry.

"What?" Peewee asked.

"Thought of you getting it on."

"What's so goddamn funny about that?" Peewee said. "You know how much sex that van has seen? I thought about marking 'em off on the fender, like a fighter pilot with kills."

"I just saw a show on television about a man about your age," Chase said. "He was having a hard time meeting women so he went and ordered one of those Japanese sex dolls. Damn, those things look real. A few of them are the same shape and size as porno stars. One of the fellas said he liked having a sex doll better because a rubber woman don't sass him. He dresses her, bathes her, takes her out in a wheelchair. Can you believe his family supports him? Calls it his life decision?"

"What the hell are you talking about, kid?" Peewee said, pushing the rest of the hamburger and fries away. "God damn."

"I'm just saying it must be hard and all to meet girls."

"I meet them all the time," Peewee said. "I meet most of them on-line. It's easier than ordering a pizza. You also go to places where you can get on a pussy hunt. Like a beer joint or Bible study. Places women go to find a man. I had lots of luck there. I met this one woman at the Baptist church who'd just lost her husband in a chainsaw accident. Damn, I never met a woman more raring to go. We was reading from the book of Colossians and got to that passage about how a woman should service her husband."

"Don't you mean 'serve'?" Chase said. "I never read nothing about a man getting serviced in the Bible."

"Same damn thing," Peewee said. "When the pastor got to that part, all of us sitting in a big wide circle, her eyes met mine and we were on, brother. I knew right then and there it was a damn done deal. Hard part was waiting through all that talking and praying, drinking coffee and eating cookies, until I could walk her out to the parking lot."

"And she just jumped into the van?"

"You better believe it."

Chase slurped some more of the shake, watching all the cars and big trucks go past on the boulevard, snaking out toward the interstate to Birmingham, down to Montgomery, and on to Mobile Bay. "Uncle Peewee?"

"Yes, sir?"

"What the hell are we gonna do?"

"Don't know."

"We got blood on our hands."

"Hush up."

"What we did with that fella's body," Chase said. "Sweet Jesus."

"I said hush your mouth."

"We ain't going back to Gordo," Chase said. "Are we?"

His Uncle Peewee just shook his head, not saying nothing, not seeming to be looking at anything in particular. He raised his hand and asked his waitress if he could get a refill of his Pepsi.

Stagg found Ringold out back of the Rebel, loading hickory wood into the barbecue pit with big black Midnight Man. Both men were sweating, as they'd chopped and stacked a cord of wood, keeping the fire going good and stoked orange-hot. Stagg never trusted a barbecue joint that didn't smoke their meat each and every day, the smell of the pit the best advertising a place can have. "How you doin', boys?"

"Smokin' turkey legs," Midnight Man said in that gruff, deep way of speaking. "Ribs. Cracklins. You want me to save you some?"

"I'd appreciate that, sir," Stagg said, patting Midnight Man on the back of his sweaty white undershirt. The man wandering on into the kitchen, knowing Stagg didn't come to Ringold to talk about pork plates.

Ringold slid his tattooed arms back into a green canvas jacket. He wore a ball cap that day, WINCHESTER ARMS. "Yes, sir?"

"Police issued four warrants," Stagg said. "Couple turds over in Alabama. And Kyle Hazlewood and our buddy Mickey Walls. Heard anything from Walls?"

"We didn't leave our last meet on good terms."

"You hurt him bad?"

"Didn't leave any marks."

"But you got his attention?"

"I did," Ringold said. "Although he kept on denying any part in it."

"Sheriff's office got hold of some cell phone records that show all four of those turds were working together," Stagg said. "They believe Mickey Walls orchestrated the whole thing while screwing Cobb's daughter down in Gulf Shores. How's that for getting back at her daddy?"

Ringold just nodded. Most of the time, Stagg could get a good read on a person, but with Ringold it was damn-near impossible. His eyes were a cold and clear blue, almost washed of all color at all. He never knew the man to laugh or be pissed-off, living in a state without any emotion at all.

"I talked to Walls twice," Ringold said. "Next time, he'll have to bleed a little more."

The iron door to the barbecue pit was open and Stagg watched the new pieces of hickory catch fire and burn down to embers. Stagg walked over to the fire, squatted down, and rubbed his hands into its warmth. The chimney above the truck stop pumped out hickory smoke just in time for the lunch rush. "Leave him be," Stagg said. "Now that the law is involved, I don't want us nowhere near him. I've done business with Walls. He ain't that smart, but he's no moron, either."

"He won't admit to a thing."

"Just how did you try and get his attention?" Stagg asked, grinning a little.

"Laid his hand on a tile saw and threatened to slice off a few fingers."

"How'd he like that?"

"He screamed a little," Ringold said, reaching into his pocket for a cigar and burning the tip with a big stainless steel lighter. There was something in the gesture of the lighting, the tobacco smoke trailing from his mouth, that reminded Stagg a great deal of Quinn Colson. He got up off his haunches and placed his warm hands into his khaki pockets, rocking back on his heels.

"All you Army boys smoke or dip?"

"Keeps your mind sharp," Ringold said.

"In some ways, you and Colson are cut from the same cloth," Stagg said. "The attitude. The training. Y'all have similar characteristics."

"Maybe," Ringold said. "But we think a lot different."

"How's that?"

"I'm a realist, Mr. Stagg," Ringold said, grinning. "Colson just could never wrap his head around what a good deal he could've had."

How can anyone live like this?" Lillie said. "This place is a complete shithole."

"Certainly misses a woman's touch," Rusty Wise said, standing next to Mickey Walls's eighty-inch television and surveying the mess of beer cans, pizza boxes, and empty bottles of Jack. Lillie acted as if she hadn't heard him, just trying to take in the kitchen, the living room, the two bedrooms piled high with more shit they'd have to search.

"It misses a human's touch," Lillie said. "Pass me that bottle next to your toe. If he and those boys were knocking a few back, maybe we can get some prints."

They'd been there nearly an hour with Ike McCaslin and two men from the MBI in Batesville. They were walking Walls's backyard with some kind of electronic tools to spot if anything might have been buried. "What the hell is this?" Rusty said, reaching for a DVD on the coffee table. "*Lesbian Cheerleaders 4*? I don't know Mickey real well but never figured him for a pervert."

"Maybe it's an art movie."

"Not from the looks of the pictures on the back," Rusty said. "Lord Almighty. Looks like she's getting a pelvic exam."

"I get the idea, Rusty."

"Reminds me of a gosh-dang frat house," Rusty said. "No rules. No one giving a damn about picking up their clothes or food. No Momma telling them what to do. You see the mess of bills by the telephone? Looks like some creditors onto him real hard."

"He was about to lose the flooring business," Lillie said. "At least

that's what Larry Cobb says. Cobb says he was about to cut off his supply. If you were him, where would you hide that money?"

"Well, we'll know more when we get his bank statements," Rusty
said.

"You think he rolled on up to the teller and unloaded a few hundred
grand?" Lillie said. "If he did, I hope to hell he got a free toaster. Or at
least a sucker."

"What would you do with that much money?"

"I'd get the hell out of Jericho," Lillie said. "I'd change my hair and
my name and leave the damn county. I'd go and raise my daughter in a
better place."

"Shoot," Rusty said. "You know that's not true. You know you love
Jericho and Tibbehah County more than anyone. You wouldn't do
all this hard work for nothing. This is your home. You want to see that
folks follow the law."

"That's me, Lillie Virgil, goddamn civic leader," Lillie said. "Remember that shit at the next pancake breakfast."

Rusty laughed and shook his head, looking a bit lost in Mickey
Walls's swirling chaos. In a back room, Ike McCaslin was searching in
closets and under the beds. Lillie knew one of them, probably not Rusty,
was going to have to crawl under the house next. In her mind, she could
see Rusty getting stuck under the crossbeams and her having to hook
his boots to her Jeep and pull him out.

Lillie had started to unzip couch cushions, knowing she wouldn't
find anything but some bottle caps and old pretzels, but wanting to go
through the process. Room by room. Inch by inch. She wanted everything done right before they allowed Mickey to come back. Rusty had
moved on back to the kitchen and took a handful of bills and loaded
them into a cardboard box. "Lillie?"

She looked up.

"I wanted to apologize for my behavior the other day," Rusty said.

"What I said wasn't any of my business, one way or another. I was trying to make a point, but sometimes my words get jumbled up in my mouth."

"Don't worry about it."

"I meant what I said about you loving Jericho," he said. "It might be as corny as all get-out, but I love it, too. When I moved down to Columbus, it wasn't home. I liked being a lawman and not having to sell dang insurance and all. But coming back here, raising my family where I was raised, really means something. Y'all are my people."

"Was it the new Walmart that sold you?"

"Shoot," Rusty said. "You know what I mean."

"Sure," Lillie said. "This place definitely has a peculiar kind of charm. Where else could you meet creeps like these?"

"You think Mickey'll talk?"

"Let's give him some time to think on things," Lillie said. "We both know it's going to take a good long while to find that money. But he doesn't know about those cell towers placing his three boys near the Cobb place."

"Calls back and forth to Hazlewood ain't enough."

"Nope," Lillie said. "But that dumb son of a bitch doesn't know it. God damn it. If we could just find Kyle, I'd play those bastards off on one another. It could be beautiful."

"What's your best guess?"

"For Kyle?"

Rusty nodded. He lifted the box up in his chubby little arms to take it back out to the sheriff's truck.

"Do you really want me to say it?"

29.

That afternoon, the horses arrived.

Jason had unloaded them from the trailer and turned them loose into the open field behind the farmhouse. For the last two weeks, he'd mended fences, tested the gates, and finished the roof on the barn. The outside needed painting but would do fine until spring. Once where there'd been only cattle, now the farm had a couple Appaloosas and an American paint horse named Bandit in honor of Burt Reynolds.

Quinn's father was out back with them now, along with little Jason and Anna Lee's daughter. The kids climbed the slat-rail fence and rubbed their hands between the giant animal's eyes. Jason had shown the children the proper way to feed a horse, flat of hand, so they didn't get bit.

"Nice," Anna Lee said. "Isn't it?"

They were seated in Quinn's living room, which at one time had probably been called a parlor. Over the years, the room had seen family members laid out on cooling boards, the arrival of a gramophone, and now a flat-screen television hung on the old beaded board. Above the fireplace was a dual gun rack filled with a vintage Winchester and an old Enfield rifle Quinn had bartered for in Afghanistan. The Enfield had been taken from the British more than a century ago and inlaid with mother-of-pearl by the Afghanis, or, as the chieftain who sold it said, "Made it our own." There were a lot of black-and-white photos of the Beckett family and a few of Quinn's time in the service. Caddy. Jason. Jean. Dead Hamp Beckett.

"You think y'all can stay for supper?" Quinn asked.

"Don't see why not."

"I told him no horses."

"But he brought them over anyway?" Anna Lee said.

"He didn't have anywhere else to put them," Quinn said. "I have the land. But you just wait, I'll be taking care of them full-time."

"You think he's going somewhere?"

"You never know with Jason Colson."

"He seems to be doing fine," Anna Lee said. "He's good with kids."

"He's always been good with kids. And animals," Quinn said. "And jumping over shit."

"Y'all look just alike," Anna Lee said. "And even little Jason. You can tell it's his granddaddy. That all y'all are related."

"You know, he asked me this morning about Caddy," Quinn said. "He wanted to know when his momma was going to get well. And quit poisoning herself. I never told him anything. Momma wouldn't say anything more than Caddy was down with the flu."

"Kids know things."

"Caddy's worried the state will try and take him away."

"They can't do that."

"She could lose her rights," Quinn said. "If Jean wanted to push things, she could get a lawyer and become Jason's legal parent."

"But she won't."

"She couldn't do it to Caddy," Quinn said. "No matter how many times she falls, Jean believes it's only temporary."

"I know y'all love her," Anna Lee said. "But as Jason grows up, you're going to have to make some tough decisions. She falls again and it's going to mess him up bad."

Quinn walked over to the window and looked through the old leaded glass, making the image of the kids on the fence seem wavy and unreal. Old Jason was on Bandit now, riding bareback, galloping around the mud and cow dung, cowboy hat raised high like Buffalo Bill Cody. The kids clapped. Quinn didn't speak.

"Maybe I'm not one to talk," Anna Lee said.

"If it comes to it, I'll take Jason," Quinn said. "Caddy and I have always had that understanding. Ever since she came back from Memphis, I promised her I'd always look out for him."

"What did she say this morning?"

"We just talked," Quinn said. "She complained about some alcoholic guitar player who did nothing but pluck away at 'Stairway to Heaven.' I brought her coffee and a carton of cigarettes."

"That's all y'all talked about?"

"That and all that happened when we were kids."

"'All that happened' covers a lot of ground," Anna Lee said. "I know something bad happened to Caddy. You've told me that much. But in all the years we've been together, you never really said what. You one time told me she had problems with boys because she'd been molested as a child. But you never said when or who did it."

"It's not something I like to talk about," Quinn said. "Besides, it's her story to tell."

"Whoever did it must be dead," Anna Lee said, giving a nervous laugh. "Because, knowing you, you'd hunt him up and kill him yourself."

Quinn didn't speak. He watched his father step Bandit forwards and then walk him backwards. He patted the animal's neck and led him back over to the fence and little Jason and Shelby. Both of the kids had

on jeans and boots, heavy wool coats and hats. Quinn let the lace curtains fall away in his hands and turned back to Anna Lee on the couch.

"That's it," Anna Lee said.

"What?"

"You killed the son of a bitch."

Quinn sat down in an old leather chair by the fire. The chair had
come from Judge Blanton's estate sale, as well as a couple tall barrister
bookshelves on the far wall filled with books Quinn loved and books
he planned to read. There was Hemingway, a lot of Russians, sport and
hunting books, and the good old stuff from the Greeks. A big red kilim
rug lay spread out under the furniture, where Hondo had found a place
to sleep. Quinn reached down and patted the dog's head.

"I like being here with you," Quinn said.

"How old were you?"

"How about we talk about supper. Or horses."

"How old were you?"

Quinn met her eyes. They were dark brown and sleepy and knew
him better than anyone. She had her fingers to her mouth, waiting for
him to answer her.

"I was ten," he said. "I had shot deer out of season and a game warden had come for me. Caddy followed me into the National Forest and
we thought we could run away."

"But he came for you?"

"It was raining and there was this barn," Quinn said. "He'd tied me
up but left his shotgun. He left it in a corncrib so he could get to Caddy."

Johnny Stagg was just about to take off for the evening when Mickey
Walls walked into his office and stood in the doorway, not sure if he
had the right to enter. Stagg pointed to a chair in front of his desk and
Walls sat down. The boy looked wrung-out and nervous as hell. Man

didn't even seem to take notice of all those framed photographs of famous Mississippians on his wall. Just the other day he'd added LeAnn Rimes to the wall after one of his dancers told Stagg she was born in Jackson.

"That linoleum you laid is holding up fine, sir," Stagg said.

"Glad you like it," Walls said, face sweaty, eyes bloodshot. "Armstrong Commercial. Tough as it gets. But I need your help with something, Mr. Stagg. I didn't want to call, have this conversation to be heard by anyone. To be honest, I don't know if the police got some wiretaps on me."

"On account of that Cobb business."

"I didn't rob Larry Cobb," Walls said. "Hell, I wasn't even in the state."

"Uh-huh."

"The cops don't believe me," Walls said. "That big woman Lillie Virgil and that fat little turd Rusty Wise are over at my property right now, going through my personal things."

"They got a warrant?"

"Of course they got a warrant," Walls said. "I'm not going to let the law root through my underwear unless they got some paper."

"Sit down."

"I'm good."

"I said sit down, Mickey," Stagg said. "You want a Coca-Cola or some barbecue? Midnight Man has been barbecuing all damn day. I think he made too many ribs. We never get a rush on ribs midweek. But, good God, how that meat falls off the bone. Melts in your mouth."

"I need you to get them off my back," Walls said. "You need to let them know I'm not a part of this. Talk to Sheriff Wise or Larry Cobb. Or whoever. But they're making me a damn nervous wreck. Shit, I can't work. My business is suffering. People are whispering that I had something to do with Kenny getting shot. God damn, I wasn't even in the state. How the hell could I rob a man from two hundred miles away?"

"They saying you're an accomplice? The ole finger man?"

"Something like that."

"Uh-huh."

"Come on, Mr. Stagg," Mickey Walls said. "You know me. You knew my daddy. You politicked for him when he ran for tax collector. My momma used to wait tables out here. She plays bridge with your wife. You ain't never used anyone else for your carpeting and flooring needs but Walls."

"You met my needs, son," Stagg said. "Sure do appreciate you."

"They're out there now," Walls said. "In my fucking house, taking shit out in boxes. There are state police over at my office, taking over my computer and looking at my hard drive and emails. I don't want anyone to see those. I have some special memories with Tonya on there. Bedroom photos of me and her, if you know what I'm saying."

"I think you got more to worry about than some policeman looking at your ex-wife's cooch," Stagg said, leaning back into his executive chair and laying his tasseled loafers on the edge of the desk. "Just what did you go and hide?"

"Nothing," Walls said. "God damn, it's hot in here. Damn. Listen, I don't have that money. But you got to hold up your end of the deal in this."

Stagg tilted his head. He reached into a coffee cup for a fresh peppermint candy. "We ain't got no deal, son."

"Didn't you send that crazy bearded bastard out to see me?" Walls said. "The one with all those wild tattoos down his arm?"

Stagg sucked on the peppermint, getting rid of the sour taste in his mouth. He lifted his chin, listening and waiting for the Walls boy to explain how the hell he thought they had a connection.

"That man threatened to cut off my fingers," Walls said. "When I wouldn't admit I'd stole from Cobb, he told me he'd put my goddamn pecker under a table saw and mail home my parts to Tonya. He wasn't joking about it. The man has crazy eyes."

"Don't I know it."

"So you admit you sent him?"

Stagg didn't answer. He wondered when Ringold would be back from town, maybe needing him to escort old Mickey Walls out of the Rebel. Walls leaned in, looking over his shoulder at the empty doorway and then back at Stagg. "You got what you wanted," Walls said. "Just give me some space to breathe."

Stagg felt a little poke at his heart, face filling with blood. "Slow down, slow down. Speak English. Just what did you hand over to Mr. Ringold?"

"Don't you know?"

Chase thought they were home free until they hit signs for Satsuma, Alabama, and noticed that highway patrolman shagging their ass. "You see him?" Chase said.

Peewee turned down the Toby Keith CD they'd been playing since Montgomery, "Drunk Americans" blaring full tilt, and glanced back in the van's side-view mirror. "Yes, sir," Peewee said. "I spotted that bastard about five miles back. I can't tell if he's following us or we just headed in the same direction."

"He don't seem to be in no hurry."

"We can just keep on riding down into Mobile or we can take the next exit and see if he follows."

"You ever been to Satsuma?" Chase said. "Don't look like much."

"I've been to Creola," Peewee said. "I fished the Mobile River one time and some of those bayous around here. Didn't catch nothing but the daughter of the fella who sold us gas. Boy, let me tell you something, that barefoot country gal sure knew how to work my pump."

"Uncle Peewee?"

"Yes, sir," he said, keeping that needle set down at sixty, easy and steady in the slow lane.

"You ever been somewhere you didn't get laid?"

"Haw, haw," Peewee said. "I'm gonna duck on down into ole Satsuma and see if that motherfucker tails us. I can't stand for him to be riding up on my asshole for the next fifty miles. At Mobile's where we take the interstate over to New Orleans and head on back to Bourbon Street. Yes, sir. Yes, sir. Temptations, here we come."

Peewee turned on his blinker and slowed down to fifty, sliding on off 65 and onto the road running into the downtown. Satsuma looked like any other town off the highway. There was an Arby's, a Subway, McDonald's, Waffle House, and a big sign for some place nearby called CATFISH JUNCTION. They hadn't eaten since back at the Denny's truck stop, but Chase didn't mention it, as that patrol car had gotten off the interstate with them, riding slow and easy past the Pintoli's Italian restaurant, China Chef, and Los Tres Amigos. Not making a move, but not slowing down, neither.

"What's he doing?" Chase said.

"Bird-dogging us."

"What're we gonna do?"

"Shake his ass," Peewee said. "Soon as I find the right road."

"You shake him and they'll know where we at."

"Hell, I know," he said. "I know. But we got to do something before we hit a goddamn roadblock. I'll pick us up another vehicle."

"How's that?"

"Son," Peewee said. "Before I was a safe man, I used to lift cars. I stole cars and semis all over Alabama and north Mississippi. We had a chop shop up in Corinth where you got cash on the barrelhead. Fine times."

"He's on us."

"I got fucking eyes," Peewee said. "Watching him in the mirror. But I ain't gonna jackrabbit off this road until he gives us cause."

Chase felt like he might get sick, reaching up under his hoodie and finding the gun he'd used to shoot the deputy. He'd told Peewee he'd tossed it in a pond back in Gordo, but he couldn't let it go. He felt the slick trigger, rough handle, knowing it was stacked and reloaded, ready to rip. Chase swallowed a bit, watching that patrol car nosing up toward their bumper, Peewee stopping at a light.

"Shit, he's got us," Chase said.

"Sure looks that way," Peewee said. "Cornholed in Satsuma."

"We gonna run?"

"Ain't nothin' left to do."

Peewee looked to be sweating a little, glancing to the highway before him and the patrol car behind him. He gripped the party van's wheel, and Chase believed the old man was about to put the pedal to the metal and speed on away from this son of a bitch and back into the nooks and crannies of Satsuma, Alabama, where they could steal some boring-ass Chevy. Damn, he hated to see the van go.

The light turned green and Peewee rolled out steady and low, following that highway for a half mile, before that dang patrolman turned his ass into a fucking Taco Bell and headed to the drive-thru for a fucking Doritos Cheesy Gordita.

"Praise Jesus," Chase said.

"We got to dump the van."

"Come on, now," Chase said. "Let's not rush it."

"Boy, we got half the state of Alabama out looking for the faces of Bear Bryant, Nick Saban, and AJ McCarron painted along the side of an Econoline. You want to take a bet on how long it takes to find us?"

30.

Two days after interviewing the fat man Peewee Sparks over in Gordo, Alabama, Lillie brought Mickey Walls back into the sheriff's office for a sit-down. No one had seen Sparks, his nephew Chase, or Kyle Hazlewood since warrants had been issued. They had a little leverage on Walls, some new evidence, but Hazlewood had been her ace in the hole. Kyle was halfway human. Mickey Walls didn't seem to give a good goddamn for anyone but Mickey Walls.

Today he'd brought his lawyer with him, a slick, bald-headed man from Memphis who rapped in his firm's commercials for local TV. They hadn't been in the room but five minutes and the lawyer had referred to Mickey as "Mr. Walls" no less than twenty times. Lillie recalled the rap going something like *Your business partner left and took all your money. / Your wife just split and got another honey. / You need a lawyer. / Yeah! Yes, you do. / You need a lawyer.*

"Always wanted to ask," Lillie said. "Do you write your own material? Or you hire someone for those commercials?"

"You can make fun all you want," the bald lawyer said. "But you remember it. Can't forget me."

"I have a mind for faces," Lillie said. "I just hate cluttering it up, is all."

Sheriff Wise walked through the open door and shut it behind him. In the corner, Lillie had set a little video camera on a tripod to take in everyone at the table, a condenser mic set in the center. Mickey Walls looked like shit. He was wearing pajama bottoms with a MISSISSIPPI STATE sweatshirt and work boots.

"Some new information has come to light," Rusty said, hands folded in front of him, earnest grin on his face. "We wanted to give Mickey— I mean, Mr. Walls—a second chance at helping us with the investigation. I've got an important member of our community wanting answers, a shot-up deputy who may always walk with a gimpy leg, and now we have three men connected to this crime running loose as fugitives. We just are looking for a little direction, Mickey."

"How many times does Mr. Walls have to tell you he's not involved?" the bald lawyer said.

"So you don't know Peewee Sparks or Chase Clanton?" Rusty said.

Mickey looked to the lawyer and the lawyer nodded.

"No, sir."

"You at least know Kyle Hazlewood, right?" Lillie said.

"You know I do."

"You heard from him?" Rusty said.

"Not in a long while," Mickey said. "I told you I'd help out if I did. I don't know what he's mixed up in, but I want to help him and y'all out."

"Appreciate that, Mickey," Lillie said. "You're real stand-up."

"Like I said, Mr. Walls doesn't need to be here," the lawyer said. "The only reason he agreed is that he wants to help law enforcement get some kind of justice. But I need to warn you, his business has suffered as well as his reputation. If you want to arrest him, I recommend you do it now. Because this cloud of suspicion over his head is taking money away from my client and food from his kids."

"He doesn't have kids," Lillie said. "Do you, Mick?"

Mickey shook his head. Man, he looked like hell. He hadn't shaved for a few days and had obviously slept in his clothes. He stunk, too. Lillie could smell him from across the table, wanting to issue him a bar of soap and toothbrush and let him head on over to the jail. If they couldn't arrest him, maybe they could just hose him off in the parking lot.

"We know you and Kyle were talking on New Year's Eve," Lillie said. "Kyle's phone records show y'all calling back and forth twelve times. You talked six times after midnight on the first."

Mickey wouldn't look up from the table, he just nodded along to show he was listening.

"I think you've already established Mr. Walls and Hazlewood are friends," the lawyer said. "Don't you call your friends on New Year's Eve?"

"Not a dozen times," Lillie said. "That would annoy the shit out of me."

"I thought you folks were headed somewhere new," the lawyer said. "My client is very tired."

"We want to ask him about Peewee Sparks and Chase Clanton," Rusty said.

"He told you he never met those gentlemen," the lawyer said. "Never heard their names."

"I met Peewee Sparks," Lillie said. "I assure you, he's no gentleman."

"Regardless, I don't understand why you wanted my client to return to the sheriff's office," the lawyer said. "As I've said, this presents an air of guilt in a small community. Money is lost. Trust is eroded."

"Do you know them?" Lillie said.

Mickey looked to the lawyer. The lawyer again gave his blessing.

"No, never met them."

"Have they ever been in your house?" Lillie said.

"He said he didn't know them," the lawyer said.

Rusty Wise stood up, really getting into the role of sheriff now, even Lillie finding his act credible in some small way. He walked away from the table and stretched off camera but spoke loud enough for all of them to hear. "Funny, we got a bunch of beer cans and likker bottles out of your house with those boys' prints all over them," Rusty said. "Looks like y'all had a hell of a party, watching football and maybe some adult films."

"Bullshit."

"We got 'em," Lillie said. "So why don't you quit jerking us around, Mickey. You lied about knowing Sparks and Clanton, and you lied about talking to Kyle. You ran the whole damn operation from down in Gulf Shores, and when it went to hell, you boogied on back up the highway to get things straight. You want me to keep going?"

"What else do you have?" the lawyer said. "Because I'm not hearing a word that links my client to a shooting of your deputy or the burglary of Mr. Cobb. If we're done here, I need to get on back to Memphis."

"Shooting another commercial?" Lillie said. "Can't wait."

"Mickey?" Rusty said, leaning onto the conference table, mouth close to the mic. "We're going to go ahead and place you under arrest for working as an accomplice to the robbery of Mr. Cobb. But I'll tell you, I'm working like hell to show you were running those sonsabitches when they shot Kenny. I'll nail your ass for that."

Lillie smiled. She looked up at Rusty Wise with a grin to show her appreciation of his cussing and sticking it to Walls like he needed.

"Y'all are making a hell of a big mistake," the lawyer said. "Do you know how much revenue this man has lost already?"

"Mickey?" Lillie said. "You want to say something?"

Mickey looked down at the table, head slung down, rounded back and flat face. He shook his head and closed his eyes. "I'm just tired," he said. "I'm so goddamn tired."

"I know you want to help," Lillie said.

"Mr. Walls—" the attorney said.

"I didn't want to," Mickey said.

"Mr. Walls—" the attorney said.

"They came over," Mickey said, not moving a bit, speaking in almost a whisper. "Kyle wanted to get back at Cobb after what he'd done. He brought along those two boys from Alabama. They had a plan, they wanted me to be a part of it."

"And what did you say?" Lillie said.

"I told Kyle I didn't want no part of it," Mickey said. "I tried to get him to change his mind. I wanted to help him. I told him those two boys were bad news and they'd sell him out for a nickel."

"Do you think he's dead?" Rusty said.

Mickey stayed silent for a half minute. A tear ran down his left cheek as he then said, "Can someone get me a glass of water? Damn it, Kyle was a good man. One of my best friends."

Johnny Stagg pulled into the Piggly Wiggly on his way home, his wife telling him he needed to pick up a bottle of Diet Pepsi, a loaf of Wonder Bread, and some Triscuits. He parked in the cripple space, since he had one of those tags hanging from his ElDo's rearview. Ain't no one in Jericho gonna ask Johnny Stagg if he had the right or was he a cripple, they'd just assume it was something official. Stagg had crawled out, heading to the Pig's front door, when he saw that official black car slide down the row of cars and park right behind his Cadillac. The Trooper got out of his vehicle, nodding to Stagg, leaving his fucking door open and engine running like Johnny was supposed to hop up into the car like a dog or some truck stop whore.

"Come on, Stagg," the Trooper said as he'd gotten within earshot.

"No, sir," Stagg said. "I don't think so. Last time I seen you, you put a nine-millimeter in my mouth like it was a man's peter. I think I'll go about my grocery shopping without any interference."

"Didn't you make a call to the good senator?"

"That's between me and him," Stagg said. "Now, how about you get the hell out of my way."

"Fine by me, Johnny Stagg," the Trooper said. "But don't you want to know what I've found out?"

Stagg stepped close, leaned in to the man's old, gray buzz-cut head, and whispered, "I told Vardaman that you were a stone-cold nut. They need to lock your ass up in Whitfield. You weren't acting on no one's authority but your own. I'll cut your ass down at the knees."

"C'mon, Johnny," the Trooper said. "Let's take a ride."

Stagg brushed past the Trooper, walking toward the image of that big smiling pig wearing a butcher's hat, just as pleased as punch that the grocery was cutting off his hog parts, wrapping them up, and parceling them out to folks. The Trooper grabbed his arm and said, "Can't you see I'm trying to help you?"

"How's that?" Stagg said. "Or you want to try and violate me again in public?"

"I want to violate something, I'd do better than a broken-down crook like you, Stagg."

"Get the fuck out of my way."

"You need to listen up."

"I may not win, sir," Stagg said, stepping toward him, "but I'll go down with fists flying and teeth gnashing."

"Your boy Ringold ain't what you thought."

Stagg stopped cold. Parked by the front door, Miss Dorothy Castleberry, garden club president ten years running, tooted her horn and waved her fat arm out the window. Stagg parted lips, showed his teeth, and grinned, waving back, the Trooper's hand feeling like a vise on his arm. "Who is he?" Stagg said through clenched teeth.

"Your boy is a goddamn federal agent," the Trooper said. "Unless you get your head out of your ass, everything you got in this county is about to burn to the ground."

"Bullshit," Stagg said. "Why the hell should I trust a man like you? I'd just as soon trust a piss-sucking goat."

"'Cause you're the one who made the call," the Trooper said. "'Cause you doubted him first. You fault ain't in your fucking stars, Johnny. It's up your goddamn ass."

The man turned his back, walked back to his cruiser, and sped away. Stagg shook his head, marching on, not knowing if anyone had just seen what had transpired in open view. He still had Diet Pepsi, Triscuits, and Wonder Bread to bring home and that bastard wouldn't shake it.

Quinn and Lillie met late afternoon at a turnaround along Jericho Road, not far from the Choctaw Lake pier. You could see the water from where they'd parked their vehicles, Quinn now driving the old Ford truck, a nice gold glow setting down across the rippling cold water. Lillie had on her sheriff's office jacket and sunglasses. "I feel like I've been living the redneck version of *Rashomon*. Not one of those shitbirds has told their story straight."

"How about Mickey Walls?"

"He's the worst of them," Lillie said. "And, unfortunately, the only bird in hand at the moment. He's blaming the whole damn thing on Kyle Hazlewood. Says Kyle wanted to get back at Cobb for fucking him over on that dozer work and that he's the one who recruited Sparks and Clanton. Mickey said Clanton shot Kenny and now believes those two turned on Kyle."

"Mickey thinks Kyle's dead?"

"Yes, sir," Lillie said. "Said that a couple weeks ago, Kyle had come to him and wanted to turn himself in and give back the money. Mickey thinks those Alabama boys took it all and buried his ass deep."

"You'll find them."

"Yeah," Lillie said. "They're running together. Got some video of them both at a truck stop outside Birmingham. Looks like Sparks had arranged the meet before he had a sit-down with us."

"How'd that go?"

"Sparks calls his busted-ass van a rolling sex palace," Lillie said. "Apparently, he just has to slide open that door and women will jump in."

"Is he a handsome man?"

"If you call five-five, two-fifty, and a face like a bulldog handsome."

"Someone for everybody."

"We've charged Walls as an accomplice to the burglary and shooting," Lillie said. "But, damn, I'd hoped we could have gotten Kyle. You know as well as I do we could have reasoned with him. It makes sense what Mickey is saying about him stepping forward, but I don't believe for a second that Mickey is clean. Or that this was all Kyle's idea. He's no schemer."

"Got any idea on where Sparks and Clanton would go?"

"After they busted through Cobb's house, they kept on rolling down to New Orleans," Lillie said. "They spent more than five grand at a titty bar on Bourbon Street in New Orleans. They were staying at the Holiday Inn by the Superdome and ran up some incredible charges there. Security finally had to ask Sparks to leave, he had so many hookers coming and going out of the place. The guard down there I spoke to said they left their hotel room looking like something inside a monkey cage. Apparently, they had to replace the carpet and burn the bedding."

"And folks from Alabama look down on us."

Lillie shook her head, the sun shining white and cold down upon the lake. The only activity came from a handful of ducks and a big mess of Canada geese. By summer, the lake would be filled with bass boats and kids in inner tubes, old men stalking the edges with their fishing poles trying to break bass and crappie records. Quinn pulled a cigar from his coat and leaned against the old truck built eight years before he was even born. The truck a faded two-tone blue and white. The stock AM radio inside still worked and picked up racist talk radio and good old-fashioned gospel.

"Listen, you need to know something," Quinn said.

Lillie turned her head, Quinn catching a glimpse of himself in her sunglasses before she turned back to the lake. Her hands were deep in her satiny coat. "If this is about you and Anna Lee, I'd rather you keep personal matters to yourself," Lillie said. "I imagine you both think you're both meant to be, but I'm waiting for the demolition derby to start."

"Appreciate that," Quinn said, flicking on his lighter, burning the tip of his cigar. He held it out in his hand, watching the end burn. "But, no."

They stood so close to each other at the grille of the truck that their shoulders touched. Lillie had her legs out straight in front of her, butt leaning against the truck, grinning, glad she'd maybe hit a nerve. "The heart wants what it wants," she said. "I think I read that on a greeting card at Walmart."

Quinn had the cigar clamped in his back teeth. "There was more in that safe than just buckets of cash."

"Please, God, tell me there aren't photos of Larry and Debbi doing it."

"Yes, Lillie," Quinn said. "A whole photo album of Larry in a double-XL pink nightie."

"I know he had some pistols," Lillie said. "A rare Civil War pistol.

Some old coins and earrings he gave Debbi for their thirtieth anniversary. He wrote out a list."

"And some books," Quinn said. "Solid, handwritten records of the last decade of dirty deals with folks in Jackson. Roadwork, bridge building. Larry kept details of every kickback he received and the bank accounts where they traded."

"Son of a bitch."

"And there's more," Quinn said, grinning.

"Goddamn Johnny Stagg."

"Some good stuff, Lil," Quinn said. "Some really, really good stuff."

"Are you sure it's January?"

"Why?"

"Because, god damn, it feels like Christmas," she said. "Who has this stuff?"

"FBI office in Oxford," Quinn said. "I'm expecting the Rebel to be raided just about any day now. Stagg will be charged with so much dirty shit, he'll never get out."

"This is it," Lillie said. "I know you love Anna Lee. But, god damn, isn't this why you stayed? Now, get out of this shithole."

Quinn smiled. The bare trees shook in the wind as a dust devil kicked up some dead leaves in the gravel, scattering them out onto the lonely road. Lillie took off her sunglasses and placed them in an inside pocket. "Do me a favor?"

"Anything."

"Talk to Rusty," she said. "If your contact's got raids coming down on Tibbehah, we should know. We can help. It's a respect issue. Besides, I'd like to be there when they snatch up Stagg's ass."

Quinn nodded, puffing on the cigar.

"Is it someone I know?" Lillie asked.

"What's that?"

"Y'all have someone inside," Lillie said. "Who is it? One of his pole dancers? Can you imagine busting your ass through Quantico and then having to show your tits and ride the gold pole for Johnny Stagg?"

Quinn winked at Lillie, pushed himself off the old truck, and walked around to the driver's-side door.

31.

Figured you'd want to know we're bringing in Stagg tomorrow," Ringold said. "Larry Cobb, too, and a few other local shitbags."

"Who?"

Quinn wasn't a bit surprised when he heard their names, asking when the roundup might start. The two men stood together along the Trace but at another marker, another burial mound, about twenty miles north of their regular meet. The sun would be going down soon and the temperature had dropped nearly twenty degrees. Some snow was expected in Little Rock and Memphis, but it didn't look like Tibbehah County would get more than some cold rain and sleet.

"We're still pushing some paper around," Ringold said. "But if all goes as expected, I think Johnny Stagg might have a real shit morning."

"Y'all need some local help?" Quinn said.

Ringold smiled. "I'd do about anything to see you slap those cuffs on Johnny Stagg," he said. "You know I would. But we got to do everything right. You can't give that bastard an inch."

"Have you talked to Sheriff Wise yet?"

"I planned to make that call on short notice," Ringold said. "Can I trust him?"

"Lillie thinks so," Quinn said.

Ringold nodded, stroking his big black beard. Everything was turning to shadow around them, dark creeping up on and over the mound, sunlight shrinking back to the edge of the woods. He had on his green parka with the fur hood dropped over his bald head. When he pulled his sunglasses off, Quinn could see his light, almost spooky-looking eyes. "Maybe you can tip him a raid is going to happen," he said. "Just don't tell him who or where. I know Stagg doesn't trust him, but that doesn't mean he wouldn't want to curry some favor."

Quinn nodded. "Just how good is that shit you have in Cobb's books?"

"Larry Cobb was so damn paranoid about not getting his cut, the bastard wrote down every nickel, every slush fund account. This all is going to embarrass some known people."

"God bless him."

"If they hadn't shot your deputy," Ringold said, "I'd be inclined to give those safe-busters some kind of citation. Or at least go easy on them."

"But they did shoot Kenny," Quinn said. "Almost killed him."

"I'm sorry."

"And now Lillie thinks the crew is turning on each other," Quinn said. "Mickey Walls says Kyle was behind everything. But he also believes Kyle might be dead."

"Son of a bitch."

"I like how it's turned out," Quinn said. "But it was born of some rotten, greedy shit."

"You'll talk to the sheriff?"

"Roger that," Quinn said, grinning. "My pleasure." He reached into his Uncle Hamp's old coat and pulled out two of his best cigars, still wrapped in cellophane. "I can't be with you. But smoke this after you bring in Stagg. OK?"

Ringold smiled and stuck out his hand. Quinn met his eye and gave him a firm shake. "Good luck."

Peewee drove on through Mississippi and into Louisiana, seeming to forget about the EMPTY gas light that had come on back in Slidell. It was dark and they hadn't stopped since picking up a new car in Mobile, a twenty-year-old Buick Park Avenue. Chase hadn't been wild about the selection, but Peewee explained he had to get an older model that didn't use those damn digital keys. They'd screwed up everything for the working man.

"You plan on us running out of fuel on the interstate?" Chase said.

"Just trying to put some distance between us."

"We got all of Mississippi between us," Chase said.

"Well, if you see a fucking service station, professor, how about you letting me know?"

"God damn, we just passed two exits full of them."

"Hell," Peewee said. "Just pass me one of them Zagnut bars."

They hadn't brought a lot with them, just a couple duffel bags full of clothes, a bag full of Peewee's bustin' tools, clean drawers, and some fancy-ass clothes for New Orleans. It had been Chase who'd had the forethought to buy the Gatorade and candy bars at the Flying J outside Birmingham. Peewee had already eaten three of them but hadn't once mentioned Chase's cut since they'd met up with Mickey Walls and gotten some more money along with that dead son of a bitch wrapped in black plastic bags.

It had been Chase who'd wrapped the man tight with duct tape and fishing line, shoring up the shit work Walls had done, fastening a half-dozen concrete blocks to old Kyle before dumping his body in the Tombigbee.

"That sign right there says Gas," Chase said.

"I can fucking read."

Uncle Peewee just didn't seem himself without the party van. The Alabama van had been a part of his identity, the way a hero of the west was tied to his horse or the way that Bobby Allison was tied to Miller beer and number 12. Chase just couldn't remember a time when Peewee wasn't running around Gordo in that vehicle, picking him up from school or when his momma had been tossed out by another uncle, not a real uncle but them fellas she dated. One time for a couple weeks he and his momma had lived in that van.

"You think we'll ever get her back?" Chase said, knowing what had put Peewee in a shit mood.

"What?"

"The van."

"It's not a she, it's just a goddamn ride."

"We partied hard in her, lots of miles between Gordo and Tusca-loosa."

"I had that van since your momma got knocked up with you," Pee-wee said. "I drove her to the damn hospital in it 'cause your daddy was too fucked-up."

"She was the first thing I drove," Chase said. "You'd let me sit on your lap and take the wheel. You had one hand on a cold can of Bud and the other on a cigarette."

"You did good," Peewee said. "Never wrecked us. How old were you?"

"Six," Chase said. "I was six, first time I got to drive."

"Well, fuck it," Peewee said. "She's gone now. Probably stripped clean by a bunch of blacks. That's why I put her out where I did. Gang-bangers probably cruising in her right now until the law shows up. And, haw, haw. Lord, ain't they gonna be surprised."

"Maybe it's for the best," Chase said. "I don't think we could ever get that smell out."

"You smell him, too?"

"Some of them trash bags were leaking and the boy's juices got into the carpet," Chase said. "I didn't want to get you all riled-up, so I tried some of that Purple Power and a little bleach."

"If cops ever pick us up, we can say we was carjacked and them blacks took Kyle with them."

"How you know it's gonna be blacks?"

"Son, it's always blacks," Peewee said. "White man wouldn't bust into a fine machine like that unless it was an emergency situation."

"Is that what we got?"

"Oh yes, sir."

"But we're just gonna lay low in New Orleans," Chase said. "Until things sort out."

"That's about it."

"Uncle Peewee?"

"Yes, sir?"

"I'd like to get my cut tonight," he said. "If you don't mind. Just in case something happens. That way, I'll have the means to move on."

"Yeah?"

"I saw how much Walls gave you back in Jericho," Chase said. "That's a shit ton of cash."

"Oh yeah?" Peewee said, taking an exit and rolling on off Interstate 10, stopping at a stoplight and looking both ways to figure out where they'd put the filling station. He leaned forward over the wheel and stared out those smudged glasses of his.

"I want half," Chase said. "I want half of that."

Rusty Wise's land used to belong to a man named Jerry Shaw before Shaw sold out and retired to Florida, leaving Jericho with a big send-off at the VFW a couple years back. Luther Varner had been there. Donnie Varner, too, before he'd been caught running guns and sent off to federal prison. It was a nice piece of land, about twenty-one acres, with a little pond and some old-growth trees. About the best part is that it ran flat against the National Forest that took up all of Tibbehah County's western border. No matter the logging around him, Rusty could count on that funnel from the forest bringing in some solid wildlife.

Quinn parked a few hundred yards from the gate, down at the bottom of the hill, near the remnants of Shaw's old trailer, set up on blocks without stairs, no one caring to haul it off or take it apart. The windows had been busted out and weeds had sprouted on the roof. A path had been cut into the mouth of the woods that would connect on into the National Forest and run for miles and miles until it was sliced through by the Natchez Trace. Before sundown, the clouds looked strange, gray and angry, rolling low over the hills.

Quinn followed the wide trail, noticing well-worn ruts from an ATV moving uphill. He didn't fault Rusty for it, but a lot of what Quinn enjoyed about hunting in the woods was leaving all man-made things behind except your gun. The moldy old oak leaves and wet brown pine needles felt good underfoot. Lillie told him that Wise was using the same deer stand that old Mr. Shaw had built, a ramshackle design of plywood and tin about a half klick from the road that fronted a wide-mouthed clearing. He'd enter from the rear, move around the back end, as not to startle Wise.

He'd tried to call, but there were no cell towers out this way. A GPS would think it was part of the National Forest, only an invisible line separating the two.

As Quinn walked, the shadows flooded the deep woods. A cold rain tapped the tree branches and dead leaves, pinging off the visor of Quinn's ball cap. He kind of wished he'd brought more than his nine-millimeter with him, maybe a thermos of hot coffee and a good rifle. Even if he didn't see a single deer, he'd be in the middle of it all as the woods became electric and alive with animals coming out, seeking supper for the bad weather. Quinn never entered these woods, the big forest, without thinking back on his walk with Caddy when he believed he'd either have to run away or get sent to jail at ten years old. Caddy believed it, too, tagging along behind Quinn when he set off with his .22 rifle and fishing pole. She'd packed some food and what little bit of money she had, not knowing where he was going or what was the plan. Quinn had believed he could find his father and a way out to California, leaving Jericho and the mess he'd made far behind. Deer had been killed out of season, he'd broken the law, and it felt like he could never make it right.

As Quinn spotted the rear of Rusty's stand, a steady rain was pelting the shit out of the woods. Quinn moved through a once-cleared space now growing up with gum trees and little pines not even kneehigh and whistled to Rusty. He wanted to make sure he was expected; it was never a good idea to sneak up on a man crouched down with a rifle. A few seconds later, Rusty crawled on down the handmade ladder and stared into the graying day. He had on a camo jacket and pants, a dark brown hat on his head. His face looked chubby and bright red in the middle of the all the dark greens and brown. "Quinn?" he called out.

Quinn waved and pushed through the growth and into the clearing around the stand. He apologized for walking up on him like that.

"I was just about to call it a day," Rusty said. "Saw a couple little does. Not worth shooting. Young and skinny. Maybe next year. My freezer's nearly full. I just had to get out of that office."

"Just wait a few months," Quinn said. "You'll want to live out here."

Rusty smiled and asked if Quinn wanted to come on up to the stand. "I got some hot coffee and biscuits," he said. "Wouldn't mind giving it another thirty minutes. Maybe that big 'un will show. What do you say?"

Quinn nodded and followed Rusty up the ladder, hammered together with scrap wood.

Up top, Rusty unscrewed the cup of the thermos and handed Quinn some hot coffee. As Quinn drank, he looked over the expanse of the green field Rusty had planted, complimenting the man on his preparation. "What are those, turnips?"

"And some rapeseed, too," Rusty said. "Deer just love that stuff. How's that coffee?"

"It's good," Quinn said, lying. "Listen, Rusty. I never would interrupt a man hunting, kind of a sacred time, but you and me need to talk."

Louisiana was some weird country. Didn't look a bit like Gordo, with that black water everywhere, having to build highways up on stilts to skim over the bayous and all those alligators. Peewee drove over a railroad track and followed the hand-painted signs along a dirt road for GAS, FOOD & BAIT, skirting more water and prehistoric trees covered in green moss. It looked like a goddamn episode of *Scooby-Doo*, Chase half expecting some Confederate regiment to raise up out of the swamp, with skeleton bodies, ragged grays, and green glowing eyes, surrounding the Buick.

"You sure this is right?" Chase said.

"What the signs say."

"You said to never follow no signs."

"I said don't follow signs like some revival preacher, thinking the Lord was showing you the way," Peewee said. "Like when ole George Strait says, 'I saw God today.' A flower growing in the sidewalk and all the horseshit. I tried to teach you how to find your own fucking way, cut your own path through the damn jungle."

They passed a few shacks, all of them up high on stilts with boats underneath instead of cars, and turned a sharp corner on toward the gas station, a blue clapboard building with neon beer signs blazing in the window. He didn't see any gas pumps, but a sign read SEE THE ATTENDANT.

"Down there," Peewee said. "Down by the boat ramp."

An old-fashioned pump, the thick metal kind with spinning numbers that didn't take credit cards, was set up on a dock. Chase got out of the car, stretched and spit and looked up to the station on stilts. "It's closed."

"How can you tell?"

"Ain't no lights on up there," Chase said. "Shit. We're gonna run out of gas in the fucking swamp."

"We can make it."

"Why?"

"'Cause I'm gonna bust that fucking padlock off that pump," Peewee said. "Use your head."

"We done a bunch of shit," Chase said. "I guess it don't matter."

"I'm sorry about the goddamn van," Peewee said. "Jesus H. It's just a van. You can buy another one, paint Nick Saban on the hood and Kenny Stabler on the rear end."

"OK," Chase said. "I can see it. Maybe get some airbrushed snake art around Stabler? A damn copperhead wrapped around his neck while he's throwing the football?"

"Now you're talking."

Peewee waddled around to the back of the Buick to fetch his tool kit, fiddling around for a bit until he found a big old pair of Ridgid bolt cutters. They'd used them things plenty when breaking into storage units around Birmingham. Sometimes Chase wondered why people even invested in a padlock when you could slice through the thing like it wasn't nothing. Sure enough, Peewee stepped up to the gas pump and snipped the lock off, tossing it far out into the water and scaring off a pelican. "Come on, drive on up some more so I can reach the nozzle."

Chase got in, reaching down for the flat-head screwdriver they'd used to bust into the steering column and get the engine started. The lights in the car flickered on and off, and it took a couple good yanks before the old car came to life and he pulled it forward on the busted oyster shells.

"Fine night for titties," Peewee said. "You know, I think I'm gonna get two women tonight. Take some of them jelly shooters off them niblets."

"How about you let me hold the money?"

Peewee stood cool, leaning against the Buick, while he pumped the gas. "We'll see."

"Last time, you spent five thousand dollars," Chase said. "I don't even know how much those whores cost."

"They weren't whores," Peewee said. "They were escorts. Lord. Ain't it pretty out here. Look at that night sky. That fuzzy shit in the trees. Man, I could just eat it up."

It was pretty, orange bleeding into the black, lots of stars popping out over all those old trees. The air smelled like salt and dead fish. Peewee filled the tank. No one came down the road or out of those stilt houses. It was quiet, about a million miles away from something.

"Tide's gonna have some growing pains this year," Chase said.

"True."

"We lost T. J. Yeldon," Chase said. "We got to get us a new running back. I seen this boy from Kentucky we got our eyes on. He's got moves like something out of the fucking *Matrix*."

"That a fact."

"You're still thinking about titties, aren't you?"

Peewee turned to him, still pumping gas, wind coming hard and salty off the swamp, or bayou, or wherever they were at, and broke into a big grin. "I want me a white one and a black one," Peewee said.

"And my money?"

"Haw, haw," Peewee said. "I'll get straight with you, boy. Don't you worry. Just don't forget, you just tailing me on this. I don't know when you started believing we were partners."

Peewee turned his head, staring out at some weird bird with tall legs settling onto the end of the pier. He reached up under his glasses to scratch his eye, taking off the frames and holding them up to the dull light swinging back and forth from the tin roof. "You remember that one girl? That skinny white girl with buckteeth? Nipples like silver dollars? Well, she told me she'd do whatever I wanted for five hundred. I think that's a money-saver right there. Maybe we should go on up to that VIP Suite and just get down to business. Hell, you get a free bottle of champagne with the servicing. Might even give you a sip."

Peewee smiled big, not even noticing his nephew was right up on him, gun outstretched in his arm, an inch or two from his ear. Didn't turn his head or stare away from the water, hearing Chase's work boots on the old boards and sensing the gun close to his head. "You're gonna kill me," Peewee said. "Ain't you?"

"Yes, sir," Chase said. "Afraid so."

"Why? Why would you do a thing like that? After all I—"

And Chase shot him. The .32 cracking big like an old bottle rocket, smoke curling up from the muzzle. "'Cause you ain't got your head in the game," Chase said. "I need me a total commitment."

I'm doing the best I can," Rusty said. "I know Debbi Cobb has been reaching out to you, thinking I don't know my ass from my elbow. But I just arrested Mickey Walls and got warrants out for the other three."

"There's more to it."

"Come again?"

"Those boys found something in that safe that's going to change this whole county," Quinn said. "I'm not trying to get involved. But something big is going to happen tomorrow and I wanted you to be ready."

Rusty smiled good-naturedly, but a little annoyed. "Can you decode that message for me a little, Sergeant?"

Quinn ran by the scenario.

"Federal agents?" Rusty said.

"Yes, sir."

"Who are they going to raid?"

"I can't tell you that."

"Or why are they coming?" Rusty said. "Or where?"

"I can't tell you that, either," Quinn said. "You just need to be on standby and trust me. They're going to need your help and support. I've been working with them for a long while. They know what they're doing."

"I may hadn't ever fought the Taliban, but I didn't fall off a turnip truck, either," Rusty said. "You're talking about Stagg. The Feds are finally going to take down Johnny. Holy moly."

"I need your word that you'll keep this quiet," Quinn said. "I may have started this, but you're going to have to finish it. OK?"

"You know how many folks the Feds are bringing?"

Quinn shook his head and drank some of that weak-ass coffee. He moved on over to the sill overlooking the green field, thinking how he might as well just go ahead and tell him all. Ringold didn't completely trust him, but Quinn did. And so did Lillie.

"I wouldn't go in holding flowers," Rusty said. "I sure don't like that man Stagg's got. The one with the beard and weird eyes? I think he'd go full auto on us without a thought."

"Y'all will do fine," Quinn said. "Just make sure to lock down everything. Make sure nothing on the property is messed with. Computers, files, that kind of thing. Protection, mainly."

"Holy moly."

"You said it."

The rain had turned to sleet in the fading winter light, hammering the tin roof above them and out in the shadowed field. Quinn was about to turn and tell Rusty the rest of it when he spotted one of the biggest bucks he'd ever seen in his life wander out to the middle of the turnips, rack held high, appraising the changing weather. At last light, deer started to move, even more reckless in bad weather, wanting to get in a good meal before everything turned to shit.

Quinn turned back to Rusty and smiled. Rusty just shook his head, out here all this time, and Quinn walks up and a big old buck shows. He walked to the corner of the stand, reached for his Winchester .308, and handed it on over to Quinn. There was no time for an argument, so Quinn raised the scope to his eye and aimed the barrel at the buck.

Quinn had the big, broad chest in the crosshairs. He could feel Rusty moving next to him, hear the heavy man's breathing, as Quinn steadied himself to take the shot.

As he started to squeeze the trigger, a single shot rang out from beyond the trees and the buck sprinted for the deep woods. Quinn dropped to the floor as a second shot punched him in the right arm and knocked him flat on his back. He called to Rusty to get down but didn't get an answer.

Quinn reached for the fallen gun, mind already jumping to a familiar place, and he saw Rusty lying on his side, chest blood-soaked and mouth working like a caught fish sucking air.

No more gunshots. Everything else still and cold. Only wind. Sleet pinged off the roof. No sounds coming from the deep woods. No breaking branches or calls from men.

Quinn crawled to Rusty. He'd quit sucking for air.

32.

Not six hours since Lillie found Rusty Wise's body, bled-out and cold in his deer stand, Caddy Colson marched through the deputies, highway patrolmen, and news folks and wanted to know what the hell had happened to her brother. Lillie had set up a command center in the sheriff's office at dawn, taking calls from sheriffs from adjoining counties who wanted to lend their support. She was on the phone, talking to the Lee County sheriff about use of their helicopter, with Caddy staring her down with crossed arms and a red face.

Her T-shirt under a loose men's flannel read ONE STEP AT A TIME.

"I'm sorry I couldn't call you back," Lillie said. "You might have noticed the shit has hit the fan around here."

"Yeah, the new sheriff has been shot," she said. "Where's my brother? Don't tell me y'all think he did it?"

Lillie leaned against the desk and took a good deep breath and said, "No, Caddy. I don't think Quinn shot Rusty. But I'd be lying to say you're the first who wondered it aloud. This office has been crawling with state people, asking a lot of questions and looking at a lot of maps."

"When's the last time you saw Quinn?" Caddy said. "I tried calling the farm, Anna Lee's, Momma. If he didn't tell you, then something real bad has happened."

"Last time I heard from him, he was headed to talk to Rusty."

"Why?"

"I can't say," Lillie said. "It was official business left over from when he was sheriff. We found Quinn's truck parked out on Rusty's land. The keys were in it. We've had folks searching the woods since three a.m."

"They killed him."

"No," Lillie said.

"They killed him," she said. "Whoever killed Rusty killed my brother. He's out there dead. Jesus God."

"Caddy," Lillie said, looking dead-eyed and serious at the messed-up girl. "I know you're going through hell. But if you ever say such bullshit again, I'll punch you right in the goddamn mouth. We're doing all we can. Quinn is out there. We'll find him. Understand?"

Caddy nodded, closed her eyes, and then, as if emptied of all her energy, sat right back in the wooden chair. She held her head in both hands and looked as if she'd started to cry. *Jesus Christ.* The last goddamn thing Lillie needed was Caddy Colson wanting some hand-holding. Quinn would be fine. He had to be fine. But, right now, she was acting sheriff with a shooter, or some shooters, out roaming a big stretch of land. She had to have a little time to think, make some connections.

"I want to help," Caddy said.

"How the hell'd you get over here from Tupelo?" Lillie said. "Don't tell me that you walked."

"I checked myself out," she said. "I'm about tired of eating Jell-O and talking to my Higher Power. Thank God, I got a ride. My brother is missing."

"Just who in the hell helped you check out of that place?"

Boom Kimbrough walked into the office, making the space seem a little smaller, more congested, with his big slumped frame. He had on an old greenish mackinaw jacket and a blue knit cap and leaned his good arm against the doorframe, staring down at Lillie. "She needed to know."

Lillie nodded. "And you gave her a ride?"

"She needed a ride," Boom said. "Quinn's got trouble."

"I know Quinn's got trouble," Lillie said. "I got trouble, too. I just got back from talking to Rusty's wife and kids for the last two hours. He hadn't been sheriff but two weeks and someone shot him dead out of his deer stand. There's blood all over that floor and walls. My God, it's a mess."

"Rusty's blood?" Boom asked.

"I don't know whose blood."

"You know patterns," Boom said. "How many got shot up there?"

Lillie gave Boom a hard stare and swallowed. She still felt empty and hollow, everything that happened almost unreal and apart from her. There had been so much crying and wailing at Rusty's, the whole house seeming to hum with their sorrow and loss. Lillie had stepped out the door as their family pastor arrived, unable to take any more. Blaming herself for not watching Rusty's back.

"Quinn's truck was parked out on his land," Lillie said.

"Ain't what I asked, Lillie," Boom said. "What'd you see in that stand?"

"God damn you, Boom," Lillie said. "We got highway patrol and MBI out, crawling those woods. If you think you can do a better job, then feel free to go on out and tramp the woods with them. I'd be out there now, if someone didn't have to run things."

"You think it's Quinn's blood," Caddy said. "Don't you?"

Lillie shook her head, looking from Caddy to Boom. Quinn's sister to his best friend. She walked over to the office door and closed it with a light click. She stood next to Boom, who'd moved into the center of the room, and looked down at Caddy. "I will not cry," Lillie said. "Not till all this is over. But, yes, it looked like two men were in that deer stand. Both of them hit. If it was Quinn, he's been wounded pretty bad. We don't know where he went."

"What the hell are we doing here?" Caddy said.

"This is what's called the command center," Lillie said. "I'm in command. I've set up roadblocks, having the woods searched grid by grid, keeping in touch with the folks out there. Did I mention, I'm working on getting a goddamn helicopter?"

"Rusty bought the old Shaw place?" Boom said. "Right? A couple miles outside Fate."

"Don't even think about it, Boom," Lillie said. "I need your help right here."

I'm not stupid," Tonya said. "You used me."

"Can this wait until I get out of jail?" Mickey said. "I got a first appearance in two hours. My lawyer says he'll argue down a decent bail."

"No, it can't wait," Tonya said. "I kind of wanted to see you like this, without the designer jeans, the fancy-ass shirt, and driving around in your red Hummer. You look more like your real self in that orange jumpsuit and behind that fence."

"It's cold out here," Mickey said. "I thought you'd come to apologize for those phone messages. You called me some real nasty shit."

The jail guard had allowed Mickey to get out of his cell, stretch, and have a smoke out in the fenced-off yard. Mommas, girlfriends, brothers, and buddies had come by that morning to exchange fried pies and cigarettes through the chain-link. There wasn't much in that yard besides some old plastic school chairs and a couple rotten picnic tables. A goddamn exhibit of Tibbehah County's finest. Jericho's own private zoo.

"Just admit you used me," Tonya said.

"How's that?"

"You didn't want to patch things up," Tonya said, wearing pink sweatpants, a big blue puffy coat, and pink cowboy boots. Her hair was the color of straw and her face that same deep brown, even without a trace of makeup. "I was a goddamn alibi while you robbed my daddy."

"Just how can I be two places at once?"

"Kyle and his buds did your dirty work," she said. "You don't even have the nuts to take care of your own business. Just like you didn't have the nuts to close the damn deal on me the other night. Didn't you see me dancing in my sheer bra-and-panty set in front of that window? At first, I thought you were having trouble with your ding-dong. But as soon as you ran for your truck, I knew there was more. I cried for you, Mickey Walls. I fucking cried for your stupid ass."

Mickey put his hand onto the diamonds of the chain-link. He offered his ex-wife his best smile.

"I sure wish I could punch your nose through this fence," she said. "People are laughing at me. Laughing for me fronting you while you embarrassed me, embarrassed my family. Son of a bitch, Mickey. I got buck-ass nekkid with you and ran into the Gulf."

"That was real," Mickey said. "That was a special night."

"So how come you ran off at the stroke of midnight?" Tonya said. "You afraid your fucking Hummer was gonna turn into a pumpkin?"

"I was drunk," he said. "I started having feelings for you. I couldn't breathe and got nervous. You just looked so beautiful on that beach."

"Freezing my titties off?"

"I got scared."

Tonya just shook her head, not buying one word of it. She put her hands into her puffy coat pockets and walked up close on the chain-link. Mickey sure was wishing the guard would call him soon. He wanted to see the judge, make that bond, and then get home for a hot shower, a cold drink, and some goddamn time to think. He could think this mess through. But whatever way it turned, he needed Tonya Cobb on his side. She goes over to her daddy and momma and there'd be a bigger fight than he wanted.

"Daddy's ulcer is back," Tonya said. "Momma is back into the wine."

"I can't help that."

"They're sleeping on my couch," Tonya said. "Daddy's carrying a gun. He keeps on saying people are coming to kill him."

"It's over," Mickey said, giving a soft, reassuring smile. "It's all over. People just want me and you to keep apart. Don't let them do that, Tonya. What we have is special. It's real."

"Daddy always said you weren't worth a shit."

Mickey's face heated up a bit, the smile dropping, as he tilted his head and looked to Tonya. Damn. There was no pleasing this woman.

"If you don't go to Parchman," Tonya said, "I hope you and Kyle sure do enjoy all that cash. I don't hate you for what you done to Daddy. But why in God's name did you have to drag me into this mess?"

Tonya turned on her pink boots and walked away. Mickey headed away from the fence, found a plastic school chair, and dragged it into a small patch of sunlight. He sat there until one of the deputies called his name.

Lillie walked out of the sheriff's office to get some air and smoke a cigarette. It had been a long while since she'd smoked, but today seemed like a hell of a day to start back. Everything had started at two a.m. when she'd gotten the call from Rusty's wife, driving down that long gravel road in the dark, seeing Quinn's old truck and knowing something horrible had happened. She had followed the path to the deer stand, seen the body and the blood smears by flashlight, and called in the deputies and the folks from MBI. She walked miles of forest until sunup, not finding a trace of Quinn. By morning, she knew she had to get back to the sheriff's office and coordinate—roads needed to be blocked off, maps laid out, and air searches begun.

She smoked and thought of where Quinn would go, who might be following, and how bad he might be hurt. The parking lot was so jam-packed with media trucks and deputies from other counties, she hadn't noticed the man in the green parka walking toward her until he spoke. "You can't find him," he said. "Can you?"

He pulled his hood back, showing his face. Goddamn Ringold, the man who walked behind Stagg. Lillie dropped the cigarette and went for her gun, pulling it on him. The man's hands shot up, him grimacing a bit as if he were hurt. "Slow down, sweetheart," he said. "Let's talk."

"Hands on the car."

"Listen to me."

"Put your fucking hands on the hood or I'll shoot you right in the fucking head."

"Yes, ma'am," Ringold said, doing as he was told.

"Where is he?" she said, reaching and finding an auto on the man's hip, running down both legs and retrieving a .38 and a knife in his boots. "You people shot him."

"It's not like that," Ringold said, gritting his teeth as Lillie touched his flank. "Let's just slow down and talk. Be cool."

"Be cool?" Lillie said. "Y'all shot Quinn. You killed Rusty. There's no slowing down. Shooting your ass would be too damn easy. I'll make you cry for it."

She punched him hard in the stomach. Ringold dropped to his knees and gritted his teeth again, unable to breathe, eyes watering. "Get up," she said. "You fucking pussy."

Ringold reached for the Jeep's hood and tried to stand, Lillie yanking him the rest of the way by the parka's hood. As soon as he'd steadied himself and caught his breath, he said, "Pull up my shirt."

"Why?"

"Shit," he said. "Just look."

Lillie pulled up the side of his parka and a thick black sweater to reveal a bloodied bandage running across his side and taped on his stomach. "I've been shot."

"He should've killed you."

"Quinn didn't shoot me," Ringold said. "God damn it. I'm working with him."

"Bull-fucking-shit."

"He told you and Wise that there was someone in with Stagg."

"Yeah, a fucking pole dancer with her hands around Stagg's unit," Lillie said. "You're too damn ugly for the job."

"You really believe that?"

"OK," Lillie said, gun still in Ringold's side. "Prove it."

"In my right-hand pocket," he said. "My shield. Call in to the Oxford office, if you want. But you know I'm right. Why else would I come here? I got nowhere else to go. Stagg knows."

Lillie found the badge, studied it, and holstered her Glock. "Son of a bitch."

"We were supposed to raid Stagg's place today," he said. "Something happened. Somebody talked and they all know about me and him. Two men came to the motel last night to kill me."

"And what happened?"

"They sucked at their jobs," Ringold said. "How many deputies can we get?"

"There's some good trackers out there," Lillie said. "A whole team of them from Jackson are taking it step-by-step from where Quinn left his vehicle and Rusty's deer stand. They think Quinn may have gotten confused and wandered into the National Forest."

"Quinn's a U.S. Army Ranger," Ringold said. "Those boys aren't known to wander. He's leading them somewhere."

"Why?"

"Because those trackers aren't on our side," he said. "Stagg goes down and a lot of important folks go with him. They want Quinn dead."

33.

The first thing you want to do after being shot is make sure you aren't shot again. Quinn had waited inside the deer stand with Rusty Wise's body for more than three hours before making a move. There was a hope, just a glimmer of it, that the man who'd pulled the trigger would grow curious and show himself in the clearing. But he never did. Whoever had done it was smart and cautious, waiting for Quinn to run for it. In the time that passed, Quinn pulled off his jacket and saw where a bullet had passed through his left forearm. There was a lot of blood. And judging from the grotesque way his arm hung, the bullet had busted through the bone.

Funny thing was, he didn't feel the pain—the deep, searing, burn through your flesh and cracked bone pain—until about an hour after the bullet passed through. When the pain hit, it hit hard.

He'd already washed it with a jug of water, wrapped and cleaned it with a snakebite kit, and fashioned a splint from some pieces of plywood and torn pieces from Rusty's shirt. At full dark, a cold rain falling in rolling sheets, Quinn scavenged all he needed from the stand and ran into the deep woods and onto a path west, away from the main road and where the shooter had been. He kept on moving through the trees and brambles until he believed he'd put a couple klicks between himself and the stand. His breath came out in spurted clouds, the rain collecting on bare tree branches and dripping down into the wet, cold ground.

He wondered how long it would take for Lillie to find Rusty Wise. And after Rusty Wise was found, how many folks might think Quinn killed the man himself? He'd been accused of worse things. After that tornado nearly wiped Jericho off the map, a local police chief named Leonard Chappel—who worked for Stagg—had turned on Quinn and his family. Lillie had killed the chief and Quinn had killed one of his officers, but there had been a third man up in the hills who they never found. A goddamn sniper who left everyone pointing fingers.

The sniper had tried to kill Quinn and Caddy and little Jason. He'd made the Good Reverend Jamey Dixon's head explode and changed Caddy's entire world. Nobody ever found the son of a bitch or knew where he'd come from. The only thing Quinn knew was that the sniper had to have operated on Johnny Stagg's say-so.

The rain stopped after midnight. Time started again for Quinn at 0100, as he marked it with a watch in his pocket since his wrist had swollen three times its size. He walked some more, the pain and the nausea bringing him back to the cold, unpleasant, never-ending time getting his ass smoked on the Cole Range and into the waist-deep muck of swamps in Florida. There was a sergeant, as Quinn had become, who delighted in the worst of it, the hell of the situation that every Ranger has to live through. You didn't just get through pain, discomfort, hardships, you learned to smile at it, make it your friend, be familiar with mud in your mouth and up your nose, nearly choking to death on green water, running with a ruck, until your body had failed but your mind kept on going. *Move, Ranger, move. Go, go, go. Speed up. Endure. Love it.*

Quinn had a compass that he didn't really need but checked in with, knowing the rolling hills and the markers since he'd been a boy. There was a pond somewhere close. A small, forgotten little pond where he'd gone with Caddy when they were kids, Caddy playing house in a homemade Indian fort while Quinn caught, cleaned, and cooked some sunfish and bream. If he could get to the lost pond, he could see back down the way he came. At first light, he'd be able to spot the enemy down in the valley and watch their movements. He just had to keep on heading to the high ground. The high ground is where he would rest.

There had been a few biscuits left, some jerky, and a jug of water. Quinn had gotten all of it on his back, along with Rusty's .308 and all the ammo he'd had on him. Quinn's own Beretta 9 fully loaded and tucked in his waistband. The hard rain had frozen on the trees, the clicks of the branches sounding like fragile bits of glass.

He'd found his way to the top, but the pond was gone. In the darkness, he could see the huge impression that it had left, with a small bit of water left in deep pockets. This is where he'd wait through the night. Once he could see again and see who was following, he'd keep moving west.

At the top of the hills, the wind was terrific and very cold. His face was frozen, only a ball cap to protect his head, and thick green barn coat to cover his body. He slid a thick wool blanket from the ruck, pulling it over his shoulder and busted arm with his good hand. The cedars were evergreens and would block the wind for the night. Even though he felt sick, Quinn forced himself to eat a biscuit and drink some water. His teeth chattered, his good hand frozen and his bad hand without any feelings at all.

Sometime later, from where he sat and watched, he saw four different flashlight beams pinging around in the valley. Toward deep night, they were all gone.

Quinn knew they'd be back. And he'd be waiting.

. . .

Wflat'd that man mean 'the party's over'?" a black stripper asked Johnny Stagg.

"He didn't mean nothing," Stagg said. "He's just a son of a bitch."

"Sure was a mess of cussing and yelling come from that back room of yours," she said. "I thought y'all were going to get down and dirty."

"I'm a Southern gentleman," Stagg said. "I don't get down and dirty."

"Mmm-hmm," the stripper said. She didn't have on a stitch, just a pair of eight-inch acrylic heels. On her long brown arm was a tattoo celebrating the birth of her son. "Is he the law or something?"

"Of a type."

"Can I get you another drank?"

Stagg nodded to the girl. She wandered back behind the bar, shuffling ice into a highball glass. "Dr Pepper with grenadine and two cherries?"

Stagg nodded again. It was nine a.m. at the Booby Trap Lounge. The Trooper hadn't been gone thirty minutes, laying out the new law of the land as relayed by Jackson. He said the whole county was in shutdown mode and damage control. He told Stagg not to even think about picking up the phone or calling a meet without his permission. The man had stood across Johnny Stagg's desk, looking down on him, finger extended, and said, "The Feds are headed this way. I'll burn this whole goddamn town before I let you embarrass my people."

And that's when Stagg had stood up and the unpleasantness started. The stripper laid the drink, popping and fizzing, on the table. "Where your boy at?" she asked.

"I don't know."

The Trooper said he was dead. Stagg didn't believe it.

"Should've been here," the stripper said. "Teach that nasty gray-headed man some manners."

"Yes, ma'am."

"When Mr. Ringold here, ain't nobody fuck with Charisma."

"Who the hell's Charisma?"

"That's my stage name," she said. "My real name is Linda. Linda Allen. You seen my G-string anywhere, Mr. Stagg?"

"You left it onstage," he said. "Last number of the night."

"Ying Yang Twins doing 'Salt Shaker,'" she said. "That's my signature song. 'Shawty crunk on the floor wide open!'"

"How 'bout 'Grandpa, Tell Me 'Bout the Good Ole Days'?" Stagg said, thinking that if Ringold was dead and Colson was dead, the bastards were tracking shit right to his back door. He'd smile and glad-hand over in Oxford at the Grove, but he wouldn't be taking the fall for the whole show. He wasn't his daddy. He didn't shovel shit for a living.

"You look sad, Mr. Stagg," the girl said, standing behind him, rubbing his shoulders. "Let me loosen you up a bit."

"Sit your ass down, Linda," Stagg said. "I'm just thinking on things. You can stay, if you like."

"Can I drink?"

"I don't care," he said. "Help yourself."

"You always saying for us to keep clean but act dirty."

"We're closed," Stagg said. "Be what you like."

The girl poured a big helping of Jack Daniel's with a little ice into a tall plastic cup. She set down the cup, fetched her G-string, and waddled into it, not fooling with covering up her drooping breasts. She sucked the Jack through a long straw like it was Kool-Aid.

"You got a family?" she asked.

"Sure."

"Boy or girl?"

"Boy."

"How old?"

Stagg watched the empty stage in the dim light, wondering how that hunt was going for Quinn Colson. Stagg telling the Trooper to shut it down and leave it, but the man wanting to close the loop. *Son of a bitch.* He'd killed Rusty Wise. The fucker killed the sheriff to shut him down. The red padded booths, the golden stripper poles shone dull in the muted stage lights. The cleaning crew would be here soon, wiping down the booths and the stage with Lysol, letting in some fresh air before the truckers came back for another round.

"How old's your boy?" Linda asked.

"I'm not sure."

"What's he like?"

"My boy?" Stagg said. "I guess he's a tricky sort."

"How's that?" Linda said, pulling off a blonde wig with short bangs. She scratched her short Afro and tilted her head, really listening, wanting to know what Stagg had to say.

"I guess I just don't trust many folks."

"That's why you check our bags before we leave?"

"Yes, ma'am."

"My son is smart," she said. "He stay with my momma when I work. I hope he never turns on me."

"It ain't a good feeling," Stagg said. "It'll play with your head."

Linda sucked down some more of her drink, telling Stagg more than he wanted to know about her ten-year-old son. She said he didn't know what his momma did, he thought she worked at the Build-A-Bear over in Tupelo. She hoped to get enough money working two jobs, her other at the new Walmart, that they could leave town, maybe get on to Atlanta. She had people there.

"You want me to leave the lights on, Mr. Stagg?" she said, calling out from the open door, letting in a rush of cold air.

"No, ma'am," Stagg said. "Shut 'em off."

Lillie walked back into the sheriff's office, realizing that she'd seen three sheriffs come and go in her time: Hamp Beckett took his own life, his nephew was voted out, and now someone had shot and killed Rusty Wise. She wondered if this whole thing wasn't a big fucking sign that maybe Jericho wasn't for her. Even if a woman could ever be elected sheriff in north Mississippi, she wasn't too sure this was a title she'd want to hold.

"I thought you'd gone," Caddy said. Lillie almost forgetting she was there, the woman sitting back in the chair her brother used to fill, fiddling around with the maps and pictures laid out on the desk.

"Caddy, please don't look through all that," Lillie said. "Those files are part of an open investigation. You don't need to be reading transcripts."

"I'm not," she said. "I'm just looking at your maps."

"Fine."

Lillie reached for her Winchester she'd left in the gun rack against the far wall. She stocked her pockets with more bullets and an extra magazine for her Glock. She'd already called up McCaslin, Watts, and Cullison to meet her at the Fate General Store and called on two more counties to meet her in Tibbehah County. She'd flush the woods with so much of the real law that the shitbirds couldn't make a play for Quinn. Ringold promised he had help on the way but was going into the woods himself to see if he couldn't get to Quinn before anyone. Nobody would be looking for him. Ringold was dead and gone, far as they knew.

"This red circle on the map where you found Rusty Wise?" Caddy said.

"Mmm-hmm," Lillie said, holding the gun and nodding for Caddy to vacate the office. "C'mon. I got to lock it."

"And down the road is where you found Quinn's truck?"

Lillie shut the door slightly and raised her voice. "Listen. I know you're worried as hell about Quinn and want to know every detail. But this isn't the time, Caddy. I got to move."

"He wasn't far from Highway 9, but y'all are making marks up into the Big Woods?"

"Where?"

"The Big Woods," Caddy said. "That's what we called it when we were kids. That's where Quinn used to hunt when he was a boy. Where he got found that time after being gone. All that stuff that was in the newspapers. 'Country Boy Did Survive.'"

"I think he knows what he's doing," Lillie said. "I never doubted that. There's just a serious fucking time factor I'm working with."

Caddy picked up the printed map and brought it over to Lillie. She pressed her thumb on a mark at the far edge of the page. "This way," she said. "That's where he's headed."

"That's a lot of woods," Lillie said. "We're talking miles and miles."

"He's trying to make the cut over to the Trace," Caddy said. "I know that trail. The exact trail. Let me show it to you."

"How about you just tell me?"

"Things might've changed," Caddy said, pulling into her heavy coat and wool hat and brushing past Lillie at the door. "I hadn't been on that trail since I was eight. I never wanted to see it again. I swore it."

"I got to go, Caddy."

"Would you listen to me?" Caddy said. "God damn it. Quinn was never lost when we were kids. I was with him. He was hiding from a bad man. We were hiding. I know where he's headed. He's taking the same path and I can take you there."

Quinn slept on and off through the darkness, waking up at the false dawn and assessing the situation. He checked and cleaned his forearm, which looked worse this morning, twisted and purple, with no feeling at all in his hand. His water jug had frozen overnight, so he used the last of the antibacterial from the snakebite kit, wrapping his arm in some clean gauze and resetting the splint. The left arm was useless. Without the injury, he could've headed right back the way he'd come, following the far northern border, and buttonhook around to the men. With some stealth and full control of the .308, he could have disabled all of them without a problem. But with one arm and use of only a pistol, the task was a little trickier. As he'd learned in the Ranger Indoctrination Program and Rogers' Rules of Ranging, sometimes you have to disperse to take a mightier stand down the road. Or as Kenny Rogers once said, "You've got to know when to hold 'em. Know when to fold 'em."

If he could keep on rucking west, the men might disperse and he could pick them off one by one. There was also some shelter he could make by nightfall, an old cattle barn deep into the National Forest. He might be able to draw a few of them into the barn and set up shop there. With a pistol, the work would come easier.

The blanket he'd used for shelter last night had frozen as stiff as a board. He'd sink it in what was left of the pond and cover his tracks the best he could along the path. The good thing about it being so cold was that the soft ground had frozen and tracking would be difficult. Quinn stared down into the valley, trying to see if the men had returned and which direction they'd headed. But the entire valley was covered in a sheen of ice, coating the heavy-weighted pines and brittle limbs of hardwoods. You could hear the branches clicking together like bottle trees.

In his coat pocket, Quinn found one last hard biscuit and ate it. He chipped some ice off a tree and sucked on it while packing the gear he'd scavenged. He had a fifteen-round magazine for the sidearm and only twelve bullets for the .308. A Bear & Son white bone bowie knife hung on his hip.

He'd need some more food. Some sleep and some medical care. If he didn't get a sweat going, he'd be at risk for hypothermia. He knew an infection was soon to follow on that arm. Of course if he'd been Rambo, he'd take the bowie knife and cut out the bullet. But his medical training had told him that was a bad idea. Sometimes that bullet is pressing just right on an artery and cutting out the bullet would just turn on the tap.

The last thing he did before leaving the dead pond was reach into his coat pocket for his cigar. He'd never give the enemy an edge with smoke. But without coffee, he needed to get a good buzz going, so he broke the end off, inserting some of the leaves behind his lip. Quinn had never been one for dipping, unlike most every other Army Ranger he'd ever known, but it would do the job.

As he set out on the western deer trail, deep into the Big Woods, he heard the heavy tramping of feet.

A man walked up within fifteen meters of where Quinn stood, stooping down and checking the water's edge for footprints. The man was in his forties, pale and thick-bodied, wearing a green puffy coat and sunglasses. His posture and haircut looked like law enforcement, but he wore no insignia on his jacket or hat.

The man squatted to his haunches, studying the frozen mud, looking like an Indian tracker from an old Western. He wouldn't see anything but raccoon and deer prints. Quinn hadn't even walked to the water's edge.

Still, Quinn took no chances, approaching the man from behind. The man carried a rifle, slung out of reach and over his shoulder. There was a chance, Quinn knew, that someone suspected him of killing Rusty. He'd been blamed for equally bad things. This could be a whole different crew than who'd been hunting him last night. They could be trying to help.

Within two feet, walking soft and slow, Quinn said, "Cold day for a hunt."

The man, still on his haunches, turned and looked up at Quinn. Quinn had the Beretta aimed dead center.

"You Colson?" the man said.

"What if I am?"

"Been looking for you all night."

"You found me."

"You've made a mite mess of things."

"Who are you with?"

"You mean like the law?"

Quinn didn't speak and shifted the gun a bit. His ruck lay waiting on the side path. All the ice in the trees clinking, sharp wind skimming the waterless pond.

"Don't be a goddamn fool."

"If you're not the law," Quinn said, "who are you?"

The man grinned, smug and self-satisfied, gathering his feet and standing up, his right hand in the puffy coat pocket. He kept on smiling, meeting Quinn's eye. "There's too many of us," he said. "Don't make it no harder."

"Take your hand out of your pocket, sir," Quinn said.

"You sure?" he said. "You got pretty shot-up last night."

"Take your hand out of that pocket," Quinn said. "Third time and I'll shoot you dead. It's too fucking cold to argue about this."

"All right, all right," the thick-bodied man said. "I got no problem showing you my—" And the man pulled out a pistol and nearly got it clear before Quinn shot him three times dead center, dropping his fat ass to his knees. The man fell back into the pond, his head breaking the ice of a little pocket of water.

Quinn walked on over and kicked him farther in. He covered the man's face with the frozen blanket and added some branches across his body. If someone wasn't looking for him, they wouldn't see him and would keep on going.

Three gunshots. Now they'd be headed this way and on his trail.

34.

The bald-headed lawyer had been worth every nickel. The only reason Mickey had used him was because he'd remembered the jingle from the commercial, with all the rapping and dancing, the 901 area code plus the number. But he'd gotten him sprung, Mickey having to come up with ten grand in cash and a hundred-thousand-dollar bond, the lawyer arguing to the judge that his client wasn't a flight risk. The man had even given Mickey a ride back from the Tibbehah County Jail, stopping off at Captain D's for a deluxe seafood platter, plus an extra order of butterfly shrimp, and a Diet Coke. Mickey walked in the house, set the paper sacks on the counter, and turned on the lights. Jesus Christ, he needed a shower.

"What you got there?" a boy said. "Sure smells good. I'm hungry as hell."

Chase Clanton was sitting on his sofa, watching the big plasma TV, Mickey and Tonya on their honeymoon trying out different and unique positions.

"What the hell you doing here, man?" Mickey said. "Are you crazy? I hadn't been out of jail but an hour. You know the cops are watching my place. Son of a bitch."

"Don't worry," Chase said. "I left my vehicle down the road. I just figured it was high time me and you talk."

"Oh yeah?"

"Yeah," Chase said. "That's right. I'm tired of you wiping your ass with me and Uncle Peewee like we just the hired help."

"Y'all were the hired help," Mickey said. "You were paid to do a job and get lost."

"And dump a body for you," Chase said. "God damn. You forget about that part? You should've heard the big splash Kyle made into the Tombigbee. I watched him sink on down to the bottom and out of sight. I think that shit kind of makes us partners."

"I don't have time for this," Mickey said. "I swear to Christ I'll call the law right now. They're already looking for you. Me and you are done."

"What'd you tell them about me?"

"Nothing," Mickey said. "Shit. Just leave. Get out of here. My fucking seafood platter is getting cold. I don't want no cold shrimp. I been hanging out with every shitbag in Tibbehah County, folks asking me all about the safe, how much we'd get, how'd we do it, and all that mess. One of the fellas in the can used to go to my church. He trimmed the hedges."

Chase had not moved on the couch, dressed in gray sweatpants and a maroon football jersey with the number 12 on the front. He had his hands down his pants, fiddling around, like it was helping him think some. On the coffee table was an open bag of Golden Flake Sweet Heat BBQ Fried Pork Skins and a can of Milwaukee's Best. They kept silent for a moment, the only sound in the room coming from the television and Tonya's groaning and giggling.

"Why don't you turn that shit off?"

"Y'all are good," Chase said. "Nothing to be ashamed of. If you let me back it up a moment, I'll show you one hell of a play. That woman—

I figure it's your wife—does a scissor kick and turn, landing on her tummy, so you can try out a different approach. I mean, it was real effortless. I could tell she had some real natural talent."

"Turn it off," Mickey said, digging into the bag for some shrimp. Damn, they were cold. "I had to listen to her bitching at me all morning. Last thing I need is to hear more screaming."

"How'd she get so tan?"

Mickey leaned against the counter, watching a side view of him and Tonya, not really thinking much about him on that eighty-inch, thinking more how'd he get this brain-dead hillbilly back on the road without calling the sheriff's office. "She owns a tanning parlor," he said. "It's more than that. You can get coffee there, too. But she likes to tan."

"Even in the wintertime?"

"Especially in the wintertime," Mickey said. "Look, Chase? Come on over here and get you a piece of fish and some fries. Get a hot meal in you and then go boogie on down the road. This looks bad. Real bad. Someone catches us together and we're looking at a better case, added time. I can drive you back to your car. But just get the hell out of Jericho."

"I want my money."

"What money?"

"Half of what you pulled out of that safe," he said. "I want half of what you promised my Uncle Peewee."

"Take it up with your Uncle Peewee," Mickey said, sifting some fries onto a plastic plate and thunking down a cold piece of fish.

"I can't."

"Why?" Mickey said, heading to the refrigerator and pulling out a cold beer, popping the top, and taking a long sip.

"'Cause I killed him."

When he turned, Chase had a gun on him.

On the television, it was Tonya's big brown ass shimmying like two old ham hocks. *Big Daddy. Big Daddy. Yes, sir, Big Daddy.* Oh, hell.

"I'll get straight with you after all this mess is done."

"You'll get straight with me now, Mickey Walls," Chase said, grinning. "It's high time you go and make things right."

Lillie drove her Jeep Cherokee down the dead-end road, past the men with rifles eyeing her, huddled around two pickup trucks, and beyond Quinn's old Ford to where the road just stopped cold in a hill.

"Who were they?" Caddy said.

"I don't know," Lillie said. "I was told they were with highway patrol."

"But you don't believe it?"

"No, ma'am," Lillie said. "I don't know. We got folks on the way. But I'd just as soon not stop and chat. Let's keep on moving ahead of them and get to where we're going."

"It's just an idea," Caddy said. "I can't be sure. But it's so close to where we got lost. If I were Quinn, that's what I'd be thinking about."

"Maybe he knows," Lillie said. "Maybe he figures you and I would talk?"

"I think Quinn hasn't figured me into the process for some time," Caddy said, Jeep window cracked, spewing smoke outside. "I think he figures me pretty much worthless."

"Come on."

"I'm not crying on it," she said. "But it sure would be nice to prove him wrong."

Lillie opened the door and walked around to the Jeep's hatch. She pulled out a backpack, her Winchester, and a handheld GPS. Cell phones didn't even register out this way. Lillie pointed into the thick woods and the gentle rising of a hill to the north.

"That way?"

"I'm not Quinn," Caddy said. "Can you show me? On the map?"

Lillie laid out the map on the hood of the Jeep, the small acre pond circled in red. She said it was a good mile into the deepest part and another mile and a quarter up to the top of the ridge.

"I have good boots," Caddy said. "Come on."

"I don't know about these folks," Lillie said. "We could wait for some help. Go in later."

"Shit."

"Yeah," Lillie said. "If we get stopped, let me talk. Don't open your fucking mouth."

Caddy nodded. She had on a waterproof woodsman camo parka and a pink Carhartt hat. Lillie figured maybe the pink would stop them from being confused with Quinn. And maybe help them from both being shot. After all, they were just helping in the search, walking the ground and marking off the grids. If there was too much trouble, Lillie had a radio. She could contact the deputies or Ringold. Ringold had moved on ahead of them to find Quinn.

Lillie kept to the GPS, heading due north, not seeing anything, not even wildlife in the frozen patch of woods. Sunlight had come on weak and white through the treetops, and every so often an icicle would drop onto the moldy wet leaves. The cedars were encased in ice, and big spread oaks seemed to be made of glass. Somewhere, far off, she heard the growling motors of ATVs, and even farther away the sound of an airplane and then a helicopter. She wondered if it was the copter she requested from Tupelo. A mile in, she and Caddy changed course and headed up into the hills and the ridge that would take them up and over into the National Forest and what Caddy called the Big Woods.

"Are you going to tell me what happened?" Lillie asked. "Because in all the time I've known Quinn, he never told me the whole story."

"He blames himself," Caddy said. "But he saved my life."

"From that man?" Lillie said. "The game warden?"

Caddy nodded under the pink hat as they walked. She kept her hands in her pockets. Lillie's hands were free and growing cold. Every so often, she'd switch up the hand holding the gun to keep the shooting finger warm, pliable, and ready. Ever since they'd found Rusty in that stand, she could not wait to use it. She didn't need much of an excuse.

"That man is dead," Caddy said. "Quinn killed him."

"He never told me that."

"He'd followed me and Quinn up to the pond up yonder," she said. "We had made a little fort with limbs. I fashioned a little broom out of weeds, sweeping the dirt floor."

"And what happened?"

"He tossed away Quinn's gun, smacked him around, tied us both up and made us walk," she said. "He told us he was taking us out and that Quinn would have to go to jail for killing those deer, running from the law. The whole time, I felt his eyes on me. Do you understand what I mean? I was only eight, but I knew what he was thinking."

Lillie didn't say anything, the hill getting a little more steep, seeing her breath come out frosty and quick, listening, watching the trees and the growth around them. She would turn and look back every so often, expecting to see one of those shitbags from the road following them. Maybe even kind of hoping that they were.

"It started to rain and that's when we found shelter in that old barn," Caddy said. "I guess the National Forest used to be part of some old farms. I didn't see a house, only the barn."

"And that's where you think Quinn will head?"

"I think if he's hurt, like you say, and cold, that's where he'd go to hide out."

"Or maybe he's leading some folks that way," Lillie said. "Quinn has taught me that it's always best if you can control a situation. A barn would be a solid enclosure for him to wrangle the bad guys into a tight space."

"It's almost pretty out here," Caddy said. "Everything seems so clean. I can breathe."

"How was rehab?"

"That's the path," Caddy said, ignoring her and pointing. "I know it. The trail we followed. Jesus Christ, that seems like yesterday. How can something be so far back but so close in your mind?"

"Bad stuff is like tar," Lillie said. "It's hard to wash off."

"I'm not going to sugarcoat it," Caddy said, walking faster, hands in her pockets. "It was as bad as it gets."

The light seemed brighter across the ridge. Morning light shining through the ice in the trees, nearly blinding, as she crested the hill and stood at the rim of the old pond. Only it wasn't a pond. It was just a big ugly mud hole with pockets of ice spread across.

"This is it?" Lillie said.

Caddy nodded.

"You sure?"

Caddy walked to the edge of the mud and ice. She stood there and looked all around her, her face frozen in cold or maybe the memory of that time. "That motherfucker raped me," she said. "I was eight years old. He's dead and gone, but I can still smell his breath every morning I wake up."

"But Quinn took care of it."

"Why should a ten-year-old need to make things right?"

"And Hamp?" Lillie said. "How'd he play in this?"

"He found us," Caddy said. "He buried the son of a bitch, took me home and got me cleaned up. Quinn got to hike out on his own. That's what happened. How he became the little lost boy who was a hero. It changed him."

"Changed you, too," Lillie said. But she wasn't sure Caddy heard her. A sharp wind cut across the top of the hills just as Caddy exclaimed a giddy shriek. She smiled big and pointed into the nothingness of the pond.

"He's alive," Caddy said. "I told you. He is here."

Lillie walked up to Caddy's shoulder and stared down into the pond, seeing an ugly man staring, flat-faced, against a thin sheet of ice. He looked bluish, taking on a quality like he'd been cured and pickled.

"Yeah, that looks like Quinn's work."

"Come on," Caddy said, walking around the pond, heading west. "Come on."

Hypothermia or some other bad shit overtook Quinn about midday. He started to shiver and his breathing came too fast, him straying off course after sighting a tree a hundred meters away. His teeth chattered, and his mind would wander, thinking back on times he'd tracked rabbit and deer in these woods with Boom. He would recognize a little creek, an oak now doubled in size, some moss on the side of a rock. Sometimes there was the smell of the rabbit over a fire, the warmth of the stones. Other times he'd be back on some rocky ledge in Kandahar Province that looked like a vista from a John Ford film, bullets ricocheting off rocks, earth shaking from air strikes. He would jolt to attention as if touched by a live wire, snapping his head to the far reaches of the Big Woods. One step at a time. *Move, move, move. Come on, Ranger, get your ass up.* Seventeen miles. Seventeen miles was a brisk jog before breakfast. Nobody cared if you were hungry or thirsty. Cold or busted-up. *Come on, Ranger. Keep moving. Don't you slow up. Don't quit. Don't you fucking quit. This is a paradise. Do you know how goddamn lucky you are?*

He was back on the Darby Queen obstacle course at Benning, on top of the Haditha Dam on night patrol with his platoon, watching a bright red setting sun as mongrel dogs ate dead Iraqi soldiers, heart sinking as Anna Lee gave him a secret smile and turned her back, driving his old '89 Ford full tilt and spewing mud, with Boom laughing at his side, and then that endless twenty-one-gun salute to old Hamp Beckett as they lowered his broken self into the ground. Quinn heard the shots and stumbled into a ravine, falling, but catching himself with one hand. The water ran under a thin sheet of ice, reddish mud covering the front of his jacket, his boots slipping, not finding purchase. *Come on, Ranger. Fucking move. Get up. Go. Go. Go.* Jason Colson gave a thumbs-up, put the pedal to the metal, and jumped that cherry-red Firebird over a broken bridge and a crooked Alabama river. *Yee-haw.*

Quinn felt like he was about to throw up. He dry-heaved and wavered on his boots, trying again to get the hell out of the crevice. He found a foothold in the ravine and was crawling up with one hand until he sighted another hand with dirty fingernails reaching for him, grabbing him by the barn coat and tugging him up onto the hard frozen ground.

"Stay down, motherfucker."

Quinn got to his knees and looked up at two men. They didn't look friendly. Both held hunting rifles and wore green puffy coats similar to the man who'd tried to kill him back at the pond. They were both white, smallish, and stubby, with red-chapped, unshaven faces. They smelled like body odor and stale cigarettes. Quinn couldn't figure out why he hadn't smelled them a mile away. They had the look of men who lived in the woods and lived to hunt. One of them carried a GPS, his jaw fat with tobacco.

Quinn gave them a hard look, about to reach for the gun at his hip. One held a rifle on him while the other pulled the Beretta and snatched the .308 off his back, slamming the ever-living shit out of his broken arm, bringing tears to Quinn's eyes and his mind back to full focus and sharpness. One of the men, just as short and ugly as the other, pulled a radio from his pocket and announced that they'd gotten the son of a bitch. "About half-dead."

The one in front of him had pocketed Quinn's Beretta. The other man had slung both rifles over his shoulder so he could work the hand-held radio, cocky and sure his buddy could control the ragged-looking man in front of him. Dead-eyed and one-armed. Quinn knew he was covered in dried mud and Rusty's blood.

Quinn kept staring at the man with the gun. He listened to the other. The pain in his busted arm was sharp and raw and felt as if the bones had ripped through the skin. His bad hand hung in a twisted and bizarre way, fingers turning black and purple.

Maybe three feet away, the man pointed his rifle at Quinn's chest. Quinn bent at the waist and started to puke, dry-heaving up a little water, retching until hollowed-out. Coughing and gagging as he looked at his boots and then at the other man's boots moving in closer. That was close enough. The men were hunters, men who lived in the woods and could follow a trail and stalk their prey. They were patient men who could walk quietly and live off the land.

But they weren't soldiers. They were sloppy and nervous, shifting from foot to foot.

Quinn came up with the bowie knife and stabbed the gunman up under his jaw and well into his head. The knife stuck hard and Quinn let go of the bone handle as the man fell, reaching into his pocket, the man going slack as Quinn snatched back his Beretta. He squeezed off four rounds into the man with the radio and another two into the man he held, before dropping him to the frozen ground.

Blood poured from the man's mouth as he flailed, rolling back and making a deep internal scream. Soon all his motion and rage stopped.

Wind came fast and hard off the western side of the rolling hills and down into the wide expanse of the forest. The trees were much older here, untouched by loggers for decades, the land growing up tall and strong and healing over the scars men had made. Everything was still and peaceful as Quinn tried to just breathe, slow himself, come back down from wherever the hell he'd been. He had blood all over his right hand and across his jacket.

"Where are you?" the radio on the ground asked. "Jesus Christ. What the fuck's going on out there?"

35.

Lillie found the dead men first, holding up her hand to Caddy on the path, telling her to stay back. "More of your brother's handiwork," Lillie said. "God, it's a mess. I'd rather you not see this shit. Try not to look down."

But Caddy didn't listen. Caddy Colson never listened to anyone, walking up to where Lillie stood and seeing the weird diorama set in dirt and ice. One man lay facedown in moldy leaves and another was flat on his back, with big wide eyes and a bowie knife stuck up under his chin and impaling his tongue. There'd been a big scuffle, lots of footprints, and more blood. It looked like a butcher's floor that needed a good mopping.

"That's Quinn's knife," Caddy said.

"So it is," Lillie said. "He can come back and get it himself. Let's just keep moving."

"What about that pack?" Caddy said, getting down on all fours and starting to rifle through a camo backpack, finding big brass bullets, a half-used roll of gauze, torn strips from a flannel shirt, and an empty bottle of water. She held up a roll of fishing line and some hooks, a book of matches. "He must've gotten this from Rusty. Why'd he leave it?"

"He took their guns," Lillie said. "A man can only carry so much."

Caddy shook her head, got to her feet, and began to follow Lillie again, Lillie glancing down every few minutes to study her GPS. She took off her hat, tightened her ponytail with a rubber band, and tugged the hat back on before heading off. The woods soon opened up into a sprawling meadow dotted with small trees. The brown grass was hip-high and brittle with ice, as they waded through. The sky was big and wide, gray and lifeless.

"It's straight ahead," Caddy said. "I remember it. Just keep walking. I know where I am. I know it."

"We're taking the long way around," Lillie said.

"Why?"

"In case someone's watching, I'd rather not have my ass hanging out," Lillie said. "Here, we can duck back into the woods."

"But I can see it," Caddy said. "I see the glimmer off the tin roof."

"And folks can see you, too," Lillie said. "Keep walking. You hear shots, run into the woods. You hear me?"

"Who are these guys?"

"In my humble opinion, I'd say professional shitbirds," Lillie said. "They're not law enforcement and don't have any authority at all out here. I see someone I don't know and I'll shoot first. I'm not asking for badges. You know, like that movie?"

"What movie?"

"Ask Quinn when we see him," Lillie said. "He'll know. He knows those Westerns."

She looked at Caddy, who'd grown very pale and silent. Her eyes, unblinking and silent, wouldn't leave that barn. Her jaw set, muscles clenching in her face.

"You OK?"

"I didn't want to come back here."

"I'm with you."

"Never," she said. "I only wanted to burn it down. I burned it down a thousand times in my mind."

They moved in a big sloppy circle, following the tree line and coming closer to the big old barn, washed and beaten of paint, leaning hard against the wind. Lillie held her Winchester as she walked, her trigger finger just outside the guard.

Up ahead, the figure of a man walked out from the shadows waving his arms over his head. "Hello, hello," he said. "Deputy Virgil?"

I don't feel comfortable doing this in the daylight," Mickey Walls said. "And truth be known, I don't feel comfortable doing this at all. Can't we get right another way? After all this shit's over and the dust has settled?"

"Dust ain't gonna settle," Chase said. "Now get out of the fucking Hummer and show me where Kyle hid my stash."

They'd come this far, might as well see this through, get this kid gone. Mickey knew any moment he'd see a Tibbehah County patrol car roll on up behind them, lights flashing. How they'd love to put him with one of those Alabama boys, try to pin Kyle on him. If they ever did find Kyle.

"So that's it?" Mickey said. "You just up and decide to take the rest of it? 'Cause you earned it."

"I'm making it right," Chase said. "I done told you, I want half. This is just between me and you now. What's right is right."

"Can I ask you something first?"

"Sure," Chase said. "I ain't got no truck with it."

"How do I know you ain't gonna use me and then shoot me right in the head like your Uncle Peewee?" Mickey said.

"'Cause you don't," Chase said. "You're thinking like the defense in the LSU game. After Saban took that time-out, they were waiting on that trick play. They changed up their defense, watching ole Landon Collins run back on the field, clock ticking down."

"I didn't see the game," Mickey said. "I don't give a damn for LSU or 'Bama."

"The ball is snapped to Mosley instead and he hands the son of a bitch off to Jarrick Williams," Chase said. "LSU knew it was coming but could never imagine it coming like this."

"So you're not going to shoot me?" Mickey said. "You're going to take your money and leave Jericho? Right?"

"Right as rain."

"Come on," Mickey said, opening the door to his Hummer, windshield wipers frozen in place. "Kyle kept it in the septic tank. Hope you don't mind the smell of shit."

S ometime on the walk out of the woods, Quinn started talking to his dead uncle.

Uncle Hamp looked to be in fine form, not even any scarring from where he'd shot himself in the head, and seemed to have lost a good bit of weight. He looked almost like the Hamp Beckett who'd come home from Korea and the U.S. Army to take over as lawman of Tibbehah County, running the back roads and trying to shut down the Colson family stills. His eyes and buzz cut were the same shade of black. His hair looked to have been varnished at some point, maybe after death.

"How'd you find me?" Quinn said.

"You used your radio," Hamp said. "Don't you remember?"

"Damn, it's cold," Quinn said. "I can't feel nothing."

"Move closer to the fire," Hamp said. "Help's on the way."

"I got rid of the guns," Quinn said. "I hid them in the creek. I couldn't carry them anymore."

"You did fine."

"I saw the barn," Quinn said. "I nearly made it. Didn't I?"

"You just needed some help."

"Won't they see us?" Quinn said. "That's a lot of smoke."

Uncle Hamp tossed on some more old twigs and the fire kicked up good and hot, crackling under that tin roof. His face was obscured with all the heat and fire, smoke twirling around him. Nothing looked the same in the barn, not as he remembered. It looked like a fun house, the whole shelter tilted and warped, walls that curved and tin that sagged. Quinn recalled a rat. There had been a rat up in the corncrib. He recalled it looked at him with those red eyes, guarding all the old corn, while the fat man crawled on top of Caddy, making those noises.

"Can I look at your arm?"

"Don't you touch it."

"Looks broke?"

"Don't touch me," Quinn said. "I swear, I'll shoot you, Uncle Hamp. I already killed plenty of men. It hurts bad. God damn, it hurts."

"I'm not your damn uncle," someone said. "Jesus Christ. Quinn? Can you even fucking see me?"

"God, there were rats up there," Quinn said. "Nasty as hell. They had red eyes."

"Just stay warm," someone said, Quinn feeling two cold fingers on his neck. "Your lips have turned blue. You can barely talk, Ranger."

Glad I found you," the man said, grinning little yellow nubs for teeth. "Help'll be here soon. We're going to try and land a chopper right over there in that field and get you two out. That's a big wide space out there in them weeds."

"Who the hell are you?" Lillie asked.

The man wore a blue jacket with an insignia for the Mississippi Highway Patrol. He took off his hat, showing his short gray crew cut, and introduced himself, giving himself the rank of captain. Lillie felt like her stomach had dropped out of her. The man Ringold had mentioned. God damn it. Caddy eyed him with some suspicion, crossing her arms over her body, and raised her eyebrows at Lillie. Her pink wool hat was far down on her head, her shoulders slumped and hands in her pockets.

"I don't want to be evacuated," Lillie said. "We just walked over twelve miles, up through those hills, to get to the middle of nowhere. I think we'll stay until we get business finished."

"Ma'am," the Trooper said. "It's nearly night. We got some good folks out here. The best. We'll find Mr. Colson and get him to answer for what he did to Rusty Wise. I guess this isn't his first go-around with a matter like this."

"I don't know you," Lillie said. "I never even heard your name. So why don't you get the fuck out of the way."

"I can't do that, ma'am," the Trooper said. "Too much blood been spilt."

"You run down Quinn Colson again and more blood's going to get spilt," Lillie said. "This is his sister with me. You hear me, old man? It's been a long day of tramping through these woods to get where we're going. Whether you like it or not, I am the acting sheriff of Tibbehah County and I'm in command of this whole show."

The Trooper grinned with those goddamn stubby tobacco-stained teeth, his face like leather. "Maybe you don't realize this ain't Tibbehah County? Now keep on walking so I can get you two little ladies on out of here. I got shit to do."

The man motioned them on, Lillie noting the gun in his hand was a fifty-cal sniper rifle made by Barrett. Someone had planted a gun just like that in her home two years ago and blamed her for killing a convict and the preacher who Caddy had loved.

Jesus Christ, it kept on getting better and better.

36.

Well, that's the last of it."

"Damn," Chase said, watching Mickey, making sure the man didn't get tricky on his ass. "Man, you right. It smells like shit."

"Maybe that's why they call it a septic tank," Mickey said, tossing the black plastic bag with the others. The man closed up the hole and kicked some dirt over it. "Drag these bags up to the sheds and count what's left. Get what you want. Just promise me I don't have to see you no more."

"I promise."

"Don't get caught," Mickey said, lighting up a cigarette, the smoke smelling good to Chase. The stink all around them and all over them. "Run far and fast. Don't look back home. You understand? Change your hair and your looks. Get a tan in Mexico. Buy a new name. Become someone else. Hell, you'll have enough money to do it."

"That's all you got?" Chase said.

Mickey grinned, flicking the ash off his Marlboro. "Don't fall in love," he said. "Pussy will fucking kill you."

"That's what my Uncle Peewee always said," Chase said, laughing. "He said he had no shame in buying his loving because it was the only honest transaction in life. How much you figure is in those stinky-ass bags?"

"Half a mil," Mickey said. "Give or take a nickel or two."

"Fifty-fifty?"

"I really don't even give a shit anymore," Mickey said, tossing the cigarette into the weeds. "How about you just get your money and get gone? I just want to be left alone and think on things."

"At least put up a fight for it," Chase said. "The whole show being your idea. Maybe something like sixty, forty. That might make me feel better."

Mickey Walls shook his head, kept on walking back to the Hazlewood house and that red Hummer with black seats and a high-powered heater. He looked like a fella who was just spent.

"Hey," Chase yelled. "Hey, you? Mr. Walls? What the hell? Mr. Walls." Chase knew he'd have to do something, call an audible right then and there. Wasn't no time for no trick plays and misdirection. "Mickey?"

Mickey Walls looked at him.

"How 'bout we warm ourselves in that shed and count it out?" he said. "Won't take long at all."

"C̱an you hold this gun?" a voice said.

Quinn turned to see Ringold standing over him, stroking that big black beard. He had on a thick parka with the hood over his ball cap.

"Yeah."

"You nearly bled out," Ringold said. "You've got hypothermia."

"Where was I?"

"Made it out the woods," Ringold said. "I dragged you here. You thought I was someone named Hamp. That mean anything to you?"

Quinn nodded and tried to swallow, but his mouth was too dry. Ringold lifted a canteen to his lips and poured more water in his mouth. Quinn drank it down. Ringold lifted it up again, water pouring down, a fresh blanket wrapping him. There was a fire. He could feel the heat in his hand and spreading across his chest and down his legs. Damn, he could not stop shivering.

"I'll leave you with a gun and the water," he said. "How many do you think are left?"

"Two," Quinn said. "Maybe more."

"You see them?"

Quinn shook his head. The fire smelled very good and warm, embers catching in the cold air and floating up to the crossbeams of the roof. He tried to stand, go out with Ringold, and finish this thing.

Ringold put a hand to Quinn's shoulder. Quinn's whole body shook, teeth chattering. "Consider it a favor," he said. "I appreciate you saving a couple bastards for me."

That's a fine weapon," Lillie said.

"Appreciate it, Deputy Virgil," the Trooper said. "But how about you shut your mouth until you're on that helicopter."

"What is that?" Lillie said. "A Barrett fifty-cal?"

The Trooper turned his thick head to stare at her as they walked, tromping through the high grass. The man walked a couple paces behind them, holding the big-ass gun up under his arm.

"You plan on running into a combat situation out here?" she asked. "You can shoot an elephant at maybe a thousand yards."

"I didn't care to come out in nature with my pants down."

"But you could make a shot that far?" Lillie said, walking side by side with Caddy Colson. "On a clear day, good light, and the right wind, you could make that shot."

"Yes, ma'am," he said. "You better believe it."

"Especially if you set up shop real high," Lillie said. "Looking down into a valley. Maybe an old airstrip where some good ole boys had gathered for a little fun."

Caddy cut her eyes to Lillie but kept walking, mouth hanging open.

"Man took a hell of a shot like that a couple years back," Lillie said. "After the twister. Could never find him. Some folks even pinned the mess on me and Quinn. Saying I'd been the one up in the hills with a fifty-cal, making that shot. You do know I was a member of the Ole Miss Rifle Team?"

The man didn't answer, turn to look, or acknowledge Lillie in any way. He just kept on following a deer path through the high weeds to that old barn. The weeds were bunched tight in the ice, boots crunching over the brown, lifeless grass.

"Figured you wouldn't," Lillie said. "You don't look like a fan of higher education."

"Shut your fucking mouth," the Trooper said. "And drop your weapon. You raise that peashooter at me and I'll blow a hole through your chest the size of a softball."

Caddy had turned white. Her shoulders shaking like a little girl from a long way back. "It's fine," Lillie said. "It's fine."

"Drop the goddamn gun."

Lillie dropped the rifle, put her arm around Caddy, and kept on moving through the weeds and briars, the scraggly pine trees. About halfway across the meadow to the barn, Lillie could smell smoke.

Someone had a fire going in that warped old structure.

. . .

Quinn lifted his head as the three of them entered the mouth of the barn. Two women and a man. They walked closer and he knew it was Caddy and Lillie. There was a hard-looking man with a gray crew cut holding a big-ass rifle, not pointing it at them but walking with it. The man raised the gun with both hands as Caddy ran toward Quinn. She was crying as she fell to her knees and touched her forehead to his. His sister hugged him close, sending a shock of pain through the bad arm, but he almost didn't mind. The heat, the feeling, was coming back into his body.

She held him closer and touched his face, telling him he had blood all over him. And he shook his head, saying he'd been shot but was fine. Quinn lifted his head at the man with the crew cut. "Who are you?"

"Doesn't matter."

"Your men are dead," Quinn said. His voice sounded hoarse and very far away.

"I know it."

"I killed them."

"Makes us about even, then," the man said.

Lillie tossed her chin at the man. "This turd killed Rusty Wise and Jamey Dixon."

Caddy's eyes shot up to the man with the gun. Quinn reached for her hand under the cover of the blanket, touching her warm fingers and squeezing her hand. The fire had kicked up a little in the wind, sending more little sparks into the barn. Ringold had busted up some old barn wood and set it beside Quinn before he left. There was plenty of heat in the cold barn. The big twin doors had fallen off long ago, leaving nothing but a big square hole showing the dark gray light of the end of the day.

"The woman's talking crazy," the man said.

"That's the same type gun seeded in my house," Lillie said. "Dumb shit's not smart enough to at least get another model."

"Women shouldn't be the law," the man said. "Got more emotions than sense."

"Did you kill a man named Jamey Dixon?" Caddy said. "Did you?"

"Sister, I ain't never heard of no man named Jamey Dixon. Sounds like some country singer outta Nashville."

"Oh, yes, sir, you sure did," Lillie said. "And I'm going to nail your old withered ass for it."

Quinn touched his sister's fingers and passed his Beretta into her hands, letting the weight of it fall to her. "He was a good man," she said. "He helped a lot of people."

I never thought I'd come back to this place," Caddy said. Lillie watched her eyes, Caddy talking as if she and Quinn were the only two in the barn. "I feel like I can't breathe in here. I knew you'd come here, Quinn. I knew it."

"Who else knows?" the Trooper said.

"You and me walked that whole way," Caddy said. "That man pushing us on with his gun and the rope. Remember how he threw away your rifle? What happened to that gun?"

Quinn shook his head. He looked skeletal, little blood in his face or much life in his eyes. His back rose and fell with each breath. There was a lot of tin leaning against a far wall. Feed signs and scraps of roofing. Some leather tack had been nailed to the wall and petrified. The wooden walls had separated, leaving a good three or four inches between them, soft white light crossing paths.

"He told me you were going to jail," Caddy said. "Can you believe that? He said he was going to take a ten-year-old boy to jail. For what?

Killing some deer? Why did it bother him so much? What was it that just ate at the man?"

"I cut his tires," Quinn said, mumbling. He grinned with the memory.

"Who else knows where y'all are at?" the Trooper said.

"I can smell his breath," Caddy said. "Even now. I can smell that rancid, horrible shit in my face. And that beard nuzzling my little neck, the weight on top of me. I couldn't breathe. He was so fat and, god damn, it hurt so much. Thank you, Quinn. Thank you for what you did."

Somewhere far off, Lillie heard a helicopter. The Trooper heard it, too, the *putt-putt-putt* sounds of the rotors growing closer, night coming on fast out the mouth of the barn. "I came to help y'all," the Trooper said. "I'm a goddamn hero. Has everyone lost their mind?"

"At first, he couldn't do it," Caddy said. "He groaned and growled. Like an animal. Pissed as hell. He spit on his hand and worked on it as he pinned me down. I just knew I was going to die. I felt like my insides would split apart."

"Come on," the Trooper said. "Get up. Get up. I don't give two shits about this mess."

"Why would a grown man do that?" she said. "What kind of horror turned him into walking evil?"

Caddy stayed at Quinn's side, arm wrapping around her older brother, Quinn's shivering, almost in a palsy, under the blanket. Through the fire and smoke, he looked up to Lillie and then with dead eyes over to the Trooper. He nodded slow and with purpose to Caddy. Caddy closed her eyes and took a deep breath. "I don't pray anymore," she said. "I think I've forgotten how."

"I didn't kill nobody," the Trooper said. "I didn't rape nobody. Come on. Let's go. I'll make sure Colson is tended to. He's in rough shape."

"He loved me," Caddy said. "God damn you. He gave me purpose."

"Who the hell you talking about?" the Trooper asked.

"His name was Jamey Dixon," Caddy said. "He had a real light about him."

Lillie saw the movement under the blanket, Quinn's resigned look at the Trooper. The Trooper recognized it and brought up that big, heavy fifty-cal. But not in time for little Caddy Colson.

Little Caddy fired twice. Only one hit him.

But it was enough. He fell hard into the fire, smothering it under his body.

Chase liked the car. A Hummer was one hell of a ride—black leather, sunroof, satellite radio, and heated seats. Never in his life had he driven such a vehicle. Uncle Peewee's van was something special, like some kind of mythical beast, but this was riding in style. A man could get drunk just on the smell of that leather. Chase checked the fuel, nearly full, and turned on the radio, finding some sports talk radio on the ESPN channel. With all that money and all that fuel, he might not even have to stop until Texas. Maybe Mickey was right. Maybe Mexico was the place for him.

Or maybe the man was talking out his ass 'cause he knew that Chase was about to drop the hammer. He tried to keep the boy off guard, see his reaction, see how the money situation worked out. He would've hated to kill the man and find out he'd been left with a few hundred bucks and some torn-up newspaper.

But deep in that shithole, Chase had found his future. Sure would be a sweet ride to the west. He wouldn't miss Gordo, Alabama. Not one bit. He had cut the money, shook Mickey's hand, and then called the play, dropping his ass right then and there. Perfect call.

ACE ATKINS

"There's no way Alabama can finish next year in the top ten. It was a hell of a run, but Saban's done lost his edge. Maybe he can do the same at some other school. I think it's time he moved on."

"Next caller?"

"Well, if he's gonna try and make things right, Saban needs to fire his special teams coach. That joker cost us the game against Ole Miss."

When he hit the Louisiana line, Chase had damn near had enough of all this crap talk. He'd gone through two different shows over the last few hours. This time some shit-for-brains was running down Alabama's recruiting and, hell, it wasn't even close to signing day. Chase picked up a burner phone he'd taken off some black guy in New Orleans and called the number for the station. After two tries and another half hour, they finally patched him through, night rolling along on Interstate 10 to the Big Easy and on toward Houston.

"That train's gonna roll in T-town, you peckerhead," Chase said. "A bad 'Bama can kick the shit out of most everyone else. So before we all start crying in our cornflakes, how about we look to the future? And I don't want none of this Saban can't adjust to no hurry-up spread horseshit. You take what comes at you in this world and turn it around in the second half. I seen it happen time and again. That's what makes a man a goddamn winner."

37.

It only took one year and nearly three months before Caddy asked, "How come you got all the credit for shooting the son of a bitch?"

"Did you really want to be dragged into that mess?" Quinn asked. "Jesus, Caddy. You have a record. You're still back and forth in rehab. How's that going to look?"

They were standing side by side on the fence railing, watching the newborn cows and a couple new horses Jason had just bought without telling Quinn. "I've been clean and sober now for ten months, thank you, sir," Caddy said. "Being an addict doesn't make me a weak person or a bad person. It's just who I am and what I've got."

"But it would have confused the issue," Quinn said. "A bad man got killed. Nobody needed to muddy that water."

It was spring again. Quinn had been gone for six months, back over to Afghanistan for a good-paying job—protection, and some training of local fighters. He might go back or he might stay in Tibbehah. He hadn't really decided. There was a special election coming up in May, the second one in six years, and he'd been asked to run. Lillie was acting sheriff, but she didn't want to run—she didn't think she'd win. She said she talked too plain and honest to make friends. Right now, Quinn was just watching the cows in the pasture. Some new calves, jumping around and nuzzling at their mothers. The trees were green again, blackberries and honeysuckle had started to grow wild at the edge of the woods.

Quinn smoked a La Gloria Cubana from a box that had been sent to his home. He still didn't know Ringold's real name. Nor had it been divulged during the inquest that followed the deaths of four known hoods and a corrupt captain with the Mississippi Highway Patrol.

"Maybe if I had been involved, it might have shed more light on Jamey's murder," Caddy said.

"That Trooper's dead," Quinn said. "He never wanted Jamey Dixon to talk, like he didn't want me or Rusty to talk about what we knew. The way of Mississippi. Corruption is all good unless someone shines a light on it. Then they scatter like fucking rats. Dixon was a good man and I'm sorry, Caddy. I don't know if I ever told you how sincerely sorry I am for your loss."

"Quinn?"

"Yes, ma'am."

A couple calves walked, cautious and slow, to the fence line, confused by the people watching them. They were pure white but splattered with mud, big eyes curious. Their ears twitched with the unfamiliar sounds.

"I wish you'd stay."

"A lot of shit has happened," he said. "I got a lot to think about."

The things Quinn noticed most after being back were the colors: all the bright greens and the deep brown of the soil. Not the dull brown-beige of rocks and sandy earth. Home smelled different, rich with growing grass and ripe cow manure. There was no more fertile place than north Mississippi in the spring.

"So that's the plan?" Caddy said. "Just sit on the front porch in a rocking chair, smoking cigars and drinking whiskey? Maybe something will come to you from some old Lefty Frizzell record. And, right then and there, you'll know."

"Maybe so."

"Doesn't work that way," Caddy said. "I take this shit one day at a time. I do believe in a Higher Power and I hand that smoldering crap of problems over to him every morning. I know what I can take on and I send on the rest."

"Next time you talk to Jesus, ask him about the election," Quinn said. "I'd like to know my chances."

"You bet I will," Caddy said. "Have you talked to Anna Lee?"

"No," Quinn said. "Haven't been home that long."

"You been home long enough," Caddy said. "Y'all left it pretty rough last time."

"She wants me but doesn't know what to do with me."

"Hard to leave alone," Caddy said. "You want to leave it, know you should, but you just can't."

Quinn turned to look at his sister's face. Small and delicate under short blonde hair. Little scars along her jawline and on her thin arms and wrists. "How'd you know that?"

Caddy smiled and patted his arm. "Addiction is a hell of a thing, brother."

The letters had come even while he'd been gone, stamped from the federal prison camp in Montgomery, Alabama. Quinn had gotten fifteen of them from "Johnny T. Stagg," with his inmate number and new address far away from the Rebel Truck Stop. The truck stop shut down a year ago, with plywood over the windows and shopping bags over the pumps. Stagg wanted Quinn to come see him. He said they needed to talk person-to-person. Man-to-man. The phrasing of it depended on the letter.

After being back home, Quinn was in no hurry to drive over and see Stagg. He helped Jason plant corn, peas, tomatoes, and peppers. He happily awoke at dawn to feed the cattle and the horses. There were fences to mend and a lot of runs to Jericho Farm & Ranch for fertilizer and dewormer. Anna Lee and Shelby spent more and more nights at the farm. On Sundays, Caddy and Jason would join them for dinner. Little Jason and Shelby loved to climb the old oak in the backyard, play on the tire swing and run wild, reminding everyone of Quinn and Caddy as kids.

No one spoke of the Big Woods. No one really concerned themselves with the trial last year in Oxford. A new pizza shop had opened up on the Jericho Square. The old movie house had been refurbished and was ready for opening night soon.

On a hot Sunday in June, Quinn got up early, ran five miles along the dirt roads around his property, fed the animals, checked on the watermelons, and drove east on Highway 82 over to Maxwell Air Force Base and the federal pen, where he'd agreed to see Stagg.

A guard brought him into a mess hall with long dining tables and hard metal chairs and told him to wait. Ten minutes later, out came Stagg, wearing comfortable-looking prison blues and a big shit-eating grin. Outside the windows, men took their exercise among manicured grounds landscaped with blooming white gardenias and purple crape myrtles. It all had the air of a good Holiday Inn.

"Appreciate this," Stagg said. "I wanted to talk straight. You know these people read your mail?"

"It is prison, Johnny."

"Oh, hell, I know," Stagg said.

Quinn sat at the table on the same side of Johnny, legs crossed and waiting to hear whatever shuck Johnny was about to lay out.

"Maybe you figure I've been reformed," Stagg said. "That I had some kind of secret pill-popping addiction and now I've changed? Or that maybe I got me one of those Gideon's Bibles and got reintroduced to the man from Galilee?"

"No," Quinn said. "I don't."

"Long drive from Jericho."

Quinn waited.

"It ain't so bad here," Stagg said. "I get three meals a day. Work some in the chow hall. Taught them how to fry chicken. I exercise every morning. Supper by four. I watch television. Been watching *Days of Our Lives* and working through those books by Bill O'Reilly. He done killed Patton, Lincoln, and Jesus Christ. Guess a lot more folks he can kill, too."

"Johnny, I don't give a shit," Quinn said.

Stagg laughed, scratched his cheek. He looked odd, for some reason, and then Quinn realized it was the hair. The high preacher hair with the ducktail had been barbered down a good bit. His hair had always been a deep brown but now was stone white.

"I didn't want you killed."

"Appreciate that, Johnny."

"I know you don't believe me," Stagg said. "But that wasn't my doing. That was the fucking psychopath, the trooper captain you killed to protect your sister. How is she? And your momma and them, too?"

"Just fine," Quinn said. "Is that it? Is that what you wanted to tell me? Because I think you wanted me to see how nice things were over here at federal camp. That however many years that you stay here, it won't change you one goddamn bit."

Stagg smiled, preacher-like, shaking his head. "You're a hard man, Quinn Colson."

Quinn started to stand. Stagg shook his head. "Hold on," he said. "Hold on. I guess everything's done, then? Them federal people ruined

ACE ATKINS

my name, my business, and shipped me off to this place. They got two
county supervisors sent to Parchman, Larry Cobb's fat ass over at Mor-
gan County in Tennessee."

"Maybe you'll learn golf."

"Already know how to golf," Stagg said. "They got me, and all those
damn morons who kicked over the anthill are dead. Every last one of
'em. You seen what happened to that one boy? The nineteen-year-old
who broke into Cobb's place? I saw it on that YouTube. They got him
in a traffic stop outside Nacogdoches, still driving Mickey Walls's Hummer. What did he say when he pulled that gun and got himself shot?"

"Roll Tide."

"Right," Stagg said, laughing and laughing. "Roll Tide. If that don't
beat all."

"Long ride back, Johnny," Quinn said. "Are we straight?"

"Almost," Stagg said. "I just wanted to look you in the eye and let
you know how you done fucked all of Tibbehah County."

"Excuse me, sir?"

"You really don't see things," Stagg said, "do you? Don't you realize
I was the one who kept the fucking order, kept everything from turning to hell on this earth. The bikers, the fucking Mexicans, the goddamn politicians who want to shake us till we bleed. I kept the
barbarians at the gate."

"Last time I heard a speech like that, I was over in Baghdad."

"You think them people are better for it?" Stagg said. "Y'all waved
the flag and hoisted Saddam high. What'd we get now?"

"International politics with Johnny Stagg," Quinn said, standing.
"Holy shit." He did not offer his hand.

"I never wanted you dead."

"Hard for me to believe."

"Maybe at the start of it," Stagg said. "When you come home. But

368

I'd like to think of us as friends. Like that ole sheepdog and the coyote from the ole cartoon."

"Be seeing you, Stagg."

Quinn turned and walked out of the mess hall, hearing Johnny Stagg's words the whole drive back to Jericho. "If you go back to being sheriff," he said, "watch your damn back, son."

Two men rode up to the Rebel on Harleys, stopped in front of the closed-down truck stop, and walked to the corrugated-tin building behind it. The BOOBY TRAP signs had been taken down some months ago, replaced with FOR SALE signs and flyers for local fish fries and dance parties. The men were muscled and bearded, both wearing sunglasses and leather vests over their sweating, hairy chests. The back of their vests read BORN LOSERS MEMPHIS, TN. One of the men, a man with a prominent tattoo on his neck, moved up to the front door of the old strip club while the other man handed him a crowbar.

A woman in a silver Lexus watched all of this from her front seat, window rolled down, checking her watch and seeing that the bastards were two hours late. Not even waiting for her to greet them.

She got out of the luxury car, slammed the door, and walked across the parking lot in a pair of black Ferragamo pumps made of soft calfskin. She had a Burberry trench coat belted tight around her waist and a light touch of Chanel Gardenia sprayed on her neck. Smelling the men under the overhang trying to bust through the door, she wished she'd put on more. Or at least on her Hermès scarf to dab under her nose.

"Didn't I say to wait?"

"I just want to see what's in there," said a grown man who called himself Rabbit. She didn't know the other man but had seen him. The tattoo on his neck said FUCK IT. Even if that wasn't his name, that's what she'd call him from now on.

Rabbit leaned on the crowbar, popping off the clasp and lock, and the three of them stepped inside. The room was dark and hot. It smelled of sweat and cheap perfume, coconut and cherry. The nasty red carpet would have to be ripped out and the horrible-looking black bar with mirrored panels removed. But the place had a reputation and a good location. A lot better than running girls down on Indian land, where you got squeezed on both sides. No white person should have to work with a Choctaw.

She reached into her pocketbook, a gold Prada, and took out a cigarette. FUCK IT tried to light it but she shooed him away, lighting the damn thing herself. Taking it all in, the titty bar, the truck stop outside, and all the business in north Mississippi and on into Memphis.

"Open the goddamn doors," Fannie Hathcock said, spewing a stream of smoke from the side of her mouth. "Let some fucking air and light into this place."